M

By the same author

Dead*lock*

Malcolm MacPherson

Simon & Schuster

SIMON & SCHUSTER
Rockefeller Center
1230 Avenue of the Americas
New York, NY 10020

Simon & Schuster and colophon are registered trademarks
of Simon & Schuster Inc.

Designed by Jeanette Olender
Manufactured in the United States of America

1   3   5   7   9   10   8   6   4   2

Library of Congress Cataloging-in-Publication Data
MacPherson, Malcolm.
Deadlock / Malcolm MacPherson.
p.   cm.
I. Title.
PS3563 .A3254D4   1998
813'.54—DC21   97-39747   CIP
ISBN 0-684-83157-0

ACKNOWLEDGMENTS

Thomas W. Ross, Superior Court District 18, North Carolina, a trial judge of twenty-two years' experience, who contributed his advice and counsel to this book.

Whitney Ellerman, an assistant United States attorney in Washington, D.C., and a friend, who offered legal guidance that included the language of the law and trial procedure.

Chuck L. White, a district court judge in North Carolina, who helped the author keep the protagonist within the constraints of judicial behavior, if not decorum.

Michael Korda, Chuck Adams, and Cheryl Weinstein at Simon & Schuster, who served in an editorial capacity that some critics of book publishing claim disappeared with tweeds.

Alan Nevins of the Renaissance Agency, who gives book agents a good name for a change by making nice things happen in the nicest ways.

Thanks to you all.

To Charlie, for all your work and
thought and effort and, not least of all,
your love.

O the mind, mind has mountains; cliffs of fall

Frightful, sheer, no-man-fathomed.

No. 65, No Worst
GERARD MANLEY HOPKINS

Prologue

Even the gentle breeze through the branches over the grave stilled in that mournful moment of parting.

"Dust to dust . . ."

With those penultimate words, Alexander Cardinal Wells, archbishop of the Catholic Metropolitan of San Francisco, transferred a fist of graveside dirt to the palm of United States Senator Stanton Hawkes, who in his sadness did not seem to know where he was. He held his hand out and looked at the dirt as though he could not figure out what was expected.

His leonine head and hawkish profile, a handsomeness and vitality that disguised his years, his straight back and tall stature—indeed, the proud if not archetypal figure of a senator from a bygone era of congressional rectitude, authority, and honor—betrayed a terrible vulnerability in the presence of the body of his beloved granddaughter, murdered in a senseless act of violence that had all America wondering what these times bode for them and their children too.

The senator focused on the grave as he turned his hand over. The dirt fell into the darkened pit onto Holly's bronze coffin like the final grains of sand through the waist of an hourglass. Tears streamed down the older man's cheeks. Around where he was standing the choking sobs and moans of others could be easily heard.

The dead girl's mother stared down into the cold grave. Any-

one who peered behind her veil would have been surprised by
eyes that burned with a rage. She could not forgive this loss of
the child she had brought into the world. Her anger had already
fused itself with her life, superceding all other emotions. She
had the rest of her life to drain from her a virtual sea of
vengeance over an evil that had ended her child's life. It would
be her final and most perfect gift.

The dead girl's father, Karl Hawkes, estranged and indifferent, looked as if he did not want to be there at all. He had
dressed in a tweed suit, which contrasted sharply with a long
braided ponytail and a string of colored beads around his neck.
He was standing with his new family, two young boys who
looked like urchins and a wife in a long pleated skirt. Karl was
dry-eyed as he watched his former wife and his father. He shook
his head with resignation more than with sadness. And even before the cardinal spoke the final words and shepherded the
mourners across the lawn to the cars parked along the cemetery
road, Karl was gone.

"*In nomine Patris et Filii et Spiritus Sancti, amen,*" said Cardinal Wells, who turned to Senator Hawkes with a consoling
look that he had practiced during hundreds of these ceremonies.
He put his hand on his shoulder with just a slight touch, as if
such familiarity were untoward. "My condolences, Senator," he
said stiffly, despite an acquaintance that went back to their
childhood, when Stanton Hawkes was Stan and the cardinal was
simply Wellsy.

Senator Hawkes nodded as one who had heard his name spoken in a dream.

"Thank you, Wellsy." Amelia, the mother of the dead girl,
spoke up for him. She raised her veil to look the cleric in the eye.
And the look of anger made her almost beautiful.

"It's over now," Wells told her.

"*Over?*" The word was bitter on her tongue. "I'd have
thought it was only beginning."

The cardinal nodded, mistaking her meaning. He thought she
had meant that the trial, the disposition of the accused, the

press, the public furor—the anger toward Chinatown's residents—were far from over. "I suppose you are right," he said. He too had an agenda. Yes, Amelia Hawkes was right, perhaps for the wrong reasons. "Please, Amelia?" he asked as she was turning to leave. "Call me anytime, for anything you need."

"I will," she said, bowing her head.

They crossed the broad swath of lawn and then boarded a limousine. The crunching of gravel followed that car and several others in a line, and within minutes they were all gone, save for one or two. The cardinal whispered a prayer into the hollow of the grave. This was his moment to be with Holly Hawkes, alone, and he did not want to waste it. She had suffered—Oh, Lord, he thought, the girl had lived through a hell on earth. Now she was at peace. He was removing the stole, the sacred purple symbol of the priesthood, when he remembered his oldest friend was still sitting there.

"A sad ending, eh?" Henry Barr, the chief justice of the supreme court of California, said in a voice that was oddly slurred. He turned in the wheelchair that a stroke had condemned his body to; his mind was as sharp as ever. He smiled across the distance at a handsome man, vibrant with youth, with black hair in a black suit, who was watching them. "Come on, Wellsy. Give me a push, will you?"

"Just a minute, Henry, please?" said the cardinal. A simple request. Only a close friend would have recognized the insistent tone.

Like two doddering men they gazed over a field of stone at a line of evergreens that formed a border between this exclusive cemetery and Golden Gate Park. The air was fresh with the scent of newly mown grass and the sea air from the Pacific. The fog had lifted and the sky was clear and sweet-smelling, with hints of the water off the bay. There was a refreshing, even bracing, breeze. For a few hours the weather would deliver what the promoters of San Francisco tourism promised, before the fog returned, with its unseasonal chill and its veiled offerings of mystery.

Neither man spoke for several minutes, enjoying the day. They were such old friends, their ability to communicate went beyond words. Henry Barr was widowed now, and Cardinal Wells was celibate. They thought like two people who had lived together for a long time, and despite their separate vows—one to God, the other to the statutes of the state of California—there was nothing that they could not share.

"Henry, you're aware of the Sacramental Seal, aren't you?" asked the Cardinal.

He was and wasn't, his look said. With some spiritual indemnity or another, Justice Barr remembered, the Catholic law ensured a strict confidentiality between a confessor and a priest.

"The Seal is inviolable," the cardinal said in a patient tone. "Its violation is a sin *ex toto genere suo*. But I have heard something which I can't keep. I have to take the risk."

Risking hell, Chief Justice Barr thought, and he looked at his friend. "Are you sure?" he asked him.

"If what I have heard remains private between that sinner and his God, I will be committing a greater sin against us all. Do I have your word that the trust will stay only between us two?"

Justice Barr didn't know if he could give it. "Why are you telling me, then?" he asked.

"Because of who you are, Henry—your rank, because of who you know, our long friendship."

Henry Barr was being asked to respect the laws of a church he did not believe in. He was being asked to share the burden of information that his oldest friend found too onerous to keep. The cardinal was no gossip. And what he had to say, therefore, was of a nature that Barr did not think he could refuse to hear.

The cardinal spoke in a whisper, ensuring that nobody but Justice Barr could hear. His lips hardly moved.

Henry Barr's face drained of color, as though a horrible vision had just presented itself before his eyes. "It's a . . . horror . . . an abomination," he said, and now the slur that his stroke had left him with thickened.

Cardinal Wells stared at him. "My single consolation is that God will find a way," he said.

"Against this even He needs our help," said the supreme court justice.

"What can *we* do?" asked the cardinal. "That's why I had to tell you. To see if you knew. My lips are sealed. I would be excommunicated if anyone were to know this came from me. You won't betray my trust, I know. Many chapters are yet to be written between now and a final judgment."

"You are suggesting, Wellsy, we wait and do *nothing?*"

"That's all *I* can do." He looked across the distance to the waiting car. He smiled at the young man in the dark suit. "Danny," the cardinal said, referring to the young man. "What a deliverance. He's like my own son."

He had never said anything of the kind about his godson before, and the remark surprised Justice Barr, who looked toward his son, then back at Cardinal Wells.

Cardinal Wells said, "I understand he was appointed to superior court," as though that were news. "A reason to be proud. Will he follow in your footsteps to the supreme court?"

"He needs seasoning," said his father, wondering what the cardinal was getting at now.

"There's nothing like a celebrated murder trial to give him what he needs," the cardinal said.

"You mean . . . ?" And Justice Barr's eyes opened wide.

"Arrange it, Henry," said the cardinal, and he looked a last time meaningfully into the open grave. "Help God find a way."

Chapter One

He gazed into the floor-length mirror behind his chamber's door, and the image that formed in his mind's eye had nothing to do with the necktie that he was straightening. For the second time, glancing at the wall clock, he slicked back the long black hair behind his ears. Nervously he shot out his cuffs from the black judicial robe, which was out-of-the-box new and too short in the sleeves.

"You look just fine, Judge," his personal assistant, Miss Hamish, a sweet older woman, reassured him. Miss Hamish had been around since Barr's father had presided here, and she fussed over him like the child he had been when they had first met.

"That's not what I'm worried about, Edith," he told her.

"I've seen the jitters many times before you," she said, brushing off a speck of lint from his shoulder. "And it never made a bit of sense. If you don't mind my saying, you're the only one who's nervous."

"No doubt," he said, unconvinced. He *was* convinced that the board had showed a singular lack of judgment in choosing him to preside over the case. The choice had surprised his colleagues, who had hoped this plum would fall into their laps. They all said his father had pulled strings to put him on the biggest celebrity case in San Francisco since the Patty Hearst trial. For weeks the press had written about little else, and Dan

Barr's celebrity had risen way above that of any other judge in America, as TV stations and the pencil press besieged his chambers with interview requests, all of which he had denied. That had not stopped them from writing things about him, of course. Most of it was flattering, but in one way or another what each had asked, however they couched the question after giving credit to his brilliant credentials, was whether he was experienced enough to handle this trial. Or was he going to make a mockery of justice, like Judge Ito in the O. J. Simpson proceedings? Indeed, everything about this trial that was about to begin had precedents there. This time, everyone, from the supreme court justices to freshman lawyers right out of law school, expected Dan Barr to show that the courts still could deliver.

Barr looked a last time at his reflection in the mirror. Far from being certain of his abilities, he had accepted the appointment more because he'd grown tired of private practice than from any desire to preside over any court of law. His old firm of Auchincloss, Collins, Conroy & Coleman recoiled at criminal cases and refused them as a matter of policy, mostly because they paid little but also for the character they reflected. White shoes didn't walk with the violent kind. And while civil litigation paid the bills, it did little to stimulate a sense of accomplishment in a lawyer with Barr's temperament.

He had reached that stage in life when he wanted new challenges. Well, he'd found one sooner than he ever imagined. And what a challenge! With this trial he might become the superior court judge with the fastest fall in California judicial history. Nothing—absolutely nothing would surprise him now. He cleared his throat, again swept back the hair over his ears, and yanked at the necktie that again had wormed off center.

The clock came around to the hour.

He picked up a file of motions and the indictments, and with a nod to Miss Hamish he headed into war.

"All rise . . ."

The assistant clerk raced through his spiel like a track announcer at Caliente. "Oyez, Oyez," brought the court to order, and he declared it in session with "God save this state as this honorable court." Then he ordered everyone to sit back down again. And with these few timeless rituals, the room was put on notice. Here dwelled people's fate. Lives changed for eternity here. This drama—and all those like it in courts all over America—defined a people and made them who they were.

As Judge Barr entered the court, his black nylon robes stirred around him like smoke on a man about to catch fire by some mysterious means. An uneven half-smile turned up the lines on his face, giving him the appearance of great curiosity as he deposited himself in the high-backed black chair. He breathed to calm his racing heart and stared at the indictment in his hands.

"All right, let's get started—the state of California versus Feng Shao-li," said Judge Daniel Barr. His voice rose and cracked. He put the indictment aside and, with a glance at the side paneled door, he ordered the jury to be brought in.

As the twelve jurors and the two alternates filed in, he watched each face, relieved to see the same worry as his own displayed there—yes, that and undisguised wariness, discomfort, and confusion too. He had seen these people before, during the two-day selection process of voir dire, but that was then, and this was now.

Made up of five women and seven men, the panel of jurors was the typical stew—four Chinese, three African-Americans, three Caucasians, two Hispanics. By the way they clasped their small court-provided spiral notebooks, he could tell they were prepared for what lay ahead. And well they might be. If they found for guilt, the defendant almost certainly would die of a lethal injection in the death chamber at San Quentin, if not next year then the year after, or the year after that. There might be postponements, but he would die, and that decision would sober any juror anywhere.

The lead prosecutor smoothed the skin on his widow's peak

in a gesture left over from the days when abundant hair grew there. He pushed back his chair, about to start his opening statement.

"A minute, please, Counselor," Judge Barr told him. And he indicated with a flutter of his hand that conveyed an unspoken apology. The prosecutor sat back down again, glancing at the assistants who flanked him at the table. "I apologize," Barr said for emphasis, and his face colored for all to see. "I guess we're all a little nervous. I forgot something I think I should mention. Bear with me." He dropped the ingratiating smile as he swiveled around to face the jury. "Ladies and gentlemen," he told them. "Before we get started here, I want to go over a couple of points. You've probably heard before of a murder trial like this one or read about them in crime novels or seen them portrayed in a movie or two. Whatever you have heard or seen, your responsibility is simple: You are to listen to what is said in this room. Many facts will be presented and debated. When I send you out to deliberate, you will use these facts as a basis for a fair judgment of a verdict of innocent or guilty. Without the facts presented here you will have no basis for informed decision. And that is your duty: to reach a choice in your own mind that is truly informed."

He looked at his hands; they were trembling with nerves. Then he looked up straight into the gaze of a woman juror named Claire Hood who offered him a radiant smile of such freshness he could hardly take his eyes away. What held his attention was that she reminded him of the victim, whom he had known as a member of a family like his own; he had already satisfied his legal duty to inform the prosecutor and the defense attorneys of this potential conflict.

The Holly Hawkes whom Barr had known had not been much older than a girl, really, and to that he ascribed a purity. Added to that, she was bright and beautiful and terribly gifted, so that the whole world of opportunity had been hers. She had seemed fresh and genuine and lovely. When she was murdered she had been about to enter Berkeley, with a career ahead in academics that coincided with her grandfather's commercial interests in the Far East. She had wanted for nothing. Some had called Holly lucky. Some may have envied her. But surely none could have wished this death on her.

He cleared his throat and turned his eyes away. Then he told the jurors, "I want to remind you, I am the judge of the law in this court, you are the judge of the facts. The case before us today is one of great seriousness. It involves the capital crime of felony murder. The accused of this crime is innocent until he is proven guilty beyond a reasonable doubt. *Innocent*. I repeat. Sitting there, the accused is *innocent*." He gave them ten seconds. "Okay, Mr. Shenon, now let's begin."

The chief prosecutor was ready to go, and he rose with a spring in his knees that was easily read. Henry Shenon had a thorough, plodding, and understated presence. He was polite and respectful, with a set of gestures that was delicate, even prissy, for a man of his girth. The bounce in Shenon's step betrayed his confidence with all the subtlety of a fist of victory hurled into the air. This prosecution was a slam dunk, and he wanted everyone to know.

He used the same boilerplate fill-in-the-blanks oration he used at this time in every trial he prosecuted. "The evidence, we believe," he said, "will demonstrate beyond a doubt that this is a case involving the unlawful killing of a human being while perpetuating a felony, which in this case was robbery. The evidence will paint a picture of a man who lured a beautiful young woman with a bright and happy future, a complete and utter stranger to him. He lured her with her own innocence. When she refused to give him what he desired, when she struggled to defend herself, the defendant stabbed her more times than the medical examiner was able to count with absolute certainty, as he himself will tell you."

Shenon took a quarter-turn. He said nothing for several seconds, which allowed the jurors to match the sight of the defendant with the charges. He wanted their imaginations to come into play. And their prejudices too. Like first impressions anywhere, the initial sight of the accused was the most important view in the whole trial.

Feng Shao-li looked unremarkable; he had a pug nose, sallow skin, lank hair, and widely spaced eyes. With a smooth round face, pouting lips, and Asian slits for eyes that to some prejudiced westerners looked deceiving, he also looked as disoriented as an alien who had entered these four walls from a distant galaxy. In fact, everything about him—his posture, his walk when he had entered the court, his expression now—seemed dead. But did he look like a killer?

"The San Francisco police found the defendant with the help of witnesses near the crime scene," prosecutor Shenon finally went on. "And when he was arrested . . ."

Judge Barr listened with half an ear to the list of particulars. He allowed his gaze to wander into the court behind the bar that separated the proceedings from the viewers. Amelia Hawkes was sitting in the second row, alone, her hands folded in her lap, her face a portrait of misery. She wore a simple flowered cotton dress, no makeup, and her hair in a chignon. Indeed, she looked as though she might have been about to begin a morning's housework. But of course she was here to observe the inexorable conviction of her child's killer, and she was telling all who saw her that her purpose was singular. Barr's glance caught hers for an instant, and the corner of her mouth rose in a shy grin of recognition. He had to fight the urge to return the same. His heart went out to her. They had been acquaintances since her marriage to Karl, whom he had known in grammar school. She was a quiet woman, not given to ostentation, but in her subdued way she was a mother who took enormous pride in her success.

Off to the right sat his own father, Henry Barr, who nodded approvingly, as if to show his support. He was in his wheelchair in the aisle beside his godfather, Cardinal Wells, who had covered his priestly robes with a black raincoat. On the complete opposite side of the room sat Senator Stanton Hawkes, the man the Forbes 400 ranked among the ten richest in America, who watched the defendant with the penetrating stare of one who willed him to die on the spot. In the weeks since Holly's funeral, Senator Hawkes had recovered his famous granite-chiseled profile, the set jaw, the sharp nose, the clear forehead, the carefully styled graying hair. But the weeks had also brought out a cruelty to the turn of his mouth and an implacable look of vengeance. The court artist, sitting against the wall, turned his appraising eye from Senator Hawkes to the defendant and sketched on a blank sheet of paper, and Barr thought how great the contrast— one famously rich and powerful, the other shrunken and disenfranchised to a point of near invisibility; one set on vengeance, the other on survival; one on clarity and direction, the other on confusion and fear.

The brevity of the prosecutor's statement caught Barr by surprise. Shenon was turning for his chair as Barr was emerging from his reverie as from a dream. He took an instant to orient himself.

"Mr. Lovelace," he said almost automatically.

"A minute, Judge," replied the defense attorney, seated beside the defendant at the opposite table.

Lovelace was a slob in appearance and as untidy in his courtroom habits. His shirt was partially untucked in front and his belly spilled over his belt. The button on his shirt cuff was either undone or off, it was hard to tell. He could never seem to do anything the court wanted him to do on time, and all these habits conformed to the gossip about him that held that he was a product of a correspondence law school based in Ottawa and that he had failed as a private attorney over in Marin County, where his specialty had been searching titles, handling divorces, and writing dowagers' wills. He had turned to the public defender's office out of financial need. But still, how he had landed this capital case was a mystery explained, Barr supposed, by a rotation system within the public defender's office, much the same as the rotation that had chosen him as the trial judge.

For all his faults, Lovelace was a man whom the same people who criticized him routinely called "sweet Tommy." He had the sunniest and most deferential personality Barr had ever seen near the business of law. He exuded understanding and great patience and was always ready to capitulate a fight he knew he could not win. He was fair and reasonable beyond anything that lawyers admitted these days, he explained, "Because there is a long view and a short view, and at my age I'm in no hurry."

"Would you care for a recess, Mr. Lovelace?" Barr asked in a gentle voice.

He responded with a shrug and sank his head between his shoulders as though he were ducking a projectile. "Minute more, Judge," he said.

Barr sighed loudly enough for the court recorder to note the sound in the trial transcripts. And while he waited for Lovelace, he gazed at the defendant, Feng Shao-li, late of Hong Kong, an illegal alien and tentative resident of San Francisco's Chinatown, a sweatshop floor sweeper, a bachelor. His eyes moved from side to side, and he leaned forward against the table to put himself out of earshot of the translator, who sat behind him.

Lovelace gave his client a tight nod as he rose to his feet and finally shuffled across the courtroom floor. The legal pad slipped from his hand, and as he bent over, a rip in his trouser's revealed a thin white strip of underpants. He paused to look for the notes he had written to remind himself of what he wanted to say.

"I have one question," he told the jury. "Why did the state accuse Mr. Feng Shao-li of murder? A good question, ladies and gentlemen. It's a question that I wish I could answer. And I honestly can't. What I will ask you to do is to listen and weigh the evidence you will hear," Lovelace told them. "Then I will ask you to ask yourselves this single question: Why did the state accuse this man of murder? Your answer will be a not-guilty verdict; not guilty because this man is not a criminal. That's what the evidence will show. Thank you."

And as he idled back across that no-man's-land to his chair, an embarrassed silence was broken by the sharp crack of Judge Barr's voice asking both lawyers to approach the bench. Lovelace's statement was a travesty, he thought. He was ahead of himself, and he had lost the jury. With Lovelace handling the defense, he had more than the jury to protect; he had the defendant too.

He said to Lovelace, "That's it? That's all?" And Lovelace blinked once slowly like an awakened sloth.

"Yes, Your Honor," he said.

"Your defense in a capital case is that the prosecution can't prove its case?"

"My client does not *have* a defense," Lovelace complained in a whisper.

"Then, why"—and Barr lowered his voice—"*in hell* did you not plead him guilty?"

"He didn't want me to," Lovelace said. "That's what he said. He didn't want to. He's his own man." His expression indicated that he could not believe it himself.

"You have talked to your client, then?" Barr asked sardonically.

Lovelace said nothing.

"What's the matter, Counselor?" Barr asked.

"I have no basis for understanding what my client wants and doesn't want."

Barr looked up. The members of the jury were casting glances around the room. He hardly blamed them for wondering what was happening. The trial had just begun and he was huddled with the counselors for as long as either side's opening statement. It looked strange to everyone, even to the legal amateurs in the press who would have a heyday with this unexpected break, and he wasn't going to allow it. He was looking like a fool, and the clock said that the proceedings had started only a half hour ago.

He spoke under his breath. "May we continue this discussion in chambers, gentlemen?" And to the court he announced in a voice he hoped conveyed a shred of authority, "I'm going to adjourn proceedings for today, to reconvene tomorrow morning." Through no fault of his own, the proceedings had gone awry, and for that he was furious with himself as much as with Lovelace. "My admonitions," he told the jurors, "are strictly in force. You are not to discuss the facts of this trial with one another or with friends and relatives outside this venue. Nobody. You are not to read about the trial in the press, and to the best of your ability you are not to watch reports of it on television or listen to the same on radio. In short, this trial stays in this court. *Dismissed.*" And he hit the gavel hard.

———

He had a strong urge to kick Tommy Lovelace in the butt as he entered the area of carpeted anterooms, dark wood paneling, muffled voices. As the most junior judge in the court, Barr's office was the farthest from the courtrooms themselves, as though getting there were perceived as a physical burden, which the oldest judge undoubtedly found to be true. As he approached her desk, Miss Hamish stood and began waving a piece of paper. "I'll sign it later," he told her. And when she persisted, he said more firmly, "*Later*, Miss Hamish. Let me deal with these gentlemen first."

The two counsels entered his chambers like truants. Barr indicated a button-backed sofa and two chairs for them to choose from. And with a sigh he started all over again.

"Mr. Lovelace, I must tell you. You are not serving your client with this kind of defense. If I sound patronizing, so be it. But I should remind you. The state requires you to represent your client *zealously* within the bounds of the law. The press are watching every move. *We* are under a microscope here. And what they are seeing so far embarrasses even me. Gentlemen, I won't have it. I can't allow it. This is important to me."

"Sorry, Your Honor," said Tommy Lovelace with a genuine look of contrition.

But Barr still wasn't finished. "You said you have no basis for understanding your client's desires and needs, Mr. Lovelace?"

Lovelace squirmed on the sofa. "Most of the time, I can't even understand the words he uses."

"He speaks no English at all?" Of course he had to speak English, or else why didn't the court know he didn't speak English? Lovelace should have filed motions to that effect, and the court would have assigned more than a single translator.

"His English is rough, let me say that. He sounds like his mouth is full of marbles. You swore in the translator, Judge. You know what I'm talking about. My client does not like her one bit. You've probably seen how he scowls at her. He won't listen to what she tells him."

"Then, find another one he will listen to," Barr said. "Good Lord, there is no shortage of bilingual Chinese in San Francisco. Chinatown is full of them."

Lovelace rolled his head on his shoulders, not convinced.

"Let me take a shot at this," said Henry Shenon, who had sat quietly, his expression like that of a cat with his mouth full of feathers.

"Go ahead, try," said Barr.

"I think my friend here, Tommy, is setting up the groundwork for an appeal with this translation business. Mr. Feng Shao-li is a dead man. . . ."

Barr said, "I believe that's for the jury to decide, Counselor."

"It's a shame to put the state through this charade."

Barr tried ignoring Shenon's self-serving remarks. "The trial is going to proceed, then, starting tomorrow morning. In the meantime, I want the public defender's office to find another translator. Got it? Damn the expense. I want the defendant to be aware of everything that is happening. And if that means, Mr. Lovelace, that you give him a tutorial, then, do it. I will allow any time you need to explain what is happening. You may take him step-by-step. Do what you need to. But do not allow the man to suffer in ignorance a minute longer. This is an important trial, important on many levels, including, gentlemen, our respective careers. The city is watching, the state and the nation are too. Nobody in the justice business is prepared to tolerate another courtroom mess like the last couple we've witnessed in L.A. Treat it likewise, gentlemen."

He dismissed them thinking that things could not get worse and, therefore, could only get better. He rubbed his eyes and was reaching for the telephone when Miss Hamish appeared in the doorway.

"Just a minute," he told her as he dialed.

"I don't think this should wait just a minute, Judge," she told him.

Whatever it was, he was certain it could wait. He counted the seconds as the phone rang, imagining his son running into the house from the side yard. He had given Roberta, their English au pair, a portable phone and a cellular car phone, but no matter what he told her about the importance of instant communication, she was blissfully out of touch. He listened as the phone rang and rang and Miss Hamish stood in the doorway.

"But Judge . . ." she said.

His son, Morgan, was out of breath. "Hi, Daddy" he blurted into the phone. Barr held up his finger for Miss Hamish. The sound of his son's voice made him smile. Such an enthusiastic greeting was one of the payoffs of being a single parent with too little time and too much love. He felt like a circus juggler—each ball in the air representing a different emotion. If one ball fell, they all would fall, and the desperation of keeping them in the air was often exhausting.

"Have you had lunch yet, sweetheart?" he asked him.

"We built a kite, Daddy. Will you fly it with me?"

"Yes!" he said and meant it.

"'Berta says we're having lunch in the gazebo."

"Honey, tell her to wait till I get there, okay?"

"Sure, Daddy."

"I love you," he said.

"Bye, Daddy," and he hung up.

Barr looked at Miss Hamish. Her persistence would have irritated him if her look were not apoplectic. Miss Hamish was not that kind of a woman. Where others fell apart, she went home for the day. "What is it, Edith?" he asked her.

She held up a sheet of paper, letting it dangle by its edge. "This was left on my desk when I went to the ladies' room; security doesn't recall anyone coming in. I asked. You were in court, Judge. When I got back, it was sitting there. . . ."

Barr stood up stiffly and took the paper from her hand. Attached was a plain envelope with his name on it. Someone had cut out letters from a magazine and, like a ransom note, had pasted them on a clean sheet of white paper. He parsed the words with a strange and growing sense of unease. He turned the paper over.

"This is obviously a hoax, Miss Hamish," he told her, adding sardonically, "What won't they think of next?" He watched as she shook her head and turned back to her outer office, knowing that she would not breathe a word of the note to anyone.

Then he looked again at the paper that trembled in his hands:

The killer

of Holly Hawkes

is Sitting on Your jury

Chapter Two

The mob of reporters and cameramen surged around him as he left the courts building. He had seen many others on television being engulfed by this media frenzy, but nothing in his imagination had ever prepared him for this reality. He felt trapped and violated and he surprised even himself when he took the steps three at once, and still they raced after him.

"Judge, give us your impressions of the trial," one yelled at him.

"No comment," he said in a quiet voice.

"Did the senator use his influence to keep the cameras out of the court?"

"No," Barr said.

"Why do you think none of the city's more prominent lawyers stepped forward to represent the accused?"

Good question, he thought. "You'd have to ask them, but the PDO does a decent job." Emphasis on *decent,* he thought. The legal stars, like F. Lee Bailey and Johnny Cochran and Alan Dershowitz and Robert Shapiro, had stayed away, Barr had heard, because of the defendant and the details of the crime itself.

He looked into the lights that even in bright daylight were blinding. He held up his hand, worried that he was going to be pushed over backward. His half-smile turned into a look of determination. "I can't answer any more of your questions," he told them. "The trial has just begun. Together we will see how it will unfold." He wanted to be polite. He wished they would try to understand. He knew they knew the rules.

One of them shouted, "Judge, this is the most celebrated trial in America. What does it say about our society as a whole?"

Barr paused a half-beat. "That kind of analysis is your job, not mine," he told him, and he hoped the microphones on the ends of the long poles had not picked up the tone. He did not want to get on the wrong side of these people, but, at the same time, a dumb question was a dumb question. He took a step forward. The reporter, whom he recognized as the local anchor at the NBC affiliate, did not move. "Doesn't this put the whole of Chinatown on trial?" he asked.

Barr wondered what he was talking about. The defendant was Chinese, from Chinatown, yes. That much was obvious. "No, of course not," he said.

"Do you think the motive for the killing was revenge?" a woman's voice cried.

"Do you have a theory why a Chinese murdered Holly Hawkes? Was it because of her grandfather's commercial interests over there?"

"Is this the most important trial of your career?" That one came from the *Chronicle*. Barr almost stopped to reply, but thought better of it.

"Being the youngest superior court judge in the county, Judge, do you think your conduct of the trial will be scrutinized differently?" Same paper, different reporter. Barr had his head down now. Yes, he was being scrutinized: for his younger age, for his liberal opinions, for his social connections, for how he was brought up, for his father's rank on the supreme court—for every damned thing that made him who he was.

"Do you have the credibility this trial needs?"

He looked up at them suddenly. "Thank you, thank you," he said and lowered his head again and directed his body into the surging mass, slowly gaining headway.

"Judge Barr, come with me," said a woman police officer who squeaked across the lobby's floor on black Reeboks. Her message delivered, she turned and walked away. Barr hurried to follow her.

In an office cubicle upstairs, Detective Sergeant Andy Cummings was leaning his elbows on the glass desktop, staring at a calendar with the rapture of a man in need of a long rest. He was wearing a red checkered lumberjack shirt and a striped necktie, and under his arm a holster snuggled a neat 9-mm Beretta. Cummings's overall appearance was rumpled, from his face to his clothes. His jowls had succumbed long ago to the gentle tug of gravity. A big porous nose sagged over his lip. His eyes were a tired, pale gray.

"The chief asked me to see you, Judge," he explained. "He's awful busy today."

Obviously Barr's new celebrity status had no effect on Cummings, who was the gatekeeper for the chief of police. Barr did not know Police Chief Dunstan, and he did not know what to expect.

"But I asked to see Chief Dunstan, not you," said Barr. "No offense."

Cummings shrugged. "You know how it is."

Barr paused for a moment, then handed him the anonymous note. "This arrived in my chambers this morning while I was in court. I thought the chief should know about it."

Cummings read the note without reaction, then handed it back.

That was all? That was it? Barr thought.

"Any idea who it's from?" Cummings asked.

"No, of course not," Barr said as he took the paper back. "I thought the opinion of your department might be useful. Was I wrong?"

"I've never seen anything like it myself," Cummings said, shaking his head.

"As the chief's representative, can you tell me, is that all the SFPD has to say?"

"All *I* have to say." He knew he could not leave it there. "Wait here a minute. Maybe the chief isn't too busy after all."

———————

Chief William Dunstan was a florid-faced man with a smooth bald head, prominent ears, and a crooked nose. His eyes occupied the terrain of his skull like two black pebbles on a molten pool. A large, imposing man over six feet tall and two hundred pounds, he looked more theatrical than intimidating in a uniform with brass buttons and epaulets and gold braid.

He was lighting a cigar, a neat late-morning Montecristo #5. He glanced up from the match, then returned to the ritual of the flame. Finally satisfied that it was lit, he pointed Barr to a chair and blew lightly on the cigar ember, turning it cherry red.

He looked up at the wall clock. "I'd have thought you'd be presiding at the trial this morning, Judge," he said pleasantly.

"I was until this arrived," Barr said as he handed him the paper.

Chief Dunstan read the note. He coughed and his face darkened. "Hoax," he said and he coughed out of control.

"My thought too," said Barr, genuinely glad to hear his belief confirmed. So why was he not even a little relieved?

The chief pushed the paper back across the desk. He puffed on the cigar, half closing his eyes, giving the impression that he was off somewhere in a reverie.

Well, that was that, Barr thought. "I wonder who would send such a thing?"

The chief opened his eyes and smiled, compressing the lines and wrinkles around his eyes and across his forehead. "Could have been anybody," he said. "It could have been one of the judges you jumped ahead of in line to land this trial. From what I understand, your colleagues aren't too happy about how things turned out."

"I had nothing to do with that," said Barr defensively.

The smile broadened. "No, I suppose not, though your name *is* Barr, isn't it?"

"My father would never have intervened."

"No, probably not. A trial like this Hawkes thing comes along once in a generation, though. Some judges wait for them and they pounce. It's a springboard to all sorts of opportunities off the bench, and with those opportunities of course, comes money, which nobody is earning on the bench, as you know. Maybe one of them wants to make the experience of this trial as uncomfortable for you as he—or she—can. That's just speculation, of course."

The idea of a conspiracy sounded unlikely to Barr. Judges might be as petty and vindictive as the rest of the general population, but he reasoned that few of them would engage in a criminal act out of spitefulness. "What if it isn't a hoax?" Barr asked, mostly for the sake of asking.

Dunstan leaned back in his chair. "I suppose you could always declare a mistrial."

"Should I, in your estimation?"

The smile faded slowly. "That's not my field, or my decision. I'd have thought that everyone wants to put this thing behind us. I know we here in the SFPD do. A mistrial at this point?" he mused. "Well, it probably would irritate a lot of people. The courts would be laughed at. The press would have a field day, probably at your expense."

"And justice would not be served," Barr said.

"Only delayed," the chief agreed. "And confidence in the system would further erode. The defendant, if I am not mistaken, could argue his constitutional right to a speedy trial. Maybe he is let go. And you know how they are. He'd just disappear into that big sea of Chinese. Go back to Canton or Shanghai or wherever they come from. Or let's say the case went to another judge and a new panel of jurors. A new trial begins. Another note arrives, just like this. What do we do then? Do we keep throwing out juries until the notes stop?" Dunstan laid the cigar on the desk's edge and leaned forward. "By my saying it's a hoax I don't mean to sound flippant or dismissive, Judge. But I also don't need to think about it a lot either." He took back the paper and handed it to Detective Cummings. "Here, make a copy," he instructed. He paused a moment. "Let me ask you another question, Judge. If this note is real, how did the killer put himself on the jury?"

"You're right," said Barr. He had thought about it only briefly, but he didn't see any way, given how the system worked.

"Coincidence? Fate?" Dunstan asked. "Perhaps. But that works in movies and books. Rarely in life. Never like this. What that leaves us with is some prankster playing a joke." The big smile again. "You did the right thing showing me this note. But trust me, it's a joke. Detective Cummings and his crew investigated the murder like none other in the SFPD's history. The minority community in San Francisco always claims that there are two justices—one for the rich and one for them. And we tell them no. There is only one. But they are absolutely right. We give the murder of the granddaughter of a U.S. senator our full attention. You bet we do. We pour out manpower to get the job done. We leave no stone unturned. We spare no expense. As a result, we found the killer. We got all the physical evidence that the DA's office needed for an indictment. Mostly, we got witnesses. The real killer *is* sitting in your court." As if he had read Barr's thought, he added, "And he is not on your jury."

Barr asked, "Then, if I read you correctly, Chief, in so many words you are suggesting I disregard this?"

Dunstan laughed. "But please, don't get me wrong. I'm not ordering you to do or think *anything*. That's not my job. I don't care if you frame the damned letter. Just remember, we have completed *our* investigation. Nobody's going to be happy if you call for a mistrial and ask us to reopen the case, because there is nothing further for us to look into, and nothing further for us to find." He puffed on the cigar, taking the original letter from Cummings and handing the copy to Barr. "Have you told anyone else about this?" he asked.

Barr shook his head. "My assistant, Miss Hamish."

Dunstan nodded solemnly. "I have a legal duty to disclose this note as exculpatory evidence to the DA. And the DA then has a legal obligation to show the note to the defense, Mr. Lovelace. . . ."

"And by then it will be leaked to the press," said Barr, shaking his head.

"You'd be forced to declare a mistrial. So? What would you recommend I do with it?"

Barr did not reply automatically. To advise the chief to break the law by withholding the information, he would be entering into a conspiracy. What helped him decide the issue was believing what the chief said to be true—that the note was a hoax. "For now, I don't think disclosure would benefit anyone," he told him.

The chief smiled. "Of course we'll do whatever we can," he said. "We'll run the original through our lab, see what is there—fingerprints, composition of the letters, watermarks, hair and fibers. We'll do our job. We always do."

———————◆———————

Barr glanced at his watch while he made certain that the attendant parked his Spyder—a certified Porsche classic, vintage 1955, Stuttgart-built—in a sheltered bay. The little convertible was his most prized possession. With its California vanity plates stamped with the word DOOM—his wife, Vanessa, had provided these one Christmas—Barr relived his teenage fantasies as he raced the sports car at the Laguna Seca annual Salon de Concours, actually winning his class three times with an ease that had earned him a reputation for abandon and doggedness, if not finesse.

When the elevator arrived he entered and stood against the back. He was feeling guilty about Morgan, something he seemed to do more and more since his assignment to the Hawkes trial. He had not even had time to call to tell him he wouldn't be there for lunch. He told himself he'd make it up to him. His debt of "making it up" had by now grown to the size of the national deficit.

A dozen people boarded the elevator when it stopped at the ground floor. The atmosphere among them was upbeat, what with the weekend just ahead and the weather predicted to be fine. Barr was considering what his weekend promised—more time in chambers, maybe a couple of stolen hours of sailing out on the bay with Morgan—when a passenger bumped him hard.

He looked up angrily at the smiling face of Jenny Thompson, who asked him, "What brings you to our humble abode, Dan?" She pointed to a young Chinese at the front of the elevator, and in fluent Cantonese she rattled off a phrase. The Chinese man pushed her floor button and looked back at her, startled that anyone as attractive and Caucasian and Nordic as she spoke his language. "Thanks," she told him in English. Then to Barr, "Well?"

"The Legends Club," he replied. "Upstairs? My dad?"

"Ah, yes. The old boys. It still annoys me that they don't let women in."

"It smells of cigar smoke," he told her. "You're not missing a thing, believe me."

She scrutinized him. "Speaking of missing, Dan, where have you been lately?"

He shrugged; hers was a question she knew the answer to. Their affair had ended months ago. Actually, he had ended it, cravenly, quietly, by just not being there, by not calling. No fight, no sudden anger; just nothing. With her career, Jenny had little time for a relationship, no matter what she claimed. The longer she had stayed in his life, the more he had doubted their future together. The truth of the matter was that she did not meet his requirements for a mother for Morgan. At least that's what he told himself. And yet seeing her now, he was reminded of just how comfortable he always felt with her. They got along as friends first, then as lovers. And how many couples could say the same? Still, she seemed to want a commitment that he was not yet ready to give; it was like that, he reasoned. No, there had been no real end to their relationship. It kind of went along, off and on. Lately, off.

"How's the job?" he asked.

"Great, thanks for asking. Since I last saw you I made VP."

"Congratulations. Wasn't that unexpected?" he asked.

"Out of the blue. Fortunately, it doesn't add any new responsibilities. Just more travel."

"To Asia?"

"Taiwan, China, Singapore, Vietnam."

"You'll like that, huh?"

"China, you bet. Hawkes has big plans for building there."

Jenny worked for Hawkes Construction and indirectly for Senator Hawkes, who owned and ran the company. Hawkes was the second largest construction company in the world. Jenny ran the marketing division for the Far East, where the bulk of the work was done. The men at Hawkes, which built dams in Indonesia, offices in Hong Kong, roads in Thailand, and air bases in Saudi Arabia, might have dismissed her as just a bit of fluff whom the boss liked to gaze upon if not for her two real strengths: languages—her Cantonese was fluent and her Mandarin expert; and education—she owned a degree in Asian history from Stanford and a masters in engineering from Cal. Added to that, she was blessed with a presence that was impossible to ignore.

"Mom was asking about you the other day," she told him. "She wondered where you'd been. I told her I didn't know."

Everyone in the car was eavesdropping on their conversation, especially the men, who glanced furtively at Jenny. She was naturally sexy, thin and fit and wholesome, with the mouth of a truck driver. She naturally attracted men of all ages and sizes and backgrounds with the illusion of availability, which she did nothing to discourage. She created a tension that *was* purely sexual with an appeal that attracted and yet declared that she was too much a woman for any man to handle. Her very presence proclaimed a joyful and wanton womanhood: *Have fun, boys,* her presence all but seemed to shout, *but keep it strictly in your dreams.*

For their part, the women in the elevator took Barr's measure not for his minor celebrity as the Hawkes trial judge, even if they had known, but for his black hair, green eyes, and Irish good looks. Attracting women was never his problem; but as Jenny could attest to, getting the one with the right combination to fit his needs was.

"How about if we get together sometime soon, you know . . . the two of us?" she asked, her voice a playful purr.

Barr seemed to think it over. He even pursed his lips. "Sure," he said finally. "Let's talk."

The elevator stopped and Jenny stepped out, then turned around. She tilted her head with a wistful smile and folded her bare arms. One young man in the elevator moaned, breaking the tension, as some other passengers giggled while others laughed out loud. Jenny was still looking at Barr when the doors closed.

———————

The Legends Club bore the imprints of a different age. The ceiling soared as high as architects dared design them. The foyer smelled of privilege, and the comingling of bay rum, mothballs, newspaper ink, smoke, and whiskey. As Jenny had indicated, only men were allowed to join. Women visited the club at their peril, never allowed beyond the vestibule, and were made to wait in a spare chamber that contained two chairs and an uncomfortable sofa.

Henry Barr scanned the *New York Times* national edition as he sat in his wheelchair in the corner by the windows that offered a view of the entire city. A martini glass brimming with chilled vodka was set out before him, a single green olive resting in its clear depths. The tables were set with fresh white linen, small vases of cornflowers, and oversized silverware. It was early yet, and Chief Justice Henry Barr was the only Legends Club member present.

Barr took the chair opposite his father and smiled when he noticed the drink. Henry Barr usually drank martinis in the middle of the day when he was celebrating, or when he had nothing better to do, or when he was worried about something he could not control. The chief justice liked control, which to a great extent was what had attracted him to the law. Barr tried to guess which motivation had caused his father to order the martini now.

"I'll get one for you," Henry Barr said, noticing the direction of his son's eyes.

"Your docket is clear, I take it?" the younger Barr asked.

With a twinkle in his faded blue eyes, he looked at the glass and sighed. "Docket schmocket," he said, as though he were offering a toast. "Join me."

"Talked me into it," Barr said.

And now it was the father's turn to stare.

Dan Barr and Henry Barr were unusually close and loving. As fellow lawyers they shared a mutual respect for the profession of the law, but this common interest was just one aspect of their father-son relationship, which had strengthened as they had become widowers and fellows in loneliness. They were closer now than ever before, since Justice Barr had suffered his stroke. He had become more vulnerable and less imposing in his son's eyes, and this new equality had given them a new freedom to express emotions that they had long kept to themselves.

Even though the stroke had put him permanently in a wheelchair and had blurred the patterns of his speech, Henry Barr was still feared and revered by the legions in the state who called the law their business. Governor Brown had appointed him to the bench when Caryl Chessman was appealing his execution. Barr proved himself an old-fashioned fire-and-brimstone judge; his opinions were practical, logical, and as stern as the Old Testament. He had come up the hard way, earning everything he had achieved. He believed in a strict code of behavior: men were responsible for their actions; character was earned, not God-given. He believed in the virtues of suffering, sacrifice, and giving. He did not think that men should define themselves by their weaknesses, their failings, or their handicaps. As a result, some considered him out of step with a society of victimization. At their own peril, some few viewed Justice Barr as a museum piece. His son was not among them.

Henry raised his glass in a toast, then tipped the glass to his lips, savoring the taste. Dan Barr, on the other hand, gulped down his drink.

"Anything *wrong?*" Henry asked. The drained glass was clearly a statement, and perhaps even his son's silent cry for help.

Barr reached into his inner pocket for the note, which he passed across the table. Judge Barr's facial expression did not change as he read it. He put the paper down, then reached up and touched the knot of his tie as though to ensure that he didn't *look* as shaken as he felt.

"A hoax?" Dan Barr asked the only question that really mattered.

"Is that what you think?" his father asked.

"The chief of police says so. He told me in so many words to ignore it. Leave it alone. Get on with the trial, get on with my life."

"He did, did he? I'm not surprised. Do *you* think it's a joke?"

Dan Barr hesitated. "I can't say." He covered the letter with his palm.

"I'll tell you my opinion. Now listen. Hoaxes, Danny, are meant to amuse. No hoax this. An innocent man may die at the hands of the state. As the judge in this trial you are the representative of the state. It'd be like you were killing an innocent human being, given what this note might be telling you, son, if what it says is true."

Barr nodded solemnly. The gravity of his father's voice, his look, his careful choice of words, all combined to frighten him. He was receiving advice not from a father but from the chief justice of the supreme court. "I asked Chief Dunstan, Who would do something like this? Who would have a reason?"

"I know what he probably told you too," said his father. "One of your colleagues on the bench wants to make life tough. Maybe, maybe, but I don't think so."

"Should I have recused myself after all?" Barr asked.

A couple of the senior superior court judges had gently raised the question of recusal. But who of them did not also personally know Stanton Hawkes from one or another period or venue? San Francisco was not a big town in that sense. In the end, recusal was an issue that none of them cared to raise.

His father thought a moment. "How about this possibility: what if the Hawkes investigation was incomplete—you know how the SFPD and the prosecutor's office bowed and scraped over this because of Senator Hawkes. They were terrified to make a move. You know how Stanton demanded a speedy trial; he wants to get this past him so he and his family can get on with their lives. He might not even care if an innocent man is killed by lethal injection, as long as vengeance is his."

"Justice rendered but not served."

"Many possibilities lead just to one. You asked me a minute ago who would write this note. A person who knows that the real killer is on the loose and the accused may be innocent. It's that knowledge you should focus on." He thought for a moment in silence. "A killer on the jury—now, that's something different."

"But Dad, why would anyone be crazy enough to try to get *on* a jury that was judging the murder he had committed? It'd be like suicide."

He was shaking his head. "Think about it. More like insurance, I'd say. To be certain that the jury finds the defendant guilty. What better insurance could a killer ask for? My God, think about it. A killer is arguing in the deliberations for his own deliverance. After the guilty verdict comes in, he is forever a free man." The elder Barr reached across the table and patted his son's hand.

Barr felt almost sick with confusion. First Miss Hamish had shown panic at the sight of the note, then the chief of police had told him not to worry, and now his father was putting him on notice. "Okay, what if I *don't* take it lightly?" he asked.

"Verify the facts in three ways."

"I already thought about that," said Barr. "The jurors—check them out. And the defendant, is he really guilty?"

"Don't forget the family. . . ."

"Why them?" Barr asked.

"Remember who Stanton is. He has enormous wealth. He's a U.S. senator with a record of legislation that people both love and hate. Was someone trying to hurt him by killing his grand-daughter? Was the defendant merely an instrument?"

"Wouldn't Chief Dunstan have known if that was true?"

"Not necessarily. Chief Dunstan believes that the police caught Holly's killer. If the killer is loose, as the note suggests, Dunstan's competence is challenged. The SFPD doesn't want to look bad, especially to the senator."

"Is Dunstan corruptible?" Barr asked.

"Incompetent, maybe, but not that. Remember, the murder took place in Chinatown. No doubt the SFPD did the best they knew how to, but the SFPD is blind as a bat in there. Their offi-cers can't even say good morning in Chinese, much less ask in-vestigative questions." He paused, as if to ponder.

"What can I do that the police weren't able to?"

"They had all of San Francisco to sift through. You have twelve people."

Barr returned to his chambers to think things over. A couple of pink phone-message slips lay on his desk: Lovelace and Cardinal Wells had called. Both had asked to see him. He dialed the PDO, and as the phone was ringing Lovelace appeared in the doorway. Barr put down the phone. "Yup?" he asked disinterestedly.

Lovelace came in and sat down in a slump.

Barr looked at him disapprovingly. "Is this about the trial?" he asked.

"Yes . . ."

"You know it isn't permitted, Counselor," Barr told the defense attorney. "I can't discuss this case with you alone without the other side present."

Lovelace nodded. The standard was common knowledge. So was its violation. "It's a housekeeping matter, more or less," he told him.

"As long as you limit it to that, you can proceed."

Lovelace edged forward in the chair. "Following on from what you said this morning, Judge, there's something I didn't mention."

Barr looked around with a show of discomfort. "This is housekeeping?" he asked.

"Yes and no," said Lovelace. "No."

"Do you feel that Shenon should be present?"

"You can ask him to come over if you want. I don't mind."

Barr looked at the door. "Close it, then." And Lovelace did, then sat back down.

"You asked me this morning to explain myself."

"I thought I needed to hear from you," said Barr. "Your opening statement was hardly a model of the law."

"I agree," said Lovelace, ever the capitulator. "But what else was I to tell the jury? You've seen my client. You know how they are."

"They? *They?* Enlighten me," Barr said. He wondered whether Lovelace was being racist or if he actually had a point to make.

"They're in a world unto themselves," he went on unfazed. "It's more than that, Judge. This guy has thought patterns you need an oscilloscope to follow. When he says up, he means down or sideways. When he says yes, he means something not quite yes, not quite no. It's hard to pin him down, legally speaking. Talking to him in a language I hardly can understand and from a culture I don't even remotely get, it's like a hall of mirrors."

Barr stifled a smile. He understood full well how the system had not kept pace with the wave of immigrants drowning California's system of public services. The courts were Anglo-Saxon by tradition, bedrock English in custom and language, right from the Magna Carta. If a defendant did not understand English and the Anglo-Saxon sensibility, he was already out of step, a situation that Barr felt the court had a duty to rectify. "Go on, Mr. Lovelace. Go on."

"Like, he says he didn't kill her, then he starts to cry. But he confessed to the police. They've got it in black and white. Go figure. I ask him why, through his translator, why he is crying. He says because he didn't kill her. He's crying because he feels bad that such a pretty young girl was killed. I ask him, Did you or didn't you? Although, of course, it's none of my business. And he goes batshit. I have to ask a guard to restrain him. This is a violent man, Mr. Feng Shao-li. No mistaking it. He says I don't know anything. He keeps asking over and over, 'Is it true they can kill me too?' What does he mean by that *too* stuff? See, Judge? You tell me."

"Let me ask you, Mr. Lovelace. Why did this issue of understanding not come up before now?"

The public defender shook his head. "The defendant said nothing until he found out he could die by lethal jab if the jury finds him guilty."

"And, as you told the jury, you have no defense."

"No *alibi,* Judge." He thought about that. "I mean, what am I supposed to defend him with?" He laughed. "That in China it's okay to kill people because there are so many of them? And he thinks the same applies over here? He hasn't been here long, you know. Just off the boat. You see the corner I'm in?"

A defense was what it was, Barr was thinking. It could be anything, and who was he to say outside of the dictates of "adequate" and "zealous"? Lovelace had told the jury that he did not understand the charge of murder in relation to his client. Maybe he was right. And if he could not understand it, how could he defend against it? He was putting the jury on notice that the defense wasn't about facts and evidence. It was about *feeling* and

46

conscience. Barr did not have that luxury. For him only facts and evidence would do.

———————

In the clerk of the court's office, Ben Bowers stroked his feathery white mustache as he read through court papers. He looked up when Barr entered and gave him an affectionate smile. "How ya doin', kid?" he called out in a familiar growl loud enough to be heard in the hall. And when the women in the office looked at Barr, then at Bowers, Ben cleared his throat. "*Judge* Barr, yes, of course, I stand corrected," he said.

"That's okay, Ben," Barr told him.

Ben was the chief clerk of the court. Barr had known him since his father had served as a superior court judge and he had hung around the court after school. Ben had taught him, among other things, how to fold paper airplanes, which they had flown into the courthouse rotunda in the hope of spearing a lawyer on his way out the doors.

"So, what can I do for you, Dan?"

"I've got a question about how the court works," said Barr matter-of-factly.

"I thought you knew this place as well as me."

"The halls, but not the workings. Tell me, just how tamper-proof is our jury-selection system? You're in charge of that sort of thing."

Bowers leaned against his desk, the picture of assurance, solid as a rock. "It's pretty airtight. As you know, it's run out of this office." He looked around at the bevy of women who worked for him. "Everyone involved takes it seriously. Damned seriously, I'd say. I drill into my people that the jury is the cornerstone of our society. It is no less important than that, in my view."

Barr felt better already. All he hoped to find was a single fact that would certify the note a hoax. And into the shredder it would go. "I just wondered, was all."

"It ticks along pretty good, except that nowadays people are lying and cheating and every other damned thing to get out of jury duty. Scoundrels, if you ask me. You'd think it was a curse, when it should be an honor."

"The computers that select the jury pools, are they located here in this building?" Barr asked.

Ben squared his shoulders. "Computers?"

Barr thought he was kidding. "You know, Apple, IBM, Microsoft, the Internet, Silicon Valley?"

"Don't get smart with me, just because you went to Harvard. I'm still bigger than you are. I know all about computers, believe me. Everyone says they have improved our lives. Well, if you ask me, this Internet that everyone's so hot about is stealing what little of our humanity we still have left, and the people who are surfing the net, most of 'em, are wankers. . . ."

"Well, where are they . . . ?"

Bowers just looked at him and shrugged.

"You mean you don't have them?" Barr asked, his tone incredulous.

"Budgets," he explained, his voice carrying all the way down the hall. "It's always budgets, in the end. There is money for this and for that, but when it comes down to computers for jury pools, not a nickel. And you know what? I haven't pushed the issue, either."

"But every county in America uses them by now. Don't they?" Barr didn't know. It wasn't a subject that anyone wrote about, or studied. Jury selection was just done. It was, because it always was, and that was all the explanation anyone needed. Tamper with it? The thought was ludicrous. Who wanted to get *on* a jury?

Of course these were thoughts that might not have occurred if Barr had not already received the anonymous note—and if his father had not presented him with such a direct, unmistakable warning: *It would be a mistake if you took this lightly.*

"You'd be surprised how many counties do without them," said Ben. "In some places there isn't a need. Some counties in

Idaho and Utah, for instance. There just aren't enough people, and few trials. In others there's no budget. That'd be us. In a few nobody's thought about it, one way or the other. Priorities, I guess."

Barr was hearing but he wasn't believing. "We can build a new twenty-million-dollar library with computerized book sorting and we can't get computers for the courts?"

"Hey, don't blame me," said Bowers.

Without computers, Barr could not imagine the task of sorting out the registered voters in San Francisco County and allotting them to the several jury pools that formed in superior court each week. But, then, he thought, most tasks these days, including checking out groceries at the supermarket and withdrawing money from the bank, seemed time-consuming and difficult without computers. "Well . . . how *are* the pools chosen?" he asked.

Ben looked eager, as though no one had ever asked him before. "I'll show you, if you want."

"I want," said Barr.

As they walked down the hall, Ben asked, "How's my main man, Morgan?"

"He asks about you all the time," Barr said. "You'll have to come to dinner sometime soon."

"Anytime. I mean it, you just name the night and I'm there."

Ben knocked on a door with a frosted glass window.

"Minute," came a voice from inside.

A few seconds later an SFPD officer opened the door. Barr had seen him around the halls, but he was embarrassed that he did not know his name. He was outfitted in a full policeman's uniform. Ben introduced him as Sergeant Michael Elkins.

Elkins ushered them into a room that was spare and cool with a worn linoleum floor and walls that were peeling mauve paint.

"I can go through a pool for you for real, if you like," Elkins volunteered after Ben told him what they wanted. He pointed to a long table in the room's recess.

Barr wondered who else knew about Sergeant Elkins. He

guessed that this job had come his way for services beyond the call of duty rendered to a long-retired deputy chief of police or a judge; maybe Elkins had once been a hero in the line of duty. Whatever it was, something had made him special and earned him this sinecure.

Elkins went over to the table. "In case you're wondering, Judge," he said, "we've used this room for this job as long as I can remember."

"How good is your memory, Sergeant?"

"I've been here fifteen years this fall, and I know it was used before I came along."

Elkins took sheets of self-adhesive labels on which the names and identifying numbers of potential jurors were printed from computer-generated lists. "These are sent several times a week from Sacramento," he explained. "Used to be you had to be a registered voter to be on a jury list. Not anymore. You got a license to drive, you are a candidate for jury duty. The computers randomly select drivers living in San Francisco County."

Barr looked at Ben Bowers, who looked right back. "See? We're not total trogs," Ben said with a hopeful smile.

Sergeant Elkins peeled off the labels one by one and stuck them onto pieces of paper which he folded laboriously. He had already folded sixty or eighty of them, and now he added another thirty to the heap.

Elkins dropped the papers into the unhinged opening of a hollow wooden drum on the far edge of the table. The drum looked like the ones used in raffles a long time ago, before Lotto came up with numbered Ping-Pong balls.

Elkins squeezed a single drop of A-1 all-purpose oil on the drum's axle. He clasped a handle of carved ivory and turned the drum slowly at first, then picked up speed. Barr had no doubt that he was doing this now for his benefit. The fluttering sounds of the papers reminded him of the beating wings of a bird against the ribs of a cage. Elkins looked over his shoulder. "My wife sometimes, just joking, calls me Fate," he said. "I'm not religious, but she is, you know. Baptist. She says there is death in what I do, and salvation, purgatory, and hell and heaven. I don't know about all that. I know there are consequences." And around and around the wheel went until Elkins released the handle and the drum slowed to a stop.

Elkins sighed with contentment. His work was almost done. Like a man fishing down a drainpipe, he put his hand in the drum and pulled out a single piece of folded paper, which he then placed in a slot on a wooden board against the wall. He repeated this again and again, until he had filled all the slots in the board; the remainder of the folded papers in the drum he emptied into a wastepaper basket under the table. Such was jury selection in San Francisco County. It was random, all right. No computer could make it more so. There was a certain efficiency to it, Barr had to admit. Quaint, certainly. But he also admitted something else: Elkins was present throughout the entire process; indeed, he *was* the process. And from what Barr had read about computers, hackers violated their security all the time. So maybe this was better after all.

Elkins closed the lid of the drum. He unhinged and carried the board down the hall, back to the clerk's office. The women who worked there stirred themselves as Elkins placed the wooden frame on the counter.

"From now on, I put the job in these ladies' capable hands," Elkins announced to Barr.

One of the women was standing with her hip against the counter. She was of a certain age, wore no wedding ring, a tight skirt. She fluttered her eyes. Ben introduced her as Ms. Meadows, a veteran of twelve years in the office.

"When was the pool selected for the Hawkes trial?" Barr asked them as a group.

No one responded. Several women shook their heads; Elkins shrugged. Ms. Meadows referred to a register on the counter, mentioning a date as she looked at Barr with her breath drawn as though she wanted to tell him something.

Barr ignored the look, and he asked Elkins, "Do you remember going through this process that day?"

Elkins raised his eyes to the ceiling in thought.

It was apparent to Barr that that day had been no different than any other to Elkins. He wasn't surprised.

"You know," said Elkins, remembering. "Come to think of it, I wasn't here that day." He went over to the counter and turned the register around. "It says I was here, but I wasn't. I remember. I had to take the wife to the hospital that morning. It took all day."

"Who took over for you?" Barr asked.

"I did, Judge," said Ms. Meadows. It was what she had wanted to say.

Ben Bowers glared at her. "Who gave you the right?" he nearly shouted.

"Nobody, Mr. Bowers," she replied, looking sheepish. All eyes turned to her, as if she had done something wrong, which wasn't exactly true. She explained, "The selection for the pool had to be done. And the sergeant called in that morning to say he wasn't coming in. So I did it. I know it was against the procedure, but there was no other choice."

"And what else?" Barr asked her gently. "What else happened that day?"

She looked back and forth between him and Ben Bowers.

"Okay, Ms. Meadows," said Bowers. "Just explain to the judge what happens to the names from here."

She smiled at Barr. "You're the new judge, the one in the Hawkes trial, aren't you?"

"That's right."

"I knew your father. You look a lot like him." She smiled again. Then she turned to the wooden board with the slots. "Well . . . I take these out and fix the labels to a single sheet, which becomes one jury pool, and then I copy the sheet and hand the copies around to the girls." To show him she reached into the slots, careful not to chip her nail polish. "The girls type up the names and addresses on form letters, notifying each of these people to appear for jury selection, when and where, you know?" She pointed down the counter. "We type up the envelopes, put the letters in, then leave them over there for the mailroom to pick up. Voilà."

Voilà, Barr thought with a slowly sinking feeling. What did it all mean? San Francisco County had a jury-selection system that was antiquated, but he still didn't see how someone who wanted to get himself on the jury might have rigged it. And it was with this thought that he went back to his chambers, where he finished up for the day. All the time, something kept nagging at him. He hadn't figured it out yet, but something as old as their selection procedure was weak, he thought, and in weakness it was vulnerable.

———————◆———————

He steered the Porsche along the familiar stretch of Jackson Street into Presidio Heights, the neighborhood where he had grown up. Cardinal Wells lived there too, in a house adjacent to the modest single spire of St. Mary's. It was a lovely holy place that Wells himself had chosen to say mass for a congregation of his Catholic peers who had donated generously to help create for him a temporal splendor.

Inside the church, the altar was a slab of pale green Cippolino marble, which Michelangelo used for his sculptures. Dalí had painted the Stations of the Cross, and a mural by Chagal gave the choir distinction. The confessionals were carved out of ancient teak by Henry Moore. A Dutch master had hewn the pew ends, and the ornate communion rail, which one of the parishioners had brought back from France after the Second World War, bore the provenance mark of Rodin's atelier. On the front wall behind the altar hung a modern *tapisserie* after the design by Picasso.

Barr looked over the congregation and was surprised to see Senator Hawkes, white-haired and handsome, almost preternatural in his youthfulness. He was seated by himself in the first pew, wearing the same kind of tailored gray suit and white linen shirt as he had on in court. His head bowed, he kneeled forward to pray on his knees as the organ played a Bach fugue.

Barr was not Catholic—he had no religion except a kind of lazy Episcopalianism—and, therefore, the setting and the sights and sounds of the Catholic mass were hardly familiar. And, after he chose a vacant pew, he found a certain fascination in watching the figure at the altar go through motions of the mass that to Barr seemed so alien and, indeed, private. Cardinal Wells was deeply engrossed, almost enraptured, by the sacred ritual. That did not surprise Barr. Cardinal Wells represented to him a spiritual-comfort compass, which had helped him through Vanessa's death and the hard days that followed. He had been there for the whole Barr family, and Barr knew he always would be.

Cardinal Wells uttered the words of the ceremony in its ancient Latin form. At the sound of chimes Barr looked up. Cardinal Wells nodded to Senator Hawkes, who approached the altar rail alone. He placed his hand on the senator's bowed head and prayed. This mass, Barr realized, was meant exclusively for Hawkes, and by the expression on the senator's face, he took his Communion with a deep religious commitment. He was devout and humble before the glory and power of God. And for some reason, watching the passing of the bread and the tilting of the Communion chalice, Barr thought about how he wanted to find the killer on the the jury not for himself or for the law but for Holly's grandfather, the senator, and, by extension, for his own godfather and father. The violation transcended law. It exposed a flaw that went as deep, he thought, as the society in which they all lived.

"*Ite missa est,*" Cardinal Wells said moments later, ending the mass.

On his way down the center aisle, the senator saw Barr, and he hesitated, as if questioning the propriety—if not the legality—of their speaking together while the trial was going on. He was a good man, Barr thought—pious, wholesome, proud, and intelligent. And he was a sorrowful one who had lost what went way beyond money, power, and prestige. He had lost flesh and blood, which nothing, not even his faith, could replace. Barr grinned hard and nodded to him, and the senator cast him an understanding smile and kept walking; Barr was relieved. A moment later, he looked up and sighed with pleasure as he saw the cardinal walk down the center aisle. Wells seemed happy to see him, and in his rush to greet him he only passingly acknowledged the other parishioners filing out of the church.

"You looked good up there in court this morning," the cardinal told him. "I was proud of you."

"You looked good up there too just now, Uncle Wellsy," said Barr, pointing his chin at the altar. He always felt awkward as an adult calling the cardinal by this familiar name, but over the years, and with adulthood, he had tried out "Your Eminence" and "Your Holiness" and even "Cardinal Wells," and nothing worked more comfortably than a simple "Wellsy." Besides, the cardinal had always insisted on "Uncle." He said it gave him a renewed feeling of belonging, which was enough to satisfy Barr.

"I've been up on the altar a couple more times than you've been on the bench."

"Don't remind me."

"I talked to your dad before mass just now. He told me about what happened, and I wanted to put in my own two cents, if you don't mind. It's why I called." He smiled with no uncertain sympathy. "I hope you don't think I'm meddling."

"Any advice I can get is welcome," he said, meaning it.

"I have just one question: Anything I can do?"

Barr shook his head. "You know the Hawkes family better than I do, better than Dad, certainly."

"I know a few things about the Hawkeses."

"Holly, you mean."

"That's right, Holly."

"Did she come here to church?"

"She was a devout little girl. As a Catholic she went to confession every Saturday, took Communion on Sunday, even sent me mass cards, wishing me happiness. She was a dear, dear child."

"Not the kind to be murdered?" It seemed to be what he was saying.

"That still confounds me," the cardinal said.

"The man tried to rob her, the police said."

That surmise squared with the indictment. According to the SFPD, Feng Shao-li had killed Holly in an apparent—and bungled—robbery. In the court's disclosure documents Barr had read that blood—Holly's type—had dripped from the Chinese man's hands when he was seen by a witness.

"I don't understand why she was there," Cardinal Wells said.

"That's why you called me, isn't it?"

Cardinal Wells did not respond directly. He did not nod, or shake his head. He did not whisper yea or nay. By this omission of any single response, Barr wondered whether he was being given a sign of some sort. What could it be? That Holly's killing wasn't a random mistake? How could he know that? "I don't suppose it would do any good, Uncle Wellsy, to ask you to tell me straight out what you know?"

He laughed. "No good at all." His expression softened.

"Isn't that a bit unfair?"

Cardinal Wells looked at him sternly. "As an ordained priest of the Catholic Church who receives confession, I know nothing about anything, period."

"But you are telling me, Uncle Wellsy, that something is wrong with this trial. And I don't think you mean the note, either. You're saying something I can't understand, and it isn't fair, given what the stakes are for me in this case. Are you helping me, or confusing me?"

"Helping," he said emphatically, and with a soft groan of effort he pushed himself off the pew. "Now I have work to do, and so do you."

Cardinal Wells left the church a few minutes later, still in his vest-
ments for mass, which he covered with a raincoat. He drove himself to the western border of Chinatown to the small brick parish
church of St. Michael's. Heavy chains greeted him at the front
door, and, confused, he stood a moment, listening to the sounds
of children and the slap of a basketball. Chinese teemed on the
sidewalks, shopping at the stalls. Written in Chinese and English,
fliers stapled to a notice board announced concerts, rehab programs, rewards for lost animals, yoga and language classes, and
therapeutic massages. He was about to return to the car when he
saw a man staring at him from the bottom of the steps.

"Your Holiness?" the man asked in a soft voice, and slipped
his hands shyly into khaki pants.

"This is your church, isn't it? You are Father Leary?"

He wore a faded madras shirt and dirty Nikes. Nothing about
him even hinted at his calling. "I was just headed around the
back. If you'd like to join me. Some of the kids play half-court
basketball in the parking lot behind the church. Basketball
draws a bigger crowd than mass, I'm sorry to say."

Cardinal Wells replied with a nod.

"The drugs, the homeless, the new immigrants," Father Leary
went on. "I wish the priesthood still had something to do with
God. I'm more like a social worker than a priest." He looked at
the cardinal. "They don't even call me 'Father.' "

They went along an alley behind the church, and there, just as
Father Leary had said, was a small basketball court. He used his
sleeve to wipe off a folding chair for the cardinal and he squatted on the curb, and for several minutes of silence they watched
the kids play.

"I think I know why you've come," said Father Leary, looking
straight ahead.

Cardinal Wells watched the action on the court as if he had
not heard.

"I know my liability," Leary said.

"For what?" Wells asked, turning to him now with a kindly expression.

"The Seal." Then he whispered, "I know my obligation."

"You would have committed a greater wrong if you had not broken the Seal."

Father Leary looked up, genuinely surprised. "Maybe I did do the right thing, but . . ."

"Then, why are you troubled?"

"The police have asked questions. They found a mass card in the girl's purse. They asked me if I had seen her. They asked again. The first time they came I didn't know what to say. It's why I called you, Eminence."

"And what did you tell them?"

"The truth, that I hear things from many people whom I cannot identify in confession. I lied, though, if you see what I mean?"

"I understand," said the cardinal.

"Twice I told the police I didn't know whether she was here or not here the night she was killed. But I do know. She *was* here. I recognized her in the confessional. I knew her voice. I could see the outline of her face." His voice trembled. "I worry all the time about that. If I had only spoken sooner"—and here he sighed with emotion—"she would still be alive. She came here often to confession, she said because she was afraid to confess to you, Eminence. She was frightened, but she was helpless too. And then . . ." He looked back over his shoulder. "A sad thing that could have been prevented. What has this world come to? When the police asked me questions, I had to call you. I knew you would know the right thing to do. A terrible sin, that's what it is. Its consequences reach beyond my parish here. Remember?"

Cardinal Wells remembered all too well. He had been unforgiving and hard at first when Father Leary had called that night.

"Your Eminence, I must break the Seal," Leary had told him. And Wells had met his statement with a stony, cold silence. "I said, the Sacramental Seal—"

"I heard you, Father," the cardinal had told him; he had never met him, not that he remembered. He had felt no connection with him. "I heard you well the first time. But the Seal is inviolable. The Seal is *you*, Father, as an ordained priest who takes the place of Christ in the tribunal of penance. It is me. We are bound by the same laws of God. To reveal what you have been told in confession to anyone is a sin in the eyes of God for which there can be no redemption. It marks you for damnation. And as a priest in the Catholic Church, nothing should be more important, nothing in your whole temporal life. I am reminding you because I think *you* have forgotten." He had not even tried to hide his contempt for what the priest had wanted to do. "I cannot give you permission or absolution for such an act, and I cannot stop you. I'm curious, though. Why are you telling *me* about this decision?"

"Because I am afraid."

Now, as they sat watching the Chinese kids play half-court basketball, Father Leary asked, "Can you forgive me, Your Eminence? Can God? *Mene absolvis a peccates meis in nomine Patris et Filii et Spiritus Sancti? Et libera me a malo?*"

Cardinal Wells was so profoundly moved by the simple faith and goodness of this priest, he kneeled down in front of him. It was why he had come here. He placed his hand on his shoulder and he quoted Psalm 143. " 'Enter not into judgment with Thy servant: for in Thy sight shall no man living be justified.' Far from condemning you, Father," he told Leary, "I have come to thank you. Because of you, justice will be done."

At a gate overhung with moonvine, clematis, and primrose, Barr slipped a key into the lock and entered an urban paradise at the top of the western slope of Russian Hill. He walked through dappled light up slate steps toward a house that looked down over the Financial District, Chinatown, and the Bay Bridge, which at night from this height looked like a string of diamond beads. Just as lovely, the sound of laughter rang out from within the house with a kind of manic merriment.

Looking through the window, Barr saw his son, Morgan, and the au pair, Roberta reading *Pish, Posh, said Hieronymous Bosch,* which Barr knew by heart.

Morgan *was* him, he thought, watching them briefly unseen. Morgan was Vanessa too. He was a handsome child, thin and angular, with the same black hair and green eyes as Barr, but with his mother's mercurial disposition. Vanessa had died when Morgan was four and she was twenty-nine. He was a perfect composite of their characters and their most hidden selves. He had seen in Morgan a reflection of small gestures that were Vanessa's alone. In the blinking of an eye he could see her there so purely, he might have cried for the yearning he often felt for her. What Morgan meant to him he could describe as a true revelation. Barr had never imagined there could be that much wonder in a face.

In the kitchen, Morgan smiled and offered Barr an indifferent "Hi," then returned to the den off the kitchen, where Roberta was reading him the book. Barr looked in. Their cocker spaniel, Flicka, was on her rug, asleep. Flicka was an old girl with a figure that was lumpy and bordering on fat. She slept most of the day, but she looked up now. Her tail wagged twice before she lowered her head again and returned to the pleasure of her dog reveries.

"We'll be finished in a minute, Judge," Roberta told him.

Roberta was in her middle twenties, and a true English rose. Big-hipped with enviable bosoms, rosy cheeks, and a disposition as sweet and luscious as Devon cream, she had come to them through an agency and within days it seemed as though she belonged. What Barr liked about her most was that she said exactly what was on her mind, to the point of tactlessness, which she called honesty. With Roberta there were never grounds for misunderstanding. Her opinions were sharp and never wavered, and her judgment about people was always on the mark.

Morgan said, "Pish posh," as though it were an epithet. He

was mad at his father, Barr imagined, for missing lunch. He should have known better than to have promised. That's what the psychologists advised. But psychologists were not a single male parent who could never stop feeling bad for an inadequacy that he could never provide. He could never be Vanessa. And beyond even that, he did not know what ideal he envisioned for himself as a parent. Maybe he pushed himself too hard. But he still felt himself to be a failure.

Moments later, the book read, Morgan came into the living room. He had forgotten his anger. "Can we watch the movie?" he asked.

It was never *a* movie, but always simply *the* movie—*Raiders of the Lost Ark*. How many times had they seen it together? So many that by now they recited the lines of dialogue—*"Get a little backbone, will ya?" "Bad dates!" "There's a snake in the plane, Jacques." "Poison is still fresh—three days"*—with silly anticipation.

"Maybe later, okay?" Barr said. "I have to go back to work."

"Can we fly the kite now?"

Barr looked at Roberta. "Dinner won't be for a few minutes yet," she told him.

Barr followed his son out behind the gazebo. The house had once belonged to his grandfather. He had long taken for granted the unusual expanse of a property that by now was worth $2 or $3 million to a developer, with or without the old house. The place was a true anachronism. People just didn't live like this in San Francisco anymore—a half-acre of private flowers and trees and grass and shrubs with a house in the center of the second most expensive city in America. But Barr did, and he knew he was just lucky.

While Flicka sat watching them from the porch, Morgan held the kite and Barr pulled on the string and started to run across the lawn. And when the kite was in the air and leaped upward, Morgan shouted, "Daddy, let it go." And at the sound, Flicka barked and swept her tail over the porch boards.

Barr laughed to himself. He never let *anything* go. That was his problem, and always had been. Morgan saw the joy of release and freedom—the scary, even chaotic sensation that came with letting things go out of control.

The kite pulled against the wind and Barr handed the string to Morgan. Control? What about the example he set for him of rectitude, morality, hard work, and a commitment to things beyond himself? How could he ever let go, as a parent?

They lay together on the lawn, father and son, as the kite colored the dusk sky. Flicka came down from the porch and gently pushed herself up against Morgan, looking up through sleepy eyes at Barr, who gave her a loving pat.

The quiet moment—the first in days for Barr—put him in a reflective mood. He thought about fathers and sons, how the relationships changed over the years. Like now with Morgan, he was the boy's whole world. His authority went without question. Barr had felt the same toward his own father far past his own youth. As close as he grew to Justice Barr after the deaths of their wives, Barr had always kept a respectful distance between himself and his father. How else could he behave toward a man of Justice Barr's enormous stature? But the stroke recently had changed all that. Barr now looked at the stairs to the house. The difference between his feelings for his dad now and before his stroke? He had carried his father in his arms up those stairs, at first silently. Neither man had said a word, as if it were not happening. Later, they had joked about it. Now, it seemed wonderful to think, Barr looked forward to his father's visits just for that reason. He liked carrying his Dad. It had brought them closer in more ways than either man had ever thought possible.

As though he had been thinking too, Morgan turned to his father. "When can we go out together for . . . you know . . . chicks, Dad?" He bent over with childish laughter.

Barr stopped petting Flicka and stared at his son. "Chicks?" he asked.

"Babes, you know—'Berta calls them dollies."

Eight years old. "They are called women. And the answer to your question is never. We don't troll bars for a mother."

"Dinner's on," Roberta called at the side door.

"Well . . . ?" asked Morgan.

"When the right one comes along we'll recognize her," Barr said as he got up off the grass.

After a dinner of macaroni and cheese with Morgan, Barr went out again; he swung the Porsche down Union Street to Stockton, a little out of his usual way to the court, but he had intended to make this detour for weeks and somehow had never found the time. Aversion was a factor. It wasn't a trip he would ever choose to make, but it was necessary now that he had a killer to find, and find soon.

He parked the car on the Chinatown end of the tunnel and walked amid the jostle of Chinese shopping the street markets. The sights and sounds here were different enough to be another universe, he thought, amazed not for the first time at this world's propinquity, almost within sight of his house up the hill.

As he approached the tunnel, the contrasts between light and shade, understanding and ignorance, chaos and order, stood out in stark relief. He walked along the footpath on the left side of the tunnel—it was on this footpath against the tiled wall that Holly Hawkes was slaughtered. He looked up, then all around, feeling a disorientation amounting almost to dizziness. The temperature once inside the tunnel's shelter dropped by several degrees. He shook his head to clear his mind, picturing the tunnel as a warp in time. Holly's death was warped too. Prosecutor Shenon had told the court that her killer had stabbed her enough times to confound even the medical examiner. There was no mystery. The killer had wanted Holly not just dead; he had wanted her punished in some way that Barr could not fathom. She had been young, innocent, ambitious, and focused on her future. She had been bright and, he somehow imagined, happy. She had been normal, even in spite of her beauty and privilege.

Tires rolling against the blacktop, the singsong voices, sirens in the distance and car horns, the rumble of truck engines— the curving tiles of the tunnel's walls bent these sounds eerily. He looked up and back—toward Union Square, then back to Chinatown—for an unguarded moment, afraid for himself and his family. But then he caught himself. He was a grown man. He did not believe in ghosts.

A variety of odors assaulted him, a mixture of stenches. The tunnel was a filthy, alien venue, far from a place where a girl like Holly Hawkes ever went. He wondered about the sadness of her dying in a place this foreign. Had she asked in final desperation why her mother and her father and her grandfather had abandoned her? Hadn't they protected her all through her childhood? What had she done to deserve this? What had she done to earn this fate?

The tunnel walls bowed in a circle with a flat bottom. Car fumes colored the tiles a sulphurous brown, and where water had seeped down, rust cracks crossed the tiles. Decay pocked the fretwork of an ancient iron railing where Barr was standing as he looked back down the tunnel at the small circle of light in a faraway familiar world near Union Square.

On the night of Holly's murder fog had rolled up from the bay against the Chinatown end of the tunnel. The only visible light had come from a yellow lamp over the walkway. The hiss of car tires on wet pavement would have muffled her screams and the sounds of the plunging knife, then the clatter of the killer's shoes as he ran into the night.

Bloodstains that had not washed away darkened the interstices of the bricks by Barr's feet. He looked up, suddenly breathless, and afraid. A mist fell across the light, and he sniffed the air and cocked his ear, trying to imagine the violence that had taken place here, the struggle, the blows, the submission, the resignation, the whisking away of a life that brimmed with promise. . . .

Standing where Holly had fallen, he tried to imagine the mind of the killer. Whoever did this, he told himself, knew her. And then he thought of Feng Shao-li, an ugly pug of a Chinese who hardly spoke a single word of English. Something didn't fit.

———————

At the court, on his way to his chambers, Barr saw that the door to the clerk of the court's office was open, and he poked his head inside expecting to see Ben working late. Instead, he found Ms. Meadows sitting at a desk on the other side of the counter. When she saw him, her smile changed to a look of concern.

"Ben Bowers went for the day," she said. She got up and came over.

Barr leaned on the counter, giving her time.

"I like that little boy of yours," she told him. "He has a lovely smile."

"Do you have children?" Barr asked her.

"No," she said softly, and she gazed off in the middle distance. Clearly, she had wanted children, and the tragedy of her life was not having one.

"This afternoon when I was here," said Barr, "I didn't have a chance to ask you. Did anything different or unusual happen that day, the one we were talking about?" He spoke in a gentle and understanding tone. "Don't be afraid to tell me. I won't mention it to anyone."

"The day I did Sergeant Elkins's job for him?" She shook her head. "I didn't say anything to anybody about what I did, as you know, but that doesn't mean anything unusual happened. I didn't ask Ben's permission to go there and turn the handle on the drum. What's the big deal? It doesn't take genius, after all. You saw how Elkins does it. I was just helping out."

"I'm sorry if I got you in trouble with Ben," he told her. "Don't worry, I'll square it with him myself."

"I can handle Ben okay," she said, and she seemed to relax.

"You were about to tell me . . ."

She tensed visibly again.

"Beyond your doing Sergeant Elkins's job for him," he asked

one more time, "was there anything different about that day?"

"Nothing I can remember," she said.

He could sense that she was lying; she seemed almost too certain for truth.

"I kept the slot board in here with the girls and me all that day," she explained. "It was right under our noses. I don't see how anything, as you say, *unusual,* could have happened. It was just business, you know, as usual."

The lady doth protest too much, thought Barr. He saw no reason to question her further. He could not force her to tell him what she didn't want to tell. "Maybe you could think it over? I'll be working late in my chambers." He looked at his watch. "If you think of anything you might have forgotten, please stop by."

She was shaking her head slowly. "I'll do that," she said. "But, Judge, I think I'd have already remembered."

Maybe, Barr thought. But he did not have time to let up on the pressure on her. He had not really thought about the time issue until right now. But he had a juror who he suspected was in some way involved in Holly's murder. The juror might even have killed her, if the note was true. And everyone, from his father to his godfather, was suggesting that it was. A clock of sorts was set in motion by the start of the trial. It was ticking even now. When the trial was finished and the verdict was in, he told himself, he might put an innocent man in the death chamber and let a guilty man go free. And by then he would have lost the last scintilla of control. "Anything, no matter how small, could be important," he told her. He looked her in the eye. "You can't even begin to imagine how important, Ms. Meadows."

Barr stared at the computer monitor, desperate to find a way to this new, illusive truth. He assumed the San Francisco County sheriff's office, which handled this end of things, had screened the jurors as a matter of procedure. Some of the Hawkes jurors had "hits" with the FBI's National Crime Information Center's database—felons with their same names living in the Bay Area. A certain Bullock, for instance, had served some portion of a fifteen-year sentence for manslaughter. Jesse Coffer showed for grand theft, auto, in Houston; and an O. Ivy, female, was sought on felony murder charges in Seattle. Barr rubbed his eyes. By now he recognized that he was too far afield with NCIC. Of course he would find hits in such a humongous database, but these also were a waste of his time.

He accessed the data base in the city hall's computers for the data from the jurors' individual questionnaires that included the facts of the jury candidates' lives. He had heard a few of these jurors discuss themselves to some degree during the voir dire proceedings. He paused a moment to reflect. Obviously, he had not asked them the right questions. But what did he miss? Lovelace had asked nothing. Prosecutor Shenon had stuck strictly to the points given to him by a paid jury consultant. No one was looking for a perjurer trying to get *on* the jury. Barr knew how potential jurors dissembled. Nearly every one of them shaved their testimonies a bit here and there, to get out of jury duty. It was almost human nature.

Juror #5, he saw now, Adam Warmath, was single, sold insurance, and voted Democrat. Anthony Bullock, #7, was also single, and was registered an Independent. David Figueroa, Juror #1, had a wife and family and no political affiliation. Michael Eng, #8, wasn't political either, and noted his professional affiliation as director of Project Right in an area below Russian Hill.

Incomes were not listed, by law. Length of employment was noted. The jurors all appeared, for the most part, to be stable, upright men and women. Their specific companies ran the gamut of local corporations and industries, from tourism to banking and high tech, and one charity. Daniel Gee, #6, who was a bachelor, operated a restaurant in Chinatown, the Golden Dragon. He did volunteer duty ten hours a week at the Chinese-American Association. Maria Garriques, #2, one of the Hispanic jurors, worked in a beauty parlor downtown as a manicurist. Olivia Ivy, #3, was an African-American housewife.

Bessie B. Matthews, #9, was a secretary for Levi Strauss jeans. Could she have killed Holly Hawkes? Could any of them have?

Jesse G. Coffer, Juror #4, another of the African-American jurors, was young and single, a bus driver for the city. For hobbies, he had put down model railroading. Was his a profile that raised questions? Barr did not think so.

Arlene Cohen, #10, was a divorcée struggling to make ends meet who took cooking lessons as a hobby.

Kim Wen, #11? He ran a pharmacy in Chinatown and was near retirement.

Amy Wong, #12, was a housewife and had raised her own children and helped her husband run his grocery on Stockton Street in Chinatown.

Claire Hood, #8, was startling for her beauty, which Barr thought of as a combination of breeding, youth, and intelligence; she and Barr shared degrees from Harvard and hailed from the same San Francisco social stratum. Barr was surprised that he did not know her or her parents.

These questionnaries were not much to go by. The law had stripped the courts of their ability to learn more about jurors, as different interest or racial groups had challenged one question after another as invasive and prejudiced. Of course, the challenges had won in courts that were bending over backward to achieve political correctness, and as a result the questionnaire was sterilized almost to meaninglessness.

But right now, these questionnaires were all he had.

Barr looked up from the screen and leaned back in his chair. He recalled his conversations with the attorneys—the two together—during voir dire before the trial had started.

In high-profile trials hundreds of thousands of dollars went to hiring private detectives, juror consultants, psychologists, and sociologists, and even clairvoyants, to assess the jurors. Each side benefitted from knowing which way the individual jurors might vote—for or against the defendant. Would Juror X be more sympathetic to the defendant than Juror Y, or would Juror Y be more hostile to the defendant than Juror Z? With this in mind Barr had asked Lovelace about his research up to that point.

"We are limited by funds," he had told him, meaning that he had none to spare. He had limited his research on the jurors, therefore, to old-fashioned intuition.

Barr had asked him, "Do you want the funds to hire a consultant? I will see that you get them."

But Lovelace had shaken his head. "It's too late," he had replied. "Anyway, it's not my bag, Judge."

"Did *you* do any of it, then, you yourself?"

"What I could, you know?"

"And what was that?"

Barr remembered him saying, "I am mostly worried about prejudice. You know how that is. I'm worried most about that. Race plays a part nobody ever wants to admit to." Lovelace had touched the bottom of his eye with his finger. "Race alone can never be the basis for striking a juror."

"What are you getting at, Counselor?" he had asked him, annoyed.

"I am trying hard to get jurors with open minds, that's what. And I am using my preemptives to get rid of those who I think have closed minds." He had looked over at chief prosecutor Shenon. "It is that simple, and I don't mind you knowing, Henry. Remember that one lady who said she had nothing at all against the Chinese? She had her sheets washed and ironed by them for as long as she could remember?" He had laughed mellowly. "I figured she might carry a bit too much baggage, if you see what I mean."

Shenon, the trial prosecutor, had been equally candid. "I'm getting less than I want, more than I hoped for," he had said, which for Shenon had been like baring his soul.

"Have you hired a consultant?"

"Yes, of course."

"And an investigator?" Barr had asked.

He nodded.

Now, in front of a computer monitor, all this was leaving Barr with little at all. He looked at the clock on the wall. It was late and he was suddenly feeling very tired. He took his coat off the hook behind the door and left his chambers. He felt himself adrift and alone, facing a mystery that so far refused to reveal anything more than a blurred outline.

He decided to go out the front way. The reporters would be gone by now. And at the bottom of the stairs he looked for a deputy to let him out.

"Quiet around here with them gone," a deputy sheriff who was Chinese said to him. He was leaning back on two legs of a chair, his feet up against an X-ray console.

Barr offered him a nonengaging smile. He heard the chair legs bump against the floor, almost like an exclamation. Though Barr had seen the deputy before, he noticed him now: a boyish, engaging smile.

"We're like this X-ray machine, I know," he told Barr. "People look right through us."

"I'm sorry if that's the impression I gave," said Barr. "I was thinking of something else entirely."

How usual, even routine, it was, he thought, not to see, or, worse, to see *through,* people. A correspondent friend for *Newsweek* who had once covered sub-Saharan Africa from Nairobi had told him that he had looked straight through the Africans after a short while. "They were there but they weren't, Danny," he remembered him saying. "It was scary." Barr understood that now. He leaned against a pillar. "You live in San Francisco?" he asked more out of a sense of obligation than interest.

The deputy shook his head. "San Jose, if you believe it. It's a commute, but it's what we can afford. My family left Chinatown when I was a teenager."

"Was it a struggle, getting out?" he asked him, curious now.

The deputy sheriff did not seem to mind. "It took our family a hundred years, if you get my meaning," he said with a grin. "Sometimes I wonder at that. We still haven't left Chinatown completely. You know the saying 'You can take the boy out of Kansas but you can't take Kansas out of the boy'? My sisters and I feel that way. We're at home in Chinatown, when we go back there. We know the place. It's us, *in* us." He looked carefully at Barr. "You're the judge in the Hawkes trial, aren't you?"

He smiled wanly. "*The* trial, yes," he said.

"Strange to me," the deputy said, looking away. "Strange to my sisters and to my parents, too."

"It is, isn't it."

"Really, the defendant being Chinese and all."

Barr was about to ask why, but he didn't have the energy. He smiled and indicated the doors with his chin when he heard the clack and clatter of high heels rattling behind him like pistol shots off the court rotunda's marble stairs. He turned to see a woman running with one hand lifting the hem of her skirt while the other clutched a purse. He couldn't see her face because of the shadows on the stairs. "Judge, Judge Barr," she shouted. "I thought I'd catch you in chambers," she called out in a rush of words. "I was afraid I'd missed you. I saw you just now leaving." She looked around her, then back at him.

It was Louise Meadows from the clerk's office. She was twisting her fingers around the straps of her purse.

"I mean, I hope it's nothing, but it might be something. You asked me to try to remember? There is something, Judge, but it's just clerical. It's not unusual, like you said. You seemed so worried earlier. I told myself, Well, it may be nothing. But let him decide."

"Yes?" he asked hopefully.

"I don't want you to think our work in the clerk's is sloppy," she said. "We take pride in what we do. All of us girls. So does Mr. Bowers. We don't make errors . . . or hardly ever." She paused for a quick breath. "I found this wedged in the counter in our office two days ago."

She handed him one of the folded squares of paper with the jurors' names and an identifying number.

He unfolded the paper, trying hard to catch her meaning.

"Someone must have stuck it there. You see? I didn't even tell the other girls. I was terrified of what Ben would say. And until you stopped by, Judge, I didn't know how you could know. I was so worried. I still don't see how it happened."

"Slow down, Miss Meadows, please," he told her, leading her over to the stairs. "I'm not sure I follow you." And he looked again at the paper.

"We accounted for the correct number of candidates in every pool. But it still just doesn't add up."

"You mean a master list?" Barr asked.

She reached into her handbag. "Do you mind if I smoke?" And she pawed a pack of Mistys. Her fingers trembled and Barr took the little Bic lighter from her hand and fired up the cigarette. She drew in a deep breath. "This screwup was from the Hawkes jury pool. I checked the number on the juror paper that I found under the counter against the master list. I was hoping it was for a pool for a civil trial, but, Judge, it wasn't. Like I said, I really don't know what happened. This doesn't change anything, please tell me it doesn't." She dragged on her Misty.

"The names of the jurors come from the master list, don't they?" That was all he wanted to know.

"That's what I don't understand," she said, shaking her head softly. "There should have been one missing since this one was wedged up in the counter like that. One wedged should mean one missing. I would have noticed if it was. It *wasn't*. If I hadn't found the paper I'd never have known." She looked at him. "Want me to show you?"

Yes, he did, very much.

They went back up the stairs to the third floor, and in the clerk's office the fluorescents bloomed and the room flooded with light. Barr's eyes followed the counter to the far wall and the wooden board with its slots filled with the folded papers. Ms. Meadows saw the direction of his gaze.

"We didn't have time to finish up," she explained. "Sergeant Elkins brought the board in just before we quit for the day. The girls left. I stayed, because I wanted to talk to you."

"It's left out like that overnight?" he asked.

"Sure," she said. "All the time. But most of the time there

aren't the jurors' names in it. Like I said, we didn't have time to type them up. We'll get to it first thing in the morning."

Barr looked over his shoulder. "This office is open to the public, isn't it?"

She looked at him with a question. "They have to come in, if they want to submit their dismissal forms in person. We have people who come through here all day long."

"I see," he said.

He walked down to the end of the counter. "Let's go through this, step by step, okay?"

She went over to her desk and looked back at Barr.

"Fold a piece of paper just like the ones in the slots, will you?" he asked her. When she handed it to him, he said, "Now pretend you are going about your business." He put the folded paper she had just handed him into one of the slots, removing the paper that was already there, and that paper he pushed up under the edge of the counter. "Okay, I've come in and I've gone out. How can you know that I've replaced another pool candidate's name and address with my own."

She came over, concentrating. "Easy," she said. She was carrying a list. "You'll be on the master list. If you're not, you don't belong on the slot board."

"What about the names on the papers that Elkins doesn't use?" He meant the leftover folded papers in the wooden drum, once the slots in the board were filled.

"He throws them out." She thought about that. "He's very careful to get rid of them, so there's never any mixup."

"The names in the slots are on the master list."

"That's right. If not, how would they get there?"

"By someone like the person who jammed the paper up under the counter."

She was shaking her head. "But the new name—the one the person slipped in the slot board—should not appear on the master list. Should it?"

He thought about that, and he had an explanation. "Each pool has how many people?"

73

"As many as five to six hundred."

"And Elkins narrows it down to the number that's needed in the room down the hall."

"That's correct."

"What if I'm on the master list? A computer somewhere has generated my name. Or I get my name on there and I want to make damned certain my name does not end up in Elkins's wastepaper basket. I want to have my name put in a slot."

"Then, of course! You could do it!" she said, surprising herself. "But what if your name's already been chosen?"

"Then there'd be two."

"There weren't duplicates. But if there were, we'd have thought it was our mistake somehow, and we'd have thrown one out, kept the other," she said. "It's not something that's ever happened. I'd have remembered, though."

"Did you remember seeing anybody that day in the office who looked suspicious?" He asked because whoever had made the switch was concerned that he would be discovered—why else jam the piece of paper under the counter edge?

She held the cigarette out in front of her. "I've thought and I've thought and I've thought." She gave him a helpless shrug. "The only thing that comes to mind? I know it may sound crazy, but Chinese. More like an impression, like something really vague." She shook her head. "I'm sorry, but that's all I can say."

"A man? A woman?"

She shook her head. "I'm sorry, Judge. Someone who was Chinese. I wish I could be more helpful."

"You've been a tremendous help, Miss Meadows."

"What does it *mean*, Judge?"

He looked at her. "It means the selection process may have been tampered with," he told her. He saw the fear in her face. "It's not your fault, Miss Meadows. Nothing's going to happen to you. When you weren't looking, someone took the original out of a slot and replaced it with a folded piece of paper they had made up themselves." He tried to keep his voice even.

"That's a funny thing to do."

He let out his breath. "Yeah, isn't it?" he said. He wished he could laugh.

———————

Wally Howard lived in the hills overlooking Sausalito in a bungalow overwhelmed by a tangle of vines. By the time Barr got there the hillside was dark. He pushed a button on an intercom, and a hoarse voice demanded to know who was there.

When Barr identified himself, the buzz on the lock indicated that Wally was receiving, and he went up the steep ascent. He was out of breath by the time he reached the top of the steps. Wally was leaning over the railing of a terrace that cantilevered out from the hill. Behind the house gurgled a swift-running brook. Wally was in a bathrobe he must have purchased in Hong Kong on one of his tours of duty in Vietnam. It was black satin embroidered with a golden dragon that looked imposing in the shadows.

"I hope business brings you by," he said in his bottom-of-the-well voice. He was a broad man with a powerful chest, short legs, and the long, rueful face of one who has seen the worst and the best. "There's very little pleasure around here at this hour, except sleep," he said. "I can probably find you a beer."

The two men had met years ago when Wally was still on the SFPD, and even then Barr had appreciated his wit and style. They had struck up an acquaintance that turned social, with Barr attending Wally's annual end-of-summer party and, in return, inviting him to his and Vanessa's Christmas cocktail bash. In succeeding years Wally was the first to arrive and *always* the last to leave. Vanessa had thought of him as one of Barr's closer friends, considering that Barr wasn't the kind of man who easily made friends. No matter how their relationship was defined, it flourished because Wally and Barr felt comfortable with one another and shared a respect and a certain admiration for each other's history and skills. Their unspoken bond included coming to the aid of the other, no matter what, though this pact had never been invoked.

In the light of the living room, Wally said, "You look like hell, Danny, if you'll pardon the observation. Don't judges get any anymore?"

Barr laughed. "Any what?"

"I know pussy's no problem for you. Sleep, I'd say, to start with."

"The Hawkes trial, remember?"

He nodded. "I know, but it just started. If this is what you look like now, you'll be a cadaver at the finish. You could use some rest."

"In time. Right now it's more important that I to talk to you. Business. Your business."

Wally's firm, Howard & Associates, worked in the investigation field. Ex-detectives from the SFPD, disgruntled when the chief of police under Mayor—now the junior United States senator—Dianne Feinstein had started recruiting gays and lesbians on the force, had joined Wally in a new company that checked out jurors for the consultants who hired out to the defense teams and the DA's office. The company had thrived from the start. "Checked out" was the only accurate way to describe what they did. The law prevented turning potential jurors into suspects whose lives were intruded upon, so Wally used material found through computer searches, stuff basically in the public domain. No snooping in garbage cans, no taps on wires, no surveillances, none of that stuff for him. It was purely superficial, Barr knew, but it was still more than anything he could ever hope to learn on his own.

Wally asked, "Before we begin, Dan, did the DA give you permission to talk to me?"

"Specifically, no."

His eyebrows arched in concern. "He's not a client my firm can afford to lose," he said. "You know I worked for him on the Hawkes jury selection."

"That's why I'm here. Let's just say I need the benefit of your intuition." All right, he thought. Don't lie to him. "I didn't ask Shenon because I don't want him to know I'm asking. He'd raise a stink. And right now a stink is something I don't need."

"Glad to oblige, in confidence," said Wally as he went to the kitchen and opened the refrigerator for a cold beer. He held one up for Barr, who shook his head, and while Wally made himself a plate of snacks and tore back the beer's tab, Barr scanned the living room, which Wally had decorated and furnished for his convenience alone and to his own taste. He was the king of his own castle, with little room for courtiers. The cushions of one reclining chair, well worn, and one sofa had taken the form of his derriere like the pockets of an old outfielder's mitt. On a side table in a neat line sat a brace of remote channel changers that connected him to a television with a huge back-projection screen and a hi-fi surround-sound system that was powerful enough to blow the paper off the walls. Painted torsos of South Seas nudes with strutting breasts, portraits of fast and highly polished automobiles, beer signs, and the logos of the San Francisco 49ers and Giants littered the walls.

"How's the love life?" Barr asked when Wally returned. "What's the woman situation these days?"

Wally manned his reclining chair with a practiced glide. "Barbara, you remember Barbara? She's off visiting her mother in Connecticut. The old bird's ill. She left in May."

It was now August.

Barr remembered her. She was endowed with a head of blond hair that she piled up in a studied and alarming heap. She was perennially tan and she claimed she slept in tanning beds even when they weren't turned on. Her helpful and eager disposition fit her job as a manager of a hamburger chain in San Francisco called Hooters.

"Anyway, did I tell you I talked with Roberta the other day? Morgan's a lucky kid. I wish I could have an au pair like her."

Barr looked at him warily. "The rule still applies, Wally," he growled.

"She asked me if I was chatting her up." He looked at Barr for a sign. "I said sure, if she wanted me to. She's a looker, Dan."

"Good help is still hard to find." The rule between them was a strict prohibition that Barr had set down against Wally's dating Roberta. If she wanted to ask him out to dinner, that was okay. But he knew Wally's history with women, and he wasn't going to have him breaking her heart.

As if he'd read his thoughts, Wally said, "I'm a heartbreaker, that much is true." He believed it too, by the look on his face. "You?" he asked, switching the conversation.

"Me?"

"Love life."

"Jenny," Barr said without putting much into it.

"Jenny, like she's chopped liver." He laughed.

Wally treated her like she was a princess. He could be very funny without intending, making certain a chair was brushed for dust and crumbs before she sat down, delivering her drink in a glass he had wiped clean and inspected up to the light, and standing up nearly at attention when she entered a room—he was like a poor man's Cary Grant around her, as naturally and yet awkwardly a gentleman as anything Barr had ever seen.

"I don't know why you won't give her the credit she deserves," Wally went on in the same vein. "Any other guy would. She could kick me and beat me and cheat and lie and I'd still come crawlin' home." He pointed to a picture on the far wall. "You see that Ferrari up there, all red and sleek and shiny? Well, that's a metallic version of Jenny. She's a Joe Montana of a gal, if you ask me."

"I didn't ask, so let's drop the subject. What I need to ask you about is the jurors. It's why I'm here. Jurors."

"What jurors?"

"The Hawkes trial?" Barr reminded him. "The jurors? You investigated some of them for the DA's office?"

Wally paused an instant. "Them," he said with disdain. "Shenon didn't seem concerned," Wally said. "He paid for what amounted to a level-one look. That's the level that just scrapes the surface—name, date of birth, serial number, POW stuff. I spent maybe thirty minutes on each one, and that was that."

"In a trial of the Hawkes profile?" asked Barr. "I'd have thought you would have poured it on."

"Shenon has enough physical evidence to convince a blind and deaf jury to convict, and the circumstantial is pretty airtight too. It's a slam dunk. Why waste the county's money?"

"And what did you pick up on this level one?" He could tell by Wally's expression that it couldn't have been very much.

Wally said, "There's a gay guy in there, I recall, still in the closet, maybe his big toe is out, that's about it. And a woman who isn't sure what she is, man or woman. There's a workaholic and a border alcoholic, a guy who's a do-gooder social worker, and a woman who tells friends she uses dope recreationally. And there's an evangelical Bible thumper who thinks she speaks in tongues. Beyond that there is the usual degree of self-absorption and delusion you find anywhere in our charming society."

The analysis made Barr laugh. "No one stands out, though? No one who might try to come down on the others maybe a bit too hard?"

He drew on his beer. "Not a one." He smiled at Barr. "Have you ever sat on a jury?"

"No," Barr replied.

"I have, and it's a world unto itself, which you should know about. You get people who understand the facts and yet cling to a belief in the innocence of the accused because he reminds them of their father, or because of something they said that struck a sympathetic chord. You can't budge them, either. We let a rapist go when I was a juror. He got a mistrial." The memory still seemed to upset him. "You know why? Because a couple of women on the jury felt sorry for him. You see, he was raped when he was a teenager, or *said* he was. His psychologist testified that he suffered from repressed memories. The veil of repression lifted only after the indictment came down. What about the victim? Talk about repressed memories." Wally was on a role. "What amazed me, Dan, the jurors were sweet as pie when they were being chosen in the voir dire, but they all changed in the deliberations. I expected some of it. But I didn't expect that degree of change. One little old lady became a terror. She wanted the guy's head." He laughed. "I loved her for that. But the others, it was like *they* were on trial." He thought a second. "The jury system can't stand up to what our society has become. Something's gotta be done. The way it is now, nobody gets condemned for anything. And they deserve to. Back to the jurors, there's always someone who wants to be different, someone who wants to be a star. A trial last year, I don't remember the name of the defendant, but there were jurors with contracts to write books. Now, what does that do to the thinking of a juror? If I am a juror and I know a vote to acquit will help sell my book, I let the defendant go. Who am I going to look out for? The justice system or my own bank balance? Give me a break."

Barr both agreed and disagreed, but he wasn't there to discuss the state of jurisprudence in America. He decided to give Wally more of an idea of what was on his mind. "I'm looking for a juror who may have committed a felony but neither has been caught nor had it revealed in the voir dire."

"You're looking for a phantom, then." He laughed. "You, Dan Barr, could commit a felony tomorrow. I could too. But I don't see you in that way. You are not a felonious personality. You don't fit that mold. I committed felonies, as in murder, in Vietnam, again and again. It was called duty. How do you know I was a killer? You can never know what a person will do before they do it. And after, you have the same problem. It's not branded on foreheads like the mark of Cain. As to your jury, I personally checked their police records. I assume the sheriff's office checked too. None of them committed a crime above a misdemeanor, and little of that. This is a clean bunch. As juries go these days, they're qualified and responsible. That's what I certified to Shenon. I stand by it."

What Wally had said about the phantom struck a note.

"Okay, but who stands out as worth asking about? Who might be my phantom?"

"You're going to investigate them yourself?" Wally sounded disbelieving and looked as though he were about to laugh, until he saw Barr nod yes. "One question, then—why?"

Barr took in a deep breath and let it out slowly. "Because I might have an impostor on my jury." Wally was about to comment, but Barr held up his hand. "And that's not the worst of it. This impostor may also have killed Holly." And he described the anonymous note.

Wally listened in silence and then shook his head. "Sounds like a prank to me," he said as he went for another beer. "And I'm not surprised, frankly, given the notoriety of this one. It's just the kind of thing we've come to dread, if not exactly expect. Unfortunately, Dan, you were the one to draw the turkey."

"Maybe, but go along with me a minute," said Barr.

"Like, what if?"

"Like, what if it isn't a hoax?"

"Who would try such a wild-ass thing?"

"Someone crazy, or cocky. I mean, if I hadn't been tipped off, I'd have never known. And as you said, I may still be dealing with a hoax."

"Then, who wrote the note?"

Barr shook his head. "These are all *my* questions. Maybe someone who's involved and has an agenda here. Someone wants the killer caught who sees an injustice—someone who knows a lot more than I do but can't come right out and talk about it." He laughed at his own confusion. "Maybe I should just pretend I never got the note. I need this case to go smoothly. I could just let it go, duck the whole thing. But I'm not going to. My dad says to take it seriously, and my godfather is telling me the same in not so many words. I've at least got to satisfy myself that someone is not playing games with my court, that I'm not being set up." He paused. "Chief Dunstan isn't going to lift a finger, for obvious reasons."

"And that's why you sailed up to my dock."

"Exactly."

"Thanks a million." Wally slumped back into the chair, staring at the ceiling in thought.

"*I* can't check them out," said Barr. "I'm not qualified. And besides, if a juror got wind of it, he'd tell the press and all of a sudden it would blow up in my face. I would look real bad. The defense would demand a mistrial; the defendant—who may be guilty, I remind you —would go free. The court once again becomes a laughingstock. I just can't afford to let that happen."

Wally was still staring ceilingward. "You were asking who stands out. That pretty young woman, Juror #8."

Barr nodded. "Claire Hood?"

"I'm sure she'll be able to influence the men on the panel," he said. "A woman like her usually does—with the men trying to please her and the women lining up behind her, for and against—unless she's stupid. And this one isn't. I thought about asking her out to lunch." He paused, reflecting, his hand even on his chin.

"A bit tender for you, wouldn't you say?" Barr asked. "How old is she?"

"Twenty-two, but she's a *mature* twenty-two."

Barr gave him a sympathetic grin. "But she's not the one I'm looking for."

"Maybe, maybe not. The only one who doesn't stand out in my mind is the little Jewish lady, Mrs. Cohen." Abruptly, Wally walked from the room, this time into the bedroom. A minute later he was back with a manila folder, which he held out to Barr. "These are my reports on the Hawkes jurors," he said. "You're welcome to them."

Barr shook his head. "I came here for your intuition, not your reports."

Wally took several minutes to refresh his memory. "We've got murder one, victim a prominent young woman, weapon a knife, a brutal mess. I'd say a man, then, for starters." He turned to the pages of his report. "I'd try this guy Figueroa, the contractor, and Adam Warmath. Juror number five," he said. "And here, this one, Anthony Bullock, number seven. And the do-gooder, Michael Eng of Project Right, too." He scrunched up his lips in thought.

"Chinatown, remember that," added Barr. "It happened in Chinatown."

He tilted his head and a grin betrayed his excitement. "Then, I'd include *this* Chinese, how do you pronounce his name? Gee, Daniel Gee?"

"On what basis?"

"Simple: sex and age," Wally said. "You are describing a perp of a certain sex and age. Men over fifty don't kill younger women unless it's accidental or they're lunatics. This crime statistically fits in a narrow age band and locale, and all the other variables are up for grabs."

"But what about Warmath. He seems like the most normal guy on the panel," Barr said. "Bullock, I don't know. The social worker, Eng? Do you get into social work to cover up homicidal tendencies?"

"That's one group. Put the women in another one."

"Exclude them, you think?" Barr asked.

Wally gave him an impatient look. "I'm talking categories now. A woman could have done it, sure, and so could a one-legged mailman, or the ugly fucker the police arrested who's sitting in your court. Statistically, females commit about a half of one percent of all murders in America, and the victims are almost always husbands and mean boyfriends."

"This Latino, Figueroa, I wouldn't have picked him. He's married, no?"

"Married men have balls, you know. His wife is fat and ugly and he finds a willing squeeze who blackmails him and says either marry me or I tell your wife, so he kills her. It's happened. You name me something that hasn't happened."

Barr looked at him. "Having the killer sit on the jury," he said.

Wally nodded as he crumpled the beer can in his fist. "If I were this juror, you'd never find me. It's not what you want to hear. But it's true. Nobody is going to take a risk getting caught if he's already almost scot-free, unless, as I said, he's very smart or he's plain crazy." He was really into it now. "If I were him, I'd know I was buried so deep in among those eleven other jurors you couldn't find me with a miner's lamp and a canary."

"He almost certainly does not know that I know about him."

"Don't say he, say *it—it* may be a she."

"You said shes were in a different group."

"Whatever. Listen, the sheriffs didn't or couldn't spot the impostor, right, when they were vetting them? I didn't either. Hey, if I'm this *person* I'm cocky. I got away with killing the adorable granddaughter of a U.S. senator and a gazillionaire. And I'm on a jury? Life goes on, right? I'm having fun. Rock 'n' roll. Of course I'm going to lie in voir dire. Even if I know *you* know that I'm there, Dan, I'm going to make it impossible for you to find me. Believe it with all your heart."

For the second time Barr asked, "But what's the use?"

Wally stared at him. "The better question is, why hasn't anyone tried it before?"

"Maybe they have."

"And nobody's the wiser. Except this time the judge has been tipped off. Okay, I'm on the jury, right? I'm the killer. I put myself on—I don't know how—"

"*I* do," Barr said. "But go ahead."

"No one's the wiser, right? And I use all my influence short of twisting arms to get the other jurors to vote to convict. That way my life goes on when the trial is over." He paused and grinned. "Then there's the alternative view. . . ."

"Tell me," said Barr.

"I'm the killer, right? Maybe some part of me *wants* to get caught. I won't give myself up. The police can't find me. They aren't even looking, stupid bastards. I'm going to make it tough for them. That's what drives me. Man, it even excites *me*. I choose the rules of the game. I'm really clever. I put myself on the jury. You don't know I am one of the twelve, so I leave you a note. Find me, Judge Barr. I want to mess with your mind, see how close you can get. Let's play, huh? I'm watching you all day long. Yeah, I really like to play with the court—pin the tail on the donkey, courtroom-style; blind man's bluff, adult-style. And guess what, Dan?"

"Don't tell me."

"You're the blind man."

———◆———

At a stoplight at Union Street, Barr's libido fought with the hour. He looked at his watch—slightly after one A.M.—and drove straight to the marina. He'd left Wally saying he'd think about what he could do to help, and Barr had crossed the Golden Gate needing to unwind before he could even consider bed.

The street he pulled into was quiet. He cut the Porsche's engine and looked across the street. Jenny's town house was a three-story building—she occupied all of the ground floor, which she had insisted on because she was afraid of earthquakes. A light in the front bay window let him know she was still up. A woman's silhouette suddenly was backlit against the curtains. With expectation quickening his pulse, he watched a taller silhouette enter the scene. And he thought that they embraced.

He turned the key in the ignition, jealous in spite of himself. Jenny had crooked her finger at him and he had come running. Wally had said to give her a chance. He had hoped for a night's surcease. Now he saw that she had moved on.

The light came on and the front door swung open. Jenny stepped outside. She was wearing an evening gown. The man with her was in a tuxedo. His silvery hair glimmered in the moonlight. He was tall and erect and reminded Barr of Jenny's patrician-looking father. She was standing near the older guy, suggesting intimacy, but a certain distinct distance and formality too.

With just another glance he saw who it was. It was Senator Hawkes. Sure, Jenny worked for him, but . . . Barr slipped the clutch and crept around the corner and out of sight. As he'd already just told himself, Jenny was moving on.

The doorway to the mansion was darkened. But no sooner had he rung the buzzer than the light went on and his father appeared at the door. When he saw Barr he looked concerned. "I'm glad you came by. Come in."

Barr felt a familiar comfort here as he followed his father's wheelchair down the hall. He had been brought up in this house, which stored childhood memories good and bad. It no longer looked the same since his mother died, and since the place had been rearranged to accommodate his father's wheelchair, but the house would always reflect his father's strong and interesting character.

Absolutely nothing in the decor was obvious or direct. Subtlety defined the features, as it defined his dad. The painting over the mantel looked like a few dashed black lines on a canvas, but in fact it was by Matisse, and it was distinctly Justice Barr's. He had not acquired it in a heated auction at Sotheby's or through some Manhattan dealer. He had commissioned the artist himself to do the portrait in 1952, only two years before he'd died. And Matisse had chosen to draw the bare outline of a woman's face, four brush strokes in black. The woman was Ellie Morgan Barr, whom Barr saw more clearly in the Matisse than in the several framed photos of her on the tables.

The Jean Arp on the living room table was a sculpture of a woman's abundant form emerging through smooth white stone. Again, the subtlety, the economy, the contrast—these motifs were like a theme that played through the other objects on display, from the Japanese carvings of songbirds to the ivory bookmarks and tortoiseshell pillboxes and bibelots on the end tables. Over the dining room table an Alexander Calder never seemed to move but presented the eye with different angles each day.

"You were up, I take it," Barr said, following his father's wheelchair toward the back of the house, which bordered on the Presidio.

"Up like Hamlet's ghost. The worst side effect of this stroke, for some reason, is insomnia. Just think of all the time I wasted when I was your age, sleeping. . . ."

They went into the library. A spiraling narwhale tusk hung over the door like a twisted rapier. Several rare seventeenth-century Rajput miniatures seemed almost to hide on the walls. Henry Barr parked his wheelchair by a stack of old art and antiques magazines. Dan Barr perched on the fender of the unlit fireplace with his chin in his hands and asked his father, "You seemed so certain this afternoon that this note isn't a hoax. Can you tell me why?"

"Drink?" he asked. Barr shook his head. "I talked to poor Amelia after court today."

"Oh?" Barr asked. "I didn't know you are friendly."

"Neighbors," Justice Barr said. "We have a history." He laughed. "At my age, anyone I know who is still alive shares a history with me."

In his mind's eye Barr pictured a vision of sadness. He remembered her wedding to Karl, long ago now, at the Grace Cathedral. Amelia, he recalled, came from sturdy stock in the San Joaquin Valley near Los Banos. She met Karl at the University of California at Davis. They'd been a wholesome couple, happy yet never ecstatically so. A reserve had denoted an emotional or intellectual gap that the bridge of love did not cross.

"How's she taking it?" Barr asked.

"Part of her died that night too," his father said. "She's glad you are handling the trial. She trusts you."

"What about the senator?" asked Barr. "Did you talk to him?"

He was shaking his head. "No need to," he replied. "Besides, he went out the back way. His limo was waiting for him."

"Amelia told you she was glad I was the presiding judge. Should *I* be glad?"

"I think I know what you're asking. Don't."

"A mistrial is the prudent course."

"Is that what you came here looking for?" He looked amazed. "If you declare a mistrial, Holly's killer will never be heard from again. And how do you explain it to the press? You've got a feeding frenzy out there and you take away the food? They'll tear you apart, son."

"I could always say there was a tainted juror."

"That's what alternate jurors are for. Your career will be finished, and your killer will be gone. You'd have nothing left but wreckage."

"What if I sequester them right now? As you know, sequestration puts the jury under twenty-four hour surveillance."

His father nodded. "That's one merit," he said finally. "But if I were you I'd wait. People will not be surprised by sequestration at the deliberation stage of the trial. It happens all the time. They will be surprised if you sequester now with the trial already started. They'll want to know what changed your mind, and you'll have to explain something you don't want to." He chuckled and tapped the cover of a book open on the table, John Keegan's *History of Warfare*. "Do not bring up your heavy guns at the start of battle. Keep them in reserve."

"I just came from Wally's place."

His father brightened. "Excellent," he said.

He held up his hand. "He won't commit himself. I think he's afraid what the DA's office will think."

"You can't investigate the jurors yourself."

He supposed not. "What about the press, Dad?" he asked. "They have a world of power. Their resources for checking out something like this are enormous. Why can't I turn it over to them?"

"I don't see how. You'd have to give the whole thing away. The minute this gets out, any chance of finding your juror will vanish. He'll be careful, and the press will never get anything, and then you really *will* have to declare a mistrial. It will be chaos."

Barr shook his head. "I know, I know."

His father tried to make himself comfortable in the hard confines of the wheelchair. "So, tell me what you plan to do."

"Conduct a murder trial," said Barr.

His father was shaking his head again.

Barr stared across the room at a painting, this one by Franz Kline. It was a brilliant interpretation in black and white of an enlarged Japanese calligraphy of which only a fraction showed, the rest to be imagined.

"Do you think it's possible that I can find out who it is, Dad?"

"I can't answer that, son. But we won't know unless you try. If you fail, you fail. But I've always taught you to try. If you don't succeed, then nobody will. The killer goes free, and Holly's murder isn't avenged. Justice dies a small death." He looked him in the eye. "You're doing fine. Give yourself credit for what you've done."

"What?" Barr asked with a self-deprecating laugh.

"Opened up a possibility, and in that you have done something quite remarkable. You have already served justice in a deeper, more meaningful way than merely running a trial—by identifying how justice can be corrupted. Keep at it. One in twelve is odds any gambler will take considering the stakes. You are a smart boy. You are my son."

———

As Barr was unlocking his front door the kitchen phone started to ring.

"Where you been, man?" Wally wondered. He sounded annoyed, as though Barr had kept him up with worry.

"A couple of detours," he replied.

"I figured you'd go by there."

"Where?"

"Jenny's. You must be very . . . shall I say, *efficient?*"

Barr shook his head. "She was otherwise engaged."

"Oh, my apologies for the aspersion. Yeah. I can't imagine too much grass growing under her pretty little . . . her feet."

"What's up?"

"Nothing interesting. But I've been thinking. . . ." And he

paused for a long time, waiting for Barr to ask what. He sounded a bit thick-tongued from a few more beverages. "You want to know what I've been thinking or not?"

"My whole life so far has pointed me to an interest in what you are thinking."

"Fuck you, Barr." It was said gently.

"How flattering." There was another silence on the line. "Okay, what?"

"You need me to check out your jurors."

"No shit," Barr said. Wally might be real slow on the uptake, but he finally uptook.

"And I have several reasons to tell you I can't."

"You called to tell me no?"

"To make you a deal."

Anything. He'd agree to any terms at this point. "Such as?"

"You let me take out Roberta, I do your snooping."

Barr didn't like it, but he didn't have a choice. "Done," he said. "Just don't break her heart."

"I have to win her heart first." He paused, breathing into the phone. Barr heard the hiss of a beer can opening. "While you're running your trial, I'll look around," Wally continued. "But I need to know timing, because once the trial goes to deliberation I got nothing to investigate, and once the verdict comes in, Holly's killer goes free. How long I got: a month?"

Barr wished. It was more like days. Shenon had a slam dunk, and Lovelace had nothing to give the jury. That much was already clear. Barr hadn't yet seen a witness list from Lovelace, which further indicated that he wasn't going to mount any defense. And that shortened the trial's time even more. "Days, I'd say, Wally," he told him. "I can drag it out by recessing, but I can't make it seem obvious. You'd better do what you're going to do in a hurry." He paused. "Listen, I really appreciate this," he said. "Mind telling me where you'll start?"

"No idea." Wally paused. "But I am thinking Chinese."

Chapter Three

"All rise . . ."

Everyone in the courtroom stood and turned toward a concealed door behind the bench proper, watching like a theater audience anticipating the rising curtain.

On the other side of the door, Barr glanced a last time at a copy of that morning's *Examiner*. He had to smile. The front page was covered with news of the trial, and he'd gotten through without a scrape. He'd read the main story. Nothing negative in the text about the adjournment, the first day—or the pitiful opening statement from Lovelace. Hopefully it was a harbinger. He checked his necktie, then went through the door.

Once seated, he hunched forward to appraise his court. The senator was there. So was Amelia. His father was absent, as was the cardinal. He recognized a few others. Out of the corner of his eye he saw a slouch he knew well. Wally was seated in the back of the room, his head nearly level with the bench back, no doubt suffering from a hangover. Barr caught his eye, held it, and they exchanged a grin so brief no one could have noticed.

The bailiff brought in the jury, and Barr watched the fourteen men and women as though he had never seen them before. While they settled in their designated chairs, he could not help but think what complete strangers they were to him. Something indefinable about their carriage, their physiques, and the composition of their features reminded him that for all his superficial knowledge of them, he really didn't know them at all. He knew only that one of them was a killer he had to find, and soon.

He glanced at Claire Hood, who reached for her spiral notebook and retracted the point of a gold pen. She seemed composed and indifferent to the presence of the other jurors, even the court. She showed that she respected the formality of the proceedings by what she wore—a black sleeveless linen shift, a discreet string of pearls, small gold studs in her ears, and little makeup. Her expression was open and attentive.

But he remembered what Wally had said about the likelihood that the impostor was a Chinese man. Why? Wally had pointed out what seemed obvious. Holly was killed in Chinatown. By a man? Men killed women, he said, and women didn't. Of course, racism was in play. Barr acknowledged how the Anglo-Saxon community demonized the Chinese. The defendant was Chinese, and an immigrant to boot. As for the jurors, four of them were Chinese, three men and a woman. Barr was going to need to examine his own racism with respect to the Chinese. He had to be careful.

He referred to the jury seating chart that lay before him and looked at them, one by one.

Adam Warmath, the insurance salesman, sat in the front row on the aisle. He was dark-complexioned, brooding in countenance. He had an athletic build, a strong back and shoulders, and a thick neck. He somehow gave Barr the impression of one who worried about keeping up, by which he intuited that he might not be too smart, although jurors, Barr had no need to remind himself, were not selected on the basis of their IQs.

Barr referred again to his chart. A black juror, Jesse Coffer, gave nothing away in his intense guardedness. He faced forward, shoulders squared, chin up. He was overweight, with a shaved head and a small gold ring in his right earlobe. His visage said he was anxious for the proceedings to begin.

David Figueroa, the Hispanic, wore a suit and tie. He gave the impression of a man whose life already had smoothed at the edges to a pleasant mellowness. He was young, a contractor, with a wife and three young kids. He probably had a mortgage on a home of modest proportions. Barr envisioned a lawn mower, a love of televised sports, and a guilt for watching them. Something about him, though, indicated that, like Jesse Coffer, he wasn't content. But were they *dis*content?

The Chinese, well . . . what could he say? Impassivity in public places was a trademark. He referred to his seating chart. Daniel Gee, the restaurateur, volunteered for the Chinese-American Association. The social worker, Michael Eng. What set him apart in Barr's opinion was his black hair cut stylishly long. Eng seemed altogether intelligent and serious, and when he looked up at Barr he offered just a polite hint of a nod. Kim Wen, the Chinese pharmacist, had a face that bespoke a whole world of hidden experience. Each of the thousand lines that crisscrossed his skin suggested a different emotion, a trial in his life, a woe and a joy and a burden relieved. His eyes betrayed his age; they twinkled and were quick, but also confused and doubtful. Amy Wong, the Chinese housewife, could have been Wen's wife. She was small and older. If she were the juror whom Barr was seeking, then he did not have a prayer. He could not begin to imagine her as a killer. He thought about that as the clerk went about the court's "housekeeping" procedures.

The other white male on the jury, Anthony J. Bullock, looked angry, as if the delay in the proceedings weighed on him. He was twenty-eight years old. Holly Hawkes had been eighteen. Bullock was thin and wiry, and had an intelligent face, a narrow head, and a scalp of healthy black hair swept straight back from his brow. His skin was an olive color, and his gray eyes were alert and clear. His clothes were expensive if a bit obvious—an Armani suit, a loose-fitting shirt with a short collar, and a necktie that seemed an afterthought. He might have been an artist, or a magazine art director. Instead, Barr knew, he was an executive, a young VP for a cellular paging company.

Barr felt almost guilty for not shining a stronger light of suspicion on the women. Women murdered, Wally had said. But women did *not* do to other women what this murderer had done to Holly Hawkes. Unless, of course, Barr was wrong about their natures. Or was he simply overlooking a culture that was alien to him? Again, stereotypes. Had a *woman* slaughtered a precocious girl, and was she now was making a desperate attempt to convict an innocent man? A lesbian? The lesbian society of San Francisco was as alien to him as the gays were. And though he had friends in both camps, he never discussed their proclivities. He believed they should go in peace. The simple maxims *"To each his own"* and *"Don't scare the horses"* had guided him. But still, was ignorance blinding him?

Arlene Cohen looked like a little Jewish woman at a Hadassah bake sale. Barr concentrated his gaze on her hands, small and delicate. These were hands used to cutting an onion, peeling a carrot, laying a Band-Aid on a child's wound. These weren't the hands to plunge a knife into a young woman over and over and over again.

What about Maria Garriques, the manicurist? She had exceptionally strong biceps for a woman. She was fit, and vital. But what did that signify? Could she be lesbian? Had Holly spurned her? She looked Barr straight in the eye and gave him nothing.

Or Olivia Ivy, the African-American housewife from Daly City. She was young enough for this rage of passion, and, given the right motives, who was to say? She was a light color, uneven in her darkness, with a nose that was aquiline. What were her feelings toward a woman as privileged and white as Holly? Might their paths have crossed?

He asked the same of Bessie Matthews, who looked younger than her twenty-three years. She was stunning, with braided hair, a thin face, and pretty eyes that betrayed nervousness and doubt. She gave Barr the impression that the slightest touch or a single word might set her running off. And what, after all, did such skitterishness mean in the context of his search?

Last of all he lowered his gaze on the defendant, Mr. Feng Shao-li, born in the People's Republic of China, an illegal alien in

America. He could discern a subtext for each juror, but this defendant presented him with an utterly blank page.

Barr asked himself, why *this* defendant in *this* of all cases, in light of what he knew? The state said that Mr. Feng Shao-li had killed Holly Hawkes with a feral need.

He might have pondered these and other questions further if he were not suddenly aware that the entire panel of jurors and the spectators crowded in court were staring at him. Barr seemed to wake up, and his fogged gaze focused. He cleared his throat. "Call your first witness, please, Mr. Shenon," he told the prosecutor.

———

Confident and calm, Detective Sergeant Cummings sat with his back three inches off the witness chair. He was one of the old boys on the SFPD, but he had been given the lead in the Hawkes murder not because of his seniority or his friendship with Chief Dunstan. Those things aside, Cummings knew more about homicide investigation than anyone else in the state of California.

Chief Dunstan was his mentor and friend, and now, a couple of years away from retirement, Cummings was thinking less of justice than of securing his retirement on the Russian River. His mind might be zeroing in on lazy days with nothing more murderous around than the gutting of pike, but, as he told the court, it became clear that he could never forget what he had seen that night.

He stated that he had responded to a call last June 23, around eleven-thirty. The police lab and forensic techies and the ME's group were already at work on the crime scene when he got there. "The ME was over the victim," Cummings told the hushed court. "He pulled back the sheet for me to see." Cummings chose that moment to reach for the water glass. He took a drink and put it back. "She was messed up," he said.

What he saw disgusted him, and it wasn't so much the gore as what the gore represented. He could still marvel at how a man's mind conjured such depravities. Even in Chinatown, where as a Caucasian he was willing to believe anything, he would never have imagined what had lain at his shoe tips. He looked, and he still did not get what he was seeing. San Francisco was not by nature a violent city. People worried more about the geological fault that zigzagged through town than about the warps of its denizens. But the remains of Holly Hawkes went beyond violence. It had amounted to a frenzy. That was it, he told the court. A frenzy that he could almost smell had suffused the air. He was looking at a language that only someone who knew about such things could translate. He said that was how he finally got it—by *not* getting it.

"Evening, Lieutenant," a duet of voices had wafted through the dim night of the tunnel, Cummings told the court. One voice belonged to a woman, the other to a man.

Cummings had made sure the corners of the shroud covered every part of the victim.

"What took you so long?" he asked the reporters.

The one from the *Chronicle* had stepped closer to the body, tilting up on his toes to see what the shroud obscured. "What have we got?" asked the woman, a reporter for KGO-TV, the local ABC affiliate.

"It's hard to say," Cummings had replied. "I'll warn you on this one." He folded back the shroud.

The man turned away so quickly he nearly fell. The woman dabbed at her eyes as she huffed to catch her breath. The man scraped a handkerchief across his mouth.

"Animal," he had said.

"That's what he said and I agreed, 'An animal,' " Cummings told the court.

Some moments later, Chief of Police Dunstan had appeared on the scene, Cummings testified. The chief had looked down, his hands buried deep in his pockets. After a long moment he had whispered something Cummings had not understood at first, but made out as he repeated it again, louder: "Mother of God," he had said over and over.

Cummings testified that the chief had crossed himself, touching his forehead and two points on his chest, not once but twice, as if he meant to protect the area around his heart.

"Why did you show them this?" Chief Dunstan had asked.

"It's routine, Chief," Cummings had replied. It *was* routine. The press was allowed to view victims.

"Her name is Hawkes," said the chief. "You know the name. Senator Hawkes's grandchild. So this is *not* routine." He had turned to the reporters. "Do either of you recognize this person? Do you *see* this?" He pointed to the body of Holly Hawkes.

Of course they saw what lay at their feet.

"No. You did *not* see it," Chief Dunstan had told them, commanding them to his view. He asked the lieutenant, "Any more of them *not* see this?"

"Just them, sir."

"Do you understand what I'm telling you?"

"But— "the reporter from the *Chronicle* had started to say.

The chief glowered. "I'm not telling you your jobs. I'm telling you for the sake of the victim's family that you will not describe this in any way as it is. You understand me? You will not." And he walked away.

"I told the ME to get her body out of there," Cummings told the court. "A mob of reporters started to arrive a few minutes later."

Cummings went on in his testimony to satisfy requirements about police procedures, evidence, and witness reports. He gave the court an overall view of the crime scene. As a professional witness he was believable, sincere, and direct, and far more descriptive than Barr thought was necessary.

"Did you have any other observations of the body?" Shenon asked him at one point.

Cummings straightened his shoulders. "The victim was stabbed multiple times."

Shenon held up his hand. "A minute, Judge?"

"Take your time, Counselor," he replied.

Shenon went over to his table, where an assistant handed him several enlarged photographs. Barr saw what he was about to do, and he admired the cleverness but he still winced. He was going to *show* the jury, right at the start, what murder looked like. He would return to the photos later, but by bringing out the pictorial evidence now he was shocking the jury into a wakefulness that would carry them through.

Barr stared at the jurors, trying to see a reaction that might tip the murderer's hand. But there were too many of them. And besides, they all registered the same degree of horror at what they were shown. Even Barr stared in disbelief. A lump of meat, a torso lying in a glistening blackened pool—that was all that the photos showed of Holly Hawkes. Worst of all, the killer's knife had created a crazy patchwork of wounds down her back.

Mercifully, the photos hid her face.

Without a word Shenon paraded the photos before the jurors' eyes. Barr watched to see who looked at them. And as he watched, he asked himself, what did a murderer look like? He glanced out at Wally, who was sitting upright, staring intensely. Amelia was looking at her lap. The senator was avoiding the sight. Barr looked back at the jurors who had finished with the photos. This documentation said that a young girl had died at the hands of the accused. No matter what the defense claimed, these photos told the jury, *"Remember!"*

The witness, Sergeant Cummings, had sat quietly during the presentation.

Shenon asked him now, "Detective, are these wounds consistent with any emotions that may come to mind?"

"Rage," said Cummings without hesitation.

"Objection," Lovelace said, stirring himself.

"Sustained," said Barr, who warned the jury to disregard the remark.

"As you can see, she was mutilated, like some animal tore her up," said Cummings.

An uncomfortable silence followed. Shenon cleared his throat. "What did you do next?"

Cummings stared straight ahead. "We cleaned up the scene

98

and got it taped off. We got everybody out of there, posted a mobile unit at the end of the tunnel to keep gawkers out. There was a mob of Chinese around, and reporters."

"When was a warrant issued for the defendant's arrest?" Shenon asked.

Cummings stuck out his neck. "The next morning," he said, looking over at Feng Shao-li, whose translator was whispering in his ear. "It happened fast."

After a few more perfunctory questions, Shenon said, "That will be all. No more questions, Your Honor."

"Mr. Lovelace?" Barr asked.

Lovelace nodded. "Only a couple of things to ask, Judge." As he crossed the distance between his table and the witness platform he smiled uncertainly at the jury, then stood a respectful distance from the witness. "What I'd like you to tell the court is this: Where is the weapon that the defendant used in the commission of his crime?"

"It was never found," Cummings replied.

"Who was in charge of the search?"

"I was, overall."

"Can you tell the jury, Detective, about the lengths you took to find the murder weapon?"

"I assigned five men who did nothing the next morning and early afternoon but search the areas around the tunnel entrance. We then called for volunteers from off-duty officers and later the kids came in from the PALs. They went over that area near the tunnel with a fine-tooth comb."

"Did you make further efforts beside these?"

"Yes."

"Can you tell us what they were?"

"We offered a reward to anyone who found the weapon."

"And was there a response to your appeal?"

"I said we never found the weapon," Cummings replied testily.

"Remind the court," Lovelace said, "is it possible to match the wounds on the victim to a weapon if there is no weapon?"

"No."

"Therefore, you do not know what weapon was used."

"A knife."

"More specifically?"

"The ME told us to look for a long-bladed knife. A tapered blade with a sharp point."

Lovelace said, "Isn't it strange no *long*-bladed knife was found?"

"Are you asking me?" Cummings inquired. "It happens all the time."

"The alleged killer was arrested in hours. In other words, I may infer that the killer was sloppy. So getting rid of the weapon would be inconsistent? Do you—"

"Objection!"

"Sustained."

"One last question." He looked at Cummings. "You saw the victim soon after her body was found, is that correct?"

"I saw her at the crime scene, yes."

"Did you examine her at that time?"

"I saw her," Cummings said. "I did not examine her."

"Did you notice if she was wearing any items of personal jewelry? A ring? A necklace?"

"No, I didn't personally."

"Thank you, that is all."

───────────

The next witness, Winston Xiao-Yang, was in his early forties, thin and elegant, with nervous eyes that jittered like beads.

Slowly and with great attention to detail, prosecutor Shenon walked him through the night of the murder.

"I saw him look behind him at the tunnel he'd just come from," Xiao-Yang said breathlessly, as though it were happening now.

"Is the person you saw that night in this court?"

"Yes," he replied.

"Can you point him out to me, sir?" Shenon asked.

Xiao-Yang aimed his finger at Feng Shao-li, who was listening to his translator. "That man sitting there."

"Mr. Feng Shao-li, the defendant. Is that correct?"

"That is correct."

"What time was that, do you remember?" Shenon asked him.

He did not hesitate. "Eleven o'clock," he replied nervously. "I looked at my watch."

"And why did you do that?"

"Because I had an appointment. I had finished dinner. I did not want to be late. I did not want to arrive at this meeting late."

"And did you know the person you saw running out of the tunnel?"

"Yes."

"How did you know him?"

"He's been to my office many times. "

"And that night, what did you do then?"

"I went into the tunnel."

"Weren't you afraid of what he had been running from?"

"No, it wasn't like that."

"And what happened then?"

"I stumbled over the body of the girl lying there on the walkway. Steam was rising out of her wounds. Steam. Hot meat."

Barr's eyes went to Amelia, who drew in a sharp breath. He felt sorry for her beyond mere sympathy. He wanted to protect her from what was to come, which he knew would get even worse.

"That is all," said Shenon, swallowing hard.

On cross, Lovelace mumbled a single question. Xiao-Yang cocked his head as if to say he could not hear.

"Speak up, Counselor, if you please," Barr told him.

"What was the weather like the evening you say that you saw the defendant near the tunnel?"

"I don't remember," Winston Xiao-Yang replied.

"Your eyeglasses, Mr. Xiao-Yang? Were you wearing them the evening you say you saw the defendant come out of the tunnel?"

"Yes."

"Thank you," Lovelace said. "No more questions, Your Honor."

Mindfully, Barr glanced at his watch. The jurors had enough to contemplate for one day. It was a good place to break.

———◆———

Minutes after Barr had adjourned the court, he entered the jury room, where the fourteen men and women were already reaching for their coats.

"I hope you don't mind," Barr said as he looked in on them, as if he were merely passing by on his way out of the building. He knew a judge's contact with jurors was frowned upon and even the basis for reversible error if he discussed anything relating to the trial without the defense and prosecution attorneys present. Maybe it was risky— even stupid; but it was something that the factor of time was forcing him to do. The trial was going faster than he had ever imagined, which meant he needed to take shortcuts.

The jurors looked stunned to see him in what they had already come to think of as their sanctuary, a bare windowless room without amenities except for fourteen chairs and a large, scarred table. Their eyes asked, what did he want, and why had he come here? To admonish them? To praise? They stopped what they were doing and for an instant stood frozen. His presence held them there, and this restraint made them visibly uncomfortable.

"From time to time," he explained, "I'll be stopping by, like this." He shook his head indifferently as though he were performing a perfunctory duty. "Because I'll want to see how you are handling the pressure. We are all in this together. Right at the outset I'd like to know if you have any complaints or needs or suggestions."

As though they had switched lenses, they looked at him now through different, more charitable eyes. He wasn't their enemy. They had heard him say that he was their ally, their benefactor,

and that seemed to please them. He could almost see them relax, though clearly they still felt the discomfort in this close
proximity.

For Barr's part, this small, close room gave him angles of
sight that the court denied him, and he walked among them like
a man lost and looking for the way out. He wanted to study
their faces. He could smell them now and see them in all the fine
detail of how they stood—placing their hands on their hips,
crossing their arms, tilting their heads, parting their lips—and
even how they breathed. He wanted to dwell on these details,
adhering them to his memory. He wanted them to see him too, to
appear before them as real. He had to understand each of them.
He kept telling himself, one of these twelve jurors had gutted a
young woman like an animal.

He saw, for instance, that Jesse Coffer wasn't nearly as angry
as he had appeared in court. His anger was a façade that he presented for protection, Barr guessed, almost as something expected of a black man his age.

The do-gooder, Mr. Eng, was shy, as Barr had almost expected. Without a word to the others Eng slipped out of the
room. So did Anthony Bullock, the cellular company exec, who
struck Barr as worried. He wondered why. What did he have to
worry about?

He could not judge any reactions with certainty. And even to
try was a mistake. Much had appeared about him in the press.
Personal stuff, his history, quotes from him from the past, and
about his famous supreme court justice father too. These jurors
knew him better than he knew them. What he represented in
their minds was impossible to say. In everything he had ever felt
and done, Barr had kept himself apart. Private, with few friends,
he was hardly one to seek out the spotlight. This distance, cou-
pled with what the jurors knew about the privilege of his up-
bringing and education, made him seem lofty. And this loftiness
skewed their view. Because it wasn't him, wasn't real.

How possible was it to know *anyone?* Barr wondered. All that
anyone saw of the interior lives of other humans was what stuck

up above the surface. Of course, Barr wasn't searching for the jurors' inner selves. A killer was what he wanted here. All he sought was a shred of evidence. But even that was hard to pinpoint. He knew little enough about these people. The law forbade him from knowing more. Eng's leaving the room so soon—was that suspicious? Should it have been? Anthony Bullock's doing the same—was that worthy of a closer look? Which of the two was more likely to have killed Holly? Barr thought of the enormity of his task and the speed that the trial required of him to find the killer. What else could he do but try any theory or any means that he might imagine?

Kim Wen, the old man from Chinatown, went into his canvas ditty bag and came out with a glass jar which he held out to Barr.

"Ginseng, keep you alert," he said, pushing the jar forward.

Barr smiled his appreciation, and he looked at the old man whom the court had described as a pharmacist. But he was no doubt a homeopathist trained in the salutary effects of garlic and ginseng and bear liver oil and a thousand different items from nature that Barr had never even heard of. And if Wen believed in these potions, how different from Barr did that make his thinking? How could he possibly read him like a book written in a language he didn't know?

David Figueroa was Barr's age, and Hispanic. Barr saw him as basically normal—meaning he had a family, and his family was his whole life. He would split the world in two: working people like himself, men who earned their wages with their hands; and people like Barr, who used their brains. Figueroa would not begrudge Barr his world. He would not understand it. In that fertile field, might suspicion grow? Barr asked himself, what would Figueroa have been doing near Chinatown with a girl like Holly? It seemed a stretch.

Daniel Gee, the Chinatown restaurateur, bristled at the sight of Barr, who imagined that he would be quick to anger. He'd be proud to a point of vanity and no doubt knew more about the

Hawkes murder from Chinatown gossip than he would ever let on.

Last among the men, Adam Warmath seemed easy. Big and bearish, handsome in a conventional salesman's smooth way, he looked like the kind of guy who enjoyed Wally's choices of simple pleasures—TV sports, a few beers, a woman around to clean up the mess, strictly no expectations. Too smart to be merely a bozo, he was still sophomoric, immature, and lazy. Barr guessed him to be someone for whom the effort of reaching the Stockton tunnel and wielding a knife over Holly Hawkes was simply too great.

He told them, "I want to thank you, personally, each of you. This trial is a huge responsibility, I know. You are engaged in the most important civic duty you will ever perform. I want you to know how much I appreciate your honesty, your sacrifice, your sense of duty. Our society would not be what it is without people like you."

Arlene Cohen shyly raised her hand. "Judge," she whispered, and she looked to be on the verge of tears.

"Yes, Mrs. Cohen?"

"You said just now about appreciating our honesty. Judge, I'm *not* honest," and her tears flowed. "I lied to the court."

"What about, Mrs. Cohen?"

"My past," she told him.

"That's all right, Mrs. Cohen," he said. "I'm sure you just forgot."

"No. I lied. I *didn't* go to college. . . . I thought you'd think I was stupid if I said only high school."

He offered a soothing smile, which succeeded to make her dry her tears. The others relaxed, the ice broken. Some of them seemed less interested now in leaving. Indeed, Mrs. Garriques put down her coat as though she were taking this opportunity to get to know him better.

Claire Hood stood watching him as though she were trying to get his measure if for no other reason than feminine curiosity, because she was a woman and he was a man, he was judge, and she a juror. She was composed, quiet, and thoughtful, and her beauty was hard to ignore for long.

Amy Wong, the Chinese housewife, older and shrunken with a large mole on her cheek, asked, "Judge, can I bring in a pillow? Those seats are uncomfortable."

"Certainly," he told her. "Your comfort is important. Bring anything that helps you as long as it doesn't distract the other jurors."

Olivia Ivy, the African-American housewife from Daly City, said, "Judge, I got the press parked in front of my house half the night. Can you tell them to get out of there? My neighbors are complaining."

He had already instructed them not to speak to the press. "You haven't talked to them, have you?" he asked.

"No, sir, just like you told us," she replied. "It's kind of hard, though. They're there. They're *always* there. They shout questions when I get out of the car to go inside. I'm like their prisoner. I don't like to be rude. . . ."

"Don't be, but you don't have to answer them either. I'll have the sheriff's department drive over. Anyone else with this problem?"

Bessie Matthews raised her hand. "They've been calling me," she said.

He nodded. "I'll have a word with them, then." He thought he already had.

He looked at the women, more or less as a group. If people in general were difficult for him to judge, women were impossible. He could not connect any of them to this bloody, insane murder. He knew he was wrong to think that way, but he was still an innocent where human depravity was concerned. And women did not kill this way.

Mrs. Garriques was signaling to him. For privacy, she went over to the corner of the room, where he joined her.

"Judge," she said in a pathetic voice just above a whisper, "my head is splitting." Then, for emphasis, she added, "Like an ax was stuck there."

"I'm sorry to hear that," he told her.

She looked at him, blushing vividly. "It's because of Mr. Garriques," she explained. "He's a pain in the ass—excuse me, Your Honor."

Barr bent closer. "What does your husband have to do with this court?"

"He's a hemorrhoid sufferer," she said in heavily accented English. "I tell him not to eat the *picante salsa, muy malo, muy caliente.*" Her dark eyebrows raised. "Last night he could not help himself. It was *fútbol,* Mexico versus Argentina. He ate the whole jar and this morning when he woke up he was on fire down there. And I am usually at home to help him out when he forgets."

Barr nodded. What was there to say?

"I blow up his little inner tube"—and she formed her hands in a circle—"like a doughnut when there is an eruption down there. Otherwise he lies in bed all day long watching soap operas and his neck gets stiff, and then he has a pain in his neck. Judge?"

"I think I understand," he said, looking away. "Did you mention his problem during jury selection?" He didn't recall, but he didn't think so.

"*¡Jo!*" she said, her eyes widened with surprise. "I forgot."

"There's not a lot we can do now," he said.

"Judge, these *bombas* last a day, maybe part of a day, that's all," she said, her brow furrowing.

"So, you want my permission to do what exactly?"

"Nothing right away. I want you to know it happens."

"I see no reason why the court should cause your husband unnecessary pain and suffering," he told her. "If he watches *fútbol* and eats the salsa again and there's an eruption, Mrs. Garriques, ask one of the bailiffs or one of the deputies to tell me. We'll arrange something." He sighed and turned to the room. "Well,

I've taken up enough of your time. You must be tired and anxious to get home," he said with a smile. "Thank you again. Have a good evening, and I'll see you all tomorrow."

Mrs. Garriques picked up her coat and started out. She stopped as she went past Barr. She put her hand on his arm. "You are a nice man, Judge," she said.

"Thank you, Mrs. Garriques," he told her.

A few minutes later he was leaving, and one thought lingered in his mind. How could any of those people have killed Holly Hawkes?

———

Fog diffused even the blazing TV lights that met Barr halfway down the courthouse steps. He could have sneaked to the parking garage around the back, protected by deputies. But the very idea that he needed protection from the press galled him. They had their rights, just has he had his, and the two could coexist. He wanted nothing from these working people who formed a gauntlet of lights and searching faces. What did they want from him? The truth, he hoped.

Down the steps one reporter shot him questions, and he kept his gaze forward. A knot of them stood at the edge of the sidewalk, their microphones and snub-nosed cameras pointed.

"Are you going to sequester the jury?" one of them yelled.

Hadn't he answered that? Didn't they read their own articles, watch their own broadcasts? He went around with a polite "Excuse me."

"Do you plan to admonish Lovelace for inadequate defense?"
"No."

"How long, in your opinion, will the prosecution's case last?"
"Don't know."

They moved closer.

He stepped over to the sidewalk through a couple of hundred of them, their numbers swollen from the day before. He wished himself to disappear, thinking this had been a mistake.

"Goin' my way, handsome?" he heard a familiar voice call.

Jenny was sitting in a tomato-red Ford Mustang with a broad green racing stripe, its convertible top down, its powerful engine throbbing. He stared. He wanted to get away and yet he did not want the press to see him jump into a car with a gorgeous blonde who had used her sexiest voice to ask him if he wanted a ride. Her hair was piled up under a baseball cap with PROZAC stitched across the front in red letters and she wore an open-necked white linen blouse that was unbuttoned halfway down. A wool plaid kilt fell halfway down her thighs.

He glanced over his shoulder, then opened the car door and slid in.

Jenny peeled out with a chirp of the tires.

When they were out of sight around the corner, she said, "You looked like you needed rescuing."

"I could have handled them."

She laughed out loud. "You just can't say thank you, can you?"

"Thank you," he told her softly. "I appreciate it. Now, please take me around the corner to the garage."

"I could use a drink."

He looked at her, marveling at her spirit.

"How's about Sam's?" she suggested, not waiting for his reply.

Sam's, over in Tiburon, was known for its garbanzo bean salad, Ramos gin fizzes, and sourdough hamburgers alfresco. The crowd was raucous and touristy, and by this hour cowboy music would be blaring on the jukebox and all that tiresome posing and pretending would be in full swing. Barr hated Sam's. Crowds annoyed him. He hated gin fizzes. And the seagulls at Sam's forced themselves on the patrons, who thought of them as cute.

"Tell you what," he told her.

"Not Sam's," she said.

"Take me to Chinatown."

She looked over at him, just to be sure. "You're kidding."

"I'm not."

"You hate Chinatown."

"It's where I want to go."

"Why?"

"I want to know your interests," he said, glancing at her to see if she believed him. She didn't.

"Chinatown isn't one of my interests."

"You told me once you hung out in Chinatown."

"I did, a long time ago. Now, what's this all about?"

He ignored her question. "Where did you study Chinese?"

Her brow furrowed. "How long have we known each other?"

"Years. I don't remember."

"Engineering and Chinese at Stanford, Chinese studies and Chinese at Cal. Anything else from my résumé?"

"Is Chinatown the briar patch I think it is?"

"To me it isn't. That doesn't mean I *know* it. I know my way around it. Are we going to a place with just drinks, or drinks and dinner?"

"Drinks."

She smiled at him. "A romantic interlude?"

"Who said romantic? You said a drink."

"One can lead to another."

"Yes, one can." He looked at her and winked.

She rattled off a phrase in Cantonese, then smiled at him sweetly. She steered the Mustang north on Van Ness, then east on Sutter, and down a hill on the bay side to Stockton, where she went north again. Ahead was the Union Square end of the tunnel's mouth, where Holly had died.

"Slow down, slow down," Barr told her. As they entered the tunnel the temperature dropped and a dampness filled the air. The sound of the car closed in and echoed out. "This is where it happened," he told her.

Jenny floored the accelerator. "Gives me the willies," she said and they sped into the open air. She glanced over at him. "That's your thing, Barr, not mine. I don't want to know about it."

She went right on Clay, braking for the pedestrians who

spilled into the street, a whole regiment of men and women and children who looked and sounded so different. The effect was startling. Indeed, in only a matter of yards, as though the Stockton tunnel were a form of time machine, they had traveled from the familiar to the exotic, from the here and now to yesteryear, when San Francisco was a shanty of gold prospectors, hooligans, sailors, and hide merchants.

A moment later Jenny parked up on the sidewalk.

"You're leaving it here?" he asked her, incredulous that she could be so inconsiderate.

She saw nothing wrong, and her look said as much.

"It's on the sidewalk," he pointed out. "Sidewalks are for walking on. That's why they are called side*walks*."

"Don't be patronizing," she told him. And she started to walk down the narrow street.

"You're walking where you're supposed to park. You're going to leave your car here, on the sidewalk, with the top down?" he asked.

"Get over it, Barr," she advised, but she was laughing. "This isn't a place you know anything about."

"Laws don't apply?"

"Not the ones you studied."

"You'll get a ticket."

She faked a look of horror.

"Your car will be vandalized."

She put her hands on her hips. "The Chinese's respect for another man's property is sacrosanct," she told him. "Confucian. Lesson number one. Don't ask why. Take my word."

Barr shrugged. He didn't care; it was her car anyway. He was trying to be helpful. He followed her down one street and up another until he was not just lost, he was totally disoriented. Then along a dank and fetid alley to an unmarked door, which a Chinese man in a double-breasted suit with wide lapels opened for them from inside. He greeted them with a quick smile meant for Jenny, and with a whisking and impatient sweep of his hand he indicated for them to go inside.

At the end of a narrow hallway the room they entered was choked with acrid pipe, cigar, and cigarette smoke. Mah-jongg tiles clattered in one corner and men at tables drank tea from clay cups, played fan-tan, and talked in a nasal singsong. For the most part they dressed in frogged cotton quilted jackets in black, gray, or a faded blue, baggy cotton pants, and black cloth slippers. Some even wore braids and black skullcaps.

Barr turned around to make sure Jenny was still there. At a table, he leaned forward on his elbows, and when a waiter shuffled over Jenny ordered drinks in Cantonese.

Barr said, "Thanks again for coming to my rescue back there. I'm glad you showed up when you did."

She shrugged. "You think that was a coincidence?"

"I guess."

"It wasn't, just like it wasn't coincidence your showing up at my place last night. I saw you. If you had waited another minute you could have come in."

He looked at her sheepishly. He knew he should just let it be, but his mouth said what his heart felt. "Working late? What is it these days? Triple overtime after nine?" His smile was like a cheap mask. "What's expected?" he asked. "I mean, out of curiosity."

"Later, Barr," she growled.

"Later? What, later? Why not now?"

"What's your point?"

"You."

She looked off in the direction of the bar, drumming her fingers on the table, then, as if she took the challenge, she turned to him. "He's my boss. Okay?"

"There's nothing going on?"

"Between Stanton and me?" She groaned.

"What's his interest in you?"

She gave him a pitiful look. "What's his interest? What was yours, stopping by at one in the morning?"

"I refuse to answer on grounds that might incriminate me," he said.

"I thought so. Now can we drop it?"

But Barr wasn't done. "He's married, isn't he?"

She sighed. "I guess. I don't know that part of him. And I don't care to know. I figure he's a big boy. If he wants to take me to the ballet, I'll go if I feel like it. You didn't ask me out for last night. He did. You and I aren't going out. Where's the attachment? Besides, Stanton can do things for my career. A whole lot of things, frankly. And he's interesting, to boot. Real interesting. Good enough?"

"Does he really like the ballet?" Barr asked.

"He wants to be *seen* at the ballet, which is different from liking it. He wants the public right now to think he has put the death of his granddaughter behind him. He does not want his political opponents and his business competitors to think that her death has wounded him. Appearances are important to him. He's a good man," she said immediately. "In spite of all his money and the Senate seat, he's decent at heart."

"He made his fortune in Asia, am I right?"

She leaned back in her chair. "The company history says that he took over his father's company and he grew it large, mostly in Asia. He went to the Far East when he was young. He tells people he was like Lord Jim. He was a roughneck. He learned about Asia from the bottom up, not from books."

"Whose bottom?"

She smiled but she didn't think it was funny; Hawkes as a subject was serious to her. "I have no doubt that he could tell some tales out of school. He prevailed. Men like him always do. He beat the Asians on their home turf."

"By their rules?"

"Of course." She thought about that.

"And he goes to the ballet."

She looked surprised by the observation. "He has a cultured side, though I have no doubt that some things he has done would make your hair stand on end."

The drinks arrived, a beer for Barr and a whiskey on ice for her. The glasses were grimy and chipped.

"Why'd you want to come to Chinatown, really?" she asked.

"I wanted to see it anew," he told her. "It's been a long time. I wanted to see if I can understand it."

"It's not for your sensibility, Barr. You're too direct. The Chinese enjoy a different pattern of thought."

"Deceptive, you mean?"

"That, and more than that. Learning Chinese was a struggle for me because in all languages the culture is indivisible. To learn French you must know how the French think. They don't think like we do. For Chinese, there's a refinement that includes great subtlety."

"What about including criminal behavior?"

She was beginning to see. "There's that too. What the Chinese allow and what they do not allow would make your head swim. There is unimaginable cruelty and selfishness in their character. If you ever want to know about man's inhumanity, study the Chinese. It bends the known rules. Your courts couldn't handle it, Barr."

"Just so long as it was written they could."

She shook her head. "They've had time over the millennia to develop behavior that we would consider shocking. We're a young country by their standards. We haven't caught on to the refinements of immorality and criminality."

"And that's here, in Chinatown?"

"Of course it is."

"Give me an example."

"Concubinage is one, but first I'll mention the most famous one: foot binding. The feet of girls who were being raised as concubines were wrapped so tightly in bandages the pain was excruciating, though they were not so tight that the bones would crack. These girls grew up deformed. Their feet looked like filets of meat. The pain was horrible. Thousands and thousands of girls endured this treatment. You know why? Because rich men were making love to these young girls, and binding kept them from running away. These girls had to be carried everywhere. They could not walk. Their lives were spent in bed,

screwing old men. And when the girls got a little bit old themselves, they were thrown out. Rich Chinese men like their girls
young."

"Are you saying it still goes on?"

"Officially, no. Practically, yes."

"Does Senator Hawkes buy into all this?"

She laughed. "Senator Hawkes? What are you talking about?
He and I sometimes discuss China and the Chinese, politics, history, the culture. But never that seamier side to things. Those
things aren't discussed between Chinese men and women, or between him and me, anyway. I would doubt, though, that he finds
the Chinese shocking in any of their practices, past or present."

"Young girl prostitutes with smashed feet?"

"Like I said, we don't talk about it."

"What else can you tell me about Chinatown?"

"My impressions? Does this place suggest anything to you?"
She leaned back in the chair, watching him as he gazed at the
men in the bar. To them Barr and Jenny were nearly invisible.
They did not look at them, refer to them with any obvious gestures, or speak to them. Their intensity was remarkable, whether
it was aimed at mah-jongg or fan-tan or just in rapt discussion.

"It suggests that your college days were different from mine, if
you hung out here," he said.

"I'd practice Chinese on the old guys, and in return I'd let
them beat me at mah-jongg. I'm a round-eye, but they accepted
me because I was young and a student and I suppose they found
me pretty. If I were a Chinese woman they wouldn't have let me
in. I amused them. I'd like to know, though, what *you* see?"

"I see a place that tells me I've lived in San Francisco my entire
life and didn't know this was here."

"The killer, Feng Shao-li, is from Chinatown, isn't he?" she
asked. "That's why you're asking these questions."

"I'm asking, Jenny, because I feel like I'm being used as a
pawn in something that I can't even begin to fathom."

"Who's using you?" she asked.

"If I had to guess? My father, my godfather, and just who else

I don't know. It's a feeling, nothing more. But that feeling is as mysterious to me as Chinatown. Dad and Uncle Wellsy know something I don't, something they can't say straight out. It's a subtext that I'm seeing, that's all. For instance, my father was a little too insistent about something I told him the other day. You know how he is. Dad never really tells me anything. Yesterday, he told me. And my godfather, Cardinal Wells, claimed to be helping me when he made a suggestion that he then denied. It's weird, what's happening, Jenny, as weird as this place." He looked around. "But, yes, specifically, the *accused's* being Chinese is why I am asking you these questions about Chinatown. It's why I'm curious. I'm looking for help anywhere I can find it, because I'm short on time. To answer your question, the SFPD picked Feng Shao-li up in Chinatown."

"I can't help you with your father, but I can answer your questions about Chinatown. From what I've read, Feng Shao-li is a recent immigrant. That struck me as strange."

"Why's that?"

"Think about it, in relationship to Holly Hawkes."

Barr raised an eyebrow; he had heard something similar, he recalled, from the Chinese deputy sheriff at the courthouse door last night. "You tell me."

"You don't hear English spoken around here, do you?" She wasn't looking for an answer. "You don't see any people like you and me here either. If you had stood in front of that door we came through to get in here, it would not have opened for you. In that sense, Chinatown is like it always was. It is not integrated the way we like to think of America. Diversity as a concept would be laughed at here. If the Chinese were African-Americans, Chinatown would be branded a ghetto. Why is the blacks' area a ghetto and this is simply Chinatown? That's both the question and the answer. There is a clear message here, if you look and listen, Barr."

Barr shook his head. "I'm looking and I'm not seeing it."

"Do these old guys window-shop in Union Square? Do their wives frequent Hermès and Gucci and Neiman Marcus?"

Barr laughed. "They probably wouldn't let them in."

"Yet you see blacks and Hispanics and Native Americans in those shops."

"But never the Chinese."

"Chinese who live in Chinatown have nothing to do with that other side of town—and by that I mean on the south side of the Stockton tunnel. They live with their traditions and culture like it's a different continent and century. Like they just arrived on a sailing ship from Shanghai or Canton. They have *nothing* to do with us. The Chinese boys do not mix with the Caucasian girls. They have never heard of schools like the Alliance Française. They don't meet those girls, talk to them, see them, date them. You know what else, Barr?"

"Don't tell me," he said.

She nodded. "If you ask me, they don't *kill* them either, unless there is something very odd about the murder. And whatever that was, it wasn't because Feng Shao-li was trying to rob her."

"Thanks for the tour," he told her later, parked by the curb in back of the courthouse. Barr was reaching for the door.

She looked straight ahead. "Tell me something, Barr, before you go. Would you have called if I hadn't rescued you?"

"I'd planned to spend the night with Morgan, if that's what you mean."

"Nothing wrong with that. I love you for that. But don't you see, between you and me, someone's got to take that first step?"

"I thought we covered that ground," he told her.

"We never did. What am I supposed to think? In case you haven't noticed, I don't need to throw myself at men. At you, I do. I don't even know why I bother. Sometimes you catch me, sometimes you don't. It hurts when I fall. Is that all I can expect from you?"

"For right now," he told her honestly.

"That's what you always say. There is always something.

There's Morgan, or your father, or a race you are sailing or driving in. I have a life to get on with too," she told him, almost sadly.

"I have a trial to run."

"You'll have trials as long as you're a judge, some less important, some more important, than this Hawkes one."

"This one is different," he said, telling her more than he should. "Something is wrong with it. Something, Jenny, is flawed. I'm being shown that flaw from a difficult, oblique angle. I'm not seeing it either."

"I'm sorry to hear that," she said. "I guess I'm different too, as different as this trial. I don't want to complain, but while I'm young I want to start a family of my own." She seemed surprised by the observation. "That's right, Barr, children."

"*And* a career?"

"You bet," she said. "A career can be as satisfying as rearing kids. It's not that I don't want them. I want to spend *good* time with them, not maintenance time. I do not want to bicker with them day in and day out over picking up their clothes and finishing their asparagus."

"Children are day in and day out."

"But you have your career. What's the difference between you and me?"

He couldn't think of one. "I'm a man and you're a woman."

"You frustrate me, Barr," she told him. "Because you try to put me on the defensive. You are self-centered and egotistical and you'd probably be just as happy on your own. You have Roberta to cook for you and take care of Morgan. You have Miss Hamish to do this and that for you at court. You have that Hispanic lady, Maria, to clean the house and wash the clothes. You have your freedom to sail. You do whatever you like with your men friends. And you have work that you love. You don't need a woman. Or, if you do, you don't need me."

He shook his head. "Tell me what you want?"

"To be included in your life if I am going to *be* in your life. I do not want to be a Seven-Eleven you stop at now and then. I can get that anywhere."

"And Morgan?"

"I love him. In some ways I love him more than I love you." She held up her hand for him to let her talk. "But I need to be included, as an equal, Barr. I want to be a part of your work, I want to know what you are thinking, what you are doing—dammit, I want the intimacy that I deserve."

"Aren't you really talking about marriage?"

Her eyes flashed with anger. "You think that's what I'm about? The big bad woman is trying to trap you? If you think I haven't included marriage in my thoughts about us, you are wrong. It is often a part of the female method of defining a relationship—permanence. Maybe it will happen. It is *not* what I am talking about, because as far as I'm concerned, we're miles from the altar. I'm talking about honesty and intimacy, and you are thinking . . . God, Barr, you really are a dope."

"Can I go now?" he asked her.

An instant later her tires screeched as she sped off, leaving him standing in the dark, alone on the curb.

Chapter Four

In court the next morning, witnesses portrayed Feng Shao-li as a young man forever landing in trouble. He was known in Chinatown as a cheat and a thief. Shenon called to the stand Shao-li's employer, Benjamin Tian Jiyun.

"You would describe the defendant's circumstances as what?" Shenon asked him. Tian Jiyun was a man with a wide face and puffy cheeks, eyes that registered surprise when he looked up at the court, and a shock of black hair that stood up straight, altogether giving him a remarkable, startled look.

"He's poor," Tian Jiyun replied.

"The defendant was earning a wage. Isn't that right?"

"He worked as a sweeper in one of my clothing plants."

Grandiose though Tian Jiyun tried to make them seem, Chinatown clothing plants were mean places where illegal immigrants worked piece rates, for pennies a day, in conditions that generally were appalling. The state and the INS investigated them, patrolled them, and occasionally raided them, shutting them down only to have them spring up again.

"And does a sweeper at your plant earn the money to bring a family over from Hong Kong?" Shenon asked.

Benjamin Tian Jiyun laughed behind his upraised hand.

"Share your humor with the court, please, sir," Shenon said.

He lowered his hand. "Not without help, he couldn't have brought them over," he replied.

A further witness was called, Steven Li Ruihuan, who said he had come over with Shao-li from Hong Kong, and had boarded in the same room with him before his family arrrived here. Li Ruihuan was now working in a bank, he told the court, which could have meant anything.

"Why was the defendant in such a rush to bring his family to America?" Shenon asked.

Barr looked at Lovelace. "Sustained!" Barr shouted. The attorneys looked at him, wondering if the other side had objected, then realized that Barr had sustained his own objection. And they smiled in spite of themselves. "Rephrase," Barr told the lead prosecutor.

"Did the defendant tell you why he wanted his family to emigrate to America?" he asked Li Ruihuan.

"He was afraid for them, he told me," he replied. "The Communists were coming."

"And what was the significance of that?" asked Shenon.

"The charter of the English Crown Colony of Hong Kong expired this year, and the PRC took over."

"The Communists? The ones in Beijing?"

"Mr. Shao-li was afraid that his family would fall into the hands of the same people responsible for the Tiananmen Square massacre. If he allowed that to happen through his own failure to raise the money, then he was afraid they would be literally imprisoned in Hong Kong. He would never see them again."

"Is this a common fear?"

"Many Hong Kong Chinese with assets have moved to Vancouver and Singapore, taking their money with them. To enter Canada, for instance, a net worth of two hundred thousand dollars is required for emigration. Many are wealthy and were quite prepared to buy their way in. Others arrived in Chinatown, legally and otherwise, and put their assets on deposit. Others, like Mr. Shao-li, are not rich. But rich or poor doesn't matter. People wanted to get their relatives out of Hong Kong. They were desperate."

"Cross, Mr. Lovelace?" Barr asked when Shenon was finished.
"No, Your Honor." He didn't even bother to look up.

Barr had listened to the testimony. He remembered walking
down Grant Street with his mother, not daring to venture too far
off the main thoroughfare for fear that the Chinese would kid-
nap him and send him into slavery. Chinatown, to his mother,
was a nightmare of intrigues. It was a foreign place of opium
dens, child labor, prostitutes, and gangs—indeed, a place governed by its own laws and patrolled by its own police.

The afternoon's testimony confirmed to Barr that Chinatown
was exactly what Jenny and his mother had said it was.

Young men in Chinatown, according to the testimony of Jiang
Zemin, the head of the Chinese-American Association, joined
gangs like the Three Dots, the Three in One, and the Heaven
and Earth societies, the Wah Ching. The gangs had begun years
ago as anti-Manchu resistance groups and surrogate clans of
blood brothers. With the Chinese diaspora they had become
Chinese mafias, complete with secret signs, passwords, rituals,
and the power and control of life and death among the Chinese.

Barr wondered where Shenon was heading in his questioning
of Jiang.

These same gangs thrived in Chinatown, the head of the association told the court under Shenon's direct questions. Their
leader was called the Dragon Head, or simply was known by the
number 489, which derived from the sum of three figures that
equaled twenty-one. That, in turn, was a multiple of three,
which signified the trinity of heaven, earth, and man, and seven,
which was the symbol of death. Few knew 489's true identity, or
where he worked out of—Hong Kong, Singapore, New York,
Vancouver. But a gang called the 49 Boys acted as 489's praetorian guard and were feared for their ways.

Shenon seemed almost compelled by this area of testimony,

and Barr again wondered why. Out loud he asked, "Mr. Shenon, you are skirting on irrelevance here, unless you can begin to tie it in, please."

Shenon asked the head of the association, "Is the defendant one of these Forty-nine Boys?"

"Yes, sir," Jiang Zemin replied. "I believe so."

"Objection," Lovelace said.

"Sustained," said Barr.

"How, sir, are these Forty-nine Boys identified?" Shenon asked.

"Two parallel bars tattooed here," Jiang said, and he pointed to the web of his right hand.

Shenon held up to the jury an enlarged photograph of Shao-li's torso and arms, which the SFPD photographer had taken. He turned back to Jiang Zemin: "Like this tattoo on the defendant, you mean?"

"That's the one, yes," he replied. "That's the Forty-nine Boys' mark."

Shenon said, "Mr. Lovelace, would you mind asking your client to hold up his arm for the court?"

Feng Shao-li looked frightened when the translator whispered to him. He appealed to Lovelace with a look, but Lovelace could do nothing legally to help him. Shao-li raised his arm. The two parallel bars showed boldly on the web of his right hand. He dropped his arm and pushed his hand under the table, out of sight.

"Thank you, Mr. Lovelace, Mr. Shao-li," said Shenon. He turned to the association head. "Now, I'd like to know a little something about this gang. Does this association with the Forty-nine Boys imply any kind of behavior in particular?"

Barr glared at Lovelace, who was doodling with a pencil.

"*Sustained!*" Barr shouted. "Rephrase if you want to," he told Shenon.

"Are the Forty-nine Boys known for anything in particular?"

"I don't quite know what you're asking," said Jiang Zemin.

"Violence? Benevolence? Charity?"

"Violence, definitely."

Shenon showed the jury a flier circulated to store owners in Chinatown by Jian Zemin's Chinese-American Association that warned of thieves. He pointed to Feng Shao-li's name near the top on the list.

"This must mean something," Shenon asked. "Why is his name included on the list?"

"He was seen stealing," said Jiang. "He is known."

"Objection, Your Honor," said Lovelace meekly.

Barr thought about it. He decided to let it go; he overruled.

Shenon asked the witness, "What extremes would you say that the Forty-nine Boys have gone to?"

"You name it," Jiang Zemin replied.

"Murder?"

He smiled. "That is a little bit like asking if a duck quacks."

"So, is your answer yes?"

"They are known killers," said Jiang Zemin. "Their avowed purpose, their pledge, if you will, is to carry out the will of the 489, the Dragon Head. Murder of the enemies of the Dragon Head is considered by the Forty-nine Boys to be a great honor."

"Mr. Lovelace?" asked Barr, who was starting to recognize the outlines of Shenon's case. He hoped that Lovelace did too. "Anything for this witness?"

Lovelace nodded his head. And he scraped his feet across the floor. "Hello, Mr. Zemin, how are you?" he asked.

"Fine," he replied warily.

"You just now told the court all about my client. You would make him out to be a bad person."

"Not I," said Zemin.

"I'm sorry. That's how I was hearing you. I didn't hear you say that he was kind to his mother, that he took in stray cats and dogs, that he raised canaries at home. Did I?"

"That wasn't what I was asked."

"That's why I'm here. I get to ask the nice questions. Balance things up. I'm not going to ask you whether my client helps old ladies across the street. I'm not going to take the court's time. I don't want to embarrass Mr. Shao-li. We can assume because he is poor, like poor people anywhere, life is hard. True?"

"Very, I would suppose."

"Work all day, half the night, what kind of a life is that?"

"Not much," said the witness.

Lovelace was holding a copy of the association's flier with Shao-li's name on it. "What exactly does this thing mean?"

"It means that he has been seen stealing."

"Seen? Was he charged?"

"No."

"Why wasn't he? If he was seen, and there were witnesses to his thievery, why weren't charges brought against him?"

"It's not our way. We take care of our own."

"Take care of your own." He looked ceilingward. "Your own." He cleared his throat. "Let me get this straight. Do you have any proof to offer the court that what this flier alleges bears any truth?"

Jiang Zemin looked left and right. "Not at this time," he replied.

"So let's disregard the gossip." He put the flier down. "Second, about this Forty-nine Boys. The tattoo would indicate that my client is a gang member. I do not think he would deny his membership." He smiled. "That tattoo would make denial difficult, in any case. Is there a law I am not familiar with against tattoos and gangs? No. Against Forty-nine Boys in particular? No. So by joining he has done nothing illegal."

"But—"

"Nothing, sir," said Lovelace quickly, and under his breath he uttered, "Guilt by association does not stand up even in Chinatown." He straightened up and paused for breath. "That leads me to ask a simple question you should be able to easily answer, as the head of Chinatown's government." He paused for effect. "Is Chinatown, where my client lives, governed by the same American laws as, say, Des Moines or Butte?"

"There are slight differences," said Jiang.

"Yes or no?"

"Yes," said Jiang.

"No more questions, Your Honor."

Barr kept his eyes on Lovelace but he was thinking how an odd, yet poorly defined, uniformity had characterized these Chinese witnesses so far. To his credit, Lovelace had already caught it. The defendant, Lovelace had said, spoke little English, and yet those who said they knew him well enough to testify about his character spoke English without accents. So why should someone as insignificant as Feng Shao-li have attracted the interest of Chinatown's business and government elites?

Barr pounded his gavel and called the proceedings for the weekend.

———

After he'd dealt with a few administrative details that Miss Hamish had waiting for him after court, Barr drove home.

He had just parked the Porsche in an empty diagonal slot on the street at the bottom of the property on Russian Hill, and he paused a minute to look out to the east, over the Bay Bridge, where a United States Navy aircraft carrier caught his eye. He watched the massive ship cross under the elevated spans of the Bay Bridge in the golden light of the setting sun. It was improbably large, and it held his interest for several minutes. He was just turning to climb the steps when a car braked hard and stopped in the street by the back of the Porsche. Barr thought he might know the passengers, and he smiled, and his smile fell when he saw that they were strangers, and Chinese. They were crowded in the car, and they were all looking at him as if they did not know what to expect. The driver stared at him with an implacable expression that Barr did not even try to read. It frightened him nearly breathless.

From around the other side of their car, he noticed the top of a boy's head. He heard a high, familiar voice. But it still took

Barr a second or two to realize that the mop of hair and the bright voice belonged to Morgan. And now he actually gasped with fear.

Morgan came around between the parked cars, and the Chinese sped off.

"What were you doing in that car?" Barr asked him, trying hard to disguise the fear that tinged his voice.

"They made me get in," Moran said, hugging his father around the waist. "They were waiting for me at school."

"Where were your teachers?" Barr asked, nearly incredulous. *His son had just been kidnapped.* Anything at all could have happened.

"They thought I got on the bus," Morgan said. "Daddy, the men told me to shut up." Now he started to cry, remembering.

"Did they touch you?"

He nodded and shook his head in the same motion. "They pushed me in the back and they held me down. They said they would hurt me if I didn't do what they said."

"What else did they do to you?" Barr asked, holding his son tight.

"They just drove me around," Morgan replied. "For an hour."

Barr pushed the hair back from Morgan's forehead, and, going up the steps, he held his hand with a tight grip. He had nearly lost his son to someone in Chinatown who wanted to send him an unmistakable message, though he could only guess at what it was.

Roberta was standing on the porch with Flicka at her side, looking down at Barr and Morgan with a worried expression. "Morgan, where *were* you?" she demanded. "I called the school and . . ." Seeing him safe, her fear changed to anger, and then to a visible relief. She ran down the steps and took him in her arms. Even Flicka barked, as if she too felt relieved, and she waddled down the steps after Roberta, waiting for a friendly touch from Morgan.

"I was okay," Morgan told Roberta, looking up bravely at his father. He had been terrified. Barr had drilled into him never to have anything to do with strangers. Morgan knew what had happened. He had known that he was being kidnapped, and he knew the danger he was in.

Roberta started to lead him onto the porch, but Morgan held back. She looked at him strangely, then at Barr. And she turned and went into the house alone. Morgan clearly had not finished with his father.

"Dad, they told me something I am supposed to tell you," he said softly, as though he feared that he would be blamed for what he was about to say.

"I know they did," said Barr. "Go ahead, tell me. It's going to be okay."

"They told me to tell you to stick to what you do. Does that make sense?"

"It does, son," he told him.

"And if you don't, they said we would hear from them again."

Barr tried to appear to take it lightly now. "They said that *we* would hear from them again?"

"They said that, yeah, Dad. They know all about us."

Chapter Five

The din in the Golden Dragon restaurant was practically deafening. The place reeked of fish and vinegar and whatnot from Chinese cuisine. A stooped Chinese man with crooked teeth and a white beard told Wally to wait by the door, then he ignored him. When he got tired of being passed by other customers who had come in after him, Wally went into the restaurant and sat down at an empty banquette. A Chinese waiter pushed up a trolley with small plates of dim sum that to Wally looked dead. His stomach churned and he thirsted for a cold beer.

"You can't sit there," said a voice angrily behind him.

"A beer," Wally told the waiter, ignoring the owner of the voice.

"That table's taken."

Wally turned around. The person who had spoken to him was big and powerful with broad shoulders and thick wrists, and his face was contorted into what looked like a parody of rage—all teeth and puffed-up cheeks and bulging eyes. "Who says?" Wally asked.

"This is my restaurant. . . ."

"Sit *down*," Wally commanded. The restaurant quieted instantly. Patrons and staff alike stared at Wally, who turned to the waiter and said, "Now, please, get me that beer."

Daniel Gee gaped at his temerity.

"Look," said Wally, bending sideways to reach for his wallet.

"My job is tough enough, Mr. Gee. I don't mean you personally. Don't get me wrong." He flipped open the wallet to show the dirty laminate of his SFPD ID with the CANCELLED stamp cleverly disguised. "I mean, I come in here and stand around while your maître d' gives all the tables to Chinese who were behind me in line. What kind of hospitality is that?"

Daniel Gee said nothing to Wally. "Beer," he told the waiter, then mumbled something else to him in Cantonese.

"You need to improve your style," Wally said. "It's also very rude to speak in a language that all your guests do not understand."

"I was telling him to get the beer and leave us alone," Gee said.

"Is your place this busy every night?" he asked, looking around. He didn't know what he expected to find here. But he had chosen to start with Gee simply because it was near dinnertime and he was hungry. Or he had been hungry. For now, a beer would suffice.

Gee nodded. "And it falls apart when I'm not here. And I haven't been around lately. It's why I'm on edge. If I am not tough with them, my workers take advantage of me. It's how they are. And if I am not here, it's like the cat's away, as you say."

"The trial," Wally said.

Gee flexed his biceps, which bulged with well-toned muscles. He was young, one of the jurors whom Wally placed in the zone of age and sex as someone who might kill out of passion.

"The trial?" Gee asked, surprised that he would know. "I'm not supposed to talk about it."

Wally asked him, "What's the gossip? You can talk about that. Do people around here think they got the killer?"

"The right one but for the wrong reason," he replied, nodding.

"This is interesting," Wally said. "Tell me."

"You know how everyone asked 'Where were you?' after JFK's assassination? Well, people here all know where they were the night the Hawkes girl was killed."

"Where *were* you?"

"Here, of course." He smiled. "Ask anyone." And now he laughed with a new thought. "I suppose you know I could tell you anything and you would have to believe me. That's why your side of town calls this side of town Chinatown."

"I could check."

His laughter said that wasn't true either, and Wally knew it. "Why would you care where I was?" Gee asked.

"I don't," said Wally. "My question pertained to rumors."

Gee looked serious when he said, "I was here that night because that night the streets of Chinatown were not exactly safe for Chinese. The gangs. There was fighting. People stay in."

"Everybody?" asked Wally, his voice demonstrating his surprise.

"If you are smart you don't go out after dark when there is a gang war on."

Wally was having trouble connecting the thought of a war that nobody but Chinese knew about in a city like San Francisco. There was no mention of victories and defeats in the newspapers. The TV stations did not report on tactics and interview its generals. Not one word about a Chinese gang war in Chinatown had reached the ears of the public. And yet people like Gee conducted their lives according to the risks and dangers of this war. Gee seemed to be saying that the Chinese in Chinatown believed that Holly was a casualty of a war. Isn't that what he was hearing?

Wally said, "I don't get the connection between the death of the Hawkes girl that night and the gang war."

"It's easy," Gee replied. "Holly Hawkes was killed because she was careless."

"And killed the way she was?" Wally shook his head. "Doubtful."

Gee shrugged with indifference; he did not care what Wally thought about a world he was ignorant of.

"Getting chopped up isn't the same as being caught in a crossfire," Wally said. "You get a bullet in a war, not a carving knife."

He shrugged again. "You never know what you get in a Chinese war."

"But you seem to think you do."

Gee said, "The gossip. That's all. I was just repeating what I heard. I do not know what weapons the gangs use in their war. Do you?"

"No," Wally admitted.

"Then, why are you so skeptical?"

Because Wally thought he knew better. But in his heart, he knew he was wrong.

⎯⎯⎯⎯⎯⎯

Roberta was waiting for him at the bottom of the steps, her face turned toward the setting sun. She was looking good, and the sunlight turned her blond tresses to gold. She jumped into the car when he waved. She was more subdued than he knew her to be, and he wondered why.

"Is anything the matter?" he asked.

"Something happened to Morgan that the judge won't tell me about," she said. "He looks scared. They both look scared."

Wally glanced at her. "Why wouldn't he tell you?" he asked her.

"Because he said I didn't need to know."

That was all Wally had to know. "Did he say whether he wants to talk to me? Should I call him?"

"He's very quiet," said Roberta. "I've never seen him this quiet. He just said that everything was going to be all right. He wanted me to tell you not to worry either. He could handle it, whatever *it* is." Now she tried to make light of the fear that she had felt enter the house. "He's cooking dinner, if that tells you anything."

"Dan doesn't cook," Wally told her. "Does he?"

She told him Barr had just started dinner when she said good-bye. "He is tonight. Pasta. He looked like he knew how. He wouldn't talk about what happened to Morgan. I never saw him look that way before. He said they were going to watch a movie after dinner, he and Morgan."

"*Raiders of the Lost Ark?*" he asked.

She laughed for the first time, and it was an easy, welcome sound. "That or World War Two documentaries. Something called *Victory at Sea.* Swarms of Japanese airplanes dropping out of the sky. Lots of heavy orchestral music. Very instructional. They pump the sound up. They know it by heart."

"*That* I can appreciate, but *Raiders of the Lost Ark?* It's for kids."

She shook her head. By her expression it was obvious to Wally how much a part of the Barr family Roberta was. Clearly she loved both Barr and Morgan. "The judge is the one who always wants to see it."

"Go figure," said Wally. He looked at her. He was already in love. "I never went out with an English girl before," he admitted. "Anything I should know?"

"Mind your manners."

"So, you like parties?"

"Love 'em."

He looked out the car window. "If you don't mind, I have a stop to make on the way. Maybe two. Mix a little business with pleasure?"

"The judge tells me you're a sleuth."

He looked at her. "He used that word?"

Roberta shook her head quite emphatically. "*I* used the word. The judge called you an investigator."

"Yeah, *that's* more like what I do."

"I love sleuthing."

"Then, let's sleuth together."

"Shall we?"

"We shall," he said, excitement creeping into his voice.

Michael Eng was buried under a pile of wriggling kids. "Michael, Mike . . . Mike, me . . ." they shouted in a chorus of joy.

Watching the melee from the curb, Wally was thinking how kids found goodness as if by radar. They detected false instincts and hidden agendas with an unfailing accuracy. And these kids clearly loved the juror named Michael Eng. Wally was about to drive off, but a single observation of something that seemed out of place made him stay.

As Wally watched from the curb, as sudden as a catch of breath, Eng said something to the child he was playing with. Wally could not see Eng's face, but he could see the child's, and it was as if Eng had struck the child with the force of his words. The boy stared at him, his arms at his sides. And with a look that was shocked and sad, tears rolled down his cheeks. Eng did nothing to comfort him. After half a minute, observing the sadness of the youngster, Eng reached out and touched his arm near his shoulder, and the child pulled angrily away.

Roberta had seen none of this. "He looks like a jolly one," she told Wally under her breath.

Eng's face widened in a smile now, seeing them parked by the curb. It was a smile that told people how he felt about his world. He felt safe in it, and secure. Now he looked like the kind of person who loved to reach out to help others less fortunate than himself. He pulled himself off the ground, brushed his jeans, and came down the slope to the car.

"Anything I can help you folks with?" he asked, standing on the sidewalk, looking into the car. He wore jeans without a belt, and a white T-shirt. He had rolled up the sleeves a couple of turns. Scuffed Timberland boots covered his feet.

"We were driving around," Wally told him. "We're looking for someplace called SoMa."

"You're lost, then, real lost," said Eng. And he gave them directions.

Wally thanked him, and he pointed to the playground. The kids were on the top of the slope, waiting for Eng to come back and play on a jungle gym and a slide, a swing and a merry-go-round. "Are you their activities director?" Wally asked.

"Project Right," he explained. "I'm its director, which means I get to do all the work." He pointed to the side of the swing where he was building a picnic table.

"Project Right?" asked Wally.

"Like Habitat for Humanity, Jimmy Carter's thing," said Eng, who squatted down on his heels by the car window. He nodded politely at Roberta. "We build playgrounds for the city kids." He pointed to his work-in-progress. "These kids don't have much. It only takes a few boards and a little sweat, and it means a lot."

"You good with your hands?" Wally asked.

"Pretty good."

"This is what you do, like, full-time?" Wally asked.

"We put up these things around the city. And we build houses for poor people."

A Chinese kid about seven or eight came down the slope carrying a hammer.

"Mike, can I have a nail?" he asked.

Eng showed him how to start a nail and the kid walked up the slope and started banging on the boards that were meant for the picnic table.

"These kids—the boys mostly—they don't have fathers," Eng explained. "With a man to show them how to do things, they blossom." He clearly liked his work. "You show them, and they can't do it, and they try and try again. And then suddenly it works! They ride a bike! They hammer a nail! It gives them the confidence to try different things. I know it's been like that always. But I really marvel at it."

"You sound like you have kids of your own."

He shook his head. "No," he said very shyly.

At that instant the boy with the hammer screamed with pain, and Eng reacted with a speed that surprised Wally. One instant he was squatting by the car talking to them, the next he was up the slope attending to the kid. In only a moment he distracted the kid from the pain. He was turned halfway to the street, showing the boy where he had hurt his own hand by peeling back a Band-Aid.

Wally had not noticed the Band-Aid.

"Everything all right, then?" Wally asked him when Eng came back down the slope with the injured boy, with a comforting arm around his shoulders.

Eng just smiled. "It didn't hurt as much as he thought." He looked at Roberta, then at Wally. He turned with a wave and escorted the boy up the slope. He sat him down and instructed him on how to use the tools. He wielded the hammer and guided in nails with smooth strokes and a deceptive power. Wally pulled his eyes away from the rhythmic motion as he put the car in gear and drove off.

Roberta, who had listened to their conversation without a word, asked, "I know you aren't lost. What are you looking for?"

He smiled at her intuition. "You tell me. What am I looking for?"

"A murderer," she said as though it were an assumption anyone might have made. She looked at Wally. "Silly, the judge is worried sick and you are helping him."

"Barr told you that?"

She smiled. "Feminine intuition."

"But you just said I was looking for a murderer," said Wally. "How did you know?"

"I didn't," she replied. "But you're a sleuth, and that's what sleuths do. They look for murderers. Don't they?"

Wally shook his head. "Lord help me."

———————————◆———————————

It was dark by the time they parked across from Swan's Oyster Bar on Polk, down the street from the old Alhambra movie theater. Two women agents in the MetLife office stared at them when they entered.

"How *may* we help you?" one asked him.

"I'm looking for Adam Warmath," Wally said.

"He's on jury duty," she explained. "Maybe we can do something for you?"

"Yeah, maybe." Wally smiled at Roberta, putting more in his expression than was necessary. "The little woman and I have just relocated the family to the Bay Area, and I . . ."

The agents' eyes lit up. "Oh? From where?"

"Back East," he lied. "I contacted this office—I believe it was—in June. Someone sent me information about property and car and life insurance. Then I had to postpone the move." He put his finger on his chin.

"When in June?" the agent asked.

Wally pretended to think for a second; Holly died on June 23. He gave her the date.

"It couldn't have been Adam you talked to," one of them said. "He wasn't here."

Roberta—"the little woman"—stood aside. And by the look on her face she was wondering how anyone would believe Wally's story.

"But I'm pretty certain of the name," Wally went on. "It must have been him. How would I know the name otherwise?"

"Several other men work here," said the woman. "If you think it was Adam, I'll check his diary for you."

"I wish you would," said Wally. "I feel I have an obligation to him. He sent me the material."

The other agent said, "We're always shorthanded that time of year, with the meetings and the vacations."

"He's our highest producer," said the first agent.

"Adam Warmath?" Wally asked.

"Come over to his desk with me."

The office was an open space furnished with desks set side by side without the benefit of partitions, as if the MetLife management wanted its agents out soliciting business, not in an office. She led them over to a desk on which sat several framed photos of Warmath with friends. It was the same Warmath in the photos as the one who sat on the jury, the same man with the pedestal neck and brooding eyes. Warmath did not smile in these photos, though everyone else appeared to be having fun.

The woman booted up Warmath's computer and tried to bring up a Windows Schedule+ program, which required a password. She looked frustrated. "Sorry," she said, shutting off the computer. "Unless I call Adam, I can't be sure. And he's put in a password because he doesn't want just anybody looking at his schedule."

"What would you recommend I do?" Wally asked, giving her an opening.

"I could get you started anyway, while you're here, show you what we have to offer."

"That would be nice," he said. "Like I said, I feel I owe him."

"In what category?" she wanted to know.

"Ten million plus is what I asked for term life. That was for starters."

"I wouldn't want to lose him," Roberta said of Wally with a sigh. "And if I did, no amount of money would compensate. Ten million plus would just get me by."

Wally made a face. "Thanks, dear," he said.

A large woman appeared at that moment from the back of the office wearing Elsa Peretti glasses with rose-tinted lenses and a herringbone pants suit. She came out of a door with the word MANAGER on it. She looked like one, Wally thought, watching her walk the length of the office. No, he decided after a second look. She looked like a boss.

"Our manageress," said the woman under her breath.

Eunice Holloway introduced herself. She tried to dismiss the other agent, who stayed where she was. "I'll handle this," Holloway told her.

"He was asking about Adam," she told her.

"I'm afraid he isn't here," she said and raised her finger.

"That's what I told them," said the other one.

"At least I think it was Adam Warmath," said Wally, who repeated the story.

"The twenty-third?" Holloway asked, then glanced at her coworker. "Adam was out of town at the Million-Dollar Round Table in Atlanta that whole week. I remember it well."

"Round Table?" asked Wally.

"Agents who write a hundred million in insurance get to join," Holloway explained. "Adam is a member, the only one in our office. It's honorary, and quite an honor too."

"Where in Atlanta?" he asked.

"The Peach Tree Hotel, I recall."

Wally looked at the other woman, who was shaking her head.

"You've been very kind," he told Holloway. "Come, dear," he told Roberta, and turned to leave. Eunice Holloway returned to her office. And as they walked past the other woman at the door, he put out his hand to her to say good-bye.

"Mayhew, Mayhew Allen, but you can call me May." She glanced around and in a whisper she said, "It's a lie, what Eunice said just now, all lies."

"Can you talk now?" he asked her.

She shook her head. "She'll want to know what this was all about," she said.

Wally gave her his card. "Please, call me, then." And the woman, Mayhew Allen, turned away, closing the office door behind her.

Outside on the sidewalk, Roberta said, "Whew."

"A little heavy competition, don't you think?"

"They'd kill each other if they had a chance. Over Adam Warmath, you think?"

"She said he was in Atlanta. The other one said it was a lie. Maybe he was here in San Francisco. And if he wasn't in Atlanta, I can't strike him from my list." He looked at her, smiling.

"What list?" she asked.

"My list," he said. "A list of suspects. What's your feminine intuition tell you?"

"That Adam Warmath, whoever he is, likes to play with women's hearts."

"That could be dangerous," said Wally.

"It always is," said Roberta meaningfully. "For this Warmath, I think it already is."

As they walked across Polk Street to the car, Wally said, "It's getting late for the party."

"Oh, it doesn't matter to me if we go."

He looked surprised. "You don't want to?"

"If you do, but not on my account. I'm having fun just doing this."

"You really are?" he asked.

She nodded, and a smile lit up her face when she said, "It's like being five different people in one day—first we were lost, then we were moving to San Francisco. What's next?"

Wally was besotted now. He said, "You ever play a lady cop?"

The house lay in the shadow of a power transmission pylon. The lines, which conveyed electricity from a nuclear power generating plant down the coast, emitted a sound like the hiss of snakes. The house, the same as the others built down the slope, looked scorched by electromagnetism. Faint yellow paint flaked from the siding, the pebbles had washed off the roof, and the lawn under the streetlights was a uniform burned-dead brown.

"This is a part of San Francisco I've never seen," said Roberta as they drove up.

"Twin Peaks," said Wally. "It's up-and-coming."

"It looks like it's up and gone," she said.

"You wouldn't believe the prices they get for these dumps." They walked to the front door and, standing under the porch light, Wally knocked.

A frazzled-looking woman answered. She had an infant bundled in her arms. A wisp of curly black hair fell on her face and a large wet spot stained her blouse. Mrs. Figueroa was fat and young, but clearly a woman who children—crying out of sight in the back of the small house—were pulling toward a premature middle age.

"Is your husband home?" Wally asked her.

"David is out back in the garage," she replied in accented English. "Go around if you like. You'll excuse me." And she closed the door.

They followed the driveway, guided by the whine of a power saw. David Figueroa was standing with his shirt off. He was rail thin and muscular. His hair fell across his forehead as his hands guided a board along a table saw. He look up and, seeing Wally, stopped what he was doing and flipped off the power.

Wally pointed to the wood. "What's it going to be?" he asked.

"A kitchen cabinet," he replied. He straightened up. "Do I know you?"

"You do nice work," Wally said, ignoring the question.

"Thanks. What are you, selling something?"

"The Hawkes trial?"

"So? What does that make you?"

"Interested in you," said Wally. He turned to Roberta. "This is my partner. Say hi to the man."

Roberta, stunned by Wally's boldness, nodded in a way she thought a policewoman would nod.

"I do anything wrong?" Figueroa asked.

"We're just checking up on some of the jurors. The judge in trial is concerned that the press is bothering some of you. I guess some of you complained to him. I've been asked to make sure they're keeping their distance."

Figueroa nodded. "Some of them came around here yesterday. I told them I couldn't talk, and they respected that." He shrugged; there was nothing more to say.

"Okay, then," said Wally. He looked around the garage.

Roberta asked, "How do you like jury duty?"

"It sucks," Figueroa said. "I wish I wasn't chosen, to be honest."

"Oh?" asked Wally.

"If you're like me and work for yourself, it costs you money. The city pays you peanuts." He indicated the house with his chin. "I got a family to feed."

"You could have explained all that to the judge," said Wally.

"He wouldn't have listened."

"Judge Barr?"

"He never did a day's real work in his life. What would he know? I read in the papers that he's rich, from an old family. Big house."

"What kind of jobs do you do?"

"Little ones. New kitchens, bathrooms, walls moved or additions, nothing major. I'm a builder, a contractor."

"Summers are your busy time, right?"

"You'd be amazed."

"I met your wife. Saw your baby. A nice-looking kid."

"Our third. He was born two months ago. It's been a tough time for Dolores and me."

"No sleep."

He grinned now in spite of himself. This was not a happy man. "Here and there, that's it."

"You do the birthing classes and all that?" Wally asked.

"I didn't have to," said Figueroa. "I know the drill."

"When was this latest one born?"

"The nineteenth of June. Dolores had some woman's problem, and she stayed at the hospital. Usually they send them home in a day. I had to take care of the kids that week."

"Was there anyone to give you a hand?"

Figueroa nodded again. "My mother-in-law. Hey, I'm no Superman."

"Did you get any time off for yourself?"

"Some nights I'd go out for a beer."

Wally liked David Figueroa. He was the kind of man who just wanted to get through the day; he accepted his lot, not viewing himself as anyone's victim.

"Speaking of beer, while we're talking here, can I get you something cold?" Figueroa asked him, then glanced at Roberta.

"Thanks—we got to be downtown, like a half hour ago."

Figueroa was leaning on a bench against the wall. Wally looked over his bare shoulder and noticed the pegboard on the wall behind his back. He had a collection of exotic knives—stilettos and needle-sharp daggers, bowie and skinning knives with thick blades, even a Japanese knife with a curved double-S blade. Their handles, some ornate, were fashioned of bone and ivory and rawhide bound to steel. Figueroa had made a space for each knife, lovingly displaying them, even outlining them with black paint.

Figueroa glanced over his shoulder and saw where Wally was looking. He stepped back with his hands on his hips and turned around. "Are you into knives too?" he asked. "You probably guessed I'm into them."

"Do you collect 'em or throw 'em or what?" Wally asked.

"I try to collect them, you know, from around the world. Some people collect stamps, some coins. I do knives."

"Holly Hawkes was killed with a knife," Wally said.

"Yeah? So?" he asked, leaving it there.

"An observation, that's all," Wally said. "I didn't mean anything by it."

"Kind of an odd observation, wasn't it?" he asked warily now.

"I apologize if you took it wrong," Wally said. "All I meant was, Holly Hawkes was killed with a knife, and you collect knives. Maybe you have some insight. I'm interested, that's all."

Figueroa looked very thoughtful all of a sudden. "I sure wish the police knew what kind of knife, I mean, like the make and the exact type. It interests me too."

"The detective who testified said it was long-bladed."

"I'd need to know more."

"Why?"

"It'd tell me something I would find helpful about the murderer. That's why."

Wally was intrigued. "You'll have to explain," he said.

"You look like someone who knows about knives yourself. Guys—even murderers—maybe especially them—choose knives with special care. They don't just go into Macy's basement and ask for a bread knife. They want a fourteen-inch Sabatier, or they go to a hunting store for a Ka-bar, a bowie, this or that. You see? Some guy kills with a blade, he knows the feel of it beforehand. It reflects his character and the job he means it for. Knives have character. They tell you something about the owner. If a long-bladed knife is used in a murder, that tells me the guy planned it out in advance. He wanted the blade to dig deep. He wants to kill. No mistake. No error. He wants that blade to slice deep into the heart. A short blade? The guy's saying he doesn't want to admit he's inflicting damage and if he does it isn't his fault, it's the knife's. In other words, he's fucking around with a person's life." He looked at Roberta. "Excuse the language, ma'am."

Roberta was looking around the garage, and she smiled and nodded, still trying to portray a convincing policewoman.

"Thanks for the insight," said Wally, turning to leave. He looked at his watch again. "We're really late, Mr. Figueroa. You've been very helpful."

Out in the car, even before Wally started the engine, she grasped his arm and said, "Did you notice anything odd in that garage just now?"

"No," he said, and he started the car.

"That pegboard with the knives behind Figueroa's back?"

"What about it?"

"The lines he drew around the blades?"

"Yeah, I saw those. So what?"

"The long-bladed knife was missing."

Wally thought about that. And he took the information in stride. "So?" he asked her. "What do you think that means?"

"A long-bladed knife killed Holly."

"Who said we're looking for *her* murderer?" Wally asked, struck by his own transparency. Or was it Roberta's unusual intuition? "I just said we were looking for *a* murderer."

She looked at him with a disapproving frown, as if to say he was taking her for something she wasn't and she did not like it. "What you are looking for, Wally, is who killed Holly Hawkes. It's no mystery to me." And now, with that cleared up, she took the next step. "That knife was missing from the wall. Isn't that something?"

He did not think so, but he said nothing. David Figueroa wasn't the type to murder someone like Holly Hawkes, then complicate the issue by sending Dan Barr a note telling him he was on the jury. It made no sense to Wally, who read Figueroa as a simple guy like himself, a worker, a craftsman, with a family and a mortgage. He wasn't a killer, even if his long-bladed collector's knife was missing. "It's something to think about," he told Roberta, who already had intuited more about what he was doing than he liked to admit.

"Shouldn't we go back and ask him?"

"Later," he told her, he hoped not too dismissively. "Leave it to me."

"One more stop?" Wally asked as they were driving back into downtown San Francisco, and he glanced at Roberta for a sign. "Or you want to call it quits for the night?"

She looked at her watch, smiling. "I could use a bite to eat."

"Oh, sure, oh, sure," he said, apologizing with his tone. "I forgot that. We can still go to the party, if you want."

"A beer and a sandwich would do."

He looked at her like she was Princess Di. "I can do better. You like opera?"

She thought he was kidding. She saw he wasn't. "What do you have in mind?"

"Tosca. It's a joint over on the Barbary Coast that has beers and sandwiches and operas. I love opera. I love the noise."

"They'd be flattered to hear you say that, I'm sure."

Wally was having so much fun with Roberta, he'd almost forgotten that he wanted to kiss her. He wasn't shy. Most of the time he'd usually rush to get his dates in bed, then carry on with the romance from there. He surprised himself now. He hadn't even thought about that aspect. Or not much anyway. She was like a friend, or a buddy—but one he still wouldn't mind getting in the sack, if it came to that.

When they entered Tosca, *La Bohème* was playing through the speakers loudly enough to make conversation impossible. Wally shouted at the girl behind the bar for a couple of beers and menus. Then they sat down opposite the bar near the jukebox. He could smell Roberta's hair when he leaned close to her ear to talk. He felt intoxicated, and the beers hadn't even arrived.

He was trying to make small talk, searching for areas of common interest, but the blast of sound made that impossible. Wally got up and asked the barmaid to turn it down, and the level of sound dropped so much that the room suddenly seemed almost silent. A guy came out of the back of the restaurant, where he'd been playing pool. He gripped the pool cue angrily in his fist, and he glared at the barmaid. "Why'd you turn it down, Deb?" he asked. And she nodded at Wally, whose back was turned.

"Because that guy asked me to," said Deb.

"Oh, fuck him," the man said.

Wally heard it. And he whipped around and saw who the man was. "Lieutenant Barstow," he said, and he smiled at him broadly. "I thought you were a country-western fan."

Lieutenant Barstow looked sheepish. He was a veteran of the SFPD who had been partnered with Wally for a while in the old days, and they knew each other well. "Didn't see it was you, Wally," he said.

"No hard feelings," said Wally. "Let me buy you a beer."

Barstow, seeing Roberta, smiled and came over to the table. He pulled out a chair and extended his hand politely to her. He was looking at Wally when he said, "Looks like your fortunes have changed. What'd you do, win the Lotto?"

"I let my inner personality come through, and the rest was easy," said Wally. He glanced at Roberta and winked. "The truth is, I got lucky."

Barstow turned to Roberta and asked about her accent. He

wanted to know whether she was visiting. She told him what she did.

"You probably know my boss, Judge Barr," she said.

"I've heard of him," he said. And he looked at Wally. "That trial's all the talk around headquarters. It's got us on edge."

"Ah, come on."

"From the chief down, everyone is concerned."

"But why?" asked Wally.

"The high profile," he answered simply. "Everybody who worked on the investigation is waiting to get slammed for one error on this or that. You remember what they did to the detectives in the Simpson trial? The whole L.A. force was being judged more than Simpson. We don't want the same happening here."

"Sergeant Cummings led the investigation," said Wally. "He did what he was supposed to, didn't he? What kind of an investigation was it?"

Barstow pressed his lips together. "I wasn't directly involved, but there has never been an investigation this thorough. Cummings and his crew turned over every rock. He's a good man. The best."

"No doubt about that," Wally agreed.

Barstow looked Wally in the eye. "We got the killer."

"You don't sound sure."

"I am. What we don't know is whether it will stick. And if it doesn't, the DA's office will find a way to blame us. You know how it goes. Because of Senator Hawkes, the politicians will stick their noses in and there will be investigations and whatnot. All because of the high profile of the victim. We don't want it happening here."

Roberta spoke up. "You make it sound like the murder was *her* fault."

Barstow smiled at her. "Sorry, if that's the spin you heard. Of course it wasn't her fault. The poor kid. But with her grandfather being who he is, the chief won't let us forget how much he wants a conviction."

"If Cummings investigated by the book, SFPD has nothing to worry about," said Wally.

"Think again," said Barstow with a sad smile. "In these kinds of things you never know."

"You have the right guy, right?" asked Wally.

Barstow did not answer directly. "The problem is getting a conviction in court. To be truthful, Cummings and his crew didn't give the prosecutor much to work with. There's scuttle-butt that the DA's office wouldn't have brought charges against this Feng Shao-li guy if they weren't forced to by the politics of the situation. I don't believe the scuttlebutt for a minute. This Chinaman did it. No one can convince me otherwise. But the fact remains, Cummings didn't find the smoking gun."

"The knife," said Roberta.

"Other physical evidence too. And the chief is nervous."

"Was there any tampering with evidence?" asked Wally. He looked at Roberta. "In politically sensitive cases like this," he explained, "evidence sometimes gets lost or fabricated or moved to make a suspect look like he did what he didn't do."

"A frame-up," she said.

He smiled broadly. "That's the word," he told her.

"Well?" Wally asked Barstow.

He was shaking his head. "Again, I wasn't involved with the investigation. But from what I hear, this was by the book, which explains why the prosecutor has little physical evidence to take into court. No, Cummings did this one clean. But I know what you mean." Now it was his turn to explain to Roberta. "When the victim is a somebody, the whole character of what we do changes and suddenly we are walking on eggshells."

Barstow's pool-playing partner came out of the back room. "You playing, or what?" he asked.

Barstow shrugged. "In a minute." He looked at Roberta. "Wally's a good guy, but don't believe anything he tells you." He stuck out his hand and shook hers again. He said to Wally, "Sorry about the harsh words a minute ago. You know how it is."

"I know how it is," said Wally.

A while later, after their dinner, Wally asked Roberta if she wanted to check out one more juror.

She yawned and stretched her arms to the ceiling. "I'm tired, Wally. This is hard work you do." She brought her arms down to her sides. "Don't you ever rest?"

"Sure, sure," he said. He drained the beer. "Come on, I'll take you home."

"Do you have to do this again tomorrow?" she asked.

"A full day," he replied.

Cheerily she asked, "Can I come along?"

He grinned. "I'll pick you up around eleven."

Wally watched her ascend the steps. At the gate she turned and waved, and when she was no longer in sight he glanced at his watch, needing to unwind. He headed for the SoMa district, where art dealers and artists had occupied vacant warehouses for their galleries and lofts. This was hardly Wally's domain. Something about SoMa bothered him. Even its name derived from New York's SoHo. He would have been more tolerant if the SoMa people weren't so self-conscious. He hated their pony-tails and their Vandyke beards and their black Tony Lama cowboy boots.

At that hour a gallery party was in full swing. He entered an old brick building and found himself in a crowd of beautiful people. A bright TV light shone in a corner where a reporter interviewed the featured artist, while in another corner a jazz trio struggled against the noise of laughter and loud talk. All but ignored were the large canvases that hung on the walls, and to Wally that seemed understandable. He looked at the paintings, shaking his head with wonder. White on white, the canvases were gobs of white paint on white canvas, painting after painting on three walls. Try as he might, he could see no real differences between the paint on the brick walls and the paint on the canvases.

A young woman came over and introduced herself to him somewhat officiously, asking if he were with the press.

"The police," he told her, and by her expression he must have looked that part too. She wore her hair pulled back from her face. Her neck was long and thin and her profile was quite stunning. She was wearing a pair of painter's baggy white coveralls, and from the angle at which she was standing Wally could not avoid seeing her bare breasts, small and firm, under the bib. The woman, Lindy, she called herself, was pretty; her heritage was a delicate mixture of Chinese and Caucasian. Gold rings pierced the corner of her lower lip, her ears, and one nostril.

"What can I do for you?" she asked.

"Is Anthony Bullock here?" he asked.

"He owns the gallery." She indicated upstairs with her chin. "He stepped out for a minute. You want to talk to him?"

"Yeah, I do," he said. He looked around. "I'm surprised his address is a gallery. I thought he worked for a cellular company."

She shouted to be heard. "This is a sideline," she said. "I run the gallery." She looked around. "Did somebody complain about the noise?"

"That's not why I'm here." He looked around. "Mr. Bullock is on jury duty, right?"

"The Hawkes trial," she said a bit too loudly. "Cool, huh?"

"Cool," he said. "I'm checking on the jurors to make sure they aren't being pestered by the press. The jurors aren't allowed to talk about the trial, you know."

"He knew Holly, you know," Lindy said.

That bit of unexpected information got his attention. "I guess he's talked to you about the trial," he said, trying hard to keep his voice level. "You said he knew her?"

"Her grandfather too." She nodded certainly. "Tony tells everybody."

"What does he tell everybody?" Wally asked.

"About knowing the Hawkes family."

Wally wanted to talk to him, but he knew this was not the time, or the place. He wondered why Bullock would not have told the court during voir dire that he knew the victim; that information would have excused him from jury duty, and maybe that was why. Bullock, from what Wally was hearing, liked the celebrity of duty on the Hawkes jury. It made him somebody he wouldn't have been otherwise. But he had to ask himself whether that was all that had motivated Bullock's perjury. He had lied to the court. That was certain. In every voir dire, the entire panel was asked together whether they knew the victim or the defendant, or whether they had ever had formal or informal contact with the attorneys in the case. And anyone who answered any of the questions in the affirmative was immediately excused. Bullock had lied. What else had he done?

Lindy looked suddenly worried. "I'd suggest you go upstairs," she told Wally. "But I don't think that would be such a good idea, not right now."

"Why would that be?" he asked.

"He's with somebody. You know what I mean."

He knew. "I need some information maybe you can help me with," he said.

"Sure, I'd be glad to," Lindy replied.

"Does Mr. Bullock keep a diary or some kind of schedule in his office?"

"I keep it for him."

"May I see it?" Wally asked.

"Come with me," she said.

He followed her along a wall of the white-on-white minimalist paintings, thinking that no matter how styles changed—rings in the nose, bright orange hair, Doc Martens boots—naïveté stayed in fashion. This girl Lindy, of such effortful radical chic, was every bit as simple and trusting as a flapper or a beatnik or a flower child in other eras of fashion. She showed him into a cramped back office with walls piled high with cartons and canvases on stretchers. She rifled the desk drawers, pawing at ledgers and boxes.

Wally picked a diary off the desk. "Maybe this is it," he said.

She put her hands on her hips and looked at him, then at the diary. She stood close to him, and he could feel the pressure of her breast against his arm and he could feel her soft breath. He thought of other things. He thought of Roberta. He thought of opera. He pointed to a dark line drawn through that whole week of June 23, the week that Holly was killed. On top of the page was written "Robert."

"Who is he?" Wally asked.

"A guy Tony knows. They were supposed to go away that week. They were going to the Grand Tetons. They do that sometimes."

"What happened?"

"Robert got a girlfriend," she replied.

"How indiscreet of him," he said. "And Mr. Bullock is the jealous type, am I right?"

She spoke in a conspiratorial tone. "He was furious. Not just because of the new girl. It happened before."

Wally closed the diary, which Lindy replaced on the desk. "Anything else I can help you with?" she asked.

"Thanks," he replied. "It's time I quit for the day."

"I can find you a glass of wine if you want."

"I'll take a raincheck," he told her, and he left the office and entered the noise and crowd in the gallery.

Lindy was showing him to the door when she spied Anthony Bullock in the crowd. She held Wally by the arm. "There he is, over there," she told him.

Bullock was hard to miss, dressed as he was in a midnight-blue velvet suit with a bow tie. A coterie of friends and hangers-on surrounded him, among them a young blond guy, handsome in a spoiled way. That must be Robert, Wally thought. He judged him to be one of the legions who made these evenings their life's work. He was dressed in a fifties tuxedo with a shawl collar and a white carnation, as though he had just come from a prom.

Lindy introduced Wally, and they looked suddenly sober and attentive. Lindy simply jabbered, "I told him, Tony, about how you knew Holly."

The color drained from Bullock's face.

"You remember," said Lindy. "You said you knew her."

"I may have said that."

"May have?" asked Wally. "Did you mention this in voir dire?"

"It's not what you might think," Bullock said.

"It's what *you* think that is important," he told him.

"Holly Hawkes came into the gallery once or twice with her grandfather, the senator. You know? It was a while ago. They looked around, doing the art scene together down here, I guess. They were spending the afternoon in the galleries. The senator didn't buy anything from me. I didn't know who the girl with him was until I saw her picture in the newspaper after she was killed. I recognized her grandfather at the time, of course."

"That's it?" Wally asked. "The extent of it?"

Bullock nodded, clearly relieved. "It was a judgment call that I made, whether to mention it in voir dire. I decided not to. I saw them. I didn't *know* them." And he glared at Lindy.

His friend Robert, the blond in the tuxedo, said, "You told me you talked to her. . . ."

"I *did* talk to her," Bullock said quickly. "She was here, okay? I talked to her about the paintings. She seemed nice. In fact, when I heard in court how old she was when she died, I couldn't believe it. She looked older. And she acted . . . well, how can I explain? Very mature."

Robert said loudly, "You told me you were friends with her."

"I lied, Robert," Bullock said, turning to Wally with embarrassment written all over his face. "You know how people like to pretend they're close with celebrities? Like the guy who washes Tom Cruise's car at the car wash and then tells his friends that he's pals with Tom, and that he's going to send his audition video to Tom?"

"I've heard of the type," said Wally.

"I'm guilty," he said with a small bow. "I did the same stupid thing." He turned to Robert with a shrug. To Wally he said, "I hope you don't think . . ."

The sentence went unfinished as an exceedingly flashy woman came out of the crowd and kissed Robert on the mouth, and Bullock just stared at her. She was Wasp-waisted, thin-legged, with long black hair. She was wearing leggings with leopard spots and a black bustier. Her mouth was a crimson gash. She stood back and blew the smoke of a filtered cigarette at Bullock with every intention to offend.

Wally suddenly felt sorry for Bullock. He'd just been doing what his crowd did naturally, and he was trying to keep his private life private.

"Anything else I can help you with?" Bullock asked.

"No, I'm done here," Wally said, wanting to get out of there. "Thanks for your time." He was never so glad to get outside into the cool night and breathe the fresh air.

———————◆———————

In the kitchen earlier that evening, Barr had tied on the apron that Vanessa used to wear.

"What's cooking, Dad?" Morgan asked him, drawing a bead on him with a toy gun that emitted a ratcheting explosive sound that spiraled him into a boy's fantasy of death and disfiguration. Barr looked at him truly amazed. This aggression was not from too much TV, or violence on TV, or anything that child psychologists ascribed it to. This was a young boy's "testosterone surge." If it wasn't a toy machine gun, it would have been a broom handle imagined as a toy machine gun, or a crooked stick imagined as a toy machine gun, or something else.

"They had guns, the men," Morgan said, almost offhandedly.

Barr turned suddenly. He took his son in his arms. "It won't happen again," he told him. "I promise." He held Morgan away from him. He did not want to dwell on the incident; it would only raise fears that were not already in play. He said, "If you don't want pasta, how about if we order a pizza with pepperoni and sausage and no anchovies?"

"I hate pizza, Dad," he said.

"Is that a love-it-hate-it or a hate-it-hate-it?"

"Hate-it-hate-it," he replied.

"Okay, well I could cook you a T-bone steak," Barr said. "Or how about a salmon fillet? Or maybe some broccoli? Better yet"—and he put his hands on his hips—"how about liver and bacon or sweetbreads—those are cows' brains. No? Maybe tripe—that's the lining of a cow's stomach, like, its guts. No? Not tripe? Or . . . What about my own special pasta, then?"

Morgan knew his father couldn't cook anything but pasta anyway, and even that usually tasted awful, but, anyway, he gave him a full blast of the machine gun, yelling, "Yeeeaaaaaa."

A few minutes later, as he waited for the water to boil in a stainless pot, Barr listened as Morgan practiced whistling in the other room, glad to hear that he had put the ride with the Chinese behind him. He did not know what he was going to do to protect Morgan; he had a few ideas, including asking Roberta to escort him right into his classroom, and to pick him up there too. He would call the headmistress at the school and tell her.

Morgan was still whistling, and Barr smiled affectionately, remembering. His son had picked up the whistling skill from Vanessa, of all people, who could whistle amazingly well—for a girl. She would put her thumb and forefinger in her mouth and produce a blast of sound that made people grimace. Now Morgan was softly aping the melody from *High Noon*, one of his favorites. "Do Not Forsake, Me Oh My Darlin'." And Barr praised the thin sound that came from his son's lips as he poked his head into the refrigerator for something green.

Vegetables, yes. Vanessa insisted on them, he thought. He could hear her now: five fruits and vegetables a day, she always said. He remembered her working in the kitchen with a dexterity that he loved to watch for its grace. She had been an enthusiastic cook who never once referred to a recipe, and her meals turned out as original and sturdy. That was no exaggeration. "It's only chemistry," she had been fond of saying, as though chemistry explained the love she had poured into everything she did.

Now Morgan brought his Insultinator into the kitchen; it was a noisome recording device that reproduced insults at the push of a button. Morgan's was now exclaiming in a Brooklyn accent, *"You're a totally gross boring nerd. . . . You're a slobbering greasy dweeb. . . . You're the ultimate slimy sneaky loser."*

The telephone rang. "Put that stupid slimy slobbering thing *away,*" he told Morgan as he reached for the wall phone.

It was Jenny. "I'm sorry I got heavy with you last night," she told him.

"I'm sorry too," he said. "I appreciated the tour of Chinatown. That bar was great."

"I can show you many great things, Judge Barr."

"Where are you?" he asked.

"Stuck at work. What are you doing?"

"Making dinner for Morgan."

"Oh?" And she let it hang there.

He hummed a few bars of the John Williams theme song from *Raiders of the Lost Ark.*

"You're not watching *that* again?" she asked, laughing. "You boys certainly love variety." She was quiet for a moment. "When will I see you again, Dan?"

"I'll call you," he said. "I promise." He knew he sounded vague. "How about tomorrow? I promised to take Morgan sailing for a little while. It'll do me good to get out in the fresh air. Want to come along?"

She hesitated. "You know me and the sea," she said.

Morgan asked, "Is she coming over tonight?"

Barr cupped the phone. "I don't think so, no," he replied.

Morgan groaned his displeasure as Barr said good-bye and hung up.

"I *know* you like her. But you like *every* woman I bring home," Barr told his son.

"I didn't like your lawyer girlfriend, the one with that dog," Morgan reminded him. "Yu-uck."

Barr laughed out loud. The woman's toy poodle had indeed had the most "yucky" habit of endlessly licking its balls. After a while Barr had stopped being embarrassed, and then he was just disgusted that its owner didn't do something to stop it. "I take that back," he told him. "You *don't* like every woman I bring home."

"I'd pick Jenny."

"You would, would you?" He put the pasta in a bowl in front of him. "Now eat."

After dinner, Barr hit the play button on the VCR. After *Raiders'* opening sequence Morgan was engrossed. Barr stared at the TV. Indiana Jones reached Nepal. The fight scene with Herr Mac (whom Morgan called AirMac), the Nazi nasty, was about to start. Morgan had slid off the sofa and was stretched out on the rug. He wouldn't bother Barr until Indie and Marian kissed, when he would moan and cover his eyes.

"Don't you think she looks like Jenny, Dad?" he asked, not once taking his eyes off the screen.

"Yes, only Jenny is a blonde," said Barr.

"I mean the way she socked him and stuff."

Morgan might have been obliquely referring to a horse pack trip the three of them had taken together in the Sierras a couple of years ago. Morgan and Barr knew how to ride and Jenny didn't. She had fallen off and blamed a gentle old mare. Her anger had made the men laugh. When Barr stepped off his horse to help her back on her own, he had made a derisive comment. It was all in fun. But Jenny had socked him, then instantly soothed the pain with a cool kiss.

"*I always knew someday you'd come walking through my door,*" Marian told Indie.

Barr looked up at the sound of the doorbell. Morgan flew across the room, and when he flipped on the porch light, he shouted, "It's Jenny, Dad! Dad! She's here!"

Flicka stirred herself from her rug and barked. She trotted over to the door and looked up at Jenny.

She had a huge smile. "I was in the neighborhood . . ." she said. She carried a brown grocery bag in her arms.

In the kitchen she made them sundaes with whipped cream,

and she had even thought to bring a box of dog biscuits for Flicka.

Barr found a jar of maraschino cherries on the shelf of the refrigerator door. "Two left," he said.

"Jenny can have mine," said Morgan. Barr looked at him. Morgan loved maraschino cherries.

She sprayed a dollop of cream on Morgan's fingertips, then aimed the can at him. *"I trusted you, Indiana Jones. I was young and innocent and I loved you.'"*

Back in the living room, Morgan snuggled between them on the sofa, and Flicka went back to sleep on her rug. After a while empty bowls of ice cream and popcorn and half-filled glasses of Coke littered the table. At some point Roberta came home wearing a secretive expression. She went over to the sideboard where the CDs were kept and searched until she found the one she was looking for. With a mysterious smile she held up a recording of *Parsifal,* and Barr nodded, wondering what she wanted with Wagner's opera; to the best of his knowledge, she listened only to heavy metal. Then she quietly went upstairs to her room.

After the movie ended, Barr carried a sleeping Morgan to his bedroom, and the beauty of his son's face absorbed him. Carrying him, he thought about his father. His dad was vulnerable now, with his partial paralysis and his slurred speech. But that vulnerability, like the innocence of Morgan now in his arms, had made Justice Barr more of a father than he had ever been to his son before. The tragic stroke had had that beneficial effect. It had robbed his father of the need to control, which had always stood between them. It had made Barr love him more intensely. It had made his dad less of an icon and a figure of supreme authority. It had truly made him human.

He put Morgan under the covers and tucked him in, then leaned over and kissed his forehead.

Barr turned to see Jenny standing in the doorway, the light of the hall at her back. Crossing to her, he reached out and pulled her into him. He kissed her, then he lifted her in his arms.

"Double duty," she whispered.

"A service of the house," he said, carrying her across the hall to his own bedroom.

"Good night," a child's sleepy voice called.

"Sweet dreams," they said in unison, and closed the door behind them.

———————

Barr looked at the clock on the bedside table. It was past two. And the phone was ringing.

"Hey, man," Wally said, as though it were the middle of the day.

"What's up?" Barr said, rubbing the sleep from his eyes.

"Some bits and pieces," he replied. "It's coming together, Barr—but slowly."

Barr said nothing. He was glad Wally was working on it. But clearly there were going to be no miracles. It was going to require legwork and luck, and time that Barr simply did not have. He thought about that as Wally talked. He was thinking days— hours, really. And Wally was talking about how it was coming together slowly.

"What did you mean just now, slowly?" Barr asked.

"I wish I knew," said Wally. "You're in a hurry, I know."

"If I don't find this guy before the trial ends, I'll never get him. Yes, I'm in a hurry. You'd better be too."

"Here's what I suggest," Wally said. "You go back to sleep. I'll keep digging."

"At this hour?"

Wally sounded impatient. "I'm going to spend the night looking in databases. There must be something that doesn't fit in the data of these jurors."

Wally was a whiz at computers, unlike Barr. He could find whatever he was looking for, no matter how obscure. "Didn't mean to second-guess," said Barr. "But you understand my anxiety, I hope."

"No need to be sorry," he told him. "Uh, Dan?"

"What?"

"Did Roberta get in okay?"

"Yeah, why?"

"She's a great girl, that's all. Just great. Thanks for letting me take her out."

Barr could hear it in his voice—Wally was smitten. "Glad you agree," he told him.

There was a pause. "Oh, one last thing. Project Right. You know, the charity that your juror Eng works for. Any idea how it's funded?"

"The city, I suppose. Or the state or the feds. All those charities survive on public funds of some sort."

"Yeah, yeah. I suppose they do," he said.

"Is that the direction you are headed in—Eng and Project Right?"

"Don't start breathing hard yet. I got more than one juror who makes me suspicious. It amazes me, frankly. I mean, this is what I do for a living, right? But now that I'm actually investigating jurors for a specific crime, you'd be surprised how many of them seem likely candidates."

"No, I wouldn't be surprised," said Barr. "But I am disappointed."

"What did you think, that this guy was going to be easy? I told you he would bury himself in the jury, didn't I?"

"Yup, you sure did," said Barr.

"I can solve this for you, Barr. I *know* I can."

"We don't have much time," he reminded him again; he had to make Wally aware of this fact, over and over. He did not want him telling him, after the trial was over, that the killer got away because he did not have enough time. He wanted him to be aware of that now, when there was still time.

"Oh, I nearly forgot," Wally said. "When you get up in the morning, do me a favor?"

"I'll do that," said Barr with a soft chuckle.

"You'll *what?*" Wally asked.

"Say good morning to Roberta for you."

Chapter Six

Barr looked across the bed. The morning light drew lines and shadows on the contours of Jenny's hips, the smooth lines under her breasts, through the flat of her stomach and down to her pelvis. Her eyes opened and sleepily she stared at the clock. Suddenly, she sat up. "Oh-my-God-look-what-time-it-is!" she exclaimed in a single breath.

"It's Saturday," he reminded her, gently pushing her back on the pillows. "Relax."

With a sigh she stretched her arms over her head. "I forgot."

"And you have nothing to do."

"Are you kidding?" She swung her legs out of bed. "I have work waiting for me, errands to run, dry cleaning and stuff, I *have* to go shopping. . . ." She turned and looked at him, reading his expression. "Okay, so we have nothing to do," she said. "What now?"

"Shower?"

"I thought you'd never ask."

Jenny slipped into the bathroom wrapped in a top sheet and Barr joined her a minute later. He closed the door and half turned.

"Your butt is awfully cute, Judge Barr," she told him. She let the sheet slip to the floor. Her eyes widened in mock surprise at his reaction to her nakedness. "Well, hello again!" she said.

He nudged her into the shower and they closed the door and

turned on the spray. Behind the frosted glass she wrapped her legs around him, her back against the stall. She moaned softly, then hummed, and in minutes the sound of her voice rose to a pitch that signaled an orgasm.

Barr turned off the water and Jenny opened the shower door, and as she reached for a towel she screamed. She leaped back into the stall and hugged Barr close. He looked over her shoulder. Morgan was sitting on the clothes hamper not five feet away.

"Jenny?" Morgan asked her in a matter-of-fact tone.

"Yes . . . Morgan?" She tried but failed to control her voice.

"Just now, in there with Dad?"

"Ummmm?"

"What were you doing?"

"We were showering together."

"She was singing," Barr added. "Now, can you find somewhere else to sit while Jenny dries off?"

"Like where?" Morgan asked, staring at Jenny's silhouette through the frosted glass of the shower door.

"Oh, never mind," she said.

She stepped out and put her hands on her hips. She peered down her front. "*This* is a woman, *this* is a female. You both look like sick cows." She slung the towel around herself, and as she went past Morgan she stuck out her tongue at him.

"Jenny?" Morgan asked her back.

"Yes, Morgan," she said, turning around.

"I really like it when you sing that way."

———

San Franciscans take these mornings for granted—the sun not just bright but sharp, as though filtered through a unique prism, and the air clear and fresh. There was a breeze but no whitecaps in the bay, and even Jenny seemed excited as they entered the St. Francis Yacht Club, past the trophy case and the hull models in the main hall, the bright pennants and the yellowed photos of old boats and commodores. The club's utter exclusivity meant little to Barr. His great-grandfather had helped to found it. For him it was simply a convenience, a place to moor his Swan.

After they had rigged the boat and stowed their gear, Barr motored the handsome thirty-six-foot *Bluejacket* out of the slip through the marina channel, past the stone jetty into the bay. He hooked a safety line to a heavy leather belt on Morgan's waist just as a breeze filled the sails a hundred yards offshore.

Jenny took that as a cue to go below.

The sloop heeled to the wind with Barr behind the wheel and Morgan by his side. Morgan gripped the wheel and copied his father's wide stance. They faced the wind as the water hissed under the hull in a frothing wake and the sails gave off a satisfying snap and flutter.

Bending the elements of wind and water to his purposes always changed Barr's outlook. Indeed, it made him feel fully alive. They tacked back and forth across the bay from Alcatraz to the marina to the bridge, again and again, before entering the lee of the Sausalito hills, where the sails luffed and Barr let out the jib sheet while Morgan fetched iced tea from the reefer. He came up with binoculars around his neck, and Jenny came up behind him. She was wearing a bikini now, ready for the sun; without a word she stretched out on the deck.

Morgan scanned the shoreline with the binoculars. He pointed to a yacht that was so large, a tender the Swan's length seemed small on its upper deck's superstructure. The white-hulled ship was positioned off a craggy point at the southern end of Belvedere Island, and the guests on deck were dressed as if for a garden party, with the ladies in skirts and dresses and the men in blazers and neckties. The transom bore the name *Mandarin*, its place of registry, Hong Kong. The boat, the largest private vessel on the California coast, was famous around the bay. Some yachts in Europe were longer and contained more staterooms, but reportedly none was more elegant than the *Mandarin*.

"The senator's yacht," Barr said, taking the binoculars from Morgan.

Jenny sat up to look.

Less than a quarter hour later, a small Zodiac runabout was lowered in blocks from the yacht's fantail. It headed straight at the Swan across a half mile of open water. A uniformed crewman in a striped boatneck shirt waved as he throttled back. He came around again and adeptly handed up an envelope to Barr, then gunned the throttles and sped off without saying a single word.

On embossed letterhead stationery in flowery purple ink, a handwritten note invited the "Master, crew and guests of *Bluejacket*" to join the master of the *Mandarin* and his guests for a light lunch.

"You want to?" Barr asked, and Morgan beamed. "What about you, Jenny?" he asked her. "He's your boss."

She looked down at herself. "I have nothing to wear," she said.

"We won't go, then," said Barr.

"We can't *not* go," Jenny said, smiling through her perplexity.

Barr sheered *Bluejacket* into the wind, pointing her bow at Belvedere. As they neared *Mandarin* he dropped the main, steering by the jib, which Morgan lowered on his command as *Bluejacket*, with fenders out, edged under power against *Mandarin*'s steel hull. They tied off and climbed an elegant mahogany ladder to the deck.

Senator Hawkes greeted them. He was dressed just like the mogul he was, in an elegant double-breasted blue blazer with bright brass buttons, white duck trousers, and, around his neck, a jade-green silk ascot. His smile was warm and his voice was soft and friendly, even gentle. The silvery wisps of gray-white hair gave him a kind of casual elegance and altogether he looked like a picture of leisure.

He introduced them to his guests, who were, as expected, a veritable local Who's Who—the CEOs of Lockheed, Wells Fargo, and Hewlett-Packard; the president of Stanford University's Woodrow Wilson School of International Diplomacy; the

Republican congressman from San Francisco; the head of Barr's old law firm; and an admiral from the Singapore Navy.

"I'm honored," Hawkes told Barr. He noticed Jenny's discomfort and said, "My dear, if you like, prowl around in the staterooms below. I'm sure you can find something less revealing to change into for lunch."

Jenny went off silently, embarrassed by his use of the word *revealing*.

Watching her go, they walked across the deck under an awning where a bartender mixed Barr a drink and handed a Coke to Morgan. A cheerful-looking man with a wild shrub of red beard came over and introduced himself as the *Mandarin*'s skipper. He offered to show Morgan the bridge, and when they were gone Hawkes and Barr took their drinks over to the port toe rail. Standing side by side, they looked out over the water toward Alcatraz.

"I sighted you by accident," Hawkes said. "I was looking at your sloop through the bridge binoculars. She's a rare beauty."

"How did you know she's mine?"

"I asked my captain to look her up in the registry." He laughed. "You race the Swan?"

"Yes, in the past," said Barr. "Not lately, though."

"As I recall, Swans have a fine reputation for blue-water sailing. Is it earned?"

"In my experience."

"But they can be hard to handle in certain conditions?"

"The rougher the sea, the sweeter they handle."

"And you enjoy rough seas?"

"I seek them out."

"Good, good," the senator said, smiling. He reached up with his hand and combed back his hair with his fingers in an unstudied gesture.

Only then did Barr notice he was wearing a bracelet, no more, really, than a wire of gold tied around his wrist with crudely twisted ends. The sight of the bracelet caught his eye because it seemed out of the character. The jewelry represented a vanity almost like a secret window that opened on a nature that Barr would otherwise not have suspected. He read no more into it than that.

"You seem to know about sailing," Barr said, taking his eyes off the bracelet and looking at the senator.

"I'm quite expert at it, if I do say so." He looked around. "You probably wonder why I have this huge motorboat."

"That crossed my mind."

"Face," said the senator.

"I'm sorry?"

"Image. I'd prefer to sail, but what can I do? The biggest, most expensive boats all have motors like this one. Not to show my wealth is to deny it."

"But show it to whom?" asked Barr.

"Everybody, but most particularly my enemies. This boat keeps 'em at a distance. It makes them envious, and if I control a man's envy, I control his soul. Seriously, if I were to lose face, I'd lose my defenses. My commercial empire would be threatened. The cost of a boat like this is of little consequence considering the gains. Wouldn't you agree?"

"And your seat in the Senate?"

He laughed. "You understand too well. The people who vote for me do not begrudge me these toys. They know I have earned them. And they expect a certain display of wealth. People live vicariously. If I were to own a little motorboat, people would feel disappointed. Great wealth demands certain behavior. In the Far East, face is who you are. I couldn't operate as I do without it."

As he went on about face, Barr studied the man closely. His ruddy features were hardly marked by the passing of time, and a full head of hair, despite its silver color, made him seem younger still. He would not have been able to say how old he was—fifty, sixty? He seemed eerily ageless. His shoulders were broad and square and he held himself erect. His blue eyes, even with his face in repose, gave off a spirited and hearty optimism that was hard to ignore. By any measure, Hawkes was a powerful and vibrant man, and, with or without face, he would be dangerous to cross.

"What else does face include?" Barr asked him.

"Houses, cars, *women*—not in that order, of course! Airplanes—you must have a Gulfstream IV now if you are on top of the heap. You must have in abundance what other men want but can't get or can't afford." He laughed at his own words. "And you must appear high on the Forbes annual rankings of net worth. It's why men with even greater wealth than mine do so little for charity."

Barr was amused by Hawkes's genial openness. The senator allowed information about himself as though they were friends. He wasn't hiding his feelings, or his motives, and somehow Barr had expected someone of the senator's stature to be closer to the vest.

Barr was shaking his head. "And you? What do you give to charity?"

"Me? I give generously. In Asia charity is thought to bring good fortune. I am devoted to my church, as you probably know. Even if that were not true—and it is, *very* true—I'd be expected to give. How can I introduce spending bills in the Congress to help people less fortunate than myself if I don't give my own personal share? The press used to say about my friend Teddy Kennedy that he was a millionaire who loved giving away other people's money. I don't believe you can justify government spending as a senator unless your charity begins at home." He looked over the gunwale down at the deck of Barr's Swan. "But that doesn't mean I can't dream."

Barr laughed at the irony of wealth's limits, that with his billions Hawkes could not "afford" a sloop that would have cost him what his portfolio probably earned in minutes. Senator Hawkes—the billionaire—was a prisoner of perception, or face, as he called it.

Hawkes looked up the deck, and his expression turned somber. A woman in her forties, thin, with a mournful look and a sickly pallor, was coming toward them. She had on a cotton print sundress and wore a wide-brimmed straw hat that covered her forehead and shaded her eyes. It was a look that made her seem preternaturally old, as though she had given up as a woman. Or worse, as though a quiet sickness had robbed her of her vitality.

"Lunch, Stanton?" she asked in a tired voice. She looked at Hawkes inquiringly, her arms hanging at her sides.

"Yes, Amelia, right away," he told her. "But come over here first and greet Judge Barr," he said.

She smiled at him quickly. "Oh, hello, Dan," she said, holding out her hand, surprised to see him. The smile stayed.

Barr was momentarily startled into silence. He held her hand, which felt like something that all life was ebbing out of.

"We were talking about sailing, Amelia," Hawkes said. "Judge Barr tells me he is an expert sailor."

She looked away. And as though she thought of nothing else, as though every context for conversation had only one subject, she said, "Holly loved the sea."

Hawkes looked stricken. "I think it's time we went to lunch," he said and looked around.

"Did you know that, Dan?" asked Amelia almost insistently, keeping them there. She stared at him. "That Holly loved the sea?"

"I know little about her, to tell you the truth, Amelia."

In a booming voice, Hawkes said, "She sailed with me to the Orient. Amelia is right. She was captured by the sea."

"She was captured by that trip," Amelia said, her eyes focused off somewhere. "She came back from that trip a different person." Her glance turned to Hawkes. "She watched that film *The Inn of the Sixth Happiness* when she came home. Again and again. I couldn't get her to leave it alone. You know what the sixth happiness is, Dan?" she asked. "The one you find for yourself." And then tears welled in her eyes.

The senator consoled her with a gentle touch, but she moved away from him slightly, not shrugging him off, but not permitting him the intimacy of touch either. She wiped her tears and squared her shoulders, then forced a smile. "Do you think the trial will last long?" she asked Barr.

"No, not with the witness lists I've seen," he told her. "There won't be much to it once the prosecution has laid out its case. I don't expect much of a defense."

"Good," she said very firmly, and then again, "good." She gazed out over the placid water. "Such evil. I want to see the man who killed her delivered to hell."

"No need to blaspheme, Amelia," Hawkes told her.

She fixed him with an icy glare. "Yes, there is, Stanton. More than a need to blaspheme, I have a *reason* to."

"Maybe you should join our guests," he told her. "We'll be along in a minute."

With a nod she left them, but she held Barr's eyes until the last second of parting.

"Poor Amelia," the senator said as he watch her like a wraith in a cloud of sorrow. "She won't be able to get this behind her until the trial is over. She is wounded deeply. We all are. I confess it's why I sent the lunch invitation over to you."

"Oh?" Barr said.

"Man to man, I do hope you will see that nothing is allowed to interfere with this trial."

"Like what?" asked Barr.

He looked suddenly confused. "Like sideshows. I'm only saying because I recall what a drawn-out mess the Simpson trial became. The judge was held to blame for letting everyone do whatever they wanted to. The jury was the problem, as I recall."

"How so?" asked Barr, curious now.

"You followed that trial, naturally. Some of the jurors talked about the trial, a couple of others got sick, and, as I recall, one of them was let go because she talked to a literary agent, or was it to the press? We can learn from their mistakes. We all want to get this behind us. It takes a firm judicial hand."

"The pace pretty much dictates itself," said Barr.

"That's what I thought you might say. But we both know that a trial judge can speed things along. I'm sure you will."

Barr thought, If only he knew. Barr wasn't interested in speed. He wanted to slow the trial without making it seem obvious. Even as he stood there, the clock was running out.

The senator smiled at a different thought. "I remember you as a boy," he told Barr. "There were many times when I heard about your achievements or read about them that I wished you were my own son. Your boy is like you were then. Handsome, personable."

"How is Karl these days?" he asked.

Barr had heard that Karl Hawkes lived in Sonoma County, north of San Francisco, with his new wife and family, but those were rumors that he had never found reason to substantiate. He and Karl had once been friends of sorts, but their careers and different lives had drawn them apart. He had liked Karl, but he understood with what difficulty he had grown up in the long shadow of his dominating father. All that had been left of original space for Karl to claim was a poor rebellion.

"He's living on a ranch with his urchin children and some woman who thinks she's a milkmaiden. He's happy, I believe," Hawkes replied breezily. "It is no secret that I do not approve of his reasons for leaving Amelia. He said he needed to be happy. He gave no thought to Amelia, nor to Holly. *He* needed to be happy. Very self-indulgent. But I suppose I'm glad he has found what he was looking for." He sounded tired and he looked at Barr fondly, as one would at a son. "I was pleased when you were appointed to the court," he said.

"I was lucky, I guess," Barr replied modestly.

"It took intelligence and hard work and desire to get you there, I'd say."

Barr wanted to avoid further talk of the trial. He looked down the deck and saw Jenny. "Here's Jenny now," he said.

Hawkes reached out to kiss her chastely on the temple. "You look lovely," he told her.

"I apologize if I held up lunch," she said.

"Jenny's part of my company's future, did you know?" Hawkes asked Barr. He bowed slightly toward her. Barr smiled inwardly at the obvious interest the senator took in her. "We are positioned well in China. It's going to be the largest construction job in history. Nothing less than that. With capitalism on the march there, the Chinese need everything except another Great Wall. Hawkes Construction will build modern China. We already have a partnership with certain high-level Chinese." He beamed at Jenny. "Right now this young lady is handling PR. Soon she'll take over the marketing. Then, who knows? We were talking a while ago about face. The Chinese government takes great stock in face. Hers is a lovely one. Don't you think, Judge Barr?"

"Don't you run for reelection next year, Senator?" Barr asked.

"Right you are. And another good reason to want only the best people around me."

At the sound of Morgan's voice they all turned. He appeared wearing a black striped *Mandarin* crew shirt that the captain had given him.

"Did you know this boat was made in Macao?" Morgan asked as he walked up to them. "The captain told me. Macao is near Hong Kong. He said he didn't know what it cost to build, but he bet it cost plenty." He looked at Jenny. "Do you know where Macao is?"

She smiled at him and straightened his hair. "I can tell you all about it; I've even been there," she said, and she and Morgan walked back along the deck to where the others were sitting down at a long table.

Under a bright blue awning, six crew members waited on the guests with a military bearing. Barr noticed that they were all Chinese. It was appropriate, he decided, as he walked up to the sumptuous buffet of cold lobster and salmon. Hawkes had named his boat *Mandarin*; it was built in Macao. What was wrong with an all-Chinese crew?

Barr spent several minutes helping Morgan at the buffet; then he followed him over to the table. The seating was arranged by place cards, and, despite their unanticipated arrival, there were places for each of them. Jenny was seated on Hawkes's left; Morgan was to be beside Amelia. Barr reminded him that he must hold her chair when she came to the table. He looked around and noticed her watching them. She offered Barr a wan, knowing smile, but her attention was focused on Morgan. And when the time came she allowed him to pull back her chair. "Thank you, young man," she said, and immediately she began to engage him in conversation.

Noticing that his own place was set between the wives of the congressman and the CEO of Wells Fargo, Barr took his time at the buffet. When he finally sat down, he found that his place afforded him a view of the others. He studied Hawkes, who had hardly a word for anyone but Jenny. Even from his end of the table he would have sworn they were speaking in Chinese. Their hands gestured and their faces expressed an evenness and a give-and-take that Barr was glad to see. Hawkes did not dictate to her, but seemed to seek her opinion. Barr felt a moment of fleeting jealousy for the intensity of their contact, something that he had experienced with her only in bed. Clearly Jenny was a serious and intelligent woman who was dedicated to her work. Hawkes saw her as that, and he appreciated her skills. Barr realized that he did not need intense conversation with the woman he loved. He wanted a woman, a mother, a wife, a companion. He did not want a business partner. And he did not think for a moment that Jenny did either.

Suddenly a peal of laughter rang out that stopped the conversation cold along the length of the table. Amelia had thrown her head back at something Morgan had said, and she was laughing with an openness and obvious sincerity that transformed her dour face into something that was lovely. Hawkes looked momentarily stunned, frightened even, but then he smiled, and the whole table seemed to relax. Amelia did not notice them, but as a starving person who is given food she went right back to Morgan, and the two of them talked as though they were the closest of friends—a boy without a mother, and a mother without a child.

From then on until lunch ended the spirits of the guests rose, all because of Amelia and her reaction to Morgan. Barr was reminded of just how effectively the murder had put a damper on the whole of San Francisco society. Hawkes was right, he thought, when he'd said how much they all needed to get the trial behind them. At the time, Barr thought he had referred only to the family, but he realized now that his remark had been all encompassing.

When the lunch had ended, Barr and Morgan and Jenny ambled down the deck to the gangway and prepared to descend the ladder to the *Bluejacket*. Jenny had already gone below to change back into her bikini. Barr felt a slight touch on his elbow, and he turned.

"May I have a word with you, Dan?" Amelia asked him quietly. He stepped quickly over to the other side of the deck.

"It was wonderful to hear you laugh, Amelia," he told her.

"Thank you," she said. "Your son is a joy. You have done a good job, all alone. Remarkable, I'd say. He's a genuine delight to be around."

"Thank you," Barr said.

"You have a way with him too, and I admire it," she said. "You're his friend and his father, his example, his disciplinarian. It's quite a trick, altogether, and you do it well."

"Thank you again," he said.

"Holly was wonderful too."

"So everybody says," he told her.

"You said you didn't know her," she said. "I wish you had. I think you'd recognize her in Morgan. They were alike, you know, when she was that age."

What could he say to that? She was evoking the spirit of her daughter as though she were still alive.

She looked over at the senator, who was talking to friends across the deck. "Maybe you'd stop by the house sometime. You know where it is. I could show you what she was like."

He looked at her carefully. "You're very kind," he told her.

"No, I mean it," she said. "I'd like it very much."

"Well, thank you," he said, "that would be nice."

"I wish your father were with you today," she said. "But, of course, that wouldn't have been possible, would it?"

He was surprised that she had asked about him. His dad had said that they were neighbors, and of course that was true. What Barr had inferred from his remark was that they were also friends. Amelia's inquiry almost confirmed that.

"I'm afraid Dad's sailing days are over, at least for now."

"I take him for walks, you know."

"No, I had no idea," Barr said.

"He's a dear man."

She seemed to be saying something that Barr could not hear. Nobody had ever before called his father a dear man. Until recently, since his stroke, Barr would have laughed at that characterization of his dad. He felt an intensity around Amelia that was uncomfortable. He doubted whether she said anything for idle purposes, though he did not understand her. What strains the death of her daughter must have put on her, he thought, he hoped he would never know. He wondered whether in similar circumstances he would even remain sane. He supposed that some part of his normalcy would die. And in that instant of thought, a frisson of fear came over him. He snapped his head around looking for Morgan, and he sighed at the sight of him by the ladder.

A moment later Senator Hawkes stepped over and gripped his hand. His parting words were a reminder, and he said while looking at Amelia, "Remember, the sooner we get this over with, the better we'll all be."

A short time later, when they were away from the *Mandarin*, Barr cranked the halyard's windlass while Morgan manned the sheets and Jenny held the wheel. Then, as the sails caught a gentle breeze, they had a chance to relax. Jenny disappeared momentarily to the galley below for coffee. "Dad, that was really fun," Morgan said. "The captain told me he met real pirates in the China Sea. He said that's where those men on the deck came from."

"They were crew members," Barr corrected him, thinking, however, that they had performed more like a paramilitary than like a hired crew.

"I asked the captain if they were all brothers," Morgan offered. "They looked like brothers."

"They were Chinese," he said.

"I mean, they all had the same tattoo."

Barr looked surprised. "What kind of tattoo?"

"They had marks here," and he held out his right hand and showed Barr the web of skin between his thumb and forefinger. "You know, like two lines." And he showed what he meant on his own hand.

"You are certain of that?" Barr asked.

"I saw them," Morgan insisted. "They all had them."

Barr looked thoughtfully out across the water of the bay. Senator Hawkes hired 49 Boys to work on his boat. Hadn't the witness Jiang Zemin testified that the 49 Boys were a praetorian guard—he had called them killers—of the Three Dots, the Three in One, or some gang he had identified as the Wah Ching? They answered directly to the supreme leader, the Dragon Head. Worse still for its implications, Feng Shao-li, the accused murderer of the senator's granddaughter, had shown in court the same tattoo that identified him as a member of these 49 Boys.

Barr had no doubt—none whatsoever—that the men who had kidnapped Morgan also wore the tattoo of the 49 Boys, and he would have asked if he wasn't afraid of scaring the boy.

For now, the implications of this revelation were profound, and confusing. What was the senator doing with a gang of young men who counted as a member the same young man who was sitting as the accused in Barr's court? Didn't Hawkes know that Feng Shao-li was a member of the gang? Wasn't he aware of what went on? Could this all just be a coincidence? Was it only a bizarre joining of the fact that the senator's company conducted business in China and that his granddaughter was killed on the edge of Chinatown by a Chinese man who bore the mark of the same people who worked for him? Could these Chinese gangs and their leader control the senator? Were they using him as their American pawn? And had he stepped out of line, bringing down on his family the death of the one person he loved more than any other? A thousand questions like these filled Barr's head, and he could not answer a single one.

"*I* certainly got an earful," said Jenny as she came up from below with a thermos of coffee and cups.

Barr had to make an effort to refocus. He smiled at her while she poured the coffee. He wondered where he could go for answers, and even that simple question sat without an answer. He had already seen what a stranger he was in Chinatown. How could he ever peer behind the veil of culture and language to seek answers? His father had always been his mainstay who brought clarity to moments like these, but even his dad, for all his brilliance and experience and knowledge of people was a stranger in the world that Barr now found himself in. Somehow, he had to find a way.

"I had no idea I was so much in Stanton's grand scheme of things," she said.

"It shouldn't surprise you, Jenny. You have what he needs. You have what it takes."

She didn't look convinced. "This is all so sudden," she said. "I mean, he never mentioned it before."

"But you knew you were on a fast track at Hawkes," he pointed out.

"Not this fast," she said. "I just wonder if it doesn't have something to do with you."

"Me?" Barr asked. "Why should it?"

"Because he knows I know you, Dan. He knows we're good friends." She looked at Morgan. "I told him what I feel about you."

"And?"

"And I can't help thinking that you're part of his reason for making such a big show of including me in his company's plans."

"What part?" he asked.

She shrugged. "He was asking a lot of questions about you. A lot. He wanted to know about the trial."

"The trial is why we were invited aboard," he pointed out.

"He kept insisting."

"On what?" he asked.

"If I'd heard anything from you about which way the jury is leaning."

Barr laughed. "The prosecution hasn't even finished its case."

"He asked if there was a chance they'd let Feng Shao-li off. What was I supposed to say?"

"What did you say?"

"The truth—that you and I do not talk about the trial." She was shaking her head. "Anyway, it was an odd discussion. I was deeply flattered by his remarks, but I couldn't help but think that he had an ulterior motive."

There was no answering her questions either, Barr knew. And out of a huge frustration, he jammed the wheel over and brought the sloop up higher into the wind. They heeled over at a violent angle, and Barr set his legs with Morgan standing beside him. Jenny dived for the dry comfort belowdecks as they sailed into a bay-bound sea in the direction of the Golden Gate.

Under the bridge the sight of the girders overhead and the heavy beams of its stanchions gave Barr a feeling of cutting loose; reaching this point was one of the reasons he loved to sail. Out beyond the Gate, where the swells formed into troughs, he tacked twice, fast and hard, and the sails sang up in the yards as the *Bluejacket* performed to the limit of her design. The sloop climbed up the crest of one trough, looked out, then plunged down between two green walls of water, then up, in a churning, exhilarating ride.

He kept the boat at this high pitch out to within sight of the

Farallon Islands, then hard about. He tacked once again, and with the wind at his stern he let out the sails and they rode the rolling waves one after another under the bridge.

Dried sea salt flaked their arms and faces by the time they sailed past the coast guard station, where Barr told Morgan to take the wheel, and he lowered the main and then started the engine at the entrance to the St. Francis marina. Only when they had tied up in their slip did he remember that Jenny was still below.

"Jenny?" he called down the hatch.

She came up looking both frightened and queasy. She burst into tears at the sight of Morgan. "You didn't have to do that, Barr," she told him in a dispirited voice. "You know I hate it. You could have eased off." She held his eyes. Her arms hung by her sides and her shoulders sagged. She looked up, and there was anger in her eyes. "Why does everything have to be a test with you?" she asked him. "Nothing I ever do is good enough. I can't compete. I'm sure I don't like sailing the way she probably did. Yet you won't accept it. I don't take care of Morgan as well as she did either. I don't look the way she did, or talk the way she did. I'm being constantly measured against a dead woman. And it just isn't fair, Barr." The tears rolled down her cheeks.

She refused the hand he held out to help steady her. Morgan watched with a kind of interest that children reserve for moments of genuine adult emotion. "I'm sorry, Jenny," he told her, and she clasped his small hand in her own. She climbed off *Bluejacket* onto the dock, and she cried even harder when Morgan said, "We didn't mean to make you feel bad," and looked between her and his father to make sure that everything was okay.

Chapter Seven

Wally looked disheveled from a night in front of his computer and, he admitted to himself as he ran his fingers through his hair, glancing quickly in the car's rearview mirror while he waited for Roberta to come down the steps, from a night of anticipation over what this morning's outing with her might bring. The night had seemed endless. And now, as he saw her on the stairs to the house, it was over.

She was wearing a Laura Ashley dress and sensible shoes. She had a small pad and pencil in her hand. She looked in the car window, and without even a hello, she said, breathlessly, "Where to, Holmes?" And she opened the car door and got in.

Wally looked up the steps she had just come down.

She followed the direction of his gaze. "The judge went off with Morgan and Jenny," she told him, settling in the car seat. "I told him I didn't know when I'd be back."

"I don't know either." He grinned at her. "Because we're going to places *I've* never been before."

Roberta said, "I think we should start with that woman at the insurance agency."

"We're having coffee with her at eleven-thirty. That's stop number one."

"The possibility of a short day, then," Roberta said, checking that one off in her notebook.

"Not for me," said Wally.

"You already have an itinerary?"

"I know how these things develop—one thing leads to another, half of them blind alleys, but you have to check out everything."

"Like having to go back to that Latino man with the missing knife."

He nodded. "Then we're going to Chinatown."

She nodded resolutely. "That was my third thought."

"You seemed to have done some homework."

"I watched you last night," she said. "When I got back I found a newspaper with the list of the jurors. And since a lot of them are Chinese, I thought Chinatown was where we would be spending most of the day."

"Do you have any idea *why* we're looking?"

"Do I need to?"

He laughed. "I think I'll let your boss be the judge of that."

Ten minutes later they stopped in front of Starbucks on Union Street.

Mayhew Allen recognized them as they entered and made room for them at her table. She was dressed in a skirt and blouse that were too young for her. Her hair was up in a bob. Altogether, a kind of forlorn girlishness came across as sadness.

While Roberta got Wally coffee, Mayhew told him, "My colleague, Eunice, the office manager you met, is a liar and a thief. Now I've said it again. I don't care."

"I was asking about Adam Warmath," he reminded her.

"And Eunice said that Adam was away that whole week."

"At a Round Table conference."

"*Million Dollar* Round Table," she corrected him.

"In Atlanta."

"The Peach Tree Hotel."

Roberta arrived with the coffees. Mayhew smiled at her, then she looked between Roberta and Wally.

"Did you two have a long courtship?" she asked them.

"I'll let the little woman answer that," Wally replied, giving Roberta a wink.

"It was whirlwind," Roberta said. "He swept me off my feet. Awfully good-looking, don't you think? And considerate. Not at all like most other men."

"Whirlwind romances are the best, I agree," said Mayhew. "How did you . . . ?"

"Land him?" She smiled. And as if Wally were not sitting there, she replied, "I guess I made myself indispensable."

Mayhew turned to Wally. "And what about you?"

"Bowled over from the start," he said.

"How romantic," said Mayhew. "It's what I always hoped for for myself."

"It's not too late," said Roberta.

"I'm afraid my time has passed."

"Never say never," said Roberta.

"It didn't pass either until that damned Eunice came along."

Roberta and Wally looked at each other, both having a very good idea what was in store.

"She got in the way," said Mayhew. "She told lies from the very beginning. I don't see how she gets away with it. You can't keep customers by lying to them. You say you have an allegiance to Adam, and that's okay with me. But she was trying to horn in, on me. She's always horning in on me."

"Perhaps you'll tell me what Eunice said that wasn't true," said Wally.

"Maybe I shouldn't be telling tales out of school," Mayhew said.

Wally almost groaned. "We wanted insurance, and we're getting a runaround."

Roberta brought her face close to Mayhew's. "My husband was just trying to do the decent thing. I don't know why he even bothered."

Mayhew looked exasperated as much by the complications of her office politics as by the thought that prospective clients were about to take a walk. "All I can say is that Adam wasn't there that week, so you couldn't have talked with him," she said.

"The office manager, Eunice, said he was in Atlanta," said Wally. "So who was it I talked with?"

She was shaking her head. "I don't know. I just don't know. But it wasn't him."

"Let's not make a big thing out of it, dear," said Roberta.

Wally leaned back in the chair, looking at Roberta. "She says he wasn't there. She says he wasn't in Atlanta. His boss, Eunice, said he was. I must say, I'm mystified."

"You want to know why?" Her voice trembled with hurt. "Because Adam was shacked up with Eunice all that week, that's why. They were in Mendocino, on the coast, in a comfy little B-and-B."

Wally felt relieved. "*All* week?" he asked.

"If you can believe it," said Mayhew. "A married woman too, with three kids in high school and college, and she goes up there with a man fifteen years younger."

"Did you follow her?" asked Roberta.

She hesitated only an instant before saying, "I would have blown up that romantic little B-and-B if I'd had the powder, I was so mad."

"So Eunice stole him away?" Roberta asked.

Mayhew lowered her head. "We'd made plans, he and I. I was in love with him, and she just took him away like I wasn't there."

"The dirty rat," said Roberta. "You're better off without him."

"Come along, dear," said Wally, scraping back his chair. "We have things to do today."

Roberta patted Mayhew's hand. Mayhew was weeping now, and there was nothing that either of them could do for her, although Roberta still felt pity for the woman. "If he's such a cad," she told her, "forget him, just forget him altogether." And although she knew she was about to tell a lie, some lies served a higher truth. "From now on, you're our agent." She looked to Wally for confirmation.

"No question," he said.

The high-tension electrical lines sang on the steel pylons like ci-
cadas in Southern pines.

"I figured you'd be back," David Figueroa said by way of
greeting them.

Wally and Roberta looked past Figueroa. His kids were playing games on the living room rug, and his wife was rocking the
newborn in a chair. A *People* magazine lay open on the floor at
her feet. A woman's throaty voice called out in Spanish from
deeper in the house, and Figueroa shrugged and sighed.

"This nuthouse," he said, his accent stronger than yesterday.
"You wonder why I like my garage?" And he edged out the door
and closed it behind him. They were standing on the brown
grass looking at the power lines that buzzed overhead.

"Those can't be healthy," Wally observed.

"Most of the time I forget they are there. But those pylons are
a little like having a herd of elephants in your backyard. How
can you forget them?" He smiled with resignation. "The previ-
ous owners of the house begged us to take the house. We knew
what we were getting into. I wanted to live in San Francisco. So,
we live in San Francisco. Even under these power pylons."

Wally liked the guy. He liked him a lot.

A moment later they found themselves where Wally wanted
to be, in the workshop-garage. Figueroa flipped on the table saw,
which whined loudly. "My mother-in-law thinks I come out here
to work." He glanced at the saw. "I do nothing to disappoint
her." He indicated a chair in the corner that was padded with
old cushions. "Sometimes I come out, flip on the power, and sit
down and just . . . sit." The thought made him grin. "I do not
apologize for it."

"You expected us, you said?" Wally asked.

"Yesterday you never really explained yourself. And I didn't ask
you to. But I still couldn't figure out why you came by. I figured
you would tip your hand. So what is it? Have some of the other
jurors talked to the bailiffs about what I've been telling them?"

The question confused Wally, who indicated neither one way nor another.

Figueroa went on, "About the trial's being a waste of time." He nodded resolutely. "It is my humble Hispanic opinion that the whole thing is a farce. I don't think it's a crime to tell people that." He tried to read Wally's expression. "And so that's *not* why you're here?"

Wally shook his head. "No," he said, "nothing to do with it."

"Then, why?" He followed Wally's eyes to the pegboard where he hung his knife collection.

"So that's it," said Figueroa. He laughed. "Why didn't you ask?"

Wally looked at Roberta. "It just struck us as odd, you and those knives."

"*Not* the knives. The knife that's missing." And he focused his dark eyes on Roberta and, with a playful grin, said, "That's what you were looking at when the blood drained out of your face. I saw you."

"Was I that obvious?" she asked.

"I said nothing because I couldn't figure out why. Then last night it dawned on me. You think I murdered her?" He looked incredulous. "You're looking for a murderer on the jury? The murderer of Holly Hawkes? What about the guy they have in jail?"

"I can't say," said Wally, who was embarrassed now.

"Sure, you can," Figueroa said, enjoying Wally's embarrassment. "You come here, and you accuse me without knowing the facts. It's only fair I should know what I'm being accused of."

"I can't go into it," Wally said, thinking how Barr would kill him if Figueroa talked to anyone about the questions that Wally had raised by his presence. "It's something I wish you would keep to yourself."

"Why should I?" asked Figueroa. "This may be my ticket off the jury."

"Because I'm asking you to," said Wally, who saw the need to explain some of it. "It is a very complicated issue right now. It's sensitive. We have problems, and unless we keep this very quiet, a killer might go free and an innocent man might be convicted. I'm asking you, please."

Figueroa nodded. He didn't say anything. He shut off the saw and led them into the house through the back door to the kitchen, which was filled with the aroma of roasting chicken. He introduced them to a squat older woman in jeans and a colorful tank top. He opened a counter drawer and brandished a knife by its handle. "The missing piece," he said, pointing the blade at his mother-in-law. "Nothing in this house is sacred, Mama," he said. "I have nothing to call my own." He flipped the knife expertly on his palm. "Take it," he told Wally.

A fine stiletto forged of blackened Toledo steel brought to mind the Ka-bar he'd endlessly honed to a razor's sharpness in the marines. He handed it back to Figueroa.

Figueroa said, pointing to his mother-in-law, "She cuts up chickens with it. The kitchen knife wasn't sharp enough. She blamed my wife. Blamed me. She went out to the garage and got it herself." He looked at Roberta. "I didn't notice it was missing until I saw you looking there yesterday."

Sheepishly, Wally said, "I think we'll be going now."

Figueroa walked them down the driveway and out to the street. As they were getting in the car, he said to Wally, "Mister, don't worry. I won't make trouble. As far as anyone is concerned, I never saw you."

"Thanks," Wally told him. "I won't forget it."

In the car, Wally saw how perplexed Roberta looked. As he drove off, he said, "Lesson number one: Things sometimes do not turn out the way you expected them."

She nodded, feeling disappointed. "Truth really is stranger than fiction."

"And no more conclusive."

They reached Chinatown minutes later and Wally's uncertainty was reflected in his caution, as if he had entered a country with laws he did not even recognize. Yet a simple review of the facts made the destination necessary: the murder had taken place here, and the defendant was Chinese, as were most of the prosecution witnesses. A third of the jurors came from here as well.

Still, Chinatown was a ghostly place that presented him with a mystery as deep and unpleasant, he thought, as death itself. Here, less than a hundred yards away from the familiar sights of Union Square, was a place that was alive with the bang of firecrackers. The movement and color in the streets they drove through reminded Wally of how nothing about Chinatown seemed subtle or hidden in the light of day. The Chinese worked hard, but on weekends they poured into the streets to shop and gawk and sell and talk. In a society that was increasingly cut off from itself, Chinatown pushed forward as rowdy and satisfying as a shower of Roman candles against a moonless sky.

Wally stared up at a façade old enough to have survived the 1906 San Francisco earthquake. Its bricks were discolored by grime and time, and the details of its sills and keystones and the crenelations described an earlier architecture. Paper blinds and cheap lace curtains covered the windows.

Inside the building's small foyer they faced a panel of buttons with the residents' names written in ideographs on corroded brass plaques; dull smudges almost obscured the mirrored walls. Years of traffic had worn the black marble floor to a dull finish.

"Can you read this?" Wally asked her.

She leaned closer to the plaques.

Wally reached impatiently over her shoulder and pushed the buttons, one after another. The lens of a security camera swept the space with a whirring sound. "We'll have to come back," he said, and headed back into the street. He turned and looked up, and as he did he saw someone quickly pull a curtain across a window. He realized suddenly that Roberta had not followed him out, but when he went back inside, she was gone. For a moment he thought she was playing games, and he went out in the street again. He turned in a circle, looking for her, but she had vanished as though the earth had swallowed her up.

"Jesus Christ," he muttered to himself.

He went to the end of the street and searched. But she was nowhere in sight. He was scratching his head when he saw three Chinese men no more than nineteen years old swaggering toward him, and he instinctively felt on his guard. The tallest of them pulled himself up and pointed a cigarette in Wally's face.

"A match, a match," he insisted in heavily accented English.

"Don't smoke, pal," he told him quietly.

One of the others behind him leaped on his back, gripping Wally's neck, and his weight brought Wally down to his knees. The other two immediately began kicking him in the ribs and head; silent, efficient blows knocked the breath out of his lungs and made his ears ring. No one came to help him. Pedestrians stood back against the building. They walked past in the street. They looked, then they turned away. And still he was being beaten. He shouted for help, but none came.

Suddenly, a loud scream abruptly ended the attack. Wally pulled himself up to a sitting position. The young man with the cigarette smiled and turned away, and the other two followed him down the sidewalk and into the crowd of pedestrians.

Immediately, Roberta was down on her knees bending over him. "Wally? Are you all right?" she asked, holding on to his shoulders.

He felt his hands trembling and jammed them into his pockets. "Let me get my breath back," he told her. "I'll be all right." He inhaled deeply. Slowly he got to his feet and looked about.

Roberta had fear in her eyes. "Why did they attack you?" she asked. "Did they rob you?"

"I wish I knew," he replied. He patted his pants; his wallet was there.

He was touching the bruise on his head when a man came out

of a nearby store. He was Chinese, in his late forties, thin and elegant, with eyes that seemed to move constantly behind thick glasses. His fifties-style double-breasted wool suit and a white shirt and tie lent him a formality. Though Wally didn't remember his name, he linked him with the court testimony. He was the one who had described Holly's dead body as "hot meat."

The man looked concerned, even frightened for him. "I will call a doctor."

"Please don't," Wally said.

"But you were beaten," he said.

"You could say that."

"Gang kids."

Wally leaned a moment on Roberta's arm to steady himself; he still felt dizzy. He was bruised, but there was no permanent damage and nothing was broken, though there might have been had Roberta not found him when she did. He knew he was a target, and there was nothing random about him as the choice. They were sending him a message, but just what they were trying to tell him he couldn't say, beyond warning him to stay out of Chinatown.

The Chinese man was holding out his hand. "Winston Xiao-Yang," he said politely.

Wally looked at him as if he were trying to decide whether he wanted to stay around. "Do you mind if we sit down?" he asked him as a wave of nausea swept over him.

Winston Xiao-Yang led them into the store from which he had just emerged. In the back there were folding chairs around a card table. Wally sat down heavily, and Roberta took the adjoining seat, looking at him with deep concern. She waited a minute, then got up and said she was going for a couple of cold drinks. He sat in silence, staring off into space, until she returned. The Chinese man did not move. Wally drank down a Coke, and he was starting to feel better.

"These gangs," Wally asked the Chinese man, "do they often attack visitors for the hell of it?"

"I was horrified myself," said Xiao-Yang. "I was watching

through the window there." And he pointed to a storefront. "Of course, a man like myself, I could do nothing to help."

"Neither could anyone else," said Wally. "Is this what happens around here?"

"The gangs fight one another, mostly."

"But they practice on visitors?"

"No, this was unusual. I never heard of them attacking people like you."

"How about people like Holly Hawkes?"

"No, never like that, never. Never." He seemed too certain to be convincing.

Wally's head was clear now, and he asked, "You testified that—"

Xiao-Yang said, "I had the honor of reporting that I saw the killer the night the girl died."

Honor? thought Wally. "You testified about what you'd seen that night."

"That's correct."

Wally checked his next question. "I'm curious because I work for the court," he said, looking over at Roberta. "As I remember it, you went to report what you'd seen to the head of the Chinese-American Association. And then he reported it to the SFPD. Was that how it went?"

"Pretty much, yes," he said, a distinct look of unease changing the expression on his face.

"I was in court when you testified," Wally told him. "What I don't understand was why you didn't call the SFPD yourself, right away."

"Because the association is Chinatown's police."

"Ex officio."

"Some people who live in Chinatown do not think so."

"If I remember, you didn't call Jiang Zemin for nearly an hour after you saw the body, right?"

"I don't remember exactly."

"What were you doing all that time? Why was there such a delay? It all seemed—how should I say—convenient?"

Xiao-Yang pretended for a moment to weigh the meaning of that word. He said finally, "If my English serves me, convenience implies contrivance, which means a partial lie, a bending of a truth, making things work out how you want them to." He paused. "I saw the killer. I saw him leave the tunnel. I saw the dead girl. I reported the crime. And the killer was arrested. What more could anyone want from me? As a community, we Chinese deserve credit for solving a murder that the police might still be investigating."

"Let me get this straight," said Wally. "You gave the head of the association, Jiang Zemin, a description and name of the man you saw leaving the tunnel. Mr. Shao-li, you said, is known. He is a nondescript sweeper in a sweatshop who arrived not long ago from a big place like Hong Kong and he is known to you and Jiang Zemin. You Chinese must pull out quite the welcome wagon here in Chinatown."

"He was a petty criminal. That fact brought him to the attention of the merchants in Chinatown. That is why I recognized him."

Wally dusted his hands. "Case closed."

"I do not know what I should have done differently."

"Nothing, I suppose," he said.

Xiao-Yang offered him a slight bow, as though saying good-bye.

Wally asked, "Does the SFPD have patrolmen assigned to Chinatown?"

Xiao-Yang looked up the length of the street. At the top was a glass kiosk decorated with Chinese filigrees in which sat an SFPD patrolman. He was far enough away that he had not seen the attack on Wally. Chances were that no one had reported it. And if they had, the cop was certainly taking his time. Even from this distance Wally could see that the policeman was not Chinese.

"*Chinese* patrolmen," he said, correcting himself.

"You would have to ask the association head," Xiao-Yang replied. "It's my understanding that from time to time there have been Chinese on the police force who are charged with maintaining order in Chinatown, but not now. The SFPD makes a continuous point of Chinese recruitment. They put up posters all over town. And they talk to the kids in the high schools. And I know that the Chinese-American Association asks for a liaison all the time. But it is an imperfect arrangement."

"Isn't that strange?" Wally asked. "I mean, either the association or nothing. You have no real police down here."

He nodded full agreement. "We wish it were not so."

"How do you explain it yourselves?" asked Wally.

"Do you know how many immigrant Chinese there are in New York City?"

"No, I was talking about *this* Chinatown," said Wally.

"Crime is out of sight back there in New York—the gangs, drugs, slavery, prostitution, smuggling of humans, gambling, extortion." He shook his head. "We have our problems, but we contain our crime. No one in city hall hears about it. New York isn't as successful. It needs Chinese detectives, and they hire ours away. We here are a quiet community, all in all."

"If you say so," Wally said. He guessed that the Chinese-American Association did not want the SFPD interfering. He couldn't blame the Chinese who ran Chinatown, of course. No doubt the association operated as a law unto itself, answerable to no one except the heads of the gangs and maybe a handful of the richest Chinese businessmen. One association or another probably had presided over Chinatown since its earliest days. It was a satrapy where only the richest and the most powerful survived.

At that moment a group of tourists came noisily into the store, and Xiao-Yang excused himself and went out.

Roberta smiled at Wally. "What did you think?"

Wally just shook his head. "He sounded like a fortune cookie to me."

They left the store, and around the corner at a Chinese café they found stools at the counter. They ordered iced teas, and Wally was feeling better, though the suddenness of the attack continued to unnerve him.

"I saw them walking toward you," Roberta said. "I saw one of them point at you. At first I thought he knew you. He said something to the other two, then they walked straight at you."

"What happened to you?" Wally asked. "I thought I'd lost you."

She gave him a sweet look. "You left me in that building."

He shook his head. "I looked for you," he said. "You'd disappeared."

"The inner door was unlocked, Wally. I went in." She looked him up and down. "Are you going to be okay?"

"You went *in* when I went *out*?" he asked, and she nodded. "Come on," he said, "show me."

She was right. When they got back to the apartment building, the inner door opened with hardly a sound, its locking pin gliding smoothly against the metal striking bar. It opened onto a set of stairs and an elevator, which they rode to the top. The smell of cooked fish and soy filled the air. No sound came from inside the apartments. Wally knocked on the door he wanted, opposite the elevator. He gauged this to be the entrance to the apartment where he'd seen the face in the window. A moment went by and then a chain rattled. A woman's wizened face appeared in the crack in the door.

"Eng," he said, then repeated it. "I'm looking for the Engs' apartment."

The old woman opened the door a little wider and glanced at Roberta, then smiled at her as though she were a friend. She leaned into the light; her skin was the color and texture of aged parchment and her teeth were blackened and cracked. Covering her gray hair was a Giants baseball cap many sizes too large. Wally guessed that in her loneliness she would have talked to anyone. He showed her his expired SFPD ID and her eyes widened with surprise. She crooked her finger at Roberta and whispered in her ear.

Roberta stood up. "She speaks English fine."

"Then there won't be any problem," said Wally.

"She says she's not supposed to talk to strangers." Roberta bent down. "This is the grandmother." She laughed. "She says she thinks I'm too thin. She wants to feed me. She wants to know if you like tea, or milk, or coffee, or a Fanta?"

"Tea's good," Wally said, putting a foot inside the door. "Why won't she talk to me?"

"Because she considers you a stranger. As a woman, I am her friend. She apologizes," said Roberta after further whispers. "She is sad that her family is not here to greet us."

"Where are they?" Wally asked.

"She says they leave her alone here all day."

The woman now couldn't seem to stop talking, all in a whispery voice. Her eyes widened, then narrowed, and her thin, wispy brows went up and down. Roberta was bent to her level, and the two women nodded and smiled and laughed until Wally was starting to feel left out.

The old woman led them through the apartment, which was not what Wally had expected. Much of the furniture still had plastic coverings on it, and area rugs of Chinese silk overlaid a white carpet that had the spongy feel of being new. A television as big as his own dominated one end of the room and audio speakers buttressed the screen. Bric-a-brac of carved ivory tusks, jade, and semiprecious-stone figurines sat on lacquered tables and mantels and brass filigree stands. There were four rooms with baths, and in the study a new computer sat on the desk. The kitchen included only the best and latest appliances. Wally scratched his head. Eng worked for Project Right, a poor charity. How could he afford all this? he wondered.

"Do you know that your grandson is a juror in an important trial?" he asked the old woman.

She pretended not to hear. She poured a glass of milk, which Roberta dutifully drank.

"How long have you lived in this apartment?" he asked her. And now the old woman looked worried. She crooked her finger for Roberta.

"She says that's a secret," Roberta reported. "She can't tell you. She wishes you would stop asking her questions."

"I only have one more," Wally said—the purpose of the visit, indeed, the purpose of coming to Chinatown. "Ask her," he said, "if she ever goes out."

Roberta bent down. "She says she goes for rides in the countryside on Sundays."

"Ask her who drives her?"

"She says her son does."

"No one else?"

Roberta looked at him strangely. And she asked. "There isn't anyone else," said the old woman. She looked at Roberta, whispered to her, as if by whispering she wasn't really talking and therefore disobeying her instructions. Roberta said, "I don't know, Wally. She says that there is a great prejudice against the Chinese. No one of our side of town thinks they can drive safely." She stood up straight. "Apparently it's important to her—something like that, anyway." And she circled her finger by her temple, like the old woman was screwy.

"What about her grandson Michael?" Wally asked. "Doesn't he drive her?"

The old woman shook her head.

"Tell her thanks," said Wally, and he made a move to leave.

The old woman pinched Roberta's arm when they were waiting for the elevator. She was looking at them across the hallway, an old woman with bandy legs and thin shoulders in a Giants baseball cap sizes too large. She shut the door, and the locks tumbled closed.

Out on the street again, Wally leaned back and waved at the windows. "Good, good," he said, rocking on the balls of his feet with a look of complete satisfaction. He told Roberta, "I couldn't have arranged it better. Little fish, big fish."

Roberta was perplexed. "What was that all about?"

"They know I'm here, Roberta, and they know who I've seen." He saw that she did not understand the importance of what he had just accomplished in a place that was almost completely foreign to him. "I'm stirring the pot," he said.

"Why's that?" she asked.

"To see what kind of monster floats up from the bottom."

Wally was moving fast, and after the street attack he told Roberta that he needed to work alone. He dropped her off, promising to call her later. Then he told her he was heading for one last interview.

Roberta did not quite understand, but she said nothing about her confusion. Wally had included her in every aspect of his investigation so far, or at least in as many of the aspects as she had wanted to join him in. She had never felt more alive than in these last two days. She had reveled in the gamesmanship, the surprises, the odd confrontations, and the charades. She had loved his assurance; he was what she wanted in a man. And now he was dumping her and going off solo.

Something about him had changed, she thought, watching him drive off. After Chinatown, he seemed to know something that he did not want to share with her. She wondered about that. He could not have thought that she would speak out of turn. She guessed it had to do with her own safety—after the street attack. She felt safe with him. But obviously Wally did not share her feelings. He did not have the confidence in his ability to do his job and take care of her at the same time.

Roberta turned up the steps, feeling the headiness of young love.

Downtown in the BankAmerica Building, Wally was greeted at the elevators by a Hawkes Construction executive who was on his way out. Wally looked lost. He said he was looking for the senator's office. The executive handed him over to a secretary, who brought him into the suites of offices. And in a few short minutes Senator Hawkes came out to greet him. He was wearing a blazer and white boating pants and canvas shoes.

"Mr. Howard. Pleased to make your acquaintance," he said. "You told my secretary you are doing some work for Judge Barr?

Odd, he didn't mention this to me. I saw the judge only a couple hours ago."

"I thought maybe you'd help me with a couple of questions, sir," Wally said.

"*Anything* you need," the senator replied. His charm overwhelmed Wally, who was starting to feel sheepish for coming here. The senator pointed to a chair.

"No need to sit," said Wally. "I won't take but a minute of your time, sir."

The secretary handed Hawkes a piece of paper, which he took a minute to read. "I see here, Mr. Howard, that you used to work for the SFPD."

"What else does it say there about me?"

"You'd be surprised what a couple of keystrokes on a computer will tell you about someone these days." He saw the look on his face. "Don't get me wrong, Mr. Howard," he said. "I'm a cautious man by nature. I have to protect myself. I do not know you. How do I know you are telling me the truth? It's a prudent thing for me to find out a little bit about you, don't you think?"

Wally nodded in agreement. He'd have done the same if the tables were turned.

"Marine Corps. Vietnam. Good. Quite a hero in your day."

Wally made a face. "Everybody over there got something to bring home."

"What modesty," Hawkes said. "Now, you said that you are making inquiries. About what?"

"Between you and me, in confidence, Senator?"

"Of course. Nothing you say will leave this office."

"There have been some irregularities in the trial. Did the judge tell you that when you saw him today?"

"No, we didn't discuss the trial."

"I'm curious about a Chinese man, one of the jurors, who works for Project Right."

He shook his head. "How can *I* help you?"

"I looked up Project Right's list of sponsors and benefactors on the computer last night, and I could not help but notice that you are its main source of funds."

The senator crossed to his desk, a massive slab of black marble ground to a glossy finish. "Maude, come in here, please, will you?" he asked the secretary through an intercom.

A second later she was standing in the doorway. "Yes, Senator?" she asked.

"Will you please get me a printout of the charities I give to."

"The corporation's beneficiaries too, Senator?" she asked.

"Worldwide," he told her.

Wally glanced around the office. It looked south and east over San Francisco, across the bay into Berkeley, and down as far as Candlestick Park—and the view was simply amazing. On the walls there were the usual power photographs, only with a difference. The important personages, from Ramos in the Philippines to Deng Xiaoping in China, were all looking at Hawkes as though he were the star and they were his fans. The difference was about as subtle, Wally thought, as the impact of a thousand-pound hammer.

"Did Judge Barr hire you to go around asking questions?" Senator Hawkes asked.

"I'm doing Dan a favor."

"You are old friends, then."

"We go back a few years."

"Dan Barr is good man. I've watched him for years. I'm proud of him. I know his family. But you, Mr. Howard. What about you? You quit the police. May I ask why?"

"Your piece of paper there doesn't tell you why?" Wally asked; he was a little put out by the personal nature of his questions. He wondered why he wanted to know.

"The computer just gives a couple of facts."

"Things changed on the force, is why I left," Wally said. He felt uncomfortable talking about himself. "It was time to move on. I'm actually glad I did."

"A jury consultant now, I see," he said.

"It's a nice term for what I do."

"You investigate the jurors' backgrounds and help advise your clients who to look for. Mr. Howard, who would you have chosen for the trial of my granddaughter's killer?"

"Out of the pool? I'd have eliminated the four Chinese jurors. Their sympathies almost certainly will be with the defendant."

"They can be reasonable people, the Chinese, or as reasonable as any other people."

"You asked me, sir. I told you."

"How do you think the jury will decide, given what they have heard so far?"

"Guilty."

"Yes, I'd agree."

"I'm not certain they would be right, though," said Wally.

The senator stared at him, dumbfounded. "Oh?" His eyes shone with curiosity. "You know something that the rest of us don't?"

Wally shook his head. "What I meant to say, everyone wants to get this over with, and if justice is not served, who cares? At least a painful spectacle is over."

"Justice can be served in different ways," said the senator. "I have been quite open about my desire to get this trial over with, for obvious reasons. If it means the life of one Chinese, so be it. Would you say that one life is worth an end to all this tragedy?"

"I don't know what you are talking about," said Wally.

"I assume the jury will find him guilty. He will be punished, I hope with his life. You can understand my feelings even if you don't share them. I want vengeance, Mr. Howard. The court is the instrument of that vengeance. Juries can always find a reasonable doubt. There is always an explanation why someone might not have done almost anything. No one saw Feng Shao-li kill my granddaughter. The evidence against him is circumstantial. Therefore, a piece of the puzzle is missing." He looked at the door as his secretary entered with a folder. "I see here that I give Project Right two hundred thousand dollars a year. You were correct. I am its principal benefactor."

"Do you know Michael Eng?"

"The juror?"

"The executive director of Project Right."

He showed him the folder. "This lists two hundred and twenty-seven separate charities that I contribute to. You can't expect me to know who works for them."

Wally nodded. "No, Senator, I can't." He tucked the folder under his arm. "Thank you anyway," he said.

Chapter Eight

Barr greeted his father at the gate by the sidewalk. He thanked the male nurse who transported him around in his van and told him he would take him from there. His father said nothing, sitting patiently in his wheelchair. Barr bent down and lifted him up in both arms, and he could feel his father's breath against his ear. He knew he was watching him. He could sense the direction of his eyes. He wondered what he was thinking.

"I'm either getting stronger or you're getting lighter, Dad," he told him, taking the first couple of the many steps up to the house.

The evening light was beautiful and warm and there was a gentle breeze in the trees. Off in the distance the lights of the Bay Bridge had just come on, and the city below them looked magical in its miniature, brilliant form. Barr felt his father's arm around his neck; he liked it there. He recalled a time when his father carried him around, as a child. Barr marveled at his childhood belief in his father's great, overpowering, all-encompassing strength. He still thought of him that way, as a man of exceptional power. He supposed he always would.

His father had not commented on what he had just said, as if he were enduring these moments of dependence, waiting with gritted teeth until it was over. "This makes me feel quite silly, you know," he said, and Barr actually strained to look him in the eye.

"Oh, it isn't so bad, Dad," Barr told him.

"Maybe not for you, it isn't."

Barr stopped to catch his breath. He wasn't looking at his father when he said, "Dad, tell me what's going on."

"I don't think I know what you mean."

"You *do* know, Dad," said Barr. "That's the point. It's why I'm asking. And you and Uncle Wellsy aren't telling. I want to know. Even more, I *need* to know if I am to protect my family." Then he told him about Morgan and the Chinese in the car.

His father sucked in his breath, and his eyes conveyed fear. "There is more than I've told you," he said. He struggled slightly in Barr's arms. "Put me down, please. Will you?" It was not a question.

Barr stepped over to one of the large trees on the property, and he put his father down so that he could rest his back against the tree trunk. Then he sat on the side of the step facing the tree, with his chin in his hands. His father made himself comfortable, and before long Flicka came slowly down the path and sat by Barr's side.

Softly, Justice Barr said, "I was at the symphony last night."

Barr looked at him in surprise, but he didn't comment.

"Ravel's *Gaspard de la Nuit*. Played by a Pole. Brilliant technique. Name of Ivo Pogorelich. This was glorious."

Barr studied his father. "You said that there is more than you have told me."

"*Gaspard's* third piece is 'Scarbo,'" the elder Barr said, ignoring his son for now.

"The dwarf," said Barr.

His father shook his head. "I prefer *goblin*. Scarbo is everywhere and nowhere. He grins and spins around on one foot. He is an evil monster."

"Like Kafka's Odradek," said Barr. "Or 'Gnomus' from Mussorgsky's—"

"'Pictures at an Exhibition,' I know. Who taught you so damned much about music?"

"You did, Dad," said Barr.

His father's eyes twinkled. "Well, stop showing off. As I was saying, Ravel's goblin is right out of our worst nightmare."

"Right out of my jury, don't you mean? Right out of what this note has brought about."

His father looked thoughtful. "I felt restless when the symphony was over, son. *Gaspard* made me think of what you are up against. To be honest, what motivates an old man like me is fear. Since I had this stroke, I have thought about it. My biggest fear is of chaos. The opposite, of course, is order, which the law represents. Order is everything that I hold dear, except for you and Morgan and Cardinal Wells. It's why I chose law for my life's work. We acknowledge a darker side to our nature which we constrain with law. And what can't be constrained must be coerced. Judges like you and me, we decide the form of coercion. It is all we have to keep our society from turning to chaos. And it worries me, this fragile order." He relaxed against the tree. "Injustices abound, of course. But the most threatening— and the most chaotic to an old man—is corruption."

"What you once told me greased the wheels of democracy."

"I think I said it greased the wheels of *capitalism*. What is especially hateful to me, corruption spreads out from the center, just like the contagion, and where it ends nobody knows. I am especially irritated as a judge and as a man by the one who initiates the corrupt act. The most corrupt are often the most pious. They hide themselves well. When one who has enjoyed all the privileges of education and wealth becomes corrupt, we are all wounded. The simple elegance of the jury system heals these wounds by allowing citizens to stand in judgment of this abuse."

Listening, Barr wondered whether age distilled the process of thought into a purity that youth clouded with its ignorance. And he felt ignorant before his father. But he also felt impatience, and maybe that was his youth.

"Dad, you're telling me about chaos and order, and corruption, and I have a murderer . . ."

"Yes," his father said.

"He is on my jury."

"That is apparently true."

"So why are you telling me this?"

"Listen to me," said his father. "Listen." And then for the longest time he said nothing at all. He looked up at his son, offering him a look of profoundest love. And he said, "I ran into Stanton at the concert. He asked after you."

"Do you think it matters to him, Dad, if the jury convicts the right man?"

"Or what?" his father asked.

"Or whether he just wants someone to bleed?"

"I can't answer for him, and I don't know his thoughts."

"Take a guess?"

He seemed to be more alert. "I'm saying, I suppose, that Stanton wants an eye for an eye without any doubt, and I'm sure he'd sit here and tell us both that. I'm not certain if he knows which part of him wants to make the sacrifice. I'm saying that, yes, he wants blood vengeance, of course. And yet he doesn't want it. The senator, if you haven't noticed, is a complicated man."

Barr laughed at that characterization. He mentioned Morgan's observation about the crew on the *Mandarin* during lunch. "Yes, I'd call that complicated. Maybe you can *un*complicate it for me."

His father shook his head.

"But why can't you?"

"Because it's all there for you to see."

Barr was exasperated with him now. "But Dad, we might be in danger, and you are playing games."

That infuriated him. The effect was quite startling. Barr had never seen it—or anything even like it—before. The power of his emotions slurred his speech to the point of making the words difficult to understand, but Barr heard them, and he followed.

"There is a design," his father said, struggling with the mechanics of speech. "You asked why. Now I will tell you. I love you. I love you more dearly than you will ever know. You have always been my passion. No one in my life has ever inspired more powerful feelings of love than you, Danny. I include your mother in that too. Nothing I have ever done, or ever will do, is meant to put you in danger. The same holds for my grandson. I would sooner die myself than see him hurt by anything that I did or didn't do."

"But that's what nearly happened, Dad," Barr said. "It's what someone is threatening will happen."

"Not again, they won't, not for long," said Justice Barr. "I am in possession of information about the Hawkes crime."

"And I've got a killer on my jury."

He nodded. "You must find him."

"But you know who he is, don't you?"

"Is that what you really think?" Justice Barr asked, showing his disappointment in his son's interpretation.

"Yes, it is," said Barr.

"Believe me, I do not know, and if I did I would have told you the minute I knew."

"Then, what do you know?"

"A much larger truth about the crime. Your uncle Wells knows too. It came from him. To tell you now, Danny, would breach a trust that I hold as high as my love for you." He looked at his son. "I see that you find that hard to believe."

"No, Dad, I don't," Barr said, and he meant it. Part of what he loved about his father was just that—an idealism that he lived with day after day. He did not tell lies. He did not reveal secrets. He broke no law, either of God or man. He was a man of a rectitude that came as near to perfection as anything human. And in that same sense he was as innocent as a child. Barr had loved that purity of innocence, just as he was starting to fear its consequences now.

"I am trying to help you," his father said. "You must believe that. It's why I came here tonight."

"Why?"

"To tell you what I just did."

He shook his head. "Then, I don't see it, Dad."

"You will, believe me, you will." He looked up at the house. "Now, if you please, I would like a tall whiskey, then you can take me home."

Flicka McGurrin was a handsome woman with a husky voice and a sharp eye for spotting pretense. She waved and smiled as Barr and Morgan came through the doors of Pier 23, her restaurant, located between wharves on the Embarcadero, with the bay off its deck. She ushered them to an outdoor table under the pastels of Chinese lanterns. As they were taking their seats, a ship's red and green running lights floated through a curtain of fog. Across the bay the lights of Berkeley glowed dimly up into the hills. Barr looked over the menu while Morgan climbed on a rusted bollard left over from the days when the Embarcadero lived up to its name.

Barr leaned back in his chair with a relaxed sigh. He kept an eye on Morgan, and he took a moment to look over the other guests with a kind of benevolent disinterest, when he noticed Jenny on the far side of the deck. She was laughing like she'd never had a better time with a man Barr had never seen before.

McGurrin brought him a margarita a moment later, and after she put down the drink she slid onto a chair beside him with a weary sigh. She had been a close friend of Vanessa's and was like an aunt to Morgan; Vanessa had named their cocker spaniel after her, and it seemed an honor. McGurrin understood Barr better than he knew. She laughed at his pained expression, which she deciphered easily: Barr and Jenny were a couple whom their friends admired, even envied, as attractive, intelligent, amusing, and accomplished. After Vanessa, McGurrin believed that Jenny was the woman for him.

"She came in earlier," she told Barr. "I didn't mention it because I didn't think you were an item anymore." She looked in

Jenny's direction. "She's having a good time, I'll say that much for her. That's always nice to see."

"It is?" Barr snapped.

McGurrin laughed again. "Jenny would be aware, of course, that you eat here every weekend. She would also be aware that your usual table is on this side of the deck. Presumably that's why she insisted on sitting over there."

"You think?" he asked hopefully.

"But she *is* enjoying herself," McGurrin said. "And that guy she's with is *cute*."

He turned slightly in his seat to look.

Jenny was animated one instant, serious the next, completely focused on the man she was with. Indeed, her animation bore the stamp of someone who knew she was being watched. The distance between their tables only intensified how good she looked to Barr.

The guy, whoever he was, looked younger than Jenny. He had long hair and refined features and was wearing a faded open-necked denim workshirt and a blue blazer. Barr could hear him laugh as though he too were having the time of his life.

"I just lost my appetite," Barr told McGurrin.

"Mind if I tell you something, Barr?" she asked.

"Everyone else does."

"You can't have someone like Jenny and not have her, it's that simple."

"I know, I know."

"You've got to make up your mind."

"You sound just like my father."

"Everyone who loves you wants what's right for you," she pointed out. "Every girl knows that if a guy doesn't commit after a couple months, he never will, and she might just as well pack her bags. Some women never do, though, and they get the short end for the rest of their lives." She looked in Jenny's direction. "But not Jenny. She knows when to abandon ship."

"Is it that obvious?"

She shook her head no. "What is obvious isn't what *you*

think." She smiled at his look of confusion. "You think Vanessa is watching you from heaven, judging you. Well, she'd think you were a sorry sight. She was my friend. You and she had a great marriage, a love made in heaven, as they say. But by the way you are acting, she would have every reason to think you hated what you had."

His face fell.

"You are celebrating your wonderful marriage by refusing to repeat it. Like you want to entomb it. Find its reflection, Barr. It's natural. It's a sign of life. You could tell Vanessa up there in heaven what she means to you by committing to someone like that beautiful woman over there. Think about it." She pushed back her chair with a finality. "Want another one of those?" And she pointed to the margarita. "You've drunk that one and I bet you haven't even tasted it."

"Make it a double, then, with salt."

Barr noticed that Jenny looked everywhere but at him. Then her expression changed suddenly from one of gaiety to one suffused with emotion. And for the benefit of her companion she pointed. Barr heard Morgan shout her name and watched him slip off the bollard and run over to her table. Morgan pointed to Barr. Jenny waved, but put nothing behind it, not even a smile.

Barr gulped his drink like it was lemonade. The hamburger and salad and roasted chicken he'd ordered for them both arrived and Barr pushed the food around on his plate, his appetite gone. He glanced across the deck with a pendular regularity. When finally he could stand it no longer, he scraped back his chair and walked over to Jenny's table.

"Morgan, sweetheart, your burger is getting cold," he told him with a sickening sweetness that got even Morgan's attention.

"Can't I eat here with Jenny?" Morgan asked.

Barr looked at her. "If it's okay with her."

She smiled and then introduced her date. "Do you mind, Tom?"

The man shook his head as though a strange little boy eating with them was what he wanted most in life. Barr knew the feeling. Jenny could make most men do what they didn't want to do with a willingness that passed for enthusiasm.

Her invitation was pointedly directed to Morgan alone, and Barr walked forlornly back to his table. They were deserting him, as though he were not there. He finished his dinner and the waitress cleared his plate. He was looking for McGurrin to give him the check when he saw Jenny get up and kiss her date on the cheek. Barr was about to look away when he noticed the date's polite reserve, then, to his astonishment, he watched him leave the restaurant alone.

Jenny waited several minutes, talking to Morgan, then came over and looked at Barr.

"One last chance," she said, holding out her hand.

She was back again. This time Barr planned to hold on.

───────

Barr found Roberta sitting on the front porch. He looked past her to see if Wally was inside. "Did Wally call?"

"No," she said sadly. "I've been waiting for you."

He was instantly afraid; something was terribly wrong. Roberta looked up at him and started to cry with a sorrow that made her shoulders tremble. Jenny sat down and put her arm around her.

"What's wrong?" she asked her.

Barr did not want Morgan to hear, and before Roberta could say anything, he told Jenny to get him ready for bed.

"I'll be up in a minute," he said. He watched them close the door, then he said to Roberta, "What happened?"

She was sobbing now. "She's dead," she told him. She looked into Barr's eyes and shook her head sadly.

"Who?" asked Barr.

"Flicka," she said.

His first thought was that Flicka was an old dog, and he felt almost relieved.

"She's down there," Roberta said, pointing to the bottom of the slate steps by the back gate. "I didn't touch her, Judge. But don't let Morgan see."

"No, of course," he told her. He wanted her to go inside. He took her by the arm, and he comforted her. Together, they entered the house. "Tell Jenny I'll be up in a minute," he said to her, releasing her arm. She nodded and started to climb the steps. Barr took the flashlight from the kitchen and went out behind the gazebo to a toolshed, where he found a shovel which he carried down the slate stairs. By the gate, he searched the ground for Flicka, and he nearly recoiled when the flashlight beam fell on what remained of her. He let the shovel go, and its handle clattered on the slate. He drew in his breath and kneeled down beside the dead animal, touching its old gray muzzle tenderly with his fingertips.

She had been slaughtered and carved up, and only her old head remained intact and recognizable. The words of the witness in court rang in his ears. *Hot meat.* That was what someone had made of Flicka. He found her dog collar, and he took off her tag, which he held in his hand. He believed that what had happened was part of a campaign to terrorize him, and, to the extent of his feelings right now, it was succeeding. If they had come over the wall and sought out and killed Flicka while Roberta was at home and awake, who in Barr's family couldn't they reach as easily?

He used the shovel to dig a hole, and with each effort his fear subsided one bit at a time. He was feeling a different emotion, almost to his surprise. He was angry. For the first time since this had begun he felt anger start to burn in his chest, and it felt good. He was angry for the circumstance in which fate found him; he was angry with his father for his rectitude, and with his godfather for his ancient codes. The shovel went easily into the earth. He covered over the body of the sweet old dog. He was angry with himself too. He was not seeing what he should see— that's what his father was telling him. What was right before his eyes that he did not see? But most of all he was angry with whomever had robbed the life of an innocent creature to scare him away. Their cowardice sent him over the top.

———————

That night he did not sleep. He was staring at the moonlight on the ceiling of his bedroom, listening to the soft, rhythmic breathing of Jenny beside him, when the phone rang. Barr picked up and mumbled something unintelligible.

"Judge," a voice said. "It's Lieutenant Cummings."

And though he had been awake, his mind was clouded; he could not anticipate why the SFPD would be calling him. In an instant of pure panic, he made an accounting in his mind of everyone in his family: Morgan was in bed down the hall. He had looked in on him after he had finished burying poor Flicka. He had not told his son the tragic news. He wanted to keep it from him for as long as possible, which meant the morning. Roberta: she was in her own bedroom next to Morgan's. Jenny was beside him. She was awake, sitting up. She put the light on and was staring at him with a question and no small amount of worry crossing the sleepiness on her face. His father: he was home, where he had taken him himself before they went to Pier 23. Wasn't he?

Barr cleared his throat. "Yes, Lieutenant?"

"You better come down here," said Cummings in a voice that was gravelly and tired. He told him where he was. And that surprised Barr. The lieutenant was describing the place where Holly Hawkes was killed—the tunnel on Stockton.

"Why, Lieutenant?" he asked.

"It's about a friend of yours, Wally Howard."

"What about him?"

"I'm sorry. You better come down. I tried his place over in Sausalito. No one was there. I wasn't surprised. I know he lives alone. I didn't know who to call. Then I remembered you two are close. I just thought you should know." Cummings told him again where to find him.

"I'll be right there," Barr said and hung up.

———————◆———————

It wasn't far, and Barr was struck with a sense of unreality when he soon saw the cruisers' lights ahead of him, at the Chinatown end of the tunnel.

He parked the Porsche and was getting out as Cummings walked over. He didn't say anything, just ushered him past the cop who was watching the gawkers. This was familiar ground. The fog wasn't in but the lights glared and the sounds echoed. On the narrow walkway a group from forensics and crime lab techies and ME's guys were doing what they did, popping flashes, huddled over stains and marks, combing and sifting.

Cummings stopped on the walkway about halfway down. He looked at one of the ME's technicians standing by. "Pull it back," he told him.

The sheet was removed down to the knees. The legs were akimbo, broken and pushed up under his back, one of them cracked at a sharp right angle sideways at the knee. His skull had been crushed, cracked open on the left side. He had been broken almost in pieces.

Barr stared. One, two beats. Then he turned away. He felt sick, and he walked out of the tunnel and stood sucking at the fresh air. Cummings gave him a minute, then he came out too.

"I'm sorry you had to see that, Judge," he told him. He looked past Barr, and he stiffened. A van with the logo of one of the local television stations had pulled up and a camera crew was getting out. Cummings waved to one of the uniformed cops who was standing guard at the yellow crime-scene tape. "Tell them to stay back," he ordered him. "I don't want them in there."

"They have police press passes, Lieutenant," the cop pointed out.

"I don't give a shit what they have. Keep them out."

The cop had to push the cameraman back. The reporter, a woman in a raincoat, came over to Cummings.

"What's the problem, Lieutenant?" she asked.

"There isn't one," he replied. "I don't want you taking pictures in there, that's all."

She did not flinch. "You got a homicide in there," she pointed out. "We heard it called in."

"Yeah, so?" Cummings said.

"A homicide in the same place where the Hawkes girl was found? Tell me about it."

"There's nothing to say. I'll get back to you when I have something, okay?"

"No, not okay, Lieutenant," the woman reporter insisted; she looked angry now. "A homicide in there means you either have a copycat killer or you accused the wrong guy of killing the Hawkes girl. Wouldn't you say?"

"I wouldn't say anything right now," said Cummings, but she was right.

Cummings took Barr by the arm, leading him behind the yellow tape, where they could be alone for a minute. "You okay, Judge?" he asked.

He nodded, and for a few more seconds that was all he could do. Finally, he asked, "What happened to him?"

"He was thrown there, dumped there, whatever," said Cummings. "He didn't die there. They threw him out of a car like he was garbage."

"Making a point," said Barr, as though to himself.

"Which was what?"

"A point. How do I know? I *can* tell you how he died," said Barr.

Cummings looked at him questioningly. "He appears to have been almost carved up."

"Like Holly," said Barr. "Making a point."

"If you're going to keep saying that, Judge, I wish you would explain the point," Cummings said, irritated by Barr's obtuseness.

"Wally knew something that someone didn't want him to know."

"We should have a talk, then, about what that might be," said Cummings.

"Yeah, we should." But we won't, Barr said to himself. "Call me tomorrow." He did not dare say anything more. He was very frightened. He feared for himself, for his son, for Roberta, for Jenny, and for his dad. Wally had identified Holly's killer—he knew which juror was the one. And he had paid for that knowledge with his life. Anyone else with that same knowledge risked the same fate. "Anything further you need from me?" he asked Cummings.

He shook his head. "You want me to ask one of the men to take you? We can get your car home later."

"That's okay, but thanks anyway." And on unsteady legs he crossed the street, anxious to be home.

———————

Barr knocked on Roberta's bedroom door. He heard her stir. She turned on a light.

"It's me," he said softly.

She came to the door, wrapping a bathrobe around herself. He went inside her room, suddenly realizing he had never actually been there before. Posters of English country scenes—of the Lake District and of the Royal Pavilion—and one of the Queen decorated the walls. The largest poster hung over her bed—Princess Di and Prince Charles on their wedding day, that fairy tale image that had enthralled the world.

"You better sit down," he told her.

"He's dead, isn't he?"

He looked surprised. "Yes," he replied softly.

"I knew it," she said, her face showing shock; grief and sorrow would follow later. She turned her face into his chest with a sob. Barr looked straight ahead at the wall. His mind felt numb with disbelief. His friend was no more.

Images presented themselves and formed patterns, like a kaleidoscope. He felt far from sorrow. For right now he was still struggling with disbelief. Wally was vibrant, self-sufficient, capable—he was *alive*. And the thought of him dead did not connect. He put his arm around Roberta. "I'm very sorry," he told her quietly. "That's all I can say."

"Judge, it's so unfair," she said, crying now. "He was so kind."

What could he say? What was there to say? He had an agenda: the safety of his family. Nothing else mattered to him now. He had to find out what Wally had learned. He had to find out not to satisfy a need to find a killer. He had to find out to protect his own family. He had to know what knowledge had killed Wally. He would have to retrace Wally's steps until he too had gained that knowledge. There was no other way.

"Do you feel like talking?" he asked her.

"I don't know what there is to say," she said flatly.

"I'd like to know what Wally told you. It's important, Roberta. It may be the most important thing in all our lives right now."

She breathed deeply, and she looked at him. "Like what, Judge?" she asked.

"Anything that may indicate who killed him. A minute ago, you said you knew he was dead before I said anything. How did you know that?"

"Three men beat him up today in Chinatown," she said. "Wally knew he was in danger. It was why he brought me home when he did. He did not want me to be seen with him anymore, because I think he knew what might happen to him."

"What did he tell you?"

She said very emphatically, "'It's all about Chinatown.' Those were his exact words. He said he had stirred the pot—to see what floated up from the bottom."

"What did he mean by that? He must have explained to you."

"He was making headway," she said. "He was excited. He was happy. He was helping you, Judge."

"Did he give you a name?"

"We visited several jurors." She ran down the list and what they had found. "He asked a lot of questions, Judge. I wish I knew his thinking. He didn't share all that with me." She looked at him.

"But he must have indicated which of the jurors he suspected," Barr said.

"We crossed a couple of them off his list: Figueroa was one. Wally said he felt sorry for him. He didn't think that Bullock did it, either. He mentioned some Chinese who owns a restaurant. He had an alibi. Who else? We went to Chinatown. Those three came right up to him. They beat him up, like I said. He was okay. But he knew he was warned. Then we went to an apartment—an old lady, the grandmother of Michael Eng. We'd seen Eng with a bunch of kids earlier. He looked like a nice guy, if you ask me. Then there was the insurance guy—Warmath. He didn't do it. He was too busy switching beds. That's what we did together, Judge. That, and Wally talked to some detective at a bar we went to. Tosca, it's called. He only said that the police were worried over the trial because of all the press interest, and because of who Holly's grandfather is."

Barr listened to her now with half an ear. Talking about what she had done with Wally obviously took her mind off her grief, and she talked on. But what she said held no direct meaning for him. He had feared the worst case. Now it was here. Wally had identified the juror who had killed Holly. And he had paid for that knowledge with his life. And nothing he had left with Roberta shed light on that knowledge.

Roberta got off the bed, and she went down the hall. At the top of the stairs she asked Barr, "I'm making coffee, Judge. You want a cup?"

"Yes, please," he replied.

He turned to go into his own bedroom. Jenny was waiting for him with the light on. He kissed her and went over and sat in the windowseat, leaning against the frame. He was sad, and he felt very tired. He turned to her. "How sudden it was. How unexpected. I feel cheated. I feel abandoned by a friend." He told her about Wally. She said nothing. But she sat on the bed hugging her knees, looking at Barr, who didn't speak for a long time. He was thinking about what this meant to him.

"Do you know why he was killed?" Jenny asked.

He nodded. "Because of me. I was responsible. I went to him for help. If he had not been a good friend he would still be alive."

Jenny slipped off the bed and wrapped her arms around him and kissed him on the temple.

"Part of me wants to turn this over to the FBI," he said. "Let them handle it. But I've broken the law. I should go back, because I'm afraid if I don't, someone else will get hurt—you or Morgan or my father. I have to make them pay for Wally. It's what he would do; it's the least I can do for him now. He got close. I can get closer."

Chapter Nine

The next morning, the San Francisco County Medical Examiner sat in court testifying with diagrams, charts, photos, and words that sufficed in their aggregate horror to suck the oxygen out of the room. It took him almost the whole day, through which Barr pictured a young woman finding her place in the world, an idealist, like Jenny not long ago, like Morgan in a few years. The court was told of a litany of wounds, which was what the proceedings had reduced Holly's life to. From time to time Barr looked at Amelia, who sat in the second row. She changed expression only once, when the ME placed photos of Holly on an easel. Then she flinched as though she had been nicked. The photos now showed Holly's face—for the first time, everyone could see who she was in death. And the tragic difference from these bloody swatches to the lovely vision they had all seen pictures of in the newspapers was hard to reconcile. She looked just dead, and in those eyes there was no clue to the nature of her death—only the profound evidence of agony.

If he could have, Barr would have halted the proceedings then and there. Who could have looked at this sad woman without wanting to spare her the sight of the child she had given birth to butchered this way? He thought, as he always did when the court sessions began, of the killer, not ten feet away. The complexity of the situation, and the smugness of the killer, enraged him.

"Cross?" Lovelace asked, then he cleared his throat to get Barr's attention.

"Of course," Barr replied, peeling his eyes off Amelia.

Lovelace stayed in his chair at the table. He had taken off his shoes.

"Decorum, Mr. Lovelace," Barr felt obliged to say.

Without a hint of embarrassment, Lovelace slipped the shoes back on, and without bothering to get up he turned to the ME. "Did you find any material evidence that places the defendant at the scene—prints, latent or otherwise, fibers, blood, skin, hair, clothing? You know what I'm asking."

"Yes," the ME testified.

Shenon looked at Barr. "The state will address that issue with its next witnesses," he said.

"One question, then, Your Honor," Lovelace said. He was still in his seat when he asked the ME, "Did you examine the victim at the scene of the crime?"

"Yes, I did, and so did others, including forensic experts who were not on the ME's staff. The whole procedure was thorough."

"To your knowledge, was the victim wearing any items of jewelry when she died?"

"No," was his reply.

"No rings, no necklaces, no earrings?"

"Nothing," the ME said.

"Thank you," he told him. "That's all I have, Your Honor."

———————

A human corpse has the power to express a complex and sometimes contradictory tale. And the forensic expert from the University of California at Berkeley served as a narrator of Holly's story. Working with the ME's autopsy report and his own observations, he told the court how Holly Hawkes had been struck from behind, over her right shoulder, the knife point entering her thorax. She was dragged into the mouth of the tunnel, where she was dealt a killing blow that had nearly severed her head. And those blows to her torso and upper thighs that came after? He could not address himself to those, he testified, for they spoke a language he did not understand.

This witness, Dr. Robert Byron, a young man with black slicked-back hair and a slight tan, was handsome in an unconventional way. He also seemed athletic and vibrant for one in his profession. Barr had trouble reconciling this man with the more traditional image of someone who worked with cadavers. And yet Byron had examined Holly's body. Indeed, he examined dead bodies all the time, out of choice.

"In your estimation, was the assailant male?" Shenon asked him.

Byron seemed to ponder the question as though he had an educated opinion but a fact was harder to find.

"Strike that," Shenon said. "How much did Holly Hawkes weigh?"

"About a hundred and fourteen pounds," Byron replied.

"Twelve . . ." came a small voice from the front of the courtroom.

Amelia Hawkes sat with tears rolling down her cheeks. Barr looked at her and their eyes met. He looked away with a feeling of horror. What he had felt before, seeing her on the senator's yacht, amplified that simple, pathetic comment, which only an adoring mother could have made, as though she had forgotten where she was. All she knew was that someone had described her child incorrectly. Somehow Barr couldn't bring himself, as he should have done, to call a recess and instruct Amelia to control herself, but he looked for guidance. The defense counsel should have been on his feet demanding a halt to the proceedings. "Mr. Lovelace?" he asked.

"It's okay, Judge," he replied in a soft, understanding voice. "It's okay."

That simple statement filled Barr with admiration for

Lovelace as a man perhaps of small acumen but large humanity. "Please continue, then," he told the lead prosecutor.

Shenon asked, "Did the autopsy reveal that the victim was impaired physically in any way?"

Byron looked to Shenon as if for a clarification.

"I mean to say, was she crippled or deformed?"

Byron's mouth worked but no sound came out.

"Was she a *healthy* young woman, in your estimation?" Shenon asked.

"In my opinion, yes."

"Then, was the killer a man, would you say?"

"Certainly that is indicated. A hundred"—he looked in the direction of Amelia Hawkes—"*twelve* pounds is a lot for any one person to carry or pull. And the victim was dragged, I estimate, about twenty-five yards into the tunnel along the walkway."

"There were signs of a struggle, were there not?" Shenon asked.

Byron shook his head. "Forensic medicine is an imperfect science, at best. It is interpretative and subjective. It is getting less so with DNA, it is true. But in this instance, I cannot say precisely what went on in those last minutes."

"Can you tell the court why you can't?"

"Holly Hawkes's tissue was badly damaged. To extend my metaphor, her body was like a book with no beginning, middle, or end. It was what it was. Therefore, I could not conclude that she fought her assailant. There was no residue under her nails to suggest such a struggle, no bruises or contusions which could point to that." He looked at Amelia Hawkes, then away. "I hate to say it with family members sitting here in court, but I will: this is the worst instance of mutilation I have ever seen."

"That is all," Shenon said.

The prosecution's was a memorable presentation, and like a conjurer Shenon was not showing all there was to see. He had pulled the bunny from the hat and had whisked the hat away. The trick was all in the timing.

"Mr. Lovelace?" Barr asked. "Cross?"

Lovelace stirred himself, and when he was in front of the witness box he asked Byron, "Ever read Edgar Allan Poe, sir?"

Shenon objected.

"Overruled," Barr said. "I want to see where this is going." He looked at Lovelace. "This *is* going somewhere, Counselor?"

Lovelace repeated the question with a nod. "Ever read Poe?"

"In school, yes."

"You remember 'The Murders in the Rue Morgue?'" Byron nodded. "Well, then, of course you recall the discussions the French inspectors had over how a man was able to stuff his victims up chimneys on a French street called the Rue Morgue, correct?"

"They talked about that, yes."

"It required great physical strength, did it not? That's what stumped them, the feral strength required. But it turned out the murderer wasn't a man, was it?"

"No."

"What was he?"

"A monkey, a large ape, as I recall."

"Objection!"

"Overruled," said Barr, amused by Lovelace's presentation.

"You testified just now," said Lovelace, "that the murderer of Holly Hawkes was a man because of *her* body weight and the distance she was dragged. Physically that would have been difficult for a woman, is that what you are saying?"

"Yes."

"But could the murderer have been a strong woman, or two women together, or, for that matter, a strong ape, like the one in Poe's tale?"

"I suppose," Byron conceded.

"One last question," said Lovelace. "Were there any cuts around the victim's neck where a piece of jewelry, a necklace, might have been forcefully removed from her person?"

"No, nothing like that at all," said Byron.

"That's all I have," said Lovelace, who then navigated himself back to his chair.

Minutes after Barr dismissed court he met in his chambers with
Claire Hood, one of the jurors, whom he had asked through the
bailiff to visit him. She seemed somehow different out of the
context of the courtroom. For one thing, she appeared younger
than he had thought. She had a gamine's freckles. She was not
quite a woman and yet long past being a girl, with an earnest-
ness and an eagerness that were refreshing. She was standing
with her arms folded, demurely keeping her eyes off Barr,
though she missed nothing.

"I've read your juror's questionnaire, Miss Hood," he said.
"And I hope you don't mind if I talk to you just a bit."

"Not at all," she responded. "We're at your disposal, Your
Honor, like we're in school again, doing only what we're told."

"I'm sorry if it is unpleasant for you," he told her.

"Don't get me wrong." She brushed back her hair in an un-
conscious gesture. "Until this morning I saw the proceedings as
a drama that I was detached from. It was lively and fun. And I
was at the center of attention. Any girl likes to be that, no matter what she says. And then that poor, sad woman spoke up."

"Holly's mother, yes, it was sad."

"And all of a sudden this trial and my role in it became real to
me. My heart went out to her. If you hadn't said something, I
would have cried along with her. What with all the dry scientific
stuff and the dispassionate things that the witnesses say, it's easy
to lose sight of what this is all about." She was shaking her
head. "I can't even imagine having this happen to my child. I
was sitting there, wondering how the mother lived with herself.
You could never let it go."

"You are part of something very important, being a juror, and
I'm glad you know that," he said. "What about the rest of it,
outside the court?"

"That!" And now she was animated again. "It's like being
suspended in time. I don't dare talk to my friends I'm so afraid

I'll let something slip. I went to the movies by myself, and I took the boat tour around the bay, by myself. I even went on a cable car."

"Is there anything you like about jury duty?"

"Oh, the other jurors," she said with an engaging eagerness. "Some of them are really nice. I'd never get to meet them, or them me, normally, if you know what I mean? It amazes me how fast it becomes an issue of us against them."

"Who's 'them'?"

"Everyone but us," she replied with a sudden burst of laughter.

"That always tends to be true," said Barr. "The press, the public, everyone, wants to know, and you are at the center of it all, the embodiment of a mystery. No one can know what you will decide. Eventually, you'll see that the us-and-them analogy exists *among* the jurors. One person tends to push an agenda, whether for conviction or acquittal, harder than the rest. This behavior is as old as the system itself."

"Isn't that the point?" she asked. "I mean, one person believes in the guilt and wants the others to share that view. If he can marshal facts and emotions to his side, he gets the votes."

"Natural coersion goes on. I'm talking about the unnatural kind."

"That sounds like David Figueroa," she said as she blushed.

"Go ahead, this is between you and me," Barr said.

"I wouldn't be mentioning him if not for his pretending to be so annoyed. Maybe *angry* is a better word. He told me that this whole trial was a waste of his time. And he is really mad because of it. He has a job and a family. I didn't even say anything to him. But he chose me to talk to. He said it was so obvious that Shao-li is guilty, why are they wasting our time?"

The question seemed reasonable. "And what did you tell him?" he asked.

"That we aren't supposed to discuss it." She smiled primly.

"You are doing what the court asked you to do." He rubbed his chin. "Anyone else on the jury pushing to get it over?"

She nodded assertively. "Anthony Bullock started making assumptions which I didn't care for. Whether that's pushing, I don't know."

"Assumptions about the trial?" he asked.

"Don't I wish. About *me.*" She checked herself. "I mean, we all make assumptions. He has come to the conclusion that I view Shao-li the same as he does. That has given rise to a certain familiarity. Like he holds the door for me but for none of the other women jurors. Then he follows after me. It's like he's always there. I have a feeling it's all for show, like he wants people to think he is what he isn't, but it comes out all the same as far as I'm concerned."

Barr looked at the clock. "Well, I'm glad we could have this chat," he said.

As she stood, she looked at him. "Why did you ask me here, Judge?"

"Because I wanted to hear from you how things are going with the jury," he said. And as far as it went, that was the truth. He did not know which direction to take, where to go, how to operate. He felt like he was drowning in a sea of indecision, and he had hoped to find some direction in his talk with her. But, of course, it had not worked out that way. Nothing before him was going to be that easy from now on.

———

Barr knew no one, recognized no one, and that was just as well, because he had come to say good-bye. He knelt by the casket, bowing his head in prayer, then said a last few words to his friend. He thought about Wally's uniqueness, most of all. He thought about how difficult and independent he had been, and the sum of all this was a friendship that he had trouble measuring. Someone had pinned his Marine Corps medals on the lapel of his burial suit. Barr stared at the stars on a blue ribbon around his neck. He had received the Congressional Medal of

Honor, the highest decoration for valor in the American military. Barr had had no idea. None.

The prayer spoken, the good-byes said, Barr turned to leave.

A woman who shared Wally's salient features stood in the aisle. She was heavyset, with a plain honest face and kind eyes. Her face brightened all at once when she smiled. "Thank you for coming," she told Barr. "I know Wally would have appreciated it. I'm his sister, Maude."

Barr took her hand in his own and held it as much to comfort himself as to comfort her.

"He talked about you a lot, Judge Barr." She smiled. "He kind of thought of you as his younger brother." She seemed hesitant in this setting, but nevertheless she felt compelled to ask, "Do you know how this could have happened?"

"In his line of work he made enemies," said Barr.

"Wally could take care of himself. He worried about other people more often. He felt protective. I know he felt that way toward you. He never talked to me about his work."

Barr asked, "What are you going to do about his place in Sausalito?" He was asking for a reason.

"I'll pack up his things. I called the landlord and he said Wally had paid for the rest of the month. Why? Would you like to have a look around?"

"Maybe," he told her.

Someone who entered the funeral room softly spoke her name, and Barr watched as she turned and smiled. In parting she told him, "I should greet the others. Will you do me a favor, Judge?" She handed him a piece of paper with her name and phone number. "Call me if you hear anything about who did this?"

"I'll let you know."

As he was leaving he noticed Detective Cummings. He was leaning against the back wall with a watchful gaze. He rolled a toothpick from one edge of his mouth to the other. He looked rumpled and tired.

"How's it going?" Barr asked him.

Cummings shrugged. "This one won't be easy," he said.

Not as easy as Holly Hawkes, Barr thought.

"The chief put me on it," Cummings said. "I was up to your place today."

"Oh?"

"Talking to your au pair. She was here a while ago. She left just before you arrived, Judge. She told me she was with Wally most of the day he died."

"I know. And?"

"She said to talk to you about it. To be honest, I think she was afraid she'd say something out of school." He sighed wearily. "Will you tell me, Judge, what Wally was doing for you?"

"Checking out a few things, that was all. I asked him to. I needed some information that I didn't have time to get myself."

"About?"

Barr shook his head. "Your chief already passed on that, remember?"

"You know, I'm coming up on retirement in a couple of months," Cummings said. "I've been at this work a long time. I don't make any claims to imagination. I don't need to, really. The work requires persistence. But I know that this is about the note you brought to headquarters. The chief wasn't going to help you. He said so. So you decided to go off on your own, with Wally's help. I can't say whether Wally's death was connected with you or the note. But if it was, or even if you think it was, maybe we should talk."

Barr had nothing to say.

Cummings pointed toward Wally's coffin draped in flowers. "He was a very good man," he said. "We shared some good times together." He looked at Barr. "I bet you didn't know about that Medal of Honor."

"Not a thing," Barr said.

"It embarrassed him." He saw the question on Barr's face. "They awarded him the medal for saving lives under fire; he killed an overwhelming force of North Vietnamese regulars.

Wally said no one in his right mind would have done what he did. He said he'd gone temporarily insane in those moments. It wasn't him, he thought. He did not believe that he deserved the honor, but the Marine Corps insisted."

"Temporarily insane?" asked Barr thoughtfully. "To save the lives of his friends."

Cummings nodded. "I hope what you are doing is worth his life." He looked away, then back at Barr. "I'll keep an eye out for you. The chief doesn't want me to stick my nose in your business. He still believes what he told you—that we already have the killer." He gave him a querying look. "Maybe the chief will change his mind, because of where Wally's body was found. The press is all over that. I guess you've seen it on TV. Maybe it is no coincidence. But for now, watch yourself. We wouldn't want anything to happen to you."

Barr found his father playing chess against a computer opponent. He was seated in his wheelchair in the morning room, dressed in a maroon velvet jacket with the Barr family crest on the pocket.

"I'm sorry, son, about Wally," he told Barr. "You want to talk about it?"

Barr shook his head. "I've come for other things."

Justice Barr pointed to the computer chess game. "I got carried away with too many easy wins. The machine's an idiot."

Barr watched his dad move a pawn. "I'm inclined to take some blame for Wally, but I don't see how I could have done anything to prevent it. And yet . . ."

"You don't really know why he was killed," his father said. "Do you think it was your juror?"

"That's just it. I don't know. It's possible. The point is, we'll never know now. I can't think of anyone else who would have wanted Wally dead."

"Everything will turn out all right. Believe me, it will."

Barr laughed in spite of himself. "What I've started asking myself is, why Holly? What was the motive. I know, I know—the state says it was robbery."

His father slid a knight on the board. "The state loves any convenient explanation it can get away with."

"Wally looked at the jurors, Dad, and, really, it could have been any of them."

"But it isn't *any* of them. And you know it. It is one of them."

"There's so much I don't know, and Wally's death only confuses everything. I got a killer on my jury. That's about it. I don't want to run around town like a chicken with its head chopped off. It's true, Dad. I don't know where to turn."

"Holly," his father insisted.

Barr continued, "I'm grasping at straws and I—"

"Turn to Holly," his father repeated, and now his voice lost the slur; it was clear with that single word. "Whoever murdered Holly *knew* her, knew her *intimately*. And when you find that person, you will have found her killer. Son, I have presided in courtrooms most of my life, and when I see brutality like Holly's murder I am seeing passion turned up to a kind of immolating heat."

"It was the same with Wally," he said, and, he might have added, with poor old Flicka too.

"This kind of an assault stemmed from a powerful rage. Holly's murderer must have been close to her. Do you understand? Let *Holly* lead you to the one you're looking for on your jury."

"But Dad, I don't think I have to remind you, she's dead."

"Exactly," his father exclaimed.

Chapter Ten

In court the next day, minutiae filled whatever small gaps Shenon perceived in the wall of his case. But he needn't have worried. Lovelace had slipped off his shoes again and his necktie was drawn down like a man who wasn't going anywhere. Beside him the translator whispered to Shao-li, and unless the Chinese language compressed thoughts into few words, his version of the testimony was the rough equivalent of Cliffs Notes. But translation couldn't be easy, especially with Shenon calling a parade of witnesses who laid down a quantum of evidence. These experts were telling the jury that the odds of a match of the DNA in human hairs found on Holly Hawkes's body were one person in six billion—or nearly all the humans on earth— and that the one person, according to his DNA, was the defendant, Feng Shao-li.

Shenon used science to protect himself. Even if the state did not win its case, he still won with his colleagues and political cronies. The DNA had proved the defendant's guilt, no matter what the jury finally said. Juries were conflicted by prejudices, while DNA was science. For the most part, DNA did not impress juries. And this jury reacted to the scientific testimony as though it were an insult to their purpose and intelligence, or, worse, as though they suspected that science hid the misdeeds of a state that they no longer trusted. By the end of the morning, they grew tired and inattentive. After the lunch break, Shenon knew he had lost them.

"No more questions," he said. One could almost feel the jury sigh.

Lovelace had little to add, and the jury responded with respect for his consideration of their feelings. He simply played to their natural suspicions, and with a couple of words he wiped out the prosecution's entire morning of DNA quantum. From his table, he gazed at the last witness, an expert from the Selmark laboratory in Bethesda, which had matched and typed the DNA for the SFPD. Lovelace slowly shuffled over to the witness stand like a man who was lame and halting.

"Sir, I don't want to get into a rebuttal of the DNA and hair-and-fiber evidence—because we all know it can be planted—"

"Objection!" Shenon shouted.

"Sustained," Barr said, and to Lovelace, "You know better than that, Counselor."

"Sorry, Your Honor," Lovelace said, unfazed. He had achieved what he wanted, and he meandered back to his chair. "I don't really have any questions."

That evening, when Barr stopped the Porsche by the curb, Amelia Hawkes was attending some of the flowers in her garden. She looked up and smiled under the wide brim of a straw sun hat. She took off her gardening gloves and welcomed him as a friend, showing him around the back of her house. The garden overlooked the pines and greenswards of the Presidio, and after a moment enjoying the view, she pointed to an open bottle of Napa Chardonnay sitting on a patio table.

"I never thought to drink before, and with Holly I didn't have time," she said modestly. "Now, with her gone, I open a bottle in the late afternoons. Please join me?" And she touched his arm with a certain familiarity. "I'll get you a glass."

She led him into a den crowded with remembrances. An exquisite—and almost ministerial—portrait of Holly in oil hung over the mantel. In the painting the young woman was standing against a blue sky with a soft breeze blowing a full-length skirt against her figure. Hung around her neck, and lying flat against a plain blouse, there was a simple gold heart-shaped locket. She was gazing off in the distance, smiling, as though someone she trusted, someone she loved, was watching from outside the frame. Something else in the portrait also drew Barr's interest. He would have said confusion showed in her lovely blue eyes, but the emotion he perceived there went deeper than that. Was she disturbed? Was that what he was looking at? Concern? Anxiety?

Barr searched the canvas for a clue as to who this girl had been in life.

"You might like to see these," Amelia told him. "Holly just barely tolerated having her photo taken. I had to beg her. You know how children are."

And there Holly was in scores of photographs laid out in silver frames on the tables, smiling, expansive, happy. Holly and her grandfather aboard *Mandarin*, hand-in-hand. There was Holly on horseback at a dude ranch in Wyoming, skiing in Aspen, in front of the Arc de Triomphe, in Trafalgar Square in a storm of pigeons, on the Great Wall in Beijing—all with her grandfather and no one else, except for one photo with Bill Clinton. He was shaking her hand while the senator stood in the background of the Oval Office, beaming. The photograph that caught Barr's eye, though, was of Holly standing alone by a swimming pool with an ocean of azure blue behind her. It might have been from the South Pacific, or the Caribbean, he couldn't say. She looked thoughtful, and lonely and sad. She was wearing a bikini. What caught Barr off guard was the fullness of her figure. She had long legs, a flat stomach, and breasts that were firm and ripe, with broad square shoulders and a long, thin neck. She was breathtaking to look at, and she was as sexy a woman as any man could ever wish for. The contrast between the Holly in this photo and the chaste Holly in the oil portrait threw Barr off balance, and he realized to what extent the narrow view in the court had idealized her and made her an abstraction that hardly jibed with reality. He did not give voice to these errant thoughts, and Amelia looked adrift in the images of her daughter.

She took a glass from the sideboard, then she showed him back to the garden, where a setting sun cast long shadows on the lawn. She poured Barr a glass of wine. "I wish I had something happy to drink *to,*" she told him. "I'm pleased you stopped by. It is very kind." She looked him in the eye as though she were trying to find something there. "You *are* a kind person, aren't you? Just like your father."

"I was surprised when you told me you were friends," said Barr with a look that begged for an explanation.

"He makes me laugh. He has a subtle humor. Are you the same? Subtle?"

He shook his head. "What you see is what you get. It's why I was interested in Holly's photos just now. I am curious about her. I'm glad you invited me by."

"Tell me what you would like to know."

He thought for a moment before asking, "What was she like in school? Who were her friends?"

"I never worried that she wasn't popular, if that's what you mean. You can ask her best friend, Sarah Bigelow. They knew one another as only girls that age do. They shared thoughts and dreams that were too private for mere mothers."

"On the *Mandarin,*" he said, "you mentioned a movie that was important to her."

She smiled at that recollection. "Holly attended the Alliance Française, as you know. She spoke French with fluency, but the language no longer challenged her. She was bright, and she wanted to learn. She said French was only useful in restaurants and art museums, whereas she wanted something that she could actually use. That was how the Ingrid Bergman movie came in, I believe. *The Inn of the Sixth Happiness* is set in China before the war. Ingrid Bergman plays a missionary from England. Holly was in her own missionary stage when she died. She was giving. She was always giving of herself. She couldn't say no.

Maybe she could have saved the world too. I don't know." She seemed to catch herself in a thought. "Do you know the greater tragedy in Holly's death?" And he shook his head. "It is the extinction of her promise. With someone our age, Dan, the promise is fulfilled with nowhere left to go. With Holly, a brightness burned which we will never see the fulfillment of. Isn't that a shame?"

"What about her interest in China?"

"Stanton took her to the Orient two years ago. Some part of Holly never came back. She was sixteen years old then. She left a little girl and came back older, more mature; she came back a woman. Her childishness gave way to a sudden idealism, as though it were a repentance for some wrong. She was going to study Chinese at Cal. China was her future." She looked away.

"Girls her age start to notice boys."

She brightened at that thought. "She could have been the most popular girl at the Alliance with the boys. She was beautiful, as you saw in her pictures just now." She laughed, remembering. "I had to force her to go to the school dances and mixers." She shook her head. "She gave no appearance of being interested."

"Wasn't that odd?" Barr asked.

"Nothing about children is ever odd," she said quite forcefully. "They are their own creatures up to a point."

"And the point?"

"Undue influence. We parents do not know our children, ultimately. We may think we do, and we may intuit but never really perceive. Children are a mystery which we ourselves create." She seemed to think hard about that, as though it were important. In a whisper she said, "Maybe because of her father . . ."

"Karl?" he asked.

"Children need both parents, Dan. In the absence of one there is a void, or weakness, if you will. Holly needed a father. She needed Karl. He chose instead to abandon her at a vulnerable time in her development as a woman. We never talked about it, she and I."

"When did you and Karl split up?"

"We did not split up, as you say. Marriages don't split up. He divorced me."

"And he moved away?"

"No, Karl exiled himself."

"Did Holly go to Chinatown often?"

She shook her head slowly. "Never. The place frightened her." She saw his querulous look. "That is a paradox, isn't it, if not a contradiction?"

"Maybe she was drawn to what she feared."

"My Holly was not complicated in that sense."

"Did she ever say why Chinatown had that effect on her?"

"Because she was attracted to it, I believe." She gazed at the setting sun. "She was afraid she might not come back." She turned and stared at Barr as if to tell him something with her look.

"The pictures inside are all with her grandfather. The senator seems to have filled the role of father quite well."

"Holly was his companion. He made her into that. He didn't ask her to go along. It wasn't like that. He demanded her presence."

"But her schooling . . ."

"That didn't matter to him. He took her out when it was convenient to him. He hired tutors for her. He said schooling was found in the world, in experiences, not in books."

"And you went along?"

In that instant she looked as though she had seen a frightening image. "I went along by not raising my voice. No, I didn't say a word and I should have. I tried once. It did no good. You don't know Stanton. You do not contradict his desires. You do not even object. He is who he is. He took her out of my hands."

Barr put down the glass, indicating that he was ready to leave. He felt a slight disappointment now that he'd heard what she had to say. On the yacht he believed Amelia wanted to tell him something specific and useful about her daughter, but he was hearing only memories.

"A favor, Dan?" she asked, coming closer.

"Of course, if I can," he told her.

Her voice sounded stronger. "Karl lives at Sea Ranch, you know, on the coast in Sonoma. Talk to him. You know him. I think he'd like to see you."

———

In spite of everything, he had a trial to run. And with the beat of time growing more insistent, Barr was struggling with the proceedings that were becoming a tedium. His mind wandered. The counsels once or twice reminded him of particulars. The press was whispering, and inevitably the whispers found themselves in their published reports. To them he was "distant," "withdrawn," and even "bored with the proceedings." For once he agreed with all they said. He was in jeopardy of an official rebuke if he did not clean up his act.

Not that he cared about that anymore. He had gone beyond the fear of rebukes—way, way beyond to the fear for the safety of his family. Of the two dramas, the one outside the courtroom walls held the truths he sought. That was where the real dangers lay. By comparison, what went on here in these hallowed chambers was a shadow of that other frightening reality. What kept him going, more than appearances, was the knowledge that the juror who had killed Holly—who was responsible for Wally's death —was where he could see him.

As Barr was thinking these thoughts, Shenon was calling Amelia Hawkes to the stand. He was winding up his case, and he had saved the most emotional witness for last. She was on the prosecution list. Barr was not surprised. He watched her come forward wearing a plain powder-blue suit with a small gold circle pin. And her grief—she wore it also, almost as an adornment for all to see. She folded her hands, and when she was comfortable in the chair Shenon said, "I have only a few questions for you, Mrs. Hawkes. I promise I won't keep you long."

She smiled at Shenon. And as she did Barr wondered what the

murderer thought, being this close. It was obvious from her body posture that she was trying to avoid the sight of the jury—but not of the defendant. She stared straight at him.

"Will you describe for the court what your daughter was wearing the night she was killed?" Shenon asked her.

"She left the house in jeans and a plain white T-shirt and a pair of white tennis shoes."

"Was she carrying anything?"

"Just a small purse."

He went over to his table, and his assistant handed him a piece of evidence which he gave to Amelia. "Can you identify this?" He showed her the purse.

"It's my daughter's." She opened the zipper and looked inside. She saw a Communion card from St. Michael's. She clutched the purse, and she began to cry.

The entire court stared at her in pained silence.

"Would you care for a recess, Mrs. Hawkes?" Barr asked.

She shook her head no and wiped her tears on a handkerchief.

Shenon looked up at Barr. "That's all right, Your Honor," he said. "I can dismiss the witness. I can call her some other time." He looked at Amelia. "Thank you, Mrs. Hawkes," he told her. "That is all."

Barr looked at the defense table. "Mr. Lovelace?"

"Just a quick question, Your Honor," he replied. He looked at Amelia almost fondly. "You just testified about what your daughter wore out that night. You mentioned items of clothing. You mentioned a purse. But did she wear jewelry?"

Amelia looked surprised. She had forgotten. "Why, yes," she replied. "A locket."

"And was it of any value?" asked Lovelace.

"Her grandfather gave it to her," she said. "I wouldn't know."

Lovelace smiled. "Her grandfather, Senator Hawkes?"

"That's correct."

"Did she wear it often?"

"Not often. Always."

"Thank you. That's all."

"You may step down now," said Barr.

Amelia tucked the handkerchief in her sleeve and rose from the chair. Lovelace held her elbow and led her over to the gate, which he held open for her. Every eye in the courtroom followed her, watching her go, a palpable presence of sadness.

"The prosecution re-calls Detective Cummings," Shenon announced.

Cummings today wore a suit and white shirt and tie, but no matter how he dressed, he could be mistaken for nothing but what he was.

"Detective, did you first see the defendant on the morning after the murder?" Shenon asked, leaning one hand on the prosecutor's table.

"That is correct," said Cummings, shifting in his chair.

"Where was that?" Shenon asked.

"At headquarters, downtown."

"Who delivered him there to you?"

"The head of the Chinese-American Association, Jiang Zemin."

"Did you charge the defendant at that time?"

"That is correct." He looked over his shoulder. "I had just come in to work. We'd been at it pretty late the night before. At the crime scene."

"What did you do to the defendant then?"

"I took him to the holding cells, where he was fingerprinted and photographed and the paperwork was done on him."

"Was he searched at that time?"

"Not searched, per se," he replied. "We booked him. We had no other suspect. When a suspect is booked, unless he can post bond he is held, then transferred to the sheriffs' detention facility. In the process, his possessions are taken away from him. It wasn't a search."

"And what did you find at that time?"

"A wallet, some loose change; nothing remarkable."

"What did you do then?"

"We charged him on the basis of eyewitness testimony. That

morning we got a warrant and went to the apartment where he lived and we searched the place."

"And what did you find?"

He pointed to Shenon. "A purse which we later identified as the victim's."

"No further questions," Shenon said.

Barr said, "Mr. Lovelace? Cross?"

"A couple questions only," he said. "I won't keep the court long."

"That's all right, Counsel," said Barr. "It's why we're here."

"I just don't want to belabor the obvious, Your Honor."

He navigated the distance to the witness platform, taking his time. He seemed genuinely bemused, and seeing the look on his face, Barr wondered whether Lovelace did not hide an altogether superb intelligence behind this façade of indifference. Thoughts went on in his head that small gestures alone reflected, as if he knew the utter futility of his task and didn't mind.

"Detective, you testified just now that the victim's personal property was found at the accused's apartment the morning after the murder. Is that correct?"

Detective Cummings leaned forward, to hear better. Lovelace was speaking in a tone just above a whisper. "Yes," he replied.

"Lieutenant, remind me again. Was the murder weapon ever found?"

"I already testified to that," said Cummings. "It wasn't found."

"Isn't it just a little unreasonable to believe that the accused went to great and successful lengths to lose the murder weapon, while forgetting to dispose of a personal possession he allegedly had stolen from the victim?"

"Objection," said Shenon.

"Sustained," said Barr.

Lovelace returned to the defense table. "Oh, Your Honor?" he said, almost as an afterthought. "One last question."

"Go ahead, Counselor."

He turned back to Cummings. "You testified earlier that when you saw the victim at the scene of the crime you did not notice her wearing any item of jewelry."

"That's correct."

"The ME testified the same." He looked at Barr. "I can read back that part of the transcript if you like, Judge."

Barr looked at Shenon. "That's okay, Your Honor," said Shenon.

"What I can't explain to myself," said Lovelace, "and maybe you can help me out here, Detective. I can see why the assailant would steal a purse if he intended to rob the victim. I *can't* see why he wouldn't have stolen her jewelry as well. Can you?"

"Objection," said Shenon.

"Sustained," said Barr. "Save it for closing arguments, if you please."

"That's all I've got, Your Honor," said Lovelace.

"Next witness?" Barr asked.

Shenon raised his hand. "Your Honor?"

"Yes, Counselor?"

"The state rests its case."

Barr looked down at his list. Shenon had decided to eliminate two witnesses, and Barr felt as if he had been cheated of even more time. Time, he thought. He needed time. Yet he couldn't order the prosecutor to call any witnesses he did not want to. Shenon had made his case.

To the best of its ability the state had shown that Shao-li was guilty of murder beyond a reasonable doubt.

There fell over the court a transitional stillness, as though it were shifting weight from one foot to another. Barr debated with himself about whether to call a recess. He looked at his watch. Part of him wished that one side or the other would take the decision from him. He needed time, yet he did not want to call a recess without some tangible reason, which he did not have at the moment. When he looked at the lawyers, both clearly were waiting for him to give them some direction.

"Are you ready to begin, Counselor?" he asked Lovelace.

"Um," Lovelace uttered. He found his witness list. "Your Honor, there's a problem here." He held up the list. "I think there's been an oversight."

"Counselors, approach the bench, please?" Barr asked them, glad for this irregularity, whatever it turned out to be. And when the lawyers stepped forward, he asked Shenon in just above a whisper, "Did you not inform Mr. Lovelace about the deletions in your list?"

"Didn't have a chance to," Shenon said, looking away.

"That is sheer pettiness on your part," Barr scolded him. "You should be above this kind of silly ambush tactic." His expression said, What could he do? But secretly he was thrilled for the bonus of added time. "Can you start tomorrow?" he asked Lovelace.

"Fine by me, Judge," he said.

Barr tapped his gavel. "We'll adjourn for the day," he told the court.

Barr ran a couple of yellow lights to make his appointment in time. Once he had parked the Porsche in the underground garage, he walked across Union Square along Post Street to Gump's, which was almost as familiar a sight to him as the Golden Gate Bridge.

As a boy, his grandmother had taken him shopping there. She'd always bought cut flowers from the vendors in the front sidewalk stalls. Gump's Chinese vases and bowls had decorated their house. Barr and Vanessa had registered their wedding gifts there; its china filled their cupboards, and he still told anyone he was meeting downtown to rendezvous there. No longer. Only a year ago, Gump's had sold out to a clothing chain and moved a block east, across the street, in a new, shiny building with none of the character of the old. He went through the doors and up a grand staircase overhung with huge paper constructions. An attractive young woman was waiting for him in the corner reserved for the bridal registry. She smiled at him. "I recognize your face from TV," she told him.

Sarah Bigelow was working in Gump's summer program. Her blond hair was tied back in a ponytail, which made her look even younger than her nineteen years. She wore a dark suit and sensible shoes and looked prim and businesslike. "We can go over there if you like," she told him, pointing to a quiet corner of the main selling floor. "My manager said it was okay." And as they sat down on a loveseat, Barr wondered whether all young women these days possessed her same poise.

He told her he had a couple of questions about Holly, and she replied proudly with "We were *best* friends."

"So I've been told. At the Alliance, right?"

"We did *everything* together," she told him eagerly. "We went to camp together and sometimes our parents took us skiing and stuff. Holly was like a sister." She looked at him. "Her mother said it was okay if I talked to you. I hope you don't mind. I called her after you called me. I thought it was only right."

He coughed in his hand. "Can you tell me, Sarah, what Holly was like, from your perspective?"

"You mean, was she rebellious or studious, or a goody two shoes—like that?" And he nodded. "I've thought about that since she died. I think of her a lot. I do that because I keep asking myself, why? You know, why she was killed like she was? Holly was more serious than *I* am. She was smart. She was cool. Her head was filled with dreams."

"Did she have any romantic attachments? Her mother told me she didn't, but I wanted to hear from a friend her own age."

Sarah smiled. "She didn't tell me everything, but you know how it is. I didn't tell her everything either. I do know that Holly couldn't stand the boys our age. You know how they are."

"I suppose I do," he said, swallowing.

"Holly wasn't a prude. Don't misunderstand me. Her mother probably thinks she was a virgin saint. You know how mothers are. Holly definitely liked the opposite sex, but she wanted substance in a relationship. That's what she called it. It was her buzzword. I mean, she needed *relevance*. She needed someone to talk to, and that eliminated boys our age. Boys only want to talk about themselves."

"So I've heard," he said. "You were mentioning boyfriends."

"She had someone. But it wasn't like, you know, a *boyfriend* boyfriend."

"Then, what was it?"

"Well, it wasn't like traditional dates and things, her going out to meet him at the movies and the mall and stuff. There was something she did not want me to know."

"Sex?"

Sarah shrugged, indicating neither one way nor the other. "She was very cool," she said, and she saw the look on Barr's face. She told him, "Young people have sex all the time."

"So I've also heard," he said.

"You don't approve?"

"It doesn't matter what I approve of. What about Holly?"

She thought for a moment. "Well, Holly was having sex, but it was like she didn't want to admit she was having sex. Do you see what I mean? It's a game some girls play, some guys too. You get involved and you get intimate, and you don't *want* to have sex but of course you really do, and so you have sex but later you say, well, it wasn't really sex." She laughed at her own confusion. "It sounds kind of mixed up, doesn't it?"

It sounded to Barr like sex for this girl's generation was the same big deal it was for his. Apparently, her generation felt no different, though they responded to pressures to make themselves sound cool. "Was she troubled by what she was doing?" he asked.

"That's exactly the word I was looking for." She was quiet for a moment, thinking. "The day before Holly died, we were talking. She wanted to tell me something that was troubling her. She was really worried, Judge. No, more than that. She was scared, almost like she knew what was going to happen."

Hindsight, Barr thought. "Was she always secretive?"

"Only after her parents' divorce, when she started going everywhere with her grandfather. I think she blamed herself for what happened, the divorce and all. She resented her dad. I guess she felt he had abandoned her. That was where her rebellion came in."

"Oh?"

"She told me her father didn't want her going to the Orient. He didn't like anything she did with the senator. Her father was mad at her grandfather."

Barr was trying to get it straight. "Let me see if I understand this. She wanted to keep from having sex and yet she was having sex with a boyfriend who wasn't a boyfriend as a kind of rebellion against her father and the divorce of her parents. Do I have that right?"

She shrugged, as if she couldn't explain it herself. "I guess so, basically."

"Did you ever meet her nonboyfriend boyfriend?"

She looked at him directly. "I asked her once, 'How can we be best friends if you won't even tell me his name?' It wasn't like he was a *celebrity*. It was her most passionate secret."

"A secret that she kept from her best friend?"

"Holly wouldn't tell me because she said there'd be trouble if I knew."

"But it's normal to have a boyfriend at her age. At least it used to be."

"Holly knew that I felt left out. She said she couldn't get into it. I think that she was embarrassed he wouldn't fit in with our crowd."

"Did she ever indicate to you why she felt that way?" he asked.

Sarah laughed behind her hand. "The one thing she said about him? I remember because it sounded so bizarre. She said he was old enough to be her father."

A short time later, Barr pulled up at the curb in front of the BankAmerica Building, where Jenny was waiting for him. She was talking to a man. And when she saw Barr's car, she ran across the plaza and jumped in.

"I was about to scream, I felt so trapped." She turned to Barr. "You amaze me. I was waiting a half hour for you outside, talking to the man who runs our copying department who thinks he's a Lothario. You made it sound like you needed me on the phone. You come late and you can't even say you're sorry?"

"I'm sorry," he told her. "I've had things on my mind."

She took a piece of paper from her handbag. "Barr? I called Karl for you," she said. "He told me there wasn't really anything for you and him to talk about."

"Did he say he'd see me anyway?" Barr asked.

"He said it was up to you. I guess he doesn't get many visitors."

Over the Golden Gate Bridge he swung sharply off U.S. 101 at the first exit, about four hundred yards off the northern end of the bridge, down the steep ridge that protected the north bay from the Pacific.

Jenny pointed out the obvious. "This isn't the way," she told him. "You want Route 1, not 101." She looked at Barr.

"A short detour," he explained as he sped down into the small bay-side town. Sausalito was a weekend destination, with tourist shops, restaurants, book stores, and the No Name Bar, where Barr's father used to take him for lunch over chess games he never seemed to win. They drove past the harbor and the Sausalito marina, where the senator's *Mandarin* was moored. Even from a distance the boat made a statement. It loomed over the masts of even the tallest sailing vessels, blotting out a clear view of the bay for everyone driving by that section of road.

"Face," Barr said derisively, almost to himself, as they headed up from the harbor into the hills. As high as they climbed, the *Mandarin* did not disappear, like an ocean liner in a bathtub.

"Oriental face," he repeated, and he glanced at Jenny. "Your boss told me he'd rather be on my poor little *Bluejacket*." He looked at her and he laughed. "Do you believe that?"

She was smiling. "Not for a minute."

"Then, why'd he bother to say it?"

"I suppose to make you feel good. In China, if you are a host, you are obliged to make your guests feel welcome."

Reaching the top of Wally's street, Barr slowed down. A Sheriff's Department patrol car was parked by the gate, which an officer was guarding. Barr flashed his court ID. The officer's walkie-talkie squawked on his belt.

"Mind if we go up?" Barr asked him.

"No problem, Judge," he replied. "Talk to the man at the top. Lieutenant McGuinnes."

Barr and Jenny climbed the steep stairs. A man from the Sheriff's Department came out on the deck and introduced himself as Bob McGuinnes.

"You were a friend of Mr. Howard's?" he asked.

"A buddy," Barr said. He glanced through the front window into Wally's living room.

McGuinnes sighed. "I didn't expect to find much, given where his body was found. I haven't been disappointed." He looked at Barr. "Are you okay, Judge?"

Barr felt a wave of unsteadiness, as sudden as it was unexpected. He was thinking how this was all that was left, and once it was gone there would be only memories and a grave. "Yeah, fine," he said, drawing in a deep breath. "I was out here a few days ago, under different, happier circumstances, visiting Wally. We laughed a lot together, he and I. He was a funny man." He looked toward the house. "Mind if we go in?"

The sheriff nodded. "Sure, but if you take anything, let me know. His sister's arranged to have the movers come by tomorrow to pack up."

Barr stood in the living room, with the TV screen with the surround sound on his left, opposite the stereo rack system with the shoulder-high speakers. He could almost feel Wally's presence.

"Quite a little boys' clubhouse," Jenny said, eyeing the busty Polynesian portraits on velvet, a *Playboy* centerfold tacked on the wall.

Barr walked down the hall and looked inside the bedroom. A modular desk arrangement took up all the space in the room left by the bed. Shelves contained a couple of hundred books, some of them histories of the war in Vietnam. On the bed an empty frame had held his war medals.

Barr sat down in the desk chair. He flipped through the pages of a *Playboy* desk diary. He went through the last couple of weeks, but the pages were blank, as if Wally had had nothing planned. He imagined Wally intending to pencil in his appointments but becoming distracted by the nudes that appeared on many of the pages and never getting around to the purpose of the diary. It'd be like him. He flipped on the computer's power switch. It booted up and he double-clicked the file manager icon and looked at the list of files. At the sound of a voice he looked up. Detective McGuinnes, standing in the doorway, said, "I took a look through that myself. Nothing pops out."

"You mind if I copy a couple files?" Barr asked.

He was quiet for a few seconds, deciding. "It's up to you, Judge, as long as the originals stay."

Jenny was watching him, her arms crossed, as Barr copied Wally's schedule program, reminding himself to review the disk later. While the computer transferred the data from the hard disk to a floppy, he noticed Roberta's name a couple of times and his own among the files. He pretty much knew through Roberta who Wally had seen and where he had been. It would have been unlike Wally to leave a log, and besides, Wally was moving too fast to have put his thoughts in writing.

Jenny said, "If we don't go soon, Barr, we'll never get to Sea Ranch and back to town. Unless you want to spend the night."

She was right. And he would have trouble explaining why he held up the entire legal parade for a morning. He gave her a quick smile and popped out the floppy, and in another minute he was saying good-bye to the detective.

"Good luck," Barr told him.

He watched them go. "Yeah, you too," he replied.

Sea Ranch was a straight shot up Route 1 along the coast, about ninety minutes' drive, with postcard vistas around every other turn. Built in the 1960s as a retreat, it was still a great place for hiking and watching the surf crash on the rocks; whales surfaced near shore. Every evening the fog drove in off the Pacific, burying the ranch under a thick blanket of cool cloud.

The fog made the going slower, but eventually they turned inside the main gate and groped their way up to a central pavilion, where some of the residents had gathered around a roaring fire. The pavilion still had the original "communal" feel of Sea Ranch, which people with plenty of money had built to get back to nature without the nuisance of bugs and hard ground. Barr was told just how to find Hawkes's place, which turned out to be by far the largest on the whole ranch. Indeed, even with a sod roof that needed mowing and solar panels for energy and a windmill to draw the well water and a barn for horses and sheep, the house was a huge mansion attended by various servants. One of them told Barr that the master of the house was out in the back meadow.

They found Karl Hawkes watching a sheepdog work a group of about twelve sheep. Dressed in a Barbour jacket and a deerstalker hat with Wellington boots and a shepherd's crook, Karl looked robust and rustic. He smiled at Barr when he made him out through the wisps of fog.

He shook Barr's hand and looked at Jenny with an appraising eye. "You always got the best-looking girls," he said, and then turned to lead them over the long grass and back to the house.

"I kind of imagined you in a mud yurt, Karl," said Barr.

"The hippie lifestyle never appealed to me," he said.

"You don't miss San Francisco?"

He didn't answer him.

"Everybody leaves their hearts in San Francisco," said Barr, trying to goad him.

"Not mine, Danny, not mine."

That was what he wanted, Barr thought. He wanted him to open up with his feelings about his father, his wife, and his daughter.

He pictured Karl when he was a doughy kid, poor at athletics, a so-so student who had everything given to him from the start. The other boys had considered him spoiled, and he was not liked. But because his father lorded over such privilege, some of the boys tried to be his friend for the sake of convenience and luxury—and trips to Disneyland in his father's private jet.

"A question, Karl?"

"Shoot. I'll help if I can."

"About Holly. You know, of course, I'm running the trial."

"You're doing a fine job too." They were standing on flag-stone tiles by the door, and he turned toward the meadow. "Look!" He pointed to the sheepdog, who was being challenged by a sheep. The dog, quick as the eye could register, leaped at the sheep, grasping it by the neck with its teeth. "Good! Very good!" said Karl. "The dogs can be trained to work the sheep, but they can never be trained to control them like that. That's instinct. In the blood." And he turned back to Barr with a satisfied smile.

"Amelia urged me to come up and talk to you," Barr told him. "She didn't say why."

"Oh? She did?" he asked, as if he were surprised that Amelia still acknowledged his existence.

"I had the sense that there are things she wanted to talk to me about but didn't feel comfortable saying, which was why she suggested you. Do you have any idea what that might be?"

"Yeah, I do," he said.

"Mind telling me?"

"Yes, for the same reason Amelia sent you up here to see me." He saw that Barr did not understand. "Amelia is scared to death of Dad."

"Why would that be?" he asked.

"Because he likes to control anything he can." He laughed, and he glanced at Jenny. "It's why I moved up here, to get away from his obsessive control. After a while you can't breathe around it. Your life isn't your own. My dad likes to control what Amelia thinks, what she says, what she does. And she lets him. For a price. She's like those sheep out there, and he's like that dog. Did you know that he disinherited me?" he asked. "I'm all right money-wise, as you can see. I live on what I was given when I turned twenty-one. But because I wouldn't let him tell me how to live my life, he cut me off as if I didn't exist. I'm dead, truly dead, as far as he's concerned. As dead as Holly."

"Maybe you can help me with a question."

"Sure," he replied.

"What I can't figure out is why Holly would have been in Chinatown the night she died."

"It wasn't exactly our part of town, if you know what I mean? My guess is she was running."

Barr looked puzzled. "Jogging?" he asked.

"No, *running*," Karl insisted, "as in running *from* something." He spoke with surprising bitterness now. "Families get up to some funny business sometimes—things that *nobody* sees, Dan. You'd be surprised. Or maybe you wouldn't. I don't know your family that well. Nobody knows another's family that well. I wish the police had asked me. I would have told them a thing or two."

"What, Karl? Told them what?"

He shook his head. "I never wanted her to go with him."

"You mean to the Orient?"

"I fought it," he said.

Barr imagined that his cup overflowed with anger. "But he was her grandfather," he said. "Why shouldn't she go?"

Karl Hawkes wore a caustic expression and his words grated when he said, "Dan, I'm disappointed in you. Maybe I misjudge you. Or maybe your mind isn't in the right frame. That's probably it." A woman's voice came from inside the house. Karl looked through the windows and he smiled at his wife. "I do not seek vengeance. I seek only separation. And that is what I have found here." He paused. "It's getting to be dinnertime, Dan. Early to bed, early to rise, that sort of thing. I'll have to say good-bye."

"An observation, Karl?" Barr asked, and Hawkes stopped and turned.

"Sure," he said with a hint of a smile.

"You said Amelia was scared to death of your father. But you are too." He looked around at the house, the fields, the barn. "This is where you hide because you are afraid of him. That's my guess. You say it's just a separation. I'd say it's more like terror. Maybe it's something else. I don't know. What the hell is it with you?"

That stopped Hawkes, as if no one had ever confronted him that way before. "Okay, let me tell you. Behavior, I have discovered, is like this fog. You see but you don't see. It's that way with my family. Nothing is spoken. Nothing is admitted, or confessed. Nothing can be proven, ever. But the suspicions are there. It's hard to live with suspicions, Dan. Really hard. You want to enter the Hawkes fog? Let me give you a direction. I suppose it's why Amelia asked you to come up here. She wouldn't tell you herself. Much too timid." He looked off toward the sheep. "Why don't you visit Holly's grave, maybe say a prayer over her."

"I was already there," Barr reminded him, knowing Karl had seen him at the cemetery. "Remember? At the funeral?"

"I said her grave," he said with an assertive nod. "You just think you were there."

⸺

On the way south, they stopped at a little restaurant overlooking the bay at Inverness, and by the time they got back to San Francisco they were both weary. Jenny had spent most of the ride speculating, as though Karl's suggestion presented a mystery she wanted to solve all on her own. But in the end she simply could not imagine why he had pointed them to Holly's grave. She had said, "Maybe it's just as simple as he implied."

"And what's that?" Barr had asked.

"He wants you to say a prayer for her."

"Maybe," he told her, giving her hope. Then, "But I doubt it," taking the hope away.

Now she slipped into bed, intending to read while Barr worked at his small bedroom desk, but the words in the book seeded her eyes with sleep and she was breathing steadily in no time. Barr bent over and kissed her chastely on the cheek so as not to wake her, turning out the bedside light. Over at the desk again, he leaned forward, booted up his computer, and slipped in the floppy from Wally. The room was dark except for the greenish glow of the monitor, and when the file came up he had the same feeling of dislocation he might have had had he heard Wally's voice on a message machine after he was dead. Seeing these appointments and the notations in the "Notes" box by each day's date, he felt that Wally had almost come alive. He had already noticed his own name, and Roberta's. In the first day of his effort on his behalf, Wally had jotted down a couple of telephone numbers, identifying them as INS and CDMV, which Barr took to mean Department of Motor Vehicles. He saw some of the jurors' names too—Warmath, Gee, Eng, Figueroa twice, a woman named Mayhew Allen at a Starbucks on Union. He had clearly concentrated his efforts on the Chinese, which underscored his message that it was all about them, all about Chinatown, as enigmatically as the Chinese themselves. For his last appointment of that day, Barr noticed that Wally had written, "Hawkes, ck re Eng/Right."

He clicked out of the program, and at the door looked down the hall from his bedroom. Seeing a light under Roberta's door, he knocked. She was wearing her bathrobe and looked exhausted, her eyes rimmed red, her face expressionless.

"How're you doing?" he asked her, and she nodded okay. "Everything all right with Morgan?"

She shook her head. "There's been a lot of death lately, and I think he's having trouble," she said. "He asked questions about his mother. They came out of nowhere. He never mentions her, Judge. It's always Jenny this, Jenny that, as if she were a surrogate for her. He adores her."

"I know. You think he'll get over Flicka?"

"I think so, after a time. You should just be with him too. He needs the kind of assurance from a parent —that his dad isn't going to die suddenly, like Flicka or his mother. . . ."

"Or Wally," said Barr.

"It was so cruel, Judge," she told him, leaning against the door frame. "I went to the funeral home. It was so sad seeing him like that."

"Wally begged me for months, you know, to give him permission to take you out. I didn't want him pestering you."

She smiled. "I did everything I could but ask *him* out," she replied.

"Tell me, Roberta, the first day you went with him, you went to see the Chinese juror, Eng, isn't that right?"

"He was on a playground with a group of kids. Very charming, if you ask me."

"What did Wally say about him?"

She took a minute to think. "Not much, really. He seemed interested in his abilities as a carpenter, how he handled the hammer he was using. He seemed fascinated by that. He mentioned it to me. Why?"

He shook his head. "He noted him in his computer, probably the night before he died. He went home and called me, said he was surfing the Web. He made a notation."

She thought a bit longer. "No, there was nothing remarkable, if that's what you mean. Before we left —he just sat there watching Eng."

"He made three notations, besides one about picking you up and meeting me. One about the INS—Immigration and Naturalization Service—one about the Department of Motor Vehicles. And then something about checking on Eng and Project Right." He looked at her. "Mean anything to you?"

She shook her head. "He was kind, but he wasn't going to share what went on in his head, Judge. He thought I'd be at risk. I wish I could help you."

He smiled and wished her good night. Outside her door he thought for a moment, taking stock.

Wally had left him with few clues—and less and less time to discover the juror who had killed Holly. Where Wally had already investigated, the tracks would be cold. The juror who had killed Holly knew he was known. It was why Wally had died. *That* was the point of depositing his body in the Stockton tunnel. As Wally himself had pointed out from the start, the juror would hide himself well, and now especially so, or else he would simply disappear. Barr was left with no doubt: to re-create Wally's investigation of the jurors would be a waste of time that he did not have.

He had to find another perspective. He had to see a clearing through the woods of intrigue and confusion that Wally had not seen.

He rubbed his eyes and went back to his bedroom and turned off the computer. A minute later, undressed, he slipped into bed beside Jenny. He went to sleep listening to the even rhythm of her breathing with the thought of an almost unrealistic certainty: the pieces of a puzzle were laid out. Now he had to put them together.

Chapter Eleven

"The defense calls Candice Apple," Lovelace told the court.

As he approached the witness platform with a sprightliness that the court had not seen from him before, he asked the witness, "You are a meteorologist?" and he unconsciously fussed with the knot of his tie, almost posing for Ms. Apple's approval, giving her his best profile.

"Yes, sir," and she smiled at him. "I'm the weatherperson for KGO-TV."

She then rolled her credits with Lovelace's prompting, but, in fact, her face was well known to the court. What made her popular as a weatherperson, everyone who watched her knew, was that geography confounded Ms. Apple. While explaining the weather, she called Montana Massachusetts while pointing to Idaho. Over time she had turned a real failing into a considerable strength. The viewing public loved her, simply because she was unpolished. Otherwise, she was a good-looking woman of a certain age dressed in a pin-striped blue suit and wearing no makeup except for a dash of lipstick. She sat up straight and spoke in a clear TV-trained voice.

Lovelace said, "I will remind the jury that the medical examiner testified . . ." And he paused to read from the trial transcript. "He testified that to the best of his knowledge the murder took place on the twenty-third of June between eight and eleven o'clock." He looked at Ms. Apple and his face was all business now. "Were you broadcasting the weather the night of June twenty-third?"

"For the six and eleven o'clock reports," she replied with a nod.

"Have you refreshed your memory about the weather that night?"

"I reviewed our Accu-Weather videotapes for the court, yes," she said.

"Tell the jury what you found."

"The offshore waters of the Pacific were particularly cold that day," she said. "And it was hot on land, it being June. When the afternoon winds blow the cold air in over the land, condensation, or plain fog, forms. In other words, the salient feature of the weather in the San Francisco area that evening was fog."

"We have already heard testimony of the police that the victim's body was found in Chinatown. Is the condition of fog the same around Chinatown as it is around the rest of San Francisco?" he asked.

"Fog is one reason why the Chinese were allowed to settle there," she told the court. "No one else wanted to live there, and the area was left to them. Let me explain. In the late nineteenth century fog was thought to carry diseases, or what they called pestilences. The geography that the Chinese settled in, China-town, is formed by a natural hollow on the eastern slope of Russian Hill. This hollow traps the fog. It can be very foggy there—and even foggier—long after the fog has dispersed elsewhere in the city. They didn't want to live there at first, but they did not have a choice."

"What would the visibility have been that night between eight and eleven?"

She smiled and her mouth formed a little red oval. "Pea soup," she said. "That's just what I reported on my eleven o'clock report."

"Pea soup?"

"You remember those old black-and-white Sherlock Holmes movies? Well that's another way to describe what the fog was like. Thick as pea soup. That night you could almost bump into somebody before you'd see them."

"Thank you," said Lovelace. "I have nothing more."

"Mr. Shenon?" Barr said.

"I have nothing to ask of the witness, Your Honor," the prosecutor replied.

Then, with a show of uncharacteristic courtliness, Lovelace held Ms. Apple's elbow as she rose from the chair and walked around the railing between the witness bench and the courtroom.

Lovelace turned with an afterthought. "Oh? Judge?"

"Yes, Mr. Lovelace?"

"I have nothing more."

"Yes, I got that, Counselor."

"No, I mean *nothing* more."

Barr called a recess.

Lovelace and Shenon were waiting at Miss Hamish's desk, and he invited them in with a wave of his arm. He grinned at Lovelace, who wore his usual dopey expression. He was starting to grow on Barr, at least the side that was original, clever, and even a slight bit calculating.

"You aren't obliged to mount a defense, as you know," he told him. "But you're certain you don't want to? I wanted to hear it from you directly."

"I can't put my client on the stand, Your Honor."

Barr nodded. If a defense was mounted and the defendant did not speak on his own behalf, the jury would ask, "If you are not guilty, why don't you tell us so yourself?"

"It's your call," Barr said. "Are you ready, then, for closing arguments?"

"Can we have the rest of the day to prepare?" asked Lovelace, and Shenon nodded in agreement.

"You got it," Barr said, relieved for the momentary delay. After these arguments, he would instruct the jury, which would then begin its deliberations. Unless he was wrong about the testimony he had heard, the jury would need only hours to decide a verdict. He thought about that with an anxiety that was turning to panic. He had another day, at most a day and a few hours, before the jury disbanded and his killer went free.

After the counselors were gone, he wrote out for himself an exhumation order, which he signed himself, before instructing Miss Hamish to notify the press that he was suspending the court proceedings for the day for "housekeeping," not that he needed to explain. True to form, their speculations that evening ran from a juror's chronic illness to the almost certainty that Barr was about to declare a mistrial.

Before he left the court, Barr visited Ben Bowers, who looked needlessly contrite when he walked into the clerk of the Court's office. Ms. Meadows glanced between Barr and her boss. Barr smiled at her and sounded cheerful and offhanded. But even still, Ben was on his feet with the immediacy of one who's been found guilty.

"Got a quick question, Ben," he told him.

Ben wasn't really listening. "I heard what happened, Dan," he said. "I feel responsible."

"Ms. Meadows couldn't have prevented it if she'd wanted to," he told him. "The whole damned system's to blame."

Bowers nodded, but he clearly wasn't happy.

"Remind me, Ben," said Barr. "How are the names generated in the jury pools?"

"Why, Motor Vehicles registrations, out in Sacramento."

"That's what I thought. Not from any other lists, right?"

"Not any longer." Bowers chuckled at a thought. "It was getting that people weren't registering to vote because they didn't want to get stuck with jury duty. It was changed some time ago."

"Motor Vehicles?"

He managed a smile. "What else can I do for you?"

"You can run a check for me," said Barr, turning to go. "See what you come up with when you put the Hawkes jurors' names through CDMV. And put them through INS too, just to see what happens."

"Sure," said Bowers. "ASAP? Or yesterday?"

Barr knew his day's schedule was going to keep him out of touch. "Anything but a back burner," he said, leaving it at that.

―――――

Minutes later, he was driving into Golden Gate Park. Jenny was beside him as they went through the gates of the private cemetery on the southwest corner of the park. In their silence they held a sense of expectation and foreboding, as though they were about to find a code or a secret sign. Barr saw heaps of flowers that gave away the site from a distance, for no other grave but Holly's bore the same manifestations of such powerful relatives.

After they parked they went straight to the grave, and they looked and waited in silence, as though for an oracular message. Holly's name and her date of birth and death were etched in a white marble slab that bore no words of sentiment, no lasting message, no summation of her life and character. Barr walked under a Pacific pine for a different perspective of her grave that still revealed nothing.

He put his hands on his hips. "You got any ideas?" he asked Jenny.

"We could always pray," she said.

He looked over at the car. "Let's go," he said. "This is a waste of time."

"But, Dan, Karl said—"

"He said a lot of things that didn't make sense."

Once in the car, Barr got on the mobile phone and called Information for an address. It took them only five minutes to drive from the park to Van Ness and the funeral home of Brown & Sons.

Brown & Sons had been in this same location since the turn of the century. From the outside, the building was early Victorian with gables and turrets on the corners facing the street. Up the broad set of front steps, the interior was redolent of former times, with parlors that had fireplaces, high coffered ceilings, and casement windows with lead tracings. The rooms smelled of subtle floral notes, jasmine and gardenia. The exotic birds of paradise and orchids held sway overall in vases that sat on nearly every tabletop.

Barr waited with Jenny on a silk-covered bench in the entrance hall. They both got on their feet when an elegant man in a charcoal double-breasted suit glided toward them on thick-soled brogues. He wore glasses that magnified the dark pupils of his eyes and his face was as pink and plump as a cherub's.

"I'm Roland Brown. May I help you?" he asked, bowing at the waist to acknowledge Jenny. "Are you inquiring about funeral arrangements?"

Barr shook his head. "I'm a friend of the Hawkes family," he told him, then introduced himself and Jenny.

"I know your father," said Roland Brown. "What can I do for you, Judge?"

"You handled the arrangements for Holly's burial?"

"Yes, and it was an honor."

Barr said, "I know this might sound foolish. It's hard to know what to ask. We went to the plot, and we saw the marker . . ."

He smiled anxiously. "Yes?"

Barr hesitated. The pointlessness of his questioning frustrated him. He had neither a direction nor a point of departure. He did not really know why he had come here, and most of all he blamed himself for believing Karl. He asked, "Who made the arrangements for the burial?"

"The family, of course," Roland Brown replied, looking more relaxed now, folding his arms.

"Yes, but who in particular?"

"The deceased's mother and the senator."

"Both together?"

"No, not together."

The way he said it, emphatically, made him wonder. "Then, how?"

He grinned. "Separately, of course."

"I see, they made the arrangements for a daughter and grand-daughter separately. Is there an explanation for that, Mr. Brown?"

"I'm not at liberty to say. It is a private matter."

"Who gives you liberty, then?"

He looked insulted by the question. "No one."

Barr reached into his pocket. He handed Mr. Brown the ex-humation order he had written out himself.

Brown read the order with a strained look. "Do you intend to go through with this?" he asked.

"I do," said Barr. "I am led to believe that there were irregu-larities at the gravesite. I intend to find out what they are."

Brown handed him back the paper. "I will need Mrs. Hawkes's or the senator's or Holly's father's permission to speak to you on this matter."

"Will you call them?"

"Is this going to be an official inquiry?" he asked.

"Holly's father advised me to visit her grave," Barr said. "It seemed like an odd request. We went to the grave. We saw noth-ing out of the ordinary. We now have to exhume her body to be thorough in our investigation. You understand what I'm saying? We've come to you for help, Mr. Brown. I don't want to have Holly's body exhumed. The family doesn't want that either, I'm sure. Now, do you mind calling?"

Roland Brown excused himself and then retreated down the corridor into an office at the end of the carpeted hall.

Jenny stared at him. "You're good, Barr," she said. "You touched a raw nerve."

He frowned. "These people are like priests when it comes to secrecy. He'll probably tell us that Stanton ordered the head-stone and Amelia picked out the plot."

"Did you see his face drop?" she asked. And only a few sec-onds went by when she squeezed his arm. "He's ba-ack," she whispered.

Roland Brown wasn't smiling this time. But he was carrying

an envelope. "I spoke with Mrs. Hawkes," he said. "I'll leave word with the senator later. Mrs. Hawkes confirms that you and she are acquainted, Judge Barr. She asks for absolute discretion in this matter. Now, since you asked and Karl sent you to the grave . . ." And he handed him the envelope.

———

Out in the car, Jenny looked at a card, and a slow smile crossed her face.

"Well?" Barr asked.

"Down the peninsula," she told him. "A town called Colma."

Colma was known for one thing only. It was San Francisco's main burial ground. Except for people of extreme wealth, plots were too expensive in San Francisco. Within a few acres in Colma nearly every faith maintained a private cemetery. Colma was known as "the City of the Dead." Wyatt Earp was buried there, in the Jewish cemetery.

"Odd," Barr mused.

"You won't believe how odd," she told him.

Odd was only half true.

"What do you know about Chinese burials?" she asked as they drove south along the Junipero Serra Boulevard. They passed San Francisco State's campus and the Shriners' headquarters building.

"Nothing," he said, glancing at her suspiciously.

"Then, I'd better give you a tutorial. Listen and learn," she said. "The Chinese bury their dead in separate cemeteries, like the Jews and Muslims and other religious groups."

"Nothing different as far as that goes," he said, concentrating on the traffic.

"But it *is* different, is what I'm telling you. Chinese families feel obligated to furnish the crypts richly," Jenny said. "If you are a somebody in life, your family must present you as a somebody in death. You live as long as people's memories of you stay alive. Tombs prolong that memory."

"So?" he asked.

"It's a matter of degree. The Chinese deify a variety of gods, like a Dragon God or the Goddess of Mercy or the God of Wealth. There are others, like the Temple of Measles. But like everything Chinese, it's not simple," she went on to explain. "They build little houses for their dead, with all the conveniences of a normal house, as if the spirits of dead Chinese actually *live* in the tombs. They furnish these houses with favorite photographs, and they play the deads' favorite tunes, even put their favorite sheets on the beds. The food is in the cupboards, the dishes are laid out. Every burial site has, like, a barbecue. The relatives burn what they call hell notes in denominations of ten thousand dollars. The smoke from the burned money goes to the deceased in heaven. They also burn paper replicas of Mercedes-Benz cars, paper dolls that represent chauffeurs and housemaids, and they have paper representations of mountains of gold and silver."

"Death must be welcomed, then."

"It's meant to be. If you believe what the Chinese believe, your spirit is not happy until you are genuinely at rest, and you can't be at rest without all the things that made you happy in your life. And why not? After all, you're going to be there a while."

Just then he pointed out the Jewish cemetery as they drove past. The one adjacent belonged to the Muslims, close enough for the dead of each religion to take their struggle into the next world. Down the road were the cemeteries of Buddhists, Evangelicals, Baptists, Catholics, Presbyterians, and Episcopalians. Obviously, segregation in death was perceived as a requirement of ascension, no matter what the religion.

A chain-link fence surrounded the Chinese cemetery. From a perch on a three-legged stool, an aging Chinaman tended a soaring gate made of brick and concrete and ornately decorated with golden dragons and a menagerie of other creatures, from toads to tortoises. The old man waved them to stop as they pulled off the highway. In Chinese he left Jenny with no doubt that they were not welcome here.

Barr listened impatiently, then said, "Tell him we're visiting a relative."

The old man waved his arms. He pointed them out, ordering them to leave with a bony finger showing the direction.

"He says we're round-eyes. We can't have a relative here. He says we can't go in anyway without a priest, either Buddhist or Taoist."

He watched her talk to the old man, the Chinese sounds fluttering from her mouth like they were musical notes. Listening to her but not seeing her, she might have been a stranger, Barr thought. Hearing her and watching her take command, he felt an instant of pride that was far from patronizing. The feeling surprised him. And the lens through which he viewed her changed once more.

"He says he doesn't want trouble. But he has to get permission. He wants to know who our relative is."

"Make up someone," he told her.

Jenny reached into her handbag. The man's watery eyes widened as he held out his hand, and he waved them through the gate.

"Who did you tell him?" Barr asked when they were in the cemetery.

"Old Uncle Greenback."

Past the gate, what opened before them was a wonder to behold. Ahead of them was a village of small dwellings that confounded Barr's sense of what a cemetery was meant to be. The one- and two-room crypts were built with doors and windows and strived for the same worldly comfort that would be found in a regular neighborhood. Inside one of the crypts they drove past, a woman was cleaning the windows with a paper towel.

Jenny said, "This is their Erebus, the waystop, if you will, their purgatory, a place of darkness."

Through the window of one crypt house, Barr saw a television tuned to the Weather Channel. In that same crypt a recording of a Chinese orchestra played. Ancestor scrolls of a man and a woman dressed in traditional Chinese robes hung on two walls separated by a door leading into a back room, presumably the bedroom where the coffins were kept. There was a refrigerator and a Formica table set with dishes and stemware and silk flowers in a cut-glass vase.

"Next question," said Barr. "What does this have to do with Holly?" And, he might have added, because the thought crossed his mind, what did this have to do with Holly's killer—with the man on the jury? He was moving farther afield than he liked; he was following his father's advice. He saw no other path, even if this one seemed misleading. Any direction now was better than none.

"My guess is that she's buried here," Jenny said. "What else would you think?"

He put on the brakes and they came to a stop under the overhanging limb of a live oak tree. "So she wasn't buried in San Francisco?"

"It would explain why Karl asked us to visit her grave."

"But the Chinese don't mind?"

"That only depends on who's paying."

Barr started the car again, driving slowly. They did not have directions, and they knew they could not ask, and in only a short time they had driven entirely around the cemetery's circular road and found themselves back at the entrance gate.

The old guard hobbled over to the car.

"Tell him the truth this time," Barr said.

Now the old man started shouting, and pointing them to the road out. He appeared genuinely frightened, and he stood in front of the Porsche, blocking their way.

"It means we're right," said Barr, who backed around the old man and drove back into the cemetery.

"That may be true," said Jenny. "But we'll never know."

Passing the crypts again, she concentrated on reading the inscriptions on the brass plaques bolted to the front of each one. They drove to the far end of the cemetery, past the opulent crypts, out to a kind of Chinese potter's field along the chainlink fence that formed the cemetery's boundary. Stones laid flush with plastic flowers marked the poorer plots. Holly would not be here.

Barr stopped the car and got out. With the warmth of the sun on his shoulders, he stretched up at the sky. "Are you seeing anything here I'm not?" he asked Jenny, giving it a last try.

The groan of an engine echoed through the cemetery. A backhoe tractor entered the narrow lane that they had driven down, and as Jenny and Barr wandered along the fence the tractor driver waved. He was working on a building that was still under construction. It had a sloping tile roof and burnished black marble slabs on its outer walls. Unlike any other construction in the cemetery, this building was of a considerable size, large enough to be mistaken for an administration building or an office.

Barr and Jenny looked at the building, then at each other.

"You think?" he asked her.

"Don't be ridiculous."

"Remember the *Mandarin* . . ."

They cut across the lawn to the construction site itself. The building was all but finished, and the backhoe operator was digging holes for landscaping, presumably for trees. The front was mounted by steps leading to a high glass wall. Inside was a pedestal with a black obsidian veneer, and on the pedestal sat a bronze coffin. They both looked in through the window. The room was bare except for the coffin. There was nothing on the walls. The anonymity of the place, Barr thought, was as creepy as the arcane nature of the burial itself.

"Look here," Jenny said. She stepped over to the corner of the building. A commemorative plaque was mounted on the marble veneer. The words etched into the plaque were written in Chinese ideograms.

"What does it say?" Barr asked.

"One word, besides Holly's name," she said. "'Beloved.'"

They both stood back from the wall.

"Anything else, like 'To My Granddaughter'?"

She shook her head.

"What now?"

"Nothing," she said in a distant, thoughtful voice. "Nothing."

———————

Back at Jenny's office downtown, Barr decided to park under the BankAmerica Building and go upstairs with her.

"Okay, why?" he asked her as they rode up to the forty-eighth floor. Jenny was unusually quiet, morbid, and gloomy in her few spoken utterances. "The only rational explanation I can see is that he wanted her buried under the aegis of a different religion. He doesn't want the public to know about that."

Jenny said, "I wasn't aware the senator was a Confucian, or a Buddhist."

"That's what gets me," said Barr. "You don't change religions to do business. He's Catholic. I saw him in church. No, there is some other meaning that I'm not getting."

Jenny said, "Yes, there is, but . . ."

"Go on," he said. "Tell me what you're thinking."

She paused a few seconds before speaking. "In Chinese, words have meanings that go beyond their definitions. The ideogram on her crypt. *Beloved* in Chinese isn't used in reference to a daughter or granddaughter, or any child, Barr."

"Then, what does it refer to?"

"Usually? That's what I don't get." She shook her head. "Usually a husband or a wife."

The elevator door opened and they got out. Barr followed her along a corridor of offices with panoramic views. Halfway down, she turned in, saying hi to a secretary sitting at a desk along the corridor, and the secretary came in after them.

"Louise, this is Judge Barr—Dan, this is Louise, my assistant. What's up?"

Louise handed her a call list. "You've got a conference in an hour with the Hilton people and the ministry in Beijing." Louise nodded at the fistful of call slips in Jenny's hand. "The senator called, asking you to get back to him when you get in." She raised her eyebrow. "Quiet otherwise." She smiled at Barr, and turned and went out.

Barr looked around her office. Jenny had clearly understated her position when she said that Hawkes had plans for her. By the size of this new office, the plans were behind her. She had already arrived. He went over to a wet bar set in a bookcase to examine the liquor bottles stocked there. "Not too shabby," he said.

"It comes with the territory," she said with a smile. "Everyone on the floor has the same acreage."

He sat down and looked out over the city. "You know, Jenny, I still don't get it."

She looked up at him.

"How likely is it that anyone would have come across that inscription, much less that Chinese grave?"

"Not very, considering. Not one of us round-eyes, surely. Odds against it are a billion to one, a trillion even. A Chinese cemetery in Colma, a crypt with no markings except that one inscription? And the body everybody *saw* being buried in Golden Gate Park?"

"Could it have been a mistake, the use of that particular word?"

"No question about it," she replied, then she hesitated. "At least that's what I'd assume. So there is a question, isn't there?" It was no big deal to her. From the moment she had first seen it, she had dismissed it as an error, assuming that Hawkes—or maybe some Chinese monument maker—had chosen the word carelessly or simply didn't know the difference. "The only way to satisfy your curiosity is to ask him." She pointed to the desk telephone.

Just then the senator appeared in the doorway. It was as if he had read their minds. He offered smiles all around. For all appearances he was without a care in the world. He greeted Barr. "I thought you'd be in court today, Judge."

"A procedural complication," Barr said, deciding not to elaborate. "I had to call a recess—closing arguments tomorrow."

He turned to Jenny. "I'm off to Washington tonight. I wanted to make sure we're clear on the Hilton matter before I leave. We should meet after the telephone conference, don't you think?"

She smiled. "It'd be helpful if we could, Senator," she told him.

The senator waved casually and turned to leave.

Barr said, "I was just about to call you, Senator."

He stopped and looked at Barr queryingly. "Is that so? What about?"

"I wanted to ask you about a meeting you had last Saturday."

"Saturday?" He thought for a moment. "I was on the *Mandarin* last Saturday. As were you and Jenny and your son. I don't understand."

"Later in the afternoon you had a meeting with Wally Howard."

The senator paused a second to recall. "You are right. He dropped by unannounced. Asking questions, I believe, on your behalf."

Barr was nodding. "About one of my jurors. Michael Eng."

The senator pointed his finger in the air. "Project Right. He was curious about the project's sponsors, which was how he got my name. I'm a contributor both corporately and as a private sponsor. Why?"

"Wally Howard is dead, Senator," said Barr.

He did not pause for breath. "Then, please, how can I help you?" It was as though Wally's death meant nothing. "You mentioned about Mr. Eng? Mr. Howard said there were irregularities with the jury. That's the exact word he used too."

"What did you tell him? Maybe it's important. His killer hasn't been found."

"Not much, I'm afraid. I gave him a list of my charities. I can get you the same one too. He asked me whether I knew Mr. Eng. I told him no. I didn't even recognize his organization. You should know that I was curious about who Mr. Howard was. I asked my secretary to run a computer search on him as we were talking. I think Mr. Howard was annoyed by that. I may have put him off. Anyway, he listened to what I had to say, and then he left." He lifted both hands, palms up. "And now I have told you everything I know." He looked as though he had not thought about Wally again until this moment, and perhaps he hadn't, either.

Jenny was standing quietly, watching both men.

Barr didn't know if she was going to bring up Holly's burial place, or their going to Karl's, or the matter of "Beloved." He hoped not. The senator did not need to know what they knew. He was either completely forthcoming or he knew more than he was saying. Roland Brown, the mortician, or the Chinese gate guard already could have reached him by telephone. Barr had not exactly made a secret of his day's itinerary. Besides, just bringing up the questions implied suspicion, which Barr wanted to avoid. As things stood, meddling in the senator's family affairs just wasn't done. He looked at Jenny, realizing that her self-absorption had nothing to do with Wally, or Karl, or the gravesite. It had to do with business.

She looked at her watch. "I have to make that call, Senator," she told him. And when he turned to leave she said apologetically, "You don't have to go. I'll use Louise's desk phone."

Hawkes referred to Barr with a look. "It's up to him, if he has any more questions for me."

Barr smiled and said, "Thanks for your help, Senator."

"Oh, Judge? About Mr. Howard. Perhaps I said nothing a moment ago. I know he was your friend. I'm dreadfully sorry he's passed away."

Barr forced a smile, admiring the polish of the man's veneer. What he wanted to find out now was what was beneath it.

A short time later, Barr found his father being pushed in his wheelchair by his male nurse. He was soaking in the slanting rays of sunlight in peaceful Golden Gate Park, near the Conservatory, the Victorian greenhouse. Justice Barr had a woolen blanket over his legs. Barr dismissed the nurse with a glance and, without his father even knowing he was there, took the handles of the chair and continued pushing him along the sidewalk.

"I spoke with Amelia," Barr announced himself by saying.

His father turned his head, his eyes filled with surprise at the sound of his son's voice. "Taking advantage of an old man's frailties, are you?" he said.

"I needed to talk, Dad, and I knew where to find you."

"Then, *talk*," he said, slightly annoyed at having been taken by surprise so easily.

"I'd rather *you* did, Dad," Barr said.

"Okay," he replied. "Ask."

"She told me she takes walks with you."

"Sometimes, yes, she does. Very nice too. I have a social life, so don't be too shocked."

"One that you keep a secret?"

"Private, though not intentionally. I do not hide my friends from you, son." He laughed self-deprecatingly. "Nobody asks anymore who they are, maybe because they assume they are all dead."

"Does your social circle include Stanton Hawkes too?"

"The senator is an old acquaintance, as you know. Very old. But that's all. He's much too high and mighty for me, son. What did Amelia tell you?"

"Nothing, really. But you and he were friends as kids, weren't you?"

His father looked pleased, and it was hard for Barr to know exactly why. Maybe it was the subject, maybe the day—maybe anything. He had given up reading the signs his father gave out.

"We have known each other most of our lives," Justice Barr said. "What else is there to say?"

Barr smiled. "A lot, I'd imagine."

"I can tell you that he's bigger than life."

"His boat is, anyway."

"He is interested in maintaining an imposing façade. Power is something he grasps. Stanton is about large, exaggerated statements. He must be, for what he does."

"Construction? Or the Senate?"

"Either. Or both. Take your pick. He is not like you or me."

"It was his father's business to start with."

"He made it what it is. Hawkes Construction grew with America's presence in the world after the Second World War. He's built embassies for the State Department, air and naval bases for the Pentagon, dams and roads for USAID. He'll tell you himself. During Vietnam it was said that his solution to the military stalemate, which the generals considered for a time, was to pave over the south. He builds for the Pentagon, and when our military leaves the destruction of war behind, he provides the survivors with construction. He profits both ways. Very smart, very smart."

"Construction and what else?"

"Now, that is a question more people than you have asked. I think it would be fair to say that Stanton at one point broadened his business to include endeavors that return greater profits and, let's say, require less capital investment. He is an offshore operator. He is above reproach in the United States, because he must be as a senator. But a world of intrigue may hide under shelters and shell companies offshore. Who knows? No one really does. Nobody ever will. His opponents have tried to expose something negative about him for years. They have dug deep in search of dirt, and they came away with clean hands. You figure."

They came on the meadow where a small herd of grazing buffaloes created an anomalous sight in a city as cosmopolitan as theirs.

Barr took a breath, almost a sigh. "I guess my question is, do *you* like him?" he asked.

His father seemed surprised. "*Like* him?" he asked. "What does that have to do with anything?"

He squatted down beside the wheelchair. "Maybe a lot, maybe nothing. You know him."

"Then, let me see. Do I *like* him?" He pondered that question with his elbows on the wheelchair's arms. "You know my oldest friend is your godfather. He and Stanton and I were pals, back before time began. We did everything together, and Stanton always did it better. He ran faster, looked handsomer, swam deeper, jumped higher—you name it, he excelled at it. Always competing. Wellsy and I weren't sloughers, either. It was a pretty high level of competition. After a while, when we were all around sixteen or so, Wellsy and I got bored with Stanton's excellence. We dropped him from our list, and he went his own way, but he never stopped competing with us."

"You sound bitter."

"I do not like to lose, at anything. In that respect he and I and Cardinal Wells are alike."

"Did he play fair?"

He laughed louder than Barr remembered ever hearing him. "Stanton displayed a unique combination of talents, even back then. He was a terrible bully and a marvelously gifted kisser of hems. He could beat you over the head with one hand and make you feel good for the pummeling with the other. Did he play fair? Of course he didn't. We didn't either. We were all out to win. That was all."

"You haven't answered my question."

"*Do I like him?* No, frankly, I do not. Never have. That doesn't mean we haven't seen eye to eye on a few things over the years. It can happen, you know. Some acquaintances whom you know most of your life you may not even like, or you may hate. Put Stanton in that latter category for me, will you?"

"What kind of a person is he?"

"Oh, that's easy, but I'm surprised you haven't gauged that for yourself. He hardly hides who he is."

"I'm asking you."

"Okay, then. He's a man of many parts, a clever man, I'd say, with a reach that just exceeds his grasp. He has had to deal with rather venal types in his business, officials and politicians in Asian countries. He beat them at their own game, which says something about him in itself. He told me once that he learned his most valuable lessons in Asia. He lived in Hong Kong in an era of big building in the area. He got in with the Chinese. Some say he married one." He winked. "Don't say I told you that."

"Who did he do business with?" Barr asked. "Governments?"

That made his father chuckle. "In Hong Kong he would have had to befriend the real Chinese." He saw that his son didn't understand. "The underworld."

"Three Dots, the Three in One, the Wah Ching?" Barr asked, recalling the names from the court testimony.

"Whatever they are called," he replied. "Such groupings of people run Hong Kong like they run our Chinatown."

"Aren't you exaggerating their influence just a bit?"

"Why would you think that?"

"Because San Francisco has a mayor, and city hall, a council, and courts."

"Our Chinatown has *never* been San Francisco," his father said. "San Francisco is partly defined by it, but Chinatown is not defined by San Francisco. The distinction is important. But that's not what you are asking. You are asking about Stanton. And, as I was saying, he had to work with what was given to him. You see, the construction business, what I know of it, succeeds on the availability of local labor. Unscrupulous gangs are often in charge. In order for Stanton to get contracts in Asia he needed their approval." He was about to say more, but he hesitated.

"Go on, Dad. Talk to me."

"In the days when we were just leaving university, he was interested in your mother. I never told you that. He took her away from me. He wanted to marry her." His words sounded bitter and hateful, describing emotions that rubbed raw even after all this time.

Barr knew that his mother had been one of the beauties of her generation. But he knew nothing of her romantic life. "What happened?" he asked. "It sounds like you fought over Mom."

"It is a detail of history now—"

"That still matters."

"Feelings linger. She came back to me. Still, she went away."

"What did Mother think of him?"

"That isn't fair," his father said. "But I will tell you. She never trusted him." He breathed a long sigh; the effort of conversation was tiring him, and his voice was becoming as thin as a whisper. "She called him amoral. He had a knack, let's say. But still, even as an amoralist, he is capable of great kindness. He has contributed to the De Young Museum and the symphony. He helps without fanfare or recognition."

"In other words, he is devoted to the things he loves," Barr said.

"A contradiction?" asked his father, very wearily now. "For people your age, son, contradictions are a horror of nature. While among men my own age, contradictions are part of life."

"What about this Chinese wife he may or may not have had?"

"There were rumors, nothing ever confirmed. Stanton takes what he wants. His mitts are large and love to grasp."

"Flesh."

"Your word, not mine."

"Which would put him in competition with younger men."

"Youth and virility often battle power and concupiscence over the sexual favors of younger women. It will always be. Friend against friend, enemy against enemy, stranger against stranger."

"Father against son?"

The question unsteadied his grip. "We love our sons," he answered. "And yet which of us has not measured our own decline against their rise? In Stanton, I suspect, an unavoidable competitive spirit, shall we say, drove Karl away." He crossed his hands over his stomach, and his head rolled on his shoulders with fatigue. "As with all amorality there is always doubt, and where there is doubt there is hope. Stanton assumed a family role. You are right and you are wrong. What more can I tell you?"

How easy it was in a court of law, Barr thought, with its issues of black and white, innocence or guilt, right and wrong. In the real world these distinctions blurred into something he could not name and could hardly perceive, like ghosts, which frightened him still. In his short time on the bench he had witnessed no end of absolutes. The real world, he was discovering, was awash with conditionals.

"Can I tell you something else?" his father asked. Barr nodded. "Not everything can be explained. Not everything always adds up." He looked at him carefully. "No, you don't see. You can't *see*. You are too young. You see only a distortion of a reality. Do you know the Heisenberg principle?" Barr thought so but he wanted his father to explain. "In physics, it holds that the observation of subatomic particles alters what is observed. The very act of seeing changes what is seen, and therefore nothing can ever be seen for what it may be. You are only one person, son, now with Wally gone. You have only two eyes and two ears. Try to know everything and you will drive yourself mad. It's a common failure for us judges. Try to be satisfied with what you can find. Being hard on yourself won't bring you closer to the truth."

Frustrated, Barr asked, "And in a practical sense?"

"He who grasps the obstacles to understanding grasps the truth. In other words, make assumptions." A thin smile crossed his face.

For all his advice, his father had offered him nothing in a practical sense, at least nothing that he interpreted as a design he could work with. "Nice walking with you, Dad," he told him.

He walked him back to the Conservatory, where the male nurse was waiting. He handed his father over, and he was about to say good-bye, when his father held up his finger.

He said, "Your mother always warned me that I'd start to sound like that *Star Wars* character with the big ears."

Barr patted him on the arm saying, "How many sons are lucky enough to have a Yoda of their own?"

Rabindranath Tagore was an Indian born in India, and he explained to Barr that while he was named after the Nobel Prize–winning poet, he was of no relation to him. He wore wire-rimmed glasses across the breadth of a moon face with skin the shade of khaki, and his voice carried a singsong that was pleasing on the ear. His skin smelled of an exotic mix of sandalwood and rosewater and formaldehyde.

Barr sat opposite his cluttered desk. "Thanks for finding the time to see me on such short notice," he said.

He bowed. "You are a famous judge," he said. "I see your face on TV. I do wonder, though, why a superior court judge from San Francisco would inquire of a medical examiner in Alameda County. This is a matter of some discretion for us both, is that not so?"

"You read that right," said Barr, who upended a manila envelope on Tagore's desk. "I hope you don't mind the request for confidentiality."

"I am zipping my mouth right now," he said.

Barr had found Tagore with the help of Jack Toys, a friend of Barr's from Harvard who sat on the district court of appeals. He'd called Toys for a reference right after he had recessed court. He had asked Toys to give him someone who could advise him on forensics; he couldn't ask the ME's office in San Francisco. And Toys had suggested that he try Tagore. "He's chatty," he had said. "And he has an imagination that takes him beyond the facts. Besides, Dan, you'll like him as a person."

Tagore studied the photos of Holly's autopsy, and when he looked up Barr handed him a copy of the San Francisco ME's report. "I can't ask my own people about this," said Barr. "They might think I was, let's say, unappreciative." He came around to Tagore's side of the desk. "Now, tell me what you see here, on first glance."

Dr. Tagore slid a reading light over by his elbow. He adjusted his glasses and took a long time before saying, "Medical examiners don't have the time to prepare bodies for evaluation. That's left to assistant MEs." He showed Barr a photo of Holly's frontal area. She was laid out on a stainless steel autopsy table. "These are typical shots," he said. He stacked the photos in two piles. One showed the photos taken at the crime scene that established for the court the exact location where the body was found; the other showed the procedures in the forensic laboratory. He looked up at Barr. "I'm not certain what you want from me."

"Was this a normal autopsy, from what you can tell?" Barr asked.

"Not by my standards, it wasn't, no."

Barr drew in a breath with hope.

"Indeed, it was hardly an autopsy at all," Tagore said, and then he explained. "Normally, a Y-incision runs from the shoulders, here, to the center of the chest, here, and down the front of the body to the pubic bone. I do not see the Y-incision here. Do you see a Y-incision here?"

Barr shook his head. "I see a lot of wounds."

"Mostly centered around her abdomen."

"Where the Y-incision should have been?"

"There is so much mutilation of that area, one cannot say whether there was an autopsy or not."

"What's the purpose of this Y-incision?"

"Access," Tagore said. "Some ME's assistants make long incisions, some short, some with a curve, some not. Let me explain," and he leaned back in his chair and raised his glasses to his forehead. "We medical examiners have a single function. We establish for the district attorney scientific evidence that a crime was committed, the corpus delicti. How? Well, we look at the body. That's how. It is dead." He wasn't trying to be funny. "In this case, this person did not die of advanced age. We explain to the courts how the death occurred—by asphyxiation, for instance, which may mean strangulation; trauma to organs, which may have occurred by gunshot, stabbing, traumatic impact, or poisoning, among others too numerous to mention in a single breath. There are so many ways to murder. Over the centuries people have tried to hide their deeds by clever means. They desire to create the illusion of death by accidental or natural cause.

A blow to the head which kills may have been from a brick which fell from a building or from one used as a weapon in the killer's hand. You see? Our job as MEs is to describe the wound and its effect. The police and the prosecutors interpret that against the backdrop of other direct or circumstantial evidence. So, the first thing we do is look at the body. Then we go *inside* the body. We do that to examine the condition of the internal organs and for toxicological analysis—the presence of poisons in tissue, drugs, et cetera. We take tissue samples and biopsies or slices of organs for microscopic and chemical examination and analysis. We weigh the organs one by one as they are removed. Did you know that your pancreas weighs around thirty pounds?" He looked up at Barr, expecting an expression of interest, if not surprise.

"I didn't," said Barr, staring at the photos.

"Now, as to your question. To look at all these organs as the state requires in a wrongful death, we need to open up the corpse. The larger the incision we make, the greater access we have with our hands. Some assistants use a specific knife to make this Y-incision. Others use a regular scalpel. We use shears to cut through the cartilage in the sternum, and where needed we bring out a Stryker saw, and there are several variations of these. The next time you are cutting up a chicken, think of what we do."

Barr grimaced.

"When we sew up the corpse, sometimes we put the organs back in, sometimes we don't. It's a matter of whim and costs, really. When we are cutting costs, we put the organs back in, and when not, the medical waste company arrives with its truck and eventually takes them off and incinerates them. And finally the funeral home comes with a truck for the body once the family makes the arrangements. Before we send the body over, we stitch the Y-incision closed, once, twice, and that's that. Sometimes we don't even bother at all. The mortician applies the cosmetics before the body is interred. End of story, end of existence." He stacked up the photos on the desk in a neat pile.

"And you claim the San Francisco ME's office didn't *autopsy* this person?"

"I can't tell you what they intended," said Tagore. He picked up the copy of the ME's report, which he took time to read carefully. He looked up at Barr when he was finished, his face a blank. "You sure you've got the right set of photos here?"

"Definitely," Barr replied. He had taken them out of evidence himself. And there was no mistaking them as the ones he had seen in court.

"Then, what was written in this report and what these photos show don't match." Tagore pointed to the base of the abdomen in one of the photos. "It's like someone in the ME's office started an incision then decided not to bother. It would have been an odd place to start the examination anyway, there. Would you like me to show you why?"

Barr was staring again at these photos, and he could see in his mind's eye that willowy young woman wearing the bikini in the photo on the beach.

"I see you do not like to be around the departed," said Tagore. "It's quite normal. It's why my wife never lets me tell people what I do for a living. It leads to our having no friends. She spends a whole year making new ones, then I get tipsy and tell them what I do and we don't hear from them again. She starts over. It is a sad thing. People refuse to accept what I am— I am a physician. Instead of diagnosing the living, I diagnose the dead."

Barr nodded and cleared his throat. "Of course," he said.

"I do not usually comment on other coroners' work and I am not criticizing the San Francisco ME's expertise now," Tagore continued. "It's not my style. He is a good doctor and a professional friend, by the way. He is above reproach. His history speaks for him."

"But . . ."

"But we coroners are sticklers for detail, if nothing else. If we overlook a single detail in our work, we could miss the whole picture. A little secret? We live for an inconsistency which we can't explain. We are connoisseurs of the enigma. We, you and I, will get to the bottom of this little one, believe me."

He rummaged in his filing cabinet like a boar for truffles. He returned to his desk with the autopsy photo of a male laid out on his back—a young black man who was heavily muscled around the shoulders and upper chest.

"Gunshot," said Tagore, and ran his fingernail like a knife blade down the center of the man in the photo. "One starts the incision inside the shoulders, here, then cuts through the thick muscle wall down to the pubic bone. A steady pressure is what it takes, not finesse. It's why we turn the job over to less-well-trained assistants. This is not brain surgery." He looked up at Barr, then went on. "If you compare the incision in your photos of the woman with this photo, Judge, you will see that that cut was three or four inches, I would say. Maybe the assistant ME went to lunch or the bathroom and he forgot to continue what he was doing."

"Aren't you just being charitable?" Barr asked.

"Oh, it happens. He might even have left the knife in, like a ham you're carving when the doorbell rings. Don't think of it as suspicious. Phones ring and you have to answer them, your hand gets slippery with whatever, and you lose your grip, or you may find a blockage by a calcified organ, and then you leave it and forget."

"Have you ever seen anything like this before?" Barr pointed to the photographs of Holly Hawkes.

"Yes, I have, from time to time."

"Then, from time to time, what does it tell you?"

"What I just mentioned, of course: expedience, sloppiness, a job left undone, for whatever the reason."

"And something else, am I right?"

He shrugged. "Sometimes a cadaver is left untouched at the behest of the prosecutor's office, or the police, and the reason is obvious. Someone asked to stop the examination."

"But why would they?" Barr asked.

"Because an autopsy is a violation, a further indignity, that is hard for relatives to accept, because of their religion. Jews, for instance, do not want extended autopsies because of their burial practices. Hindus from my own country don't like autopsies either because of their interruption of the journey into the hereafter. Or, rather than religion, it could be because they do not want to know what they will find. In short, there can be many reasons." He held one of Holly's autopsy shots under the light. "This girl's body is clean of an ME's full incision. I would guess, therefore, that influence was brought to bear." He smiled at Barr. "Was this young woman a relative, Judge? A friend? I ask because there is nothing criminal or even wrong here. She was murdered, quite obviously, and, for reasons unexplained, the police thought that an autopsy would not help them to find her killer. Was there a witness to the crime?"

"In a sense," he replied, thinking of Winston Xiao-Yang.

"You see? I knew that was it." He breathed easier, and he looked at Barr, who did not look convinced. "You seem concerned, as though the deceased were one of your own family."

"I knew her," Barr said.

"You must be a very sympathetic man, a very nice man," Tagore said. "It is a nice thing to see, someone who cares about the dead." He looked again at the photos. "She looks young. A mere girl, wasn't it?"

"Holly Hawkes," Barr told him.

His eyes opened wide and he pushed the photographs back at Barr. "This is an oversight, then. Yes, definitely an oversight."

"I am in need of a nice quiet dinner *à deux*," Jenny said, getting in Barr's Porsche in front of BankAmerica's headquarters. With a sigh she added, "I could definitely use a glass of wine, candlelight, and thou."

He accelerated away. "And I don't have time for any of them. You don't either. How was your meeting?"

"Don't ask. What about you?"

"Something's screwy," he said, adding right away, "I don't know what, but something sure is."

"That's where I left off."

"Screwy with your boss, I mean."

She nodded as if she'd thought about it. "He was pretty cool, wasn't he? He's never popped in my office before. He's not a popper, if you get what I mean."

"I had the feeling he knew I was there."

"*And* where we had just come from." She looked straight ahead, thinking. "If you were he, wouldn't you have mentioned it at least? Like, asked, 'Why did you go to Colma? What are you trying to find out?' Why wouldn't he explain why he buried his granddaughter twice?"

"Because he doesn't need to," said Barr.

"Your appearance at the office had one effect," she told him. "Remember him saying he was flying to Washington. Guess what?"

"He isn't after all."

"He had some excuse, and he made a point of telling me." She stared thoughtfully into the distance.

A few minutes later they were walking through the security doors of the Thomas J. Cahill Hall of Justice on Bryant. Barr showed his ID to the duty-watch officer, and with a wave they were buzzed in. A steel door automatically pulled back along a metal rail, and a deputy behind bulletproof glass pointed them to a long row of cells. In the last one they found Feng Shao-li, sitting on the bed, his head down. He looked up at the grating of the cell door and at first did not acknowledge Barr, but he watched Jenny warily when she spoke to him in Cantonese.

Barr asked, "Do you mind if I talk with you?" He could not have known that Barr had a legal duty to notify Lovelace of this visit. He didn't care about those niceties now. "I want to help you," he told him. "But I need your cooperation."

Jenny translated, and Shao-li indicated nothing. He stared at Barr as though they were different species put together in a cage.

"It may save your life," Barr said.

Shao-li straightened up.

Barr told him, "I know that there is a gang war and you were out in the streets that night Holly Hawkes was killed." Shao-li still gave him neither affirmation nor denial.

When Jenny finished translating, Shao-li leaned forward, his elbows on his knees.

"Tell me what happened that night," Barr said. "Tell me the truth."

Without looking at either of them, Shao-li said, "I told the lawyer what happened."

"Then, tell us again."

His voice was almost a whisper and Jenny translated as he went along. "I was there, it is true. That night I was told there was a dead woman in the tunnel. If I went in there before the police found her I could rob her. I went in and I found her body. It was no big deal. I took her purse." He shrugged. "And that was all."

Barr knew that something was out of whack. "Who told you she was there?"

"One of my friends."

"Did you not wonder why your friend gave her to you to rob?"

He shook his head, as if it hadn't dawned on him until that moment. "He knew I needed money bad. He knew I'd do what I did."

"Was he a member of the gang, the Forty-nine Boys?" Barr asked.

"The leader," said Shao-li, through Jenny.

"And you were just another member?"

Jenny said, "He says no. He wasn't a member of the gang, Barr." And she listened to Shao-li carefully.

"I *wasn't* a member," Shao-li insisted, and then shook his head. "That is what I told my lawyer, but he never listened."

"Lovelace?"

"The translator was bad, bad."

Jenny held up her finger to stop him. "Hold it a sec," she said, then to Barr, "We'll have to go a little slower. I can understand the trouble with the translation, Barr. It's not easy. The tenses *was* and *is* and *would have been* and *were* are tough for me to get, and they're important."

"Please go on," Barr told Shao-li through Jenny.

"It is simple, really," he said. "I was removed as a member of the Forty-nine Boys. The leader told me I was not disciplined. You see, I had robbed some stores in Chinatown that the Forty-nine Boys were paid extortion money to protect. I didn't always do what the gang leaders told me to do. I couldn't. I had to get money."

Barr said, "But the leader of the Forty-nine Boys told you there was a body in the tunnel?"

"I was surprised, like he was helping me. I'd have robbed her anyway. And then I thought, why is the leader of the Forty-nine Boys telling me what to do? It must mean that I can become a member again."

"So you went in the tunnel. Did you see who murdered her?"

"No," he said straight, without hesitation. "She was already dead. She was lying there."

"And what did you do then?"

"I took her purse. I was scared. She was very bloody. I got her blood on my hands. She was chopped up. I did not like it one bit. I ran out of the tunnel."

"And Winston Xiao-Yang was waiting for you."

"He saw me, and I saw him," said Shao-li. "We almost ran into each other."

"Like he was waiting for you there?"

"He was standing there, yes."

"Were you ever offered a deal? Like, in exchange for a few years in prison your debts would be paid and the Forty-nine Boys would send your whole family over from Hong Kong?" Shao-li made no sign. "I'm trying to save your life," Barr said.

He smiled. "No deal, no. I would have taken it if the one you just described were offered."

Barr went over and held on to the cell bars. Of course Shao-li could still be lying. Indeed, it was even likely. And yet he had just described a frame-up by members of his former gang. But why frame him? No doubt Shao-li wasn't very bright. But ignorance did not imply guilt.

"She was a mess," Shao-li said through Jenny. And he held up his palms to show Jenny where the blood had been.

———

Barr stopped for a light at the main intersection of Van Ness and Market. He explained to Jenny that he wanted to go alone to Presidio Heights. He was waiting for her to ask to go along too—she was becoming a part of everything now—when a van came up behind them and slammed into the rear of the Porsche. The impact shoved the lighter car into the intersection, and the cars traveling east narrowly avoided them. Barr put the car in gear and pulled over to the curb by a bus stop.

The van, a purple Nissan Quest with a crumpled fender, pulled up behind them.

Getting out of his car Barr groaned, thinking this was not what he needed now.

Five men—all Chinese—climbed out of the van, and the instant they faced each other, they began to berate Barr in Chinese. Clearly, this was not a simple fender bender. Without a word, Barr turned back to the car, but a heavy hand on his shoulder restrained him, and he turned to face their shouting. He was nearly hunched with expectation and fear; he knew now that these were not Chinese who had run into him by mistake.

Jenny, however, wasn't as afraid; she did not know enough to be. She'd heard all the shouts, and when she came out of the Porsche she appeared almost unhinged by anger. Like a lioness protecting her cub she screamed at them, and her use of Chinese made them stare. They moved back to the Quest under the threat of her pointed finger.

"Don't you know," she told Barr, writing down the van's license number, "a little civility goes a long way."

As they drove off Barr noticed in his rearview that the van was following them.

"Those guys knew you," Jenny told him, and Barr gave her a surprised look. "One mentioned something about the judge—that's you. They had you marked."

"No kidding," Barr said. He speeded up. The van kept pace.

"What's the hurry?" asked Jenny.

He pointed his chin at the rearview mirror, and she turned around. He stepped harder on the gas. Still the Quest stayed behind them.

"What do they want?" she asked, fear tinging her voice.

Barr slowed down to find out. Suddenly, the van pulled even with them, then veered sharply into the Porsche, which scraped against a line of cars parked at the curb. Barr hit the brakes and the van flew past.

"They're going to *kill* us," Jenny screamed.

Barr made a quick U-turn in the middle of the block. He was afraid now and his mouth tasted like cotton. He and Jenny never agreed on issues of danger. This time they did. This vanload of thugs was trying to kill them by the bluntest of means. In the rearview he saw the Quest make a U-turn as well and head back toward them. When the driver saw that Barr wasn't accelerating, he too slowed down. The van was coming straight at them. It was going to ram them broadside. Barr gave the accelerator a spurt. The Porsche flew out of the van's way, and the Quest roared past, then slewed in the middle of the street and spun around. Relentlessly, it came at them again.

In that instant, Barr spied a black-and-white SFPD cruiser parked on the side of California Street in front of a New York pizza place, and he slipped the Porsche in front of the police car and slammed on the brakes. The van skidded to a stop. The men inside glared at them as they went slowly by, their faces in the windows implacable with anger. When they had gone, Barr pulled out again and headed west on California.

The terror of the incident was reflected in Jenny's eyes. "Are we going to be all right?" she asked him.

"I don't know," he replied.

———————

"Come in, Dan, please," Amelia said, meeting him at the door.

She wore the same look of exhaustion as before, and she did not show the least bit of surprise at seeing him. Indeed, he thought, it's almost as though she had expected him.

"You look preoccupied," she observed. "Is there anything the matter?"

"Jenny and I just nearly got killed," he said, then he told her what had happened.

"Do you know who these men were?" she asked with a look of genuine concern on her face.

"Chinese, that's all I know," he said. "As Wally said, it's all connected, Amelia—through and through. It started when I took your advice and visited Karl," he told her as he stepped inside.

"I gathered you saw him," she said.

"He guided me to Holly's grave."

"That was meant to remain a secret." She shrugged, as if she did not care one way or another anymore. "I gave Stanton my word. So did Karl, I thought. I just went along with what I thought Stanton already told you." She looked him in the eye. "But I'm glad you know." Then she broke into tears. After a moment, however, she regained her composure, and, as if she were angry with her emotions, she straightened her shoulders and looked Barr in the eye. She seemed to reach a decision about him, and she asked him to join her in the den, the room in which he had seen the portrait of Holly. She poured herself a drink and then turned to the portrait. "She should not be buried among those people," she said. "They are *not her kind*."

"She was *your* daughter," Barr pointed out.

"Oh, that is true, but in the end, Stanton gets his way," she said resignedly.

"Why would he do that?" he asked Amelia.

"It was his pleasure, that's why. There doesn't need to be any other reason."

"You know what I'm asking, Amelia."

"Oh, yes, *I* know, Dan." And she looked at him strangely. "You are asking more than you realize."

"And you know more than you are saying."

"A lot more, Dan, and I've told no one for good reason."

"Which is?"

"I'm afraid, *very* afraid. I'm a woman alone. I have no support, no one to defend me, no one to watch out for me." Then she stopped herself and shook her head, unwilling for now to go further. "You asked me why? Do you want to know what I think?"

"Very much," he said.

"Stanton buried Holly among the Chinese because it raises his stature among important people in Asia. It is his strength and a source of power. By burying his granddaughter according to their customs, he shows them that he returns their feelings. He'd probably tell you himself that it involves face."

"That word again. Yes, he went into that with me."

"Don't underestimate the strength of his belief in it," she warned him. "He lives by it. He would gladly die by it too."

"Beyond that, on another level?" asked Barr.

She seemed to ponder what she dared to say. "He wanted Holly's memory all to himself, and what better way to ensure that than to bury her according to customs that were strange to everyone else in the family?"

"He wanted her to himself? I don't understand."

"In *memory,* Dan."

"'Beloved'" is what is inscribed on her crypt. Did you know that, Amelia? Jenny translated it from Chinese."

"'Beloved,'" she said, testing the word. "'Beloved'?" She was surprised and angered. "I'm sorry. You'll have to explain. I know nothing of anything inscribed on her grave."

He told her about the crypt that was being built in the Chinese cemetery. Obviously, she had never gone there.

"The meaning confused Jenny," Barr told her. "Maybe you can tell me, Amelia. In Chinese Jenny said the word was reserved usually for a beloved wife or husband."

She looked outraged but she shook her head. And then, as if fear had frozen her anger, her shoulders slumped. "Holly is at peace, no matter where she is buried," she told him. "No matter what is written on her grave." She seemed about to say something more.

"Go on, Amelia, tell me. . . . What is it?"

She looked him in the eye. "After Holly's death, about a week, I guess it was, before the start of the trial, Stanton visited me here. It was about this time of late afternoon. I'd gone in the kitchen, and when I came back, the door to the den was closed. I heard him talking on the phone about the jury. . . ." At that moment, Amelia stopped talking. She looked over Barr's shoulder, and her expression changed from thoughtfulness to one of fear, hidden poorly behind the mask of a smile.

Stanton Hawkes was in the doorway, listening.

"Good evening, Judge," the senator said in a cautious voice. "We seem to be bumping into one another a lot lately." Then he looked at Amelia. "And good evening to you, Amelia. I let myself in." He held up a key. He smiled with his mouth but his eyes were narrowed with interest. "Did I overhear you discussing Holly, something about the trial?"

Barr seized the initiative. "I was asking Amelia why Holly was buried in Colma."

He nodded recognition. "The guard at the gate called my office. I knew you were there. Her burial is a matter strictly between me and my family."

"That doesn't stop me from asking, sir."

"Nor stop me from telling you that it's none of your business."

Barr decided that it was time for him to leave. "Thanks, Amelia," he told her, looking at Senator Hawkes. "I'll be in touch."

"I'm not going anywhere," she told him pointedly. "I'll be right here."

Senator Hawkes watched them, back and forth, suspicion and confusion mixing in his eyes.

Chapter Twelve

In court the next morning, expectation filled the air. It was always that way on the final day of a trial, with the jurors able to foresee their normal lives resuming, and the public and press excited to have their opinions matched against the jury's findings.

In his summation, prosecutor Shenon touched each point of his case, and the wall of evidence and testimony was solid.

"Put these elements together, ladies and gentlemen—the *opportunity* to commit the crime of which the defendant is accused, the *motive,* and the *means.* Those are all the law requires for the state to prove its case. The defendant, Mr. Shao-li, set out to rob the victim. Something happened that upped the stakes. We'll never know what it was. A scream. A call for help. It might have been that a witness like Winston Xiao-Yang intruded on the scene. The defendant struck Holly Hawkes with a knife until she was dead, and then he fled with her belongings. No other facts should enter your deliberations. And armed with these facts, I know you will do the right thing. You will allow justice to be done. You will vote to convict. Thank you."

Barr was taken aback by the brevity of Shenon's statement; he looked at his watch. He thought he would have part of this day, but it wasn't going to be so. He looked over at the jurors, knowing that after this morning he would lose control of them forever and the killer would be gone. He went from one face to another. He knew them all now with a certain familiarity. He knew them, and he did not know them.

A moment later, Lovelace began his oration.

"You can't find my client guilty," he pleaded in a voice louder than necessary. "You just can't, ladies and gentlemen. Why? Because there is a reasonable doubt. The prosecution talks about opportunity and so on. Reasonable doubt is all the defendant has to show. No one the night that Holly Hawkes died could see their hands in front of their faces. Pea soup. Remember? So how was the defendant seen? And where is the murder weapon? Do you believe that the defendant did such a good job of hiding the knife that the best efforts of the SFPD couldn't find it, yet he kept the victim's purse in his room? Ladies and gentlemen, ask yourselves, 'Isn't there something off center about all this, something not quite right?' The victim's mother testified that the victim always wore a necklace with a gold locket that her grandfather gave her. She cherished it. She NEVER took it off. The night she died it was neither seen nor found. The next morning when the police searched the defendant's room and found the victim's purse, they did not find the victim's locket and necklace. Strange? Reasonable doubt? Are the police pulling the race card here? Did they plant the evidence of the purse and only the purse because the purse was all that they found? Reasonable doubt. A single reasonable doubt is all you need. I know you will find the defendant innocent. That's all I have to say."

Barr waited until Lovelace was seated. Then he called a recess.

Back in his chambers, he dialed Amelia's number, but still got no answer. He had tried her all last night, and the response was always the same—an answering machine that by now was filled with his repeated messages for her to call him. She had said pointedly that she was going nowhere, but she had gone somewhere she had not expected to go.

Miss Hamish came in. "I've tried all morning, Judge," she told him. "No one, not even a maid, answers."

Back in court after the recess, Barr began his last address to the twelve people who would decide Feng Shao-li's fate.

"It's my duty now to charge you before you are sent out to deliberate upon a verdict," he told them. "I hope you will listen to my charge carefully. Once you go out, I cannot sit with you. I cannot listen in to what you say. I can advise you, beyond what I am telling you now; a bailiff will stand outside the door to ensure your privacy, even from me, but if you have questions he will bring them to me. This is my last chance to instruct you on how to reach a verdict."

He referred to a boilerplate "pattern instruction for jurors." The pattern prevailed in every instance, in every trial, no matter what the crime. He explained in detail what they needed to prove in order to return "alternative verdicts"— murder one, second-degree murder, and manslaughter. The jury, he told them, could return a verdict of guilty to the ultimate charge of felony murder or to a lesser charge, or a verdict of not guilty. He advised them on how to weigh the credibility of the witnesses through their testimonies, and, after a lengthy description of the "arc of evidence," he defined the meaning of an informed verdict rather than one based on emotion and unrelated issues.

His penultimate charge defined the "elements of proof." He gave them a list of what Shenon had to have proved beyond a reasonable doubt in order for them to convict.

"Reasonable doubts," he told them, "cannot be defined by this court. You have all been raised in a society based on the rule of right and wrong. There is inbuilt in each one of you a sense of right and wrong. It takes no genius, no special religion, and no education to know the differences. If there is a reasonable doubt, a little voice in your head will whisper to you, 'It might not have happened the way the state says it did.' Why? Maybe because the arc of evidence has given you a reason. You should talk about your doubts among yourselves. Remember, this deliberation is between you and your humanity, your conscience, your experience and learning, your character—between you and who you are."

His oration bordered on the philosophical, but it was only common sense. He was telling them to let their consciences be their guide.

"I want you to listen carefully to what I have to say next," he continued. "You are deciding a man's freedom. Remember that." He paused for half a minute. "Finally, the defendant is innocent before the law unless or until you deliver to this court a unanimous vote of guilty."

He looked over the entire scene—at the spectators staring at him, the counselors, the defendant, and then back again at the jurors. Then, with a final tap of his gavel, he dismissed the court, watching the jurors leave toward a conclusion he could not have imagined.

"Of course, they're being sequestered," Barr told Lovelace and Shenon in his chambers after the court was dismissed. Needlessly, he added, "They're always sequestered at this stage."

"For the length of their deliberations," said Lovelace.

"It's none of my business," said Shenon, "but that won't take but a few minutes."

"Now, Mr. Shenon," Lovelace said. "That's enough of your opinion."

Shenon looked like he wanted to argue with Lovelace, and might have had Ben Bowers not come in with Miss Hamish by his side.

Barr dismissed the counsels with a word and addressed himself to particulars. "I want you to inform the sheriff's office to escort the jurors home after they've deliberated today," he told Bowers. "Assuming they don't come in with a verdict by then, they'll pick up their personal belongings. You know the drill. Pajamas, toothbrushes, books. They'll be taken to the Westin St.

Francis in Union Square, where they'll be sequestered." He turned to Miss Hamish. "You know who to call, what to do, to set it up, right?"

"Yes, judge, the procedures are all written down," Miss Hamish replied.

She was referring to a pattern of details for sequestration. The court needed to hire vans to transport the jurors, to inform the hotel, to organize food, to get the Sheriff's Department up and running to guard them — in short, all the things that people do in their everyday lives had to be replicated within the confines of sequestration.

Barr stood up. "Okay, let's get moving."

It was afternoon when, worn with worry over Amelia, Barr drove out to Presidio Heights. As he parked the car he looked out over the waters of the bay. The view was glorious and the fresh sea air that blew up from the bay invigorated him. Even from the heights, the white hull of the *Mandarin* loomed in the far distance.

The flowers in the garden looked cheerful; a gardener was backing a lawn mower up a trailer in the driveway. Barr went to the door and rang the bell. When no one answered, he stepped across the lawn and looked up at the windows. The house seemed quietly forlorn. Then, down the driveway, he noticed a Lexus and a Mercedes in their garage bays. Around the back at the corner of the house, he came face-to-face with the gardener.

"Do you know if Mrs. Hawkes is at home?" he asked the man.

He wore a muscle T-shirt and he pushed back a hank of hair. "Mrs. Hawkes?" he asked. "There's someone in the kitchen."

Barr climbed the back stairs and knocked on the door. He could see a woman through the glass; she was eating a bowl of cereal. At the sound of rapping she looked up and came to the door. He was disappointed that it wasn't Amelia.

"I'm looking for Mrs. Hawkes," he told her. By the look of her uniform, it was Amelia's maid. And he told her his name.

"I'll tell her when she gets back," she told him.

"Do you know where she went?"

"She left last night, right before dinner. She didn't say anything about where she was going. She didn't even pack a bag. But she didn't come home again. She must have just picked up and left. She was with the senator."

"If she calls," Barr told her, handing her his card, "make sure she gets this."

The jury room offered few distractions. There was a blackboard and twelve chairs around an oak table. That was all.

But the jurors seemed unaware of this spareness. The responsibility of the task ahead excited them. Their real duty was beginning.

After they had taken seats around the table according to their jury numbers, their first task was to elect a foreman. Daniel Gee, the Chinatown restaurateur, asked if anyone wanted to volunteer. At first, no one spoke up. Then Michael Eng raised his hand.

"Anyone else?" Gee asked.

Claire Hood raised her hand. "I might as well give us a choice," she said almost apologetically.

"Do either of you have anything to say on your own behalf?" Gee asked them.

Eng clasped his hands on the table. "Only that I'll try to make sure we don't deadlock," he told them.

The other eleven looked at him, wondering what he meant.

"I don't want to see all our effort wasted for nothing. I'll see to it that we either convict or acquit the defendant. I won't let us give up, if it comes to that."

"Ms. Hood?" Gee asked.

She looked around at their faces. "I just think we should listen to our consciences, like the judge said. If that means we don't reach a unanimous verdict, then so be it. I'll only try to make sure that we do our best."

They voted with a show of hands. Eng was their foreman.

He said, "I think we should take a straw vote right now to see how far apart we are. Can I see a show of hands, first, for a conviction?"

"Wait a minute," said Claire Hood. "I don't think this is how we should do it." She challenged Eng with a look. "I agree about a straw vote, but can't we make the vote secret?"

"If it's secret," asked Adam Warmath, "how can we know who is in the minority?"

"Anyone have an answer to that?" asked Eng. The jurors looked at each other. "Okay, let's do this one in secret. Maybe we'll take the next vote with a show of hands." He passed around pieces of paper, and when they had balloted, he collected them and asked Mrs. Garriques to count them. She made two piles.

"Ten to convict, two to acquit," she reported.

"We're closer than I thought," said Eng. "Okay, then, what are the unresolved questions?"

Claire Hood spoke up. "What bothers me is the difference between the motive and the nature of the crime. I mean, why would a killer like Shao-li, who set out to rob Holly Hawkes, kill her the way the prosecutor said he did? It makes no sense to me. He might have accidentally killed her for the purse. But why would he do what those police photos showed that he did? That's no accident. Can anyone tell me?"

"I agree," said Mrs. Cohen.

"Me too," said Mrs. Garriques, and a couple of other jurors nodded.

"Maybe she angered him," Jesse Coffer said.

"To the extent that he would do *that* to her?" Claire asked. "Not for a purse."

Mrs. Garriques was nodding.

"Look, Ms. Hood," said Eng. "If you are trying to find a reason to acquit the defendant . . ."

"It's not that," she said adamantly. "I'm trying to be fair."

"You can always find a reason why the defendant might *not* have done what he did," said Adam Warmath. "We can never know the killer's thoughts. The defendant did not testify."

"What other points don't we agree on?" Eng asked.

"I'd like to talk more about the motive," said Daniel Gee.

"What is there to say?" asked Warmath. "He took her purse."

"Isn't that where we can see room for a reasonable doubt?" asked Mrs. Garriques. "He did not take her locket."

"This is a man's life we are judging here," said Mrs. Cohen.

They deliberated back and forth for the better part of two hours, but had gotten no closer to a unanimous verdict. They were about to take another secret vote when a bailiff came in.

"That's all for today, folks," he told them. "Gather up your belongings. We'll be going downstairs to the vans in a few minutes."

"Give us another minute, will you?" said Eng.

The bailiff looked around the room, and when he saw that none of the jurors objected, he said, "Okay, five minutes."

When they were alone again, Eng told them, "We don't have to spend the night in a hotel. I mean, we can finish this up here and now."

"Let's take one more vote," said David Figueroa.

"For the sake of expedience, why don't we just show hands?" Eng said.

"I'll say again, I don't think that's how we should do it," Claire said.

"Who believes the defendant is guilty?" Eng asked, ignoring her protest.

Claire stared at him in anger. "Don't raise your hands," she told the others.

Eng hit the table with his fist. His face was livid. He took a couple of seconds to gain control of himself, but his fury was obvious.

The bailiff poked his head in the doorway. "Everything all right in here?" he asked.

Claire pushed back her chair. "I don't think you realize," she told Eng. "We are voting on a man's life."

He looked at her, his eyes alight with rage. "I do realize, Ms. Hood," he told her. "I most certainly do."

The assistant manager of the Westin St. Francis came out of a back office and walked across the carpeted lobby past a crowd of tourists. "Your Miss Hamish organized things nicely," he told Barr. Shaking his hand, he introduced himself by name as Bob Preston. "I suppose you're here to check on things," he said. "Well, we have everything pretty much taken care of. Per Miss Hamish's instructions, we've restricted the cable available on the televisions. The jurors can watch movies if they want, but none of the news programs. Likewise, the newspapers will be censored each morning by the sheriffs. The Gideon's Bibles and the books they bring with them are all they will have to read."

"And the telephones?" Barr asked.

"Pacific Telesis is working on that," he said. "Come on, I'll show you."

They went into a room behind the hotel's central reception desk where there were three women at switchboards wearing telephone headsets. A technician was working on a circuit box at the far side of the room. "He's splicing the room phones on the fourth floor to a line that the sheriffs will monitor from this office," Preston explained.

The technician looked around. "It's not a problem," he told the manager. "I'll be finished in a few minutes."

"It's an interesting challenge," Preston told Barr. "We haven't done this in some time."

Next, they rode the main elevators to the fourth floor. A sheriff's deputy had positioned a desk by the side of the doors. He had a clear view down the whole length of the hall.

"Are the jurors all present and accounted for, Deputy?" Barr asked him.

"The last one got here a few minutes ago," he replied.

"Is anyone else staying on this floor?" Barr asked the manager. Preston nodded. "The other guests won't get in the way."

Barr checked the room assignments, then thanked the manager and walked down the hall. He knocked on a door, and a minute later Claire Hood appeared. She seemed surprised to see him, but a wary expression quickly turned to a warm smile.

"Would you like to come in?" she asked, stepping back.

He shook his head. "I'm just checking to see that you are comfortable," he told her.

She leaned against the doorsill. He noticed that she was wearing the hotel's terry-cloth bathrobe. She clasped the lapels at her throat.

"How did it go this afternoon?" he asked her.

She looked nervously up and down the hall. "There was tension. Jesse Coffer looks at me like *I* was on trial. Mrs. Garriques, she's an ally. And the others . . . well. Michael Eng is a bully. I think there is a reasonable doubt. Most of the others don't."

"It's your right to hold out," he told her. "Nobody can force you." But he knew better; he wanted the killer to force the issue. He wanted him to force it on Claire Hood.

"Michael Eng insisted on a show of hands."

"Oh?"

"He tried to make us," she told him. "He's our foreman. He doesn't want a deadlocked jury. He told us so himself. He was incredibly angry. In the van on the drive over here he asked me what proof I needed. He said he was there to help me."

Barr smiled at her. "You're doing fine," he said. He looked at his watch.

"Mrs. Cohen invited some of us by her room later for pizza." She glanced up at Barr. "Will you visit again?"

He was uncertain of what to say. "Visit? Yes, I will," he said.

Barr walked the short distance from Union Square to the Mark Hopkins on Nob Hill, where Jenny and his father were waiting for him in the main downstairs dining room.

"Congratulations," his father told him.

Barr didn't think he had earned anyone's congratulations. "What for?" he asked.

"It's customary," his father pointed out.

"We still don't have a verdict," he said as he sat down. "And I still don't know who the killer is. Either he gets a conviction of Feng Shao-li, or if the jury deadlocks, he goes his own way. I will never see him again. He can now do pretty much what he pleases."

"So your juror has gotten away with murder," said his father. "Ask one of the other jurors to hold out."

"I can't *order* anyone to do that," Barr said. "But that's what I'm doing. That's what I'm hoping for, Dad. But I can only hope."

Barr looked across the room. The maître d'hôtel was pointing someone to their table, and Barr saw that it was a deputy sheriff. He pushed back his chair and greeted him with a surprised look.

He was out of breath. "We've been looking everywhere for you, Judge," he said. "Ben Bowers says it's important to find you."

With just a glance at his father and Jenny, Barr was on his way.

"I must sound like I'm always offering apologies," said Bowers when Barr rushed into the clerk of the court's office.

"Tell me," said Barr, mentally bracing himself for what he had to say.

"I was just going to ask you the same," Bowers said.

"Come on, Ben," he said irritably. "You sent the deputies to find me."

"You asked me to run the names of the jurors through INS and DMV."

"And? What did you find?"

Bowers chuckled softly. "Calm down, sonny," he said. "The INS was a wash. That much was true. They had nothing to offer. That took time."

"And?" he asked.

"Next, the DMV. They couldn't understand the mix-up. They brought in their computer people. They had *them* take a look, and they said they'd been hacked—that's a new term, Dan . . ."

"I know, Ben, I know," he said impatiently. "Tell me what happened."

"They ran a check on your list of jurors. Each of them has a valid current California driver's license. That checked out. They found nothing unusual until later, when they checked the names in their full database."

"What the hell does that mean?" asked Barr.

"It means they checked not just whether the jurors have licenses. They checked to see whether there was documentation that supported each of the issued licenses. I guess it included where and when each one them took their driver's and written tests."

"And?"

"Nothing appeared in the database for Michael Eng."

Now confusion tempered Barr's excitement. He was trying to get this straight. "Michael Eng has a driver's license, doesn't he? What more is there?"

"Dan, he never took the tests. And if he didn't take the tests, he couldn't have a valid, *legal* license."

"So, what was his name doing on the jury-pool list?"

"The DMV thinks that somebody hacked into their computers. Somebody put Eng's name on the list of the jury pool that comes from DMV. But that same somebody didn't have time to put in the background data on the full database, or they couldn't find a way to access it. They just didn't have time or the knowledge that was needed to do the job right."

Barr took a moment to think. Wally was killed before he had

a chance to check the jurors' names against the DMV's computer files. But Wally had pointed him that way. Now, almost by mistake, Wally had found the killer. Barr asked to be sure, "And DMV is positive about this?"

"Yup. The one you're looking for, Danny, is Michael Eng."

The sheriff's car with Barr inside braked under the iron portico in front of the Westin St. Francis. In the next few seconds, other police cars pulled up and deputies got out. The whine of sirens in the distance grew nearer as more police cars converged on the hotel.

The manager, Bob Preston, met him in the lobby.

"Has anyone checked his room?" Barr asked.

"I called the deputy on duty in the hall. He said the jurors were all in one room. They are having a party. A pizza delivery guy just arrived."

Barr asked him to bring a house key card. Then, with a couple of the sheriff's deputies accompanying them, they took an elevator to the fourth floor.

Down the hall they could hear the sounds of laughter coming from Mrs. Cohen's room. The door was ajar, and when Barr went in, followed by the deputies, everyone became suddenly quiet. Claire Hood was there too. "Was Michael Eng here earlier?" he asked Mrs. Cohen.

"Yes, but he said he was tired," she told him. "He went back to his room about a half hour ago."

The manager opened the door to Eng's room. Barr felt a cool breeze blowing through the open door. Across the room, the sheer window curtains billowed in the breeze. Barr switched on the light and moved inside. Eng had disturbed nothing in the room, as if he had not planned to spend the night, no matter what. He had not hung clothes in the closet. The bathroom sink was clear.

Barr craned out the opened window and looked down an iron fire escape into a dank alley. He did not know how Eng had known to run. All that mattered now was that he was gone. And that he had to find him.

———

Stubbornness and frustration compelled Barr to look with his own eyes, which strained through the dimming light to see into the face of every Chinese who went past him along Chinatown's Grant Street. The police were out looking, but their ability to search was limited here. He listened to unfamiliar sounds of singsong voices; a grating music played somewhere out of sight. He smelled the aromas of unfamiliar foods. His ignorance about the place made him feel alien and alone, and vulnerable.

On Waverly Place, a block-long street of Chinese benevolent associations, sweatshops, stores, and restaurants, Barr leaned up against a wall. Where he was standing was the heart of Chinatown, a byway with an infamous past for gambling, bordellos, and opium dens. Across the street he noticed a sign for the Sue Hing Benevolent Association; above was a Buddhist temple. Men and women in quilted jackets walked past on their way home from work carrying plastic shopping bags heavy with vegetables. From a room above where he was standing came the clatter of men shuffling mah-jongg tiles, joined by the background hum of the machines in a sewing factory.

An early fog was descending on Chinatown, and Barr felt a sudden chill. He looked at his watch, knowing he should leave the search for Eng to the SFPD.

Suddenly, from out of nowhere, he was surrounded by a group of young Chinese men, and when he stopped walking, two of them grabbed his arms. He started to complain, but he knew it was useless; besides, he was interested to see what they would do. They did not threaten him. They said nothing to him.

What intrigued him—and kept him from shouting for help—was that they led him quickly through one back alley after another, obviously with a specific destination in mind. They stopped in front of a building that had gilded dragons over the doors like the ones that he had seen on the cemetery gate in Colma. Police, all heavily armed and dressed in SWAT armor, stood by the doors like members of an invading army.

Clearly, the Chinese man who met him was terrified. He led Barr down a long, dimly lit corridor that was crowded with other young Chinese men. All were expressionless as they watched him pass.

At the end of the corridor he entered a large room in which fifteen or so young Chinese sat on chairs and broken-down sofas. They were smoking cigarettes and playing cards, and they looked up, watchful and wary. At the sight of Barr they stamped out their cigarettes, and without a sound they picked up rifles and automatic weapons that were leaning against the walls and filed out a back door.

Barr noticed that one man in the room did not leave with the others.

He looked, then stepped closer with an awkward fascination. The man was dead, his body laid out on a long table on one side of the room. The corpse bore atrocious gunshot wounds and his blood pooled under him and dripped to the floor. Barr took a breath and then looked at the door through which the young men had just left. Standing there now was Chief Dunstan. He wore no expression. He neither smiled nor frowned. He seemed intrigued, if anything, by the circumstances—them meeting in a place like this in front of a Chinese casualty.

Chief Dunstan pointed to the naked body on the table. "I wanted to speak a little reason with you, Judge. Consider this chat to be a charity of mine. I like to help reasonable men to find reason."

"I'm listening, Chief."

"Let me give you an important lesson. It does matter to the

dead what happens to the killer. What matters is that the deceased's memory is honored."

"A question?" Barr asked.

Chief Dunstan stepped into the room. "Be my guest."

Barr's anger showed when he asked, "You didn't even *try* to find the juror, did you? His name, by the way, is Michael Eng."

"Judge, you are too young to understand that higher laws have their courts too. SFPD does its utmost to serve this city. None does better. Sometimes we succeed; sometimes we fail. And where we fail sometimes we also succeed according to this higher court. Everyone wins, no matter what. Everyone that matters, Judge Barr. To coin a phrase, to get along you must go along."

Barr did not know what to say. "That's not how I operate, Chief."

"There is a war on," he stated simply, as if to explain himself better. "There is fighting between the Chinese and *only* the Chinese."

"What was Wally?" Barr asked.

"He got in the way. This was not about him. It is strictly not our concern. And even if it were, we are lost here. This is not about the city of San Francisco. This is not about you, either, Judge Barr. I am trying to save your life."

Barr pointed to the corpse. "That dead man is a casualty of this war?"

Chief Dunstan glanced distractedly at the body. "Most nights two or three are killed," he said.

"How many *civilian* casualties like Wally has this war produced?" Barr asked almost cynically.

"No one is counting," said Dunstan.

"Was Holly Hawkes one of them?"

He looked surprised, and then he sighed. "You have stumbled across a revolution, Judge. That is what we wanted you to know. Hong Kong. 1997. A shift in power started this war. The fighting spread to Singapore and Taipei before it arrived here. It is going on in New York and London."

"Where does Senator Hawkes fit in this war? He is involved, am I right?"

He nodded. "To an extent," he said. "The senator has affiliations in Asia."

"We're talking about San Francisco's Chinatown."

"Here too."

"He has ties to the gangs fighting this war, correct?"

"He has thrown his weight behind one of the sides in the conflict," said the chief.

Barr asked outright, "Is Senator Hawkes the Dragon Head?"

Dunstan had to think what to say about that. "The Chinese make mysteries of nothing at all. I understand that it's in their nature. My friend Stanton Hawkes has enemies in Chinatown. They killed Holly in order to wound him. Holly flew close to the flame. That night she was killed, she was in the wrong place at the wrong time. A tragedy."

Barr was not convinced. "And you are still going to tell me that Feng Shao-li was the killer?"

The chief looked at him, wondering what to say. "No," he said.

"Then you framed Feng Shao-li?"

He shook his head. "Me? No. Not strictly speaking, I didn't. The SFPD stayed out of it. Chinatown framed him. We needed a defendant. That much is true. We had to go full circle. We couldn't have left the murder unresolved. Too many questions, a celebrated victim—it wouldn't have done. The circle is now closed. Everyone is satisfied."

"Except for me." Barr felt disgusted, and he shook his head, looking again at the naked corpse.

"Now you know the secrets," said the chief.

"If I know everything, then why do I still feel like I know *nothing*?"

The chief turned to leave. "Come on, Judge," he said, opening the door. "We have lives to live."

Trying to leave Chinatown, Barr got lost.

He made his way to the end of the street, stopping for a minute at the door of the Golden Gate Fortune Cookie factory. He was about to ask an elderly woman the directions to Grant Street, but he realized she wouldn't understand English. For a minute he watched her remove the baked circles of dough from small griddles and, by hand, insert paper strips of fortunes into each. He had lived in this city all his life too. He shook his head and continued walking.

As he went past a herb emporium, he hesitated just a half-step. In that instant he saw a face and he almost mouthed the name.

Eng saw him and ran into the building with a deliberateness that frightened Barr with the thought that he was being led into a trap. The emporium owner and his wife stood up straight behind a counter and watched in fearful silence as Eng went out the back door while Barr shouted for him to stop, then shouted for someone to help him.

He followed him out the back door into the fading light. Eng turned his head before vaulting a low barrier over a narrow walkway between two brick buildings. An instant later, Barr went over the wall and scraped along the walkway, as Eng, just ahead of him, ran into Washington Street.

Barr would have lost him there if everyone else in the street wasn't either walking slowly or standing still. Eng was running, and Barr saw him turn into an alley that ended with a wall. When Barr got there, Eng was nowhere to be seen. The iron fire escapes clinging to the sides of the buildings were hung with drying clothes and birdcages and potted plants. A sign for the Rainbow Anne Sewing Company spluttered neon light into the gathering darkness. Barr edged forward past the doorway of a benevolent association, where a group of elderly Chinese men huddled over a mah-jongg game. The door was iron mesh, and when he rapped his fist on its frame, the players looked up at him, then back at their game again, as if he were invisible.

Next door, Bo Bow's had a small neon sign with a glowing martini glass and a bright green olive. Inside, the bar was nearly empty. The burning cigarette of the woman behind the bar rolled out of an ashtray, while doubt and fear registered on her face. Barr went over to her, and she cocked her head in the direction of a side room, where a group of musicians was setting up drums and electronic amplifiers.

Barr had no more than turned into the room when he felt himself being pulled backward, an excruciating pain around his neck. Eng's arm came around with a knife in his fist and began slashing at him with thrusts. Barr dropped down with his full weight and threw Eng off balance, and the two men struggled on the floor. Eng slashed the knife back and forth. Barr caught his wrist and held on, turning it over until Eng dropped the knife. Holding his wrist, Barr saw the web of Eng's hand: Eng carried the same gang tattoo as Feng Shao-li and the other 49 Boys, as well as the crew of Senator Hawkes's *Mandarin*.

Eng punched Barr in the face, then, with both fists balled, pounded his chest, knocking the wind out of him. The ceiling above Barr started to spin. Eng hit him again and again before leaning over to reach for the knife.

Barr heard an explosive sound. One of the musicians struck Eng with an instrument. Barr pushed Eng away, and someone shouted in Chinese. The woman at the bar screamed for help. Eng was standing up over Barr, looking around the room. Then, without warning, he turned and ran out of the bar.

Less steadily than before, Barr followed him into Commercial Street, which narrowed as it sloped down a hill toward the Chinese Cultural Center. At the moment that Barr thought he might catch up with Eng, a large crowd of Chinese poured out of the doors of a theater under a bright marquee, and Eng disappeared in the throng. Barr pushed from one Chinese to another, looking in their faces, but he knew he had lost him.

Minutes went by. And when all the audience had filtered out of the theater and headed off, Barr was standing alone.

———————

Jenny was sitting in a circle of light on Barr's front porch. She looked up at the sound of his footsteps on the slate steps. He sat down and put his arm around her, and she leaned into him comfortably.

"Eng got away," he told her, and when she turned to look at him, he explained what had happened.

"What will you do now?" she asked.

"I'll declare a mistrial tomorrow. Feng Shao-li will be released." He looked into the night.

"It's over?" she asked.

He laughed quietly and without humor. "It's not *over*, Jenny. But I just do not know where to turn anymore for answers to the questions that won't go away."

"You just told me that there is a gang war. That explains everything, doesn't it?"

"That's what Chief Dunstan hopes."

"If Holly was not killed in the gang war, then, how?"

"It doesn't add up."

"And yet it forms a sort of tally."

"A *Chinese* tally," he said.

"Now *I* don't understand," said Jenny.

"You just said this gang war explains everything. A war is going on. It is real. But I believe it was used as a smoke screen, Jenny. Wally and Holly Hawkes were not victims of war. They were murdered. Deliberately tracked down and murdered."

"Wally was killed because he was on to Eng."

"Because of Holly. That's what I think."

"But Michael Eng is a member of the Forty-nine Boys," said Jenny.

"And the senator controls them. He's their Dragon Head."

"What you are saying, Barr, is that he ordered one of his sol-
diers to murder his own granddaughter? Please. It just can't be."

"That's what I think."

"Then, tell me *why*? Why would he do that?"

He kissed her on the cheek. "We'll never know," he said with
a shrug. He stood up a moment later, stretched his arms, and
gazed at the moon. He was trying to shake off the emptiness of
defeat that overwhelmed him.

He was going into the house when Jenny said, "I forgot to tell
you. Just before you got back, a few minutes ago, a woman
called." She handed him a piece of paper. "I wrote this down.
She wouldn't tell me her name." She saw the look on his face.
"What's wrong?"

"What did she sound like?" asked Barr.

"Hurried. She said if you didn't get this, to tell you good-bye
for her."

He left the Spyder in the unloading-only zone and ran inside.
The number for the Alitalia flight to Rome blinked on the de-
partures board beside the gate number. At the metal detector
some guy in front of him wore a ring of keys. A security officer
was scanning him; he wasn't letting anyone else through.

They had closed the flight by the time Barr reached the gate.
An Alitalia ticket agent was locking the ramp door. When Barr
showed her his ID and told her what he wanted, she called air-
port security. Only seconds later Barr was explaining his story
while the Boeing 747 was preparing to pull back.

The Alitalia attendant called the cockpit, and the airplane's
door was opened for him. Moments later Barr ran down the
ramp. Aboard the airplane, he turned toward first class. Amelia
was sitting against the bulkhead beside a man with silver hair.

Barr looked at her, and the sight of him made her stifle a
scream. The man sitting beside her turned to him, surprised and
angry. And only then, Barr saw he was a stranger.

"Will you come off with me, Amelia?" Barr asked her.

She had been crying. Reluctantly, she gathered up her belongings. She allowed him to take her elbow.

Barr said, "I thought for a minute that was Stanton."

Her eyes widened with renewed fear. "I am running from him. I was afraid he would follow me. I had to get away. He forced me—"

"I've been trying to call you since yesterday," he said.

"Stanton forced me to leave the house," she told him. "I couldn't call you." She looked away. "We all are afraid of him. His son is, I am, Holly was."

"But why?"

"Because when he is through with you there is nothing left."

"But why did he take you away? And why are you running away from him now?"

She shook her head. "He warned me not to speak to anyone. It's a warning I'd be foolish to ignore."

"What is it that you know, Amelia?"

"I *know* nothing, Dan. That's the truth. Don't you see? I can *prove* nothing." She seemed exasperated by his lack of understanding.

"I know who killed Holly," he said. And he explained. He was taken aback by her reaction, which he had not expected at all.

"You think that's all?" she asked him. "You think that's all?"

He shook his head. "You have to help me if it isn't."

"It is too dangerous. Stanton warned me. Many people have died. I don't want to be one of them. I have to watch out for myself."

"Okay," he said. "Where is he now?"

She shook her head. "I don't know. I don't *want* to know."

"Where did he take you?"

"To that boat of his. He's leaving tonight for Asia."

He helped her up from the chair. "Until this is over, Amelia, stay with me and Jenny. You'll be safe with us."

She shook her head. "You haven't been listening to me, Dan Barr. There is a last flight tonight—to Paris. I'll be on it."

"But—"

"You don't get it, Dan. You just don't get it. This is evil like you've never even heard of." Then she turned resolutely away.

———

Barr was driving back to San Francisco when the cell phone in the Porsche rang. He thought it would be Jenny. He was surprised when it wasn't.

"It's Bob Byron," the caller said. "I'm sorry to be bothering you, Judge. Someone named Jenny at your house gave me this number."

Barr looked at his watch. It was nearly midnight. "Who?" he asked, trying to connect the name.

"Dr. Robert Byron, Judge—the forensic guy from Cal. I testified for the prosecution?"

Now he remembered Byron, his compact build and slight tan. He was the one who didn't look the type, he recalled. "Yeah, I remember you," he said. "What's up?"

"Rab Tagore phoned me. He's an old friend. He told me he talked to you."

Barr could hear the sounds of laughter and loud music in the phone. "Where are you?" he asked.

"The Red Bar on Sutter." He slurred his words; he sounded like he'd had one too many. "I've been trying to decide whether to call you."

"But you *are* calling," Barr pointed out.

"It's no big deal." He sounded like he was ready to hang up.

"No big deal, but you are calling me."

He sounded offhand. "I thought it over. It's up to you if you want to talk to me."

"Okay," he told him. "What have you got to tell me, Dr. Byron?"

"Not on the phone," Byron said.

Barr sighed. "Then, I'll meet you."

"I know a place that isn't noisy," Byron said, and he named it.

About fifteen minutes later Barr was driving along Bay Street to the western end of Crissy Field. He turned back on the paved access road by the water's edge in front of the United States Navy's Electronic Silencing Station, which was a small white wooden-frame building with a red roof and a lookout. It was protected by a chain-link fence. The station held equipment that demagnetized the steel hulls of warships heading out of the bay to sea. At this hour this was the most private place in all of San Francisco.

Barr waited long enough to conclude that Byron wasn't coming, and he was about to leave when he saw a car turn off Marina Drive. A few seconds later, Dr. Byron was walking toward him.

"Sorry to take so long," he said.

"So, what's this all about?"

Byron looked out into the darkness. "Rab told me you were asking him about Holly's autopsy."

"My conversation with him was confidential."

"Don't blame Rab," Byron was quick to say. "You presented him with an enigma. Rab hates enigmas. He called me because I worked on Holly Hawkes, as you know. He had a few questions that he thought I could answer."

"I sought him out for his opinion," Barr explained. "I needed to talk to someone who wasn't involved."

"I understand," said Byron. "You showed him the photos. *That's* what intrigued him."

"He said that the ME didn't do much. He thought it was a matter of expedience. What did he think you could tell him?"

"He asked me if I knew whether it was political," said Byron.

"Well, was it?"

He smiled. "Expedience is the same as political. He wanted to know the details. I told him that nothing criminal went on."

Barr stared at him through the darkness. "Tagore told me that the ME did not follow normal autopsy procedures."

"Strictly speaking, he was right. The ME told me that word came down to leave this one alone." He shrugged as if to say it happened all the time. "The ME knew Holly had been murdered. He knew a knife was used as the weapon. He also knew that slicing her up in an autopsy wasn't going to tell him anything he didn't already know from just looking at her."

"But the report . . ."

"Have you actually *read* the report, Judge?"

"No, and I probably wouldn't understand it anyway."

"It lays out the necessary information, as if there had been a thorough internal examination. That was what confused Rab."

"Then, why am I standing here in the dark talking to you?"

"Because of what was *not* in the report. Like I said, no big deal. The ME and I were having lunch a few weeks before your trial began. I didn't think anything about it until Rab called me. In autopsies there's no set rule. But we are all creatures of habit. I guess the ME's assistant who first looked at Holly sent out blood and urine for serology and chemical analysis before the word came down. Her body was sent over to the funeral home. A few days later, the lab analyses came back."

"And?" Barr asked, impatiently.

"Holly Hawkes was pregnant when she died."

"Hold it," said Barr, feeling as if his breath had been taken away. *"Pregnant?"*

"In the first trimester," Byron said matter-of-factly. "Not enough to show. But the fetus was there."

"Why wasn't it reported?"

"Oh, it was, in an internal memo from the ME's office to the chief of police. Everything was legal, as far as that goes. The police didn't see any connection between her pregnancy and her murder. It was considered a private matter and irrelevant to the case. And it was treated that way." He looked at Barr. "It happens, Judge. Young female cadavers come in pregnant. Sometimes the fact appears in the ME's report, sometimes it doesn't. Most of the time it isn't mentioned in trials, either. It's usually incidental." He tried to read Barr's expression. "It was incidental, *wasn't* it, Judge?"

Chapter Thirteen

Barr made his way along the wooden pier toward a looming white shape by the water's edge. Diffused light poked through the heavy fog as he reached the side of the yacht. He ignored a sign that warned trespassers in English and Chinese. He unclipped the chain and climbed the ladder, looking up, and when he reached *Mandarin*'s deck, towering over him was the ship's captain, who did not give the impression that he was happy to see him.

"Get off," he told him, pointing the direction down.

Barr stood his ground. "Is the senator aboard?" he asked.

"Get off, I said. Or I'll throw you off," and the captain took a threatening step forward.

"You'll have to answer to the senator, then. He asked me to wait for him," said Barr.

He stopped in midstride and he shook his head. "No guests are permitted onboard, sir, unless the senator's here," he said.

"He specifically requested it," Barr insisted, seeing that the captain was uncertain.

"I'll tell him you came by." He looked down at the ladder, then off toward the dock. "You can't stay onboard."

"You know who I am? The judge in the trial of his granddaughter. Senator Hawkes said he'd be along soon. Can you try to reach him by phone?"

The captain shook his head again. "Not unless he's in his

limo." He hesitated, looking closely at Barr. "You're the one with the good-looking woman from the other day, and Morgan, he's your son?"

"That's right. We sailed up in the Swan."

He nodded and cast Barr a grin. "A nice kid, your son, lots of questions," he said. And he scooped his hand, indicating for Barr to follow him. He turned down the deck and entered the main cabin. "Like I said, the senator doesn't allow guests on-board without him here, but in your case, Judge . . . since he asked you . . ."

The salon they entered was as opulent as any room Barr had ever seen—almost like a museum, with precious Oriental vases and carvings in ivory and jades of differing colors. The walls were hung with paintings that Barr had no doubt were worth a small fortune. One was an astonishing ancestor scroll of a wiz-ened man in a blue silk gown seated at a desk. Yet there was not a photograph or a single portrait of a contemporary person whom Barr recognized. He had expected to find the same suffo-cating collection of photos of Holly here as he had seen at Amelia's.

The captain opened a set of teak cabinets along the bulkhead and asked Barr if he would like a drink while he waited. Barr said no and settled on a sofa against one bulkhead wall. He picked up a book and began to look idly through its pages. The captain stood there as if trying to decide what to do. He wasn't a steward, and he didn't like being used for one. "Will you ex-cuse me a minute, Judge?" he said. "I have work to attend to." And with a polite nod he was gone, doubtless worried less about Barr than if the senator came aboard and he wasn't on deck to greet him.

Barr stood and went to the stern end of the salon. He turned the handle of a center door, which led down a companionway to the decks below. He listened for sounds warning him of the sen-ator's arrival. He walked down a carpeted hall of staterooms and cabins. At the far end, a brass plaque on a door of teak lou-vers proclaimed this one to be the owner's.

Barr was facing the doors, drawn by a light that shone dimly through the louvers. He knocked softly, then tried the brass handle, which did not move. He was not about to force the door; the sound would be heard throughout the ship, and he would bring down the wrath of the captain if he did. He was turning around to head back along the companionway when the door suddenly burst open, and just as suddenly he was staring into the face of Holly's killer.

Michael Eng held a pointed gun at the level of his waist, aimed at Barr's stomach, about five feet away. He observed Barr with a strange curiosity, as though he were trying to place him aboard the yacht, wondering how he had come here. He slowly shook his head, as if to say that he was amazed at Barr's persistence.

"We are leaving tonight," he said. "I'm afraid the senator isn't going to like your being here one bit." Eng wagged the barrel of the gun to indicate to Barr to enter the cabin. "We may ditch your body at sea," he said, stepping back as Barr passed him, entering the cabin. "Before we do that, there's something you might want to see." As if he were a guide, he indicated the interior of the cabin with his free hand.

Barr was amazed by what he saw in the dim light.

On the shelves sat scores of framed photographs of Holly. The light from two overhead spots shone on her portrait over a king-size bed. It was a duplicate of the portrait he had seen over the mantel at Amelia's, only vaguely different. He went past the rows of photos on the bookcase shelves—those of Holly with many men and women whom Barr recognized as famous and accomplished and celebrated. But always, in each of these pictures, Stanton was somewhere in the frame, in either the background or the shadows, watching Holly, always watching, his eyes on her—not on the camera, not on the celebrity, but on *her*. The senator's was the look of absolute concupiscence, which Barr, in his innocence, had mistaken for control.

He turned away as a loud shout from the far end of the companionway shattered the quiet and Eng's expression froze. Eng glanced nervously at Barr, then turned his head to try to see who was making the noise. In that instant, Barr lunged at the gun, which fired with him grasping the barrel. He held on, snatching it out of Eng's grasp. He turned it on Eng, fumbling for the trigger, as Eng jumped at him.

Barr felt the pressure of his finger against the trigger. He jerked at it again and again.

The impact tossed Eng backward on the bed; he struggled but his wounds held him down. Barr could see that he had shot him in the middle of his chest. He brought the pistol over and down on his face; he was prepared to fire at his head if he moved. This time he wasn't going to let him get away. Eng looked over to his right. Then his eyes went flat.

At the door, Barr turned to look at the room a last time. He glanced up at Holly's portrait, and that's when he saw it.

He went over and stood on the bed. He reached up to the portrait. The canvas ripped around Holly's neck and down her chest to her shoulder. The precious locket which she had worn the night she was killed came free in Barr's hand.

"Put that down!" Senator Hawkes was standing in the doorway. He looked angry enough to use the gun in his hand. "Give me that necklace, now!"

Barr did what he asked. "A dangerous sentimentality, Senator," he told him, trying to calm his voice.

Hawkes clenched the locket in his fist. "Dangerous? Why would you think this is dangerous?"

"Because she was wearing it when she died."

"Chief Dunstan gave it to me," he said.

Barr could almost see his mind dissembling. "Sorry, Senator," he said. "Only her killer could have taken those from her body. *You* killed your own granddaughter. She was pregnant with your child, Senator, and you could not live with the consequences. You made the choice. *You* had her killed."

"You don't know what you're talking about," Hawkes said impatiently.

Barr pointed to Holly's portrait. "Did you think hanging her jewelry around her neck would bring her back to life?"

"What I think is none of your business." He stared at Holly's portrait. In a voice filled with emotion he said, "I'm sure you can't understand this, but I truly loved her. She was a woman." Tears welled up in his eyes. "She betrayed *me* in the end."

"She was a girl, Senator."

"I couldn't let it happen."

"But you didn't stop it."

"Do you know how it began?"

"I have no idea, Senator."

"One thing, then another, and suddenly we were lovers, and neither of us admitted it openly, even to one another, until it was too late. We were alone on the boat for that summer. We were in Asia. Everything there is different. It began between us, and we never talked about it. We never acknowledged it until the night she told me—"

"The night she died."

"She told me about her condition."

"*Not* a condition," Barr said. "She was pregnant. With your child. Your granddaughter was carrying your daughter or your son."

"One thing led to another," he repeated to himself.

"They were not *things*, Senator. They were crimes."

He looked at Barr, appealing for his understanding. "You sound horrified. Why?"

"What you did *was* horrible."

"She begged me to help her."

"You used your power to corrupt her. You took away her youth. You robbed her of everything. I'm surprised she didn't kill herself. Maybe it was an act of mercy, what you did."

"She said she wanted to."

"And you couldn't even give her that," said Barr.

He shook his head. "You are naïve as a child, Judge Barr," he said, wiping the tears from his eyes. "You know how children are? You warn them, you say no, you tell them every way you can to protect themselves, and they ignore you anyway. That's *you*, Judge."

"This is not about me. It's about her. She was the child. You didn't warn her of the consequences of what the two of you did. You didn't say no to her. Your own daughter-in-law called you evil tonight. She knows you better than anyone. But I think she was being kind. You are a monster, Senator."

He looked at Barr, disregarding him. "Holly meant more to me than anything in my life."

"Anything, you mean, except for face. I'm going to see that you are punished for it."

As if the thought had not dawned on him until now, his stature altered. "Ultimately God will judge me," he said as if to himself.

"He'll have to wait in line," said Barr. "*I'll* start right here on earth. You are answerable to the law." Barr looked at him, amazed at the man's arrogance. "You put Michael Eng on the jury. Did you really think I wouldn't find him?"

"Eng was a tool to be used, and putting him on the jury was his price. I needed this affair to be put behind me. I needed it over with."

"And your Forty-nine Boys framed Feng Shao-li. Winston Xiao-Yang was standing there, waiting to identify him. Do these people all work for you, Senator?"

He nodded. "I have influence over their lives."

"Chief Dunstan too?"

"The chief did nothing on my behalf but choose to ignore those portions of the autopsy results."

"What did you give him?"

"My word of honor that the pregnancy had nothing to do with her death. I said it was a private family matter."

"It certainly was that, Senator."

Hawkes opened his fist. Holly's locket shone in his palm. "It is your word against mine, Judge," he said. "I have my wealth, my reputation, my standing as a senator. I am respected. I am a man of honor. I will be leaving the country in a few hours."

"I have what I need, Senator."

He jangled the jewelry on the chain. "I should have dropped this in the sea. I'll put them where they will never be found."

"You will still be punished," said Barr.

"What if you too became a casualty, Judge?"

"Sorry, Senator. Jenny and Amelia know everything," he lied. "The truth will be told."

"Without the cross, without this locket, no one will believe you," Hawkes said.

Barr did not have to think about that. "I have Holly and her unborn child on my side."

Hawkes looked at Barr, and for that moment he was speechless.

"That's right," said Barr. "I have already written out a court order. It is with my last will. Jenny has instructions to open it if I die. It is an order for Holly's exhumation. That's the first thing. As you recall, I know where her body is."

"The fetus was destroyed," said Hawkes.

Barr smiled wickedly. "How do you think I found out about her pregnancy?"

He shook his head. "Dunstan, I suppose."

"The medical examiner did not autopsy her as he was commissioned to do. But his assistant, before the word came down, sent samples of the fetus's blood out for analysis. You ever hear of DNA matching? Science has more ways of connecting a father to a child than you can imagine, Senator." He folded his arms. "I hope I preside at your trial. It'll be a joy." He glanced up at Holly's portrait.

Too fast for Barr to react, Hawkes raised the pistol. There was a metallic click, followed instantaneously by an explosion. A gout of blood shot out from the senator's skull with the trajectory of the bullet, across the plane of the bed, splattering against the portrait.

Epilogue

"Earth to earth, ashes to ashes, dust to dust . . ."

The sky was bright and the branches over the gravesite rustled in the breeze. Those few who attended the funeral watched the proceedings, listening to the words of Cardinal Wells, but they might have been watching almost anything.

Barr's father had not come to say good-bye but to make certain that Hawkes was actually buried. On the way to the cemetery, he had told Barr, "In this, son, I am a literalist. Terrible shame Stanton won't be buried with his Oriental friends," and his face was serious, befitting the tragedy.

"A lonely wanderer for all eternity," said Cardinal Wells without a hint of pity. He looked down into the senator's grave and carelessly let a handful of dirt fall into the hole.

"Lovely day, altogether," said Barr's father, looking up at the sky and breathing in the park air. They were in a corner of a cemetery far away from Golden Gate Park, where Holly was now buried. The senator's grave, in a site chosen by Amelia, was as close to a potter's field as she could find. It overlooked the smog and roar and lights of the main artery that connected Fresno with San Francisco.

"Dad," said Barr in a sobering voice, "please don't gloat."

"Why not? The senator has been punished," his father said.

"God has his ways," the cardinal said.

"God didn't tell *you*," Barr said to his father.

"Sadly, He doesn't speak to me. He may try to communicate with Wellsy. I can't speak for him." He noticed the look of annoyance on his son's face.

"Did you arrange for me to preside at the trial?" Barr asked.

His father looked away. "I arranged nothing," he told him. "I was proud of how you handled yourself."

"There's no reason to be, Dad," he said. "None at all."

A month later, an orchestra played under a blue-and-white-striped marquee while celebrants lined up at a buffet table for champagne and wedding cake. The reception was already in full swing in the back garden of Justice Barr's house overlooking the Presidio park, and the day was warm and very clear. Jenny looked resplendent in her white wedding dress. Morgan went up to her and pulled her onto the dance floor. His morning suit made him look like a penguin. But he had served San Francisco's most attractive newly married couple as best man, handing over the gold wedding band the moment the cardinal had asked for it.

Barr was standing off to one side by his father's wheelchair. His father was eagerly awaiting the delivery of a martini, and Barr held a full glass of champagne in his hand. At one of the corner tables Lovelace had pulled up a chair next to Roberta. Lovelace was looking happy. He had every reason to be. He was talking to a pretty young woman.

Cardinal Wells came over to Barr with a Bloody Mary in his hand.

"Thank you, Uncle Wellsy, for making this a perfect day," Barr told him.

"The honor is mine," he replied with a cheery smile. "It was something I hoped I'd be asked to do. You make a fine couple, you and Jenny. I hope you have many children."

A waiter brought up a martini for Barr's father. "Didn't I tell you, Wellsy," he said. "Amelia telephoned me. She is coming back from Europe. It'll be nice to see her again."

Morgan came running off the dance floor. "Okay Acapulco, Dad," he said. "Jet skiing, fishing, and scuba diving."

Jenny followed him over, and Barr and his father kissed her on the cheek, and Cardinal Wells squeezed her hand.

"Jenny said she'll take me fishing for a black marlin," Morgan reported.

Barr stared at her. "You told him he could go? On our honeymoon?"

She hugged his arm. "We'll talk about it later," she said.

Roberta came over. "A family picture, please?" and she raised a camera to her eye. "You all look so lovely," she told them.

Justice Barr's eyes twinkled. "You should see the pictures of *my* wedding," he told her. "Now, that was a ceremony."

"I'd love to see them," Roberta said.

Bubbling over with enthusiasm, Justice Barr turned to his son. "Go upstairs to my study and get the album for me, will you, son? You know the one."

Barr had to go into the house anyway. He excused himself and ran upstairs to the study. On the top of his father's desk, bibelots, correspondence, magazines and books, and framed photos of Barr, his mother, and Morgan each had a certain place. Barr pulled out the drawer where he knew his father kept several leather-bound photo albums. His hand fell on a magazine lying on top: *Connoisseur,* to which his father subscribed. He was pushing it aside when he noticed that its cover had been cut up with scissors. His hand stayed where it rested, and he thought for a moment. He upturned the magazine. Scraps of paper fluttered out onto the carpet.

Barr squatted down over them. Like a jigsaw puzzle he was trying to figure out, he laboriously placed each cut-out letter right-side up on the carpet. At first he wondered why his father would have wanted to cut letters from a magazine. Then he concentrated on the hollow letters themselves, trying to form them into individual words. The first one he put together was KILLER; the next one was HOLLY, and the next, SITTING. After he had found JURY, he did not need to bother with the rest of the letters. He stood up, went into the bathroom, and dropped the scraps in the toilet. He looked out the window at the scene on the grass of the wedding reception. He caught sight of his father in his wheelchair trying to "dance" with Roberta. Over the sounds of the flushing, through the window Barr could hear him laughing.

About the Author

Malcolm MacPherson, a foreign correspondent for *Newsweek* based in Chicago, Los Angeles, Nairobi, Paris, and London, and a senior writer for *Premiere,* has written eight books, most notably the acclaimed Holocaust history *The Blood of His Servants* and the fictional depiction of Disneyland's creation, *In Cahoots.* He lives with his wife and two children in northern Virginia.